LISA REGAN

COLD-BLOODED
By Lisa Regan
Copyright © 2015 Lisa Regan

ISBN-13: 978-0-9967159-2-8

All rights reserved. Except as permitted under the U.S. Copyright Act of 1976, no part of this publication may be reproduced, distributed, or transmitted in any form or by any means, or stored in a database or retrieval system, without prior permission of the author.

The characters and events in this book are fictitious. Names, characters, places, and plots are a product of the author's imagination. Any similarity to real persons, living or dead, is coincidental and not intended by the author.

Cover Design by Forward Authority Design Services
Interior Design by Integrity Formatting

Praise for
COLD-BLOODED

"*Cold-Blooded* is the embodiment of a top-notch, great thriller. Lisa Regan will make you thankful for your safe, comfortable bed while you're hiding under the covers reading this quintessential, calculated, maniacal masterpiece. *Cold-Blooded* is a mix of gripping terror and tension." — Dana Mason, Author of *Dangerous Embrace*

ALSO BY LISA REGAN

Praise for **HOLD STILL**

"Hold on tight when you read *Hold Still,* for the Lisa Regan roller coaster has taken thrill rides to a whole new level! She sends you up that first hill and then just drops you into a twisting, turning maelstrom of breathtaking suspense! *Hold Still* is one of the most captivating books I've ever read!" — Michael Infinito, Author of *12:19* and *In Blog We Trust*

"Tense, harrowing, and chillingly real, Regan weaves yet another engagingly sinister tale that will leave your nerves on edge right up to the frightening end." — Nancy S. Thompson, Author of *The Mistaken*

Praise for **FINDING CLAIRE FLETCHER**

"Readers should drop what they're reading and pick up a copy of Finding Claire Fletcher." — Gregg Olsen, New York Times bestselling author

"Author Regan keeps the tension alive from the first page. Her psychological insight into her characters make the story as intriguing as it is real as today's headlines. This is a well-written and thought-provoking novel that will keep you riveted until the conclusion." — *Suspense Magazine, Sept/Oct 2013 issue*

Praise for *ABERRATION*

"With Kassidy Bishop, Lisa Regan has created a character that's not only smart, but vulnerable. It's that kind of complexity that lifts her novels from others in the suspense genre." —Gregg Olsen, New York Times Bestselling author.

"*Aberration* is a sophisticated and compelling suspense novel. Just when you think you know what's next, the story whips you around a corner into shocking new territory and you discover nothing is quite what it seems. *Aberration* will keep you reading, and guessing, until the very end, when not one but two shocking twists await the reader. Lisa Regan has also created that rarity, a wonderfully original and complex heroine in Kassidy Bishop, who is a tough and bright FBI agent but also refreshingly human. Someone to root for, fear for, and hope we meet again in another Lisa Regan novel." —Mark Pryor, author of *The Bookseller (Hugo Marston series)*

DEDICATION

In loving memory of Walter Conlen
and for Shilie Turner

NOTE TO READERS

Many of the places mentioned in this novel are real places, businesses, et cetera in Philadelphia. I try to make the setting as authentic as possible. However, sometimes it is necessary to fabricate certain things. For example, Dirk's Gameplex is fake, and Franklin West, the high school mentioned throughout this book, is complete fiction. I made it up and all of the events that took place within it. Franklin West figures heavily in another novel, HARM, unrelated to this book, which will be released in 2017. It is in that book that the 2006 school shooting mentioned herein occurs. Also, in service of the story, I have occasionally taken liberties in order to move the plot forward. So if you find yourself saying, "That's not entirely accurate," you would be right. This is, after all, a work of fiction.

CHAPTER
1

May 9, 2000

She'd gotten a late start. It was a quarter after seven as Sydney Adams jogged that evening along Boxer's Trail, a path for runners that meandered through Philadelphia's Fairmount Park east of the Schuylkill River and looped around the outside of the park's athletic field. But it was May, and the sun still strained on the horizon, not willing to give up the fight, even at this late hour. Soon though, night would descend. She didn't like to start so late, but her grandmother had made breaded pork chops, and Sydney had gorged herself until she felt bloated and lethargic. She'd almost skipped the run. Track and Field season was nearly over. What was one practice run?

But she needed to think. She needed to be alone.

Columns of sunlight filtered through the thick copse of trees on her left. The air had cooled since that afternoon but only slightly. It had been a nearly ninety-degree day, and she'd sweated it out gracelessly with the rest of her classmates at Franklin West High School. Now the humidity lingered, clinging to her bare thighs, condensing into a fine sheen of perspiration.

Sydney pushed herself, running faster than usual. She passed a couple jogging with their dogs—a greyhound and a husky—a bicyclist, and then a knot of teenage boys whose catcalls trailed after her. She picked up her pace, ears pricked to any sounds behind her that might suggest someone approaching. The tension in her body eased when she'd gone another quarter-mile without incident. The light was seeping away, the shadows around her lengthening. All she could hear now were the sounds of her raging heartbeat, her labored breath, and her sneakers pounding the trail.

None of it drowned out thoughts of him—of what had happened between them.

Mentally she calculated the days. It had been twenty-one days since he had kissed her, touched her, taken her. She had let him. There was no denying that. She could have stopped him at any time. She should have. He was older. He was married. And he was white.

And yet . . .

She willed her burning leg muscles to move faster, harder. Her entire body was slick with sweat. It ran in fat drops down her face and neck, pooling between her breasts, sliding down her spine and gathering at the cleft of her ass.

What would Lonnie think?

A lump formed in her throat, and she swallowed quickly. Her boyfriend would never know. No one would ever know. Only the two of them. It had happened one time because they both wanted it, and now it was in the past. She might be a teenager, but she was far from naïve. She knew exactly how scandalous the situation was, and she had no interest in continuing with it. She had a future. She had Lonnie and Georgetown and a grandmother she didn't want to disappoint. A grandmother who had worked hard to raise her and her sister after her parents had died. A grandmother who had moved heaven and earth so Sydney could afford to go to college in the fall.

Their flirtation, or whatever it was, had to be over. Still, she thought of his hands gripping her hips, his breath hot and rapid on the back of her neck. *His mouth—*

She stumbled, crying out as her left foot tangled with a rogue tree root poking up through a crack in the concrete. Her hands shot out, prepared to break her fall, but her legs stuttered, almost of their own volition, finding purchase. She stopped, leaning against the offending tree. Her chest heaved. Sweat ran down her forehead and into her eyes, irritating them. Laughter erupted from her diaphragm. How many times had she run this path? Hundreds. Sprained ankle by way of tree root was a rookie move. This was exactly the problem. This distraction.

Pop.

It sounded like a firecracker and registered as a searing, stabbing pain in the back of her right thigh. Like a hot poker. Before she could react, another pop sounded, this one closer. Then two more. She suddenly tasted dirt in her mouth, and her temple was resting on that damn tree root before she could even begin to process what was happening to her. Her legs wouldn't work. Panic, hot and frenzied, closed in on her. What was happening?

"Help," she said, but her voice came out small and squeaky. She thought she heard footsteps approaching from behind. Sydney willed her legs to move, to stand, to scramble, to run. She reached forward with her right arm, feeling for the base of the tree. She had to get up. As her surroundings began to fade to an inky, charcoal blackness, she felt a tug on her lower body.

"Please," she croaked.

Then the darkness swallowed her.

CHAPTER 2

CHAPTER

October 14, 2014

It was the Tuesday after Dorothy Adams' funeral. Knox woke up with the hangover of the century, which was saying a lot, considering how much and how often he drank. He was facedown on the couch in the same clothes he'd been wearing for the last three days. As he raised his fuzzy head from the couch cushion, which bore a Rorschach of foul-smelling drool, he realized he was starting to smell. The putrid scents of Chinese takeout, moldy coffee, and stale beer were all in attendance. He peeled himself off the couch and rubbed the sleep from his eyes. The phone was ringing. His landline. But he couldn't find it.

"Moira," he called before he was fully awake enough to remember that his wife had left him almost ten years earlier. This wasn't even the home they'd shared. It was a low-income apartment he'd rented . . . he couldn't remember when. But evidently he'd had a landline installed. Or it had come with the place.

He reached toward one of the end tables and pushed aside a stack of unopened mail. The envelopes fluttered to the floor, along with two crushed beer cans. Pabst Blue Ribbon. Nausea assailed him at about the same time that something inside him thirsted for one. The digital clock on his cable box said eleven fourteen in the morning. The ringing was making his head rattle. Finally, his hand closed over the receiver. He pressed it to his ear.

"Knox," he said.

Jynx Adams sounded like she was out of breath. Then again, she was eight months pregnant and looked like she was carrying around a litter. Everything made her out of breath. "It's Jynx," she said. "Why aren't you answering your cell phone?"

"I dropped it in a puddle when I was leaving your grandmother's funeral. Haven't had it fixed yet."

"Oh. Well, do you think you can come out to her house? There's something you need to see. It's about Sydney."

"Sure," Knox said, glancing at the wallet-sized photo of Sydney Adams that her grandmother had given him fourteen years earlier, after her murder. It sat in a tiny frame on his coffee table — a reminder of his greatest professional failure. He managed to keep the trash that accumulated on his coffee table away from the photo. He had to have focus. Sydney Adams' unsolved murder had ended his marriage and his forty-year career. Well, his ex-wife would say it wasn't the murder itself, but his obsession with it, that had done him in. What he had now was this photo.

"Knox," Jynx said, drawing him out of his mental fog.

He reached up to his forehead. Pain pulsed behind both his eyes. "Yeah."

"This is important."

In other words, don't show up drunk. The Adamses knew him well, and they never judged.

"Yep," he said. "I'll be there in a half hour."

He hung up, stood and stripped out of his smelly clothes before heading to the shower. Afterward, he found a pair of slacks and a black button-down shirt that wasn't too dirty. He bypassed the refrigerator and the twenty or so cans of Pabst sitting in it. Outside, the sun was bright and prevented his eyes from focusing right away. *Where the hell is my car?* Nothing but blinding white light filled the designated parking spot where his car was supposed to be. Knox's head swam, and he swayed as a wave of nausea churned through his stomach. He thought of returning inside for just one beer. But Jynx had said it was important. The beer could wait.

A stroll around the parking lot left a fine sheen of sweat on his brow, in spite of the cool October air, but brought him no closer to finding his vehicle. With a heavy sigh, he hobbled the three blocks to one of his neighborhood's main thoroughfares, Ridge Avenue. Public transportation would get him to Dorothy Adams' house in less time than it would take for him to figure out what happened to his car. The bus ride didn't help his nausea.

Dorothy had raised her two granddaughters in a small row house on Dauphin Street in the Strawberry Mansion neighborhood of Philadelphia. She had been able to support them working as a secretary at Swartz Camp & Bell, a defense firm in center city. Dorothy had always spent whatever money she brought in on her girls, leaving her house dated and in ill-repair. Dark, faux wood paneling covered the walls. The carpets were worn threadbare from decades' worth of foot traffic. Sydney's room, which was where Knox found Sydney's sister, Jynx, hadn't changed all that much in the fourteen years since her death. Dorothy had gone through Sydney's things and given most of them away after her death. The furniture remained—a twin bed stripped to its mattress, an empty nightstand, and a dresser. Sydney's bed and dresser had become a sort of storage area for Dorothy and Jynx's things—holiday decorations, rarely used kitchen implements, and folding chairs. It looked as though Jynx had been packing everything into boxes.

Knox sat on the bed, wiping the sweat from his forehead with a crumpled tissue he pulled from his pocket. It wasn't hot in the house, but he couldn't stop sweating. Jynx had opened almost all of the windows to let the crisp fall air in. She stood near the nightstand. Knox watched as she leaned back, both hands at her lower back. She blew out a breath, then moaned. She wore a forest green cotton shirt and tight, black stretch pants. There was nothing elegant or dressy about her ensemble. It clung to every curve of her body, and there were plenty. She looked even more pregnant than she had at Dorothy's funeral, and that had been less than a week ago.

Jynx caught him staring and raised one brow, twisting her lips in what Dorothy always referred to as Jynx's "oh no you didn't" look. She said, "If you ask me about twins, I will knock you down."

Knox's gaze flitted to the floor. He scratched his nose to hide a smile. "That's not what I was going to say," he lied.

She kneaded the muscles of her lower back and rolled her eyes. "Really?"

Knox stood and walked over to the cherry dresser, which was nicked in about a hundred places and covered in a quarter-inch-thick layer of dust. He touched its edge, dislodging a clump of dust and leaving half a hand print. He studied the photos atop it. Dorothy and Sydney. Dorothy and Jynx. Sydney and Jynx. The girls together and apart as teenagers, their eyes bright, their faces wide open, unguarded, unlined by the travails of living. It was hope, Knox realized. He was staring at hope in its purest form. That was the transcendent quality he saw in both their faces. Everything was in front of them. Nothing had gone wrong yet, and everything was possible. They had no idea the world was about to reach out with its nasty, unforgiving talons and snatch one of them up, destroying the beautiful hope that marked them.

"Knox?"

He turned toward Jynx, feeling dizzy and disoriented. "Yeah."

"Where'd you go?"

He smiled and shook his head, walked back over to the bed. "Nowhere. I was just thinking you shouldn't be moving this stuff alone. Where's Myron?"

"Working. He's pulling doubles till the baby comes."

Her hands slid around to her belly, resting on the sides of it. She motioned to the nightstand, which she'd managed to pull away from the wall. Behind it, a piece of the brown carpet had been peeled back. "That's where I found them," she said. She waddled back to the bed and plucked an old photo envelope from the top of a box she'd already taped up. "I couldn't lift the table up, so I was dragging it and dragging it, and it pulled the carpet right up. Otherwise, I never would have found them. Looks like

7

she cut a flap in it to stick them under there."

Knox's fingers quivered as he turned the envelope over and shook out the photos. He tried not to get excited or to get his hopes up. He knew smoking guns were rare in a mythical kind of way, like unicorns and women who liked giving blow jobs. Still, his heart pounded a little. The photos were old and somewhat faded. Not near the kind of high-definition quality that society had grown used to with the advent of smart phones with built-in cameras and all things digital. Some of them had gotten moist or hot, maybe, and were hopelessly stuck together. Most of the photos were of students on Sydney's track team; some were of Dorothy. Disappointment crept into Knox's posture, his shoulders rounding, knees bending to meet the edge of the bed.

There was a photo of Sydney's track coach, Cash Rigo, in his classroom, surprised by the camera but smiling. There was one of Sydney's grandmother loading dishes into the dishwasher, bent at the waist, looking over her shoulder, her eyes blank. Then there were three of Sydney herself. In each one, she was smiling coyly but playing for the camera. She wore a black sports bra and her skimpy track shorts. She was playing the sexy grown-up woman she might have become. In one, she puckered her lips, her body turned to the side, hands over her bare belly, blowing a sly kiss to the camera. In another, she was turned with her back to the camera, bent forward slightly so the camera caught the expert curve of her rear. She looked over her shoulder with a "come hither" look as she peeled one strap of her sports bra down her shoulder. The last photo showed her reaching for the camera, arms extended beyond the scope of the lens, laughing, eyes wide and bright.

Jynx sighed. "I know, I know. There's nothing there. I don't even know why she hid them. I mean, I guess Lonnie took them, but everyone saw her in a sports bra—she used to run in it. Nothing scandalous there."

"Lonnie didn't take these," Knox said. He had pulled the three photos in question out of the pile. They lay fanned out on his lap. "Cash Rigo did."

Jynx's eyes bulged. She moved her hands to the top of her belly,

8

which was now a shelf for her ample breasts. Knox thought he could see a limb poking through her belly—an elbow or a knee. He remembered when his wife was pregnant with Bianca, how toward the end, their daughter's movements became visible beneath Moira's skin. Back then, it reminded him of a bad sci-fi film, but now, having witnessed the miracle of life first-hand and the horror of death, he thought it was pretty cool.

"The coach? How do you know he took them?" Jynx asked.

Knox tapped the middle photo where the corner of the painting behind Sydney peeked out. "This painting. If you get a magnifying glass, I'll bet you'll make out the initials F.R."

Jynx stared at him, uncomprehending.

Knox said, "Francine Rigo. The coach's wife."

"The school nurse?"

"Yeah, she had just taken an art class when I visited them after Sydney's murder. She had done this painting, and it was hanging in their downstairs hallway. It was a tree in a field but it . . . there was something strange about it."

He remembered staring at it, wondering which one of them had made the decision to hang it up. Was it her own hubris or Cash being overly solicitous to keep her happy?

"Sydney was never over there. She was never at his house," Jynx said.

Knox flicked a finger off the photo. "Evidently, she was there at least once."

Jynx's mouth turned downward. "Why would she pose like that for him? There was never anything between them."

Knox chuckled. "Jynx, I never pegged you as being naïve."

She bristled, straightening her spine and trying to fold her arms across her chest. "Sydney would never have done something like that. She wasn't—she was a good kid."

Knox kept his gaze steady on her. "Lots of good kids get into situations they shouldn't. Rigo *was* older than her."

"Sydney wouldn't allow herself to be manipulated that way. I know you always thought he was a suspect."

"And you've always dismissed that notion," Knox countered. He sighed and dabbed his sweaty face again. A wave of dizziness came over him. He blinked his eyes, willing it away. "Everyone always has," he added, almost to himself.

"Okay, maybe he did it. Maybe he was obsessed with her and killed her because he couldn't have her."

Knox laughed. "Stop watching Lifetime, for Pete's sake. You mean to tell me that, as a teenager, you never had a crush on an older guy? Cash Rigo wasn't that far out of college. He wasn't even ten years older than Sydney. There could have been something. The guy was pretty broken up over her death."

"But he was married — and white," Jynx blurted.

Knox stared at her, an amused smile playing on his lips.

"No offense," Jynx said, turning away from him. She busied herself patting the flap of carpet down with her sneakered foot.

"None taken."

"I know you have your theories," Jynx said over her shoulder. "I don't think Coach Rigo killed Sydney. But I'm not a cop. My grandmother . . . she always thought you were right. She adored you."

"And I adored her."

Finally, Jynx turned and met his eyes. "She believed in you."

The words were like a knife in his heart, and as if they had conjured pain, an ache bloomed in his chest, spreading to his arms. No one believed in him. Not his wife nor his daughter. Not his coworkers. He was an epic failure. An incompetent drunk. He ruined everything he touched. But Dorothy's faith in him had been unnerving. The fact that he could not bring her granddaughter's killer to justice before her own death had broken his imperfect heart.

"With these pictures, I might be able to do right by her," he croaked. "By all of you."

He felt Jynx's hand on his shoulder, heard her whisper, but couldn't make out the words. His heart seized in his chest and he had a sudden, absurd image of his heart as an angry, clenched fist. He couldn't make it open. Then he felt light, like he was made of air, like he could float away — a balloon no one wanted.

Knox looked into Jynx's lovely, thin face. The smooth brown skin of her forehead creased. Concern pooled in her dark eyes.

Then her fingers dug into the flesh over his collarbone as the floor rushed at him. The last thing he heard was her screaming his name.

CHAPTER 3

October 14, 2014

Dying was just like everyone said, which was weird because Knox had never believed in any of the bright-light-at-the-end-of-the-tunnel crap. But then he was in a long, dark tunnel, walking toward a pinprick of light. He couldn't remember how he'd gotten there or why he was there. He wasn't even sure what he was supposed to do. His mind was a blank slate. Behind him was only darkness, so he went toward the light. It went on and on, but he didn't mind. He felt good. His body didn't ache. No pain, no headaches, no hangovers, and no thirst. He just . . . was.

Just as he reached the light, the silhouette of a figure emerged. He tried getting closer, but the figure receded.

"Hello?" he called.

The figure turned. He recognized the woman's face. Dorothy Adams. "You go on back now," she said.

Knox looked around, but there was only blinding white light. "Where's Sydney?"

Dorothy didn't answer. Instead, she turned away and disappeared into the light.

"Where's Sydney?" Knox called after her.

He cried out once more, but then he was falling, and the light was gone. He could feel himself in his body again—pain, cold, heaviness in his chest. His head felt foggy. He opened his eyes and had to blink several times to get the room to come into focus. He was in a hospital room. There was a woman on each side of his bed. One was black with a short pixie haircut, like Halle Berry's. She had a massive belly.

"Jynx?"

She squeezed his hand. "Right here."

On the other side of the bed stood a white woman with long flowing black hair, piercing blue eyes, and sharp features. His daughter. "Bianca?"

"Jynx called me," she said icily. "Technically, I'm your next of kin. She thought you were dead." She folded her arms across her chest and glared at him. He closed his eyes and focused on the feel of Jynx's hand on his. Warm, dry, reassuring.

"I called the doctor," Jynx said. "Now that you're up."

"Where am I?"

"Temple University Hospital," Jynx answered.

He heard footsteps and opened his eyes to see a man in a white coat at the foot of his bed. The doctor. He was young with dark olive skin and thick brown hair. "Mr. Knox," he said, unsmiling. "I've got good news and bad news. Which would you like first?"

Knox stared at the man, uncomprehending. An awkward silence filled the room until Jynx said, "The good news."

The doctor folded his arms over his chest, much like Bianca, except that he seemed to be hugging himself, bracing himself for something, whereas Bianca's folded arms were a defensive maneuver. She was guarding herself against him.

Not for the first time, Knox wished he hadn't fucked things up so grandly.

"The good news," the doctor began, "is that you survived a heart attack today. You didn't die. This time."

Bianca made a noise under her breath and glowered at him. "Jesus Christ. You can't even get that right. You couldn't just die?"

If he hadn't already heard such hateful sentiments from her before, he might have been upset. But this was not new territory,

13

and he knew he deserved it. The doctor and Jynx, however, were taken aback. The doctor stood silent, staring open-mouthed at Knox's daughter. The guy had a pretty abrupt bedside manner, but even he was stunned by her vitriol.

Jynx leaned over, her swollen midsection pressing against his forearm. With narrowed eyes, she pointed a finger at Bianca. "I may be pregnant, but I *will* knock you down. You shut your mouth in this room, right now."

Knox had always loved Jynx's way of handling people. She never raised her voice, never used a single swear word. But people tended to listen to her. Bianca quieted as Knox waved a hand. It was difficult getting the words out but he said, "It's fine, it's okay. Just the bad news then. Doctor?"

The doctor looked back and forth between the women as if waiting for a fight to break out. When neither spoke, he continued. "The bad news is that you've got congestive heart failure and chronic obstructive pulmonary disease, complicated by the early stages of cirrhosis of the liver."

His lungs, heart, and liver were failing — in concert. "I've had those things for a while," Knox said. "That's not news."

The doctor loosened his arms and leaned over the bottom of the bed, bracing his hands on the bedframe. "Yes, and by the looks of your tests, you haven't been managing them very well. I'd venture to say you haven't been managing them at all."

No reason to, Knox almost said. He'd been sick for a long time, but there'd never been a good reason to try and *not* be sick. Not since losing his family. Plus, he'd never been a health nut and had smoked for most of his life. Even when he was married, his diet wasn't great. Working homicide made for long hours, during which eating healthy — or at all — wasn't a priority. Greasy take-out had been a staple of his diet for decades. Then after Sydney's case, the heavy drinking started. He'd stopped smoking, mostly, but he knew the drinking and his perpetually shitty diet were driving him to an early grave. At seventy-two, he was no spring chicken either.

"Mr. Knox, your lungs are filled with fluid, your heart is straining to —"

Knox held up a hand to silence the doctor. "I don't need you to tell me what's wrong with me. It doesn't matter now. Just tell me: how much time do I have left?"

Jynx squeezed his hand so hard he thought she might break it.

The doctor said, "It's very hard to predict. There are no guarantees. Based on your labs and scans, I would say four to six months. I'm very sorry, Mr. Knox. I would suggest you do what you can to put your affairs in order."

His affairs? He nearly laughed. He didn't have any affairs left to put in order. His own child wished him dead. He could die this very second, and it would not matter.

Except.

"Sydney," he said, his voice husky.

Bianca growled. There was no other way to describe it. She had done it when she was six years old and didn't get her way. She threw her hands in the air. "It never stops, does it? On your death bed, all you care about is her."

She'd said the word "her" with the kind of venom a wife would use to refer to her husband's mistress. "You care more about dead people than anything else. Why don't you just fucking die already?"

Jynx looked horrified. Knox had never seen her at a loss for words before. But Bianca was right. For fourteen years, he had been putting Sydney before her. It hadn't started out that way. At first, it was just another case. A garden-variety random shooting. They happened every day in Philadelphia—then and now. He had never been sure what it was about Sydney's case that ignited such an obsession in him, except that, ironically, she and his own daughter had been roughly the same age. He hadn't been able to let it go. His superiors told him to move on, so he started working the case on his own time, which caused fights with his wife. Philadelphia homicide detectives didn't get much spare time to begin with. That had always been a point of contention in his marriage. He'd started drinking so he could withstand the tension at home, but it only made things worse. By then, he couldn't stop himself. Then there were the things he forgot, like Bianca's college graduation, and the things he ruined, like her wedding. He drank through it all. He drank until there was nothing left.

The only thing he had left was Sydney's cold case.

"I did die," Knox said. "There was a light at the end of the tunnel—the whole nine yards."

Jynx and Bianca stared at him, nonplussed.

He went on, even though his chest burned and his breath was raspy—even with the O₂ they were giving him. "I went to the light, but she wasn't there. Sydney wasn't there, and they sent me back."

The words hung in the air for a long moment, like a strange smell no one could identify. Then Bianca reached forward and clamped a hand over his forearm. He drew in a sharp, wheezing breath. She hadn't touched him in five years. Her hand was cold. She peered into his face, the hatred and pain in her eyes palpable.

"You know why she wasn't there, old man? Because you were at the gates of hell. That's where you're going when you die, you miserable bastard. Straight to hell."

CHAPTER
4

October 16, 2014

Jocelyn Rush pulled a crumpled black thong from the depths of her underwear drawer. The lace was coarse against her hand. She held it up and sighed. Caleb would love it, and she could picture his brown eyes lit up and hungry. But all she could think about was how uncomfortable it was going to feel to have that tiny sliver of string lodged in her ass crack for however long she had it on. She knew women who wore thongs on a daily basis—like, as their underwear. She would never understand it. Did they just get used to it?

With a sigh, she dropped her drawers, kicking off her jeans and beloved cotton granny panties. She stood before the full-length mirror affixed to her closet door and pulled on the thong. She adjusted the thin strap creeping between her buttocks what seemed like fifty times, but it never settled into anything resembling comfortable. Must be like wearing a gun, she thought. When she first wore the holster with the heavy weapon in it, it felt like she was tugging around a brick. It was bulky and unwieldy. But after weeks, months, then years of wearing it each day, she felt naked and off-kilter without it. That had to be it.

She turned and looked over her shoulder, craning to get a look at her ass. Not bad for thirty-seven. Although she had managed to avoid childbirth, Jocelyn still wore a little extra flesh that hadn't been there ten or even five years ago, but she could live with it. Maybe it was her active role as mother to her niece that allowed the additional pounds to sneak up on her. Olivia, her four-year-old daughter, was her sister's biological child whom she had taken in at just seven days old and adopted shortly thereafter. Jocelyn's sister had been a drug addict and prostitute at the time of Olivia's birth and was in no position to raise a child.

Her fingers fidgeted with the thin material over her sacrum — the tiny triangle that covered nothing and served no purpose other than to hold the pieces of floss together.

"I will never get used to this," she muttered.

She resisted the urge to dig in her ass crack. No amount of digging would make it feel better. Besides, she mused as she went back to her dresser to search for a matching bra, once Caleb arrived, the thong wouldn't stay on for very long.

She and Caleb had met about a year ago while working a high-profile case for the Philadelphia Police Department. She'd been with Northwest Detectives and he with the Special Victims Unit. Caleb's hours with the SVU were long and erratic. That, coupled with the fact that Jocelyn had neither told her daughter about Caleb nor introduced the two, mostly left them with only enough time for quickies, which gave their relationship the feel of an illicit affair. They had to steal time whenever they could — after Olivia fell asleep, on Jocelyn's lunch break, on Caleb's dinner break. Any time that they could be utterly alone for fifteen minutes or longer without Olivia finding out or it interfering with their jobs, they met. They often planned to meet at restaurants for lunch or dinner but never made it out of the car. They were like two horny teenagers.

Jocelyn's hand seized on a lacy black bra that would go with the thong, but once she held it up, she saw a nickel-sized hole in one of the cups. She poked a finger through it, wondering if Caleb would notice. The bra wouldn't stay on long either, she was certain.

"No," she said, shaking her head. She tossed the offending bra in her wastebasket. She really needed new underthings. For today, it would have to be topless with the black thong. He would like that better anyway. She started to pull her T-shirt off, imagining the feel of his heated palms on her bare breasts. A loud banging on her front door startled her. She froze, the T-shirt half off and half on. She waited. It came again, louder and harder this time. She checked her bedside clock. Caleb would be here any minute. But that wasn't him. He had a key.

Bang, bang, bang.

The whole house shook.

"Goddamnit."

She pulled her T-shirt back on, fished her jeans from the pile of discarded clothes on the floor, and yanked them back up over her hips. It was probably one of those damn hippie college kids selling electricity. Since Pennsylvania had deregulated, electricity providers competed for customers like rabid dogs. Representatives went door to door at least twice a week. They waited at the entrance to the grocery store. They were ubiquitous, persistent, and annoying. And she was going to punch this one in the face if he or she didn't get off her porch before Caleb arrived.

Bang, bang, bang.

As she reached the bottom of her steps, the thong riding up her crack, she saw the door shimmy in its frame.

"Motherfucker," she said. She stalked into the kitchen and snatched her gun from the top of her fridge, the shoulder holster sliding onto her body with the ease and comfort of her oldest, most worn pair of granny panties. She doubted she'd need it, but it was intimidating.

Bang, bang, bang.

She swung her door open and froze, the stream of expletives dying on her lips. Before her stood an old man, his frame thin and frail. He didn't look strong enough to rattle her front door in its frame, but there was no one else with him. His hair was salt and pepper, mostly salt. He wore a St. Patty's Day T-shirt and a beat-up pair of khaki slacks. His cheeks were sunken, his blue-gray eyes jaundiced. A nasal cannula rested on his cheeks, the tubes

19

snaking over his ears and down to his chest where they cinched together and ran as one to the portable oxygen cylinder he wheeled behind him on a small cart.

The electricity companies were really getting desperate. Before he could ask if she was the owner, and if he could just have a "quick" look at her electric bill, Jocelyn said the only thing that stopped them cold. "I'm a renter."

Confusion deepened the lines age had etched into the man's face. "I'm not—" he began, but she cut him off.

"And I've already been saved."

He shook his head, the ghost of a smile on his lips. "No, it's not what you—"

"And I don't need any pie."

"I'm not here to sell—wait, what?"

They stared at one another.

"People sell pie door to door?" he asked.

"Twice a year. Some church or ex-cons raising money for some charity. They do the whole block."

The man looked up and down the street as if he might spot an ex-con trying to sell pie at one of the twin houses or row houses lining the street. They were nicely kept homes, many with hardy potted mums lining their front stoops or Halloween decorations arranged on their porches. Roxborough was one of the nicer blue-collar neighborhoods in Philadelphia. "Do they sell any?"

"I wouldn't know. Look, I think you have the wrong house."

"I'm looking for Jocelyn Rush," the man said. He reached up and adjusted his nasal cannula. Jocelyn noticed a tremor in his fingers.

She suppressed a sigh. "That's me, but I really don't have time—"

"Please," the man said. "It's important."

Jocelyn looked behind him, searching for signs of Caleb. She had to get rid of this guy before Caleb showed up. In the back pocket of her jeans, her cell phone vibrated, no doubt a message from Caleb that he was on his way.

"What's this about?" Jocelyn asked.

He slid the clamp that held the two sides of the cannula tubing down and back up until it pinched the loose flesh at the underbelly of his neck. "I need to hire you. It's about a case."

Her cell phone vibrated again. She exhaled noisily. "I have an office, you know."

The man smiled. "Yes. I know. Your assistant—"

"My partner," Jocelyn corrected. "Anita."

"Your partner, Anita," he parroted, "told me you were at lunch. I would have waited, but I don't have a lot of time."

Jocelyn put a hand on her outthrust hip. The thong rode ever deeper into her crack. "Anita gave you my home address?" She asked skeptically.

The man chuckled. "No, she kicked me out. She's something, that one."

Anita was typically great with clients and generally made up for Jocelyn's occasional abrasiveness, but she took shit from no one. This guy must have been pretty persistent if Anita had thrown him out.

Jocelyn stepped out onto the porch, backing him up two steps, her posture rigid. "Who are you, and how did you find out where I live?"

He stumbled backward, his feet tangling with the portable O_2 cart. He reached out for something to help him keep his balance but found nothing. Quickly, Jocelyn grasped his arm. The last thing she needed was some guy suing her for falling on her porch. She could feel his bones beneath his crepe paper skin. She held tight to him, steadying him. When she pulled her hand away, she could see the skin beneath it already bruising where her fingers had been.

Great.

Before she could apologize for intimidating him, nearly knocking him over, and bruising his arm, he spoke again, his words spilling out so rapidly it took her a moment to process what he was saying. "Kevin Sullivan recommended you. He said you guys were partners when you were with Northwest Detectives. I'm a former detective. Homicide. Name's Knox. Knew Sully a long time. He said you were good, you were tough. I looked you up. Researched you. When your assistant—I mean partner—

21

wouldn't call your cell, I got your home address from an Accurint search. I know, I know, it's pushy and I'm sorry, but I've got CHF and COPD and cirrhosis. I've only got four to six months to live. There's this old case. I need to solve it before I—before I—you know, before I go. I found something new. I know this probably seems nuts, but like I said, I don't have much time. Please, I need to clear this one. It's important."

He stopped abruptly. His mouth moved to say more, but his lungs couldn't keep up. Jocelyn could hear him wheezing as she stared open-mouthed. He reached back, twisting some dials on his oxygen tank. He was about five shades paler than before. In the back of her mind, a little voice told her to offer him a seat before he collapsed. But then he drew himself up to his full height, only a few inches taller than she. He clenched his jaw and stared straight at her with an unflinching gaze. She had a flash of how he must have looked on the job. Strong, masculine, imposing.

"So," she said. "Knox. What is that? First name? Last name? Both? Like Cher or Pitbull?"

A hint of a smile at the name Cher, then confusion blanketed his face. "Pitbull? Who the hell is that?"

CHAPTER 5

October 16, 2014

"Pitbull is an entertainer, like Cher," Jocelyn said.

Knox scratched his head. "Oh, well, I never heard of him — it's a him, right?"

Jocelyn nodded.

Knox went on, "My full name is Augustus Knox. Everyone just calls me Knox."

Jocelyn forced a smile. Her cell phone buzzed in her pocket again. "Look, Knox. I'm sorry to hear that you're . . . sick."

"Dying."

She pulled her phone out but didn't look at it. "Okay, dying. I'm happy to help you, but right now I'm expecting . . ."

The word "someone" died on her tongue as she finally looked at her phone. Caleb had texted her several times.

> *U won't believe this but we got a warrant for the Powell suspect. I'm gonna miss our lunch.*
>
> *I'm really sorry.*
>
> *Babe?*
>
> *I'll make it up to you.*

Babe?

Jocelyn sighed.

"Get stood up?" Knox said.

"More or less . . . Tell you what. Give me a minute, and you can come back to my office and tell me about your case."

She slipped back into the house and texted Caleb.

Damn you. I'm wearing a thong. It's ok. No worries. Was about to stand you up for a client anyway. Go get em.

As she was on her way up the steps to change out of the offending thong, he texted her back.

Keep it on. I'll be over tonight.

"Sure you will," she muttered as she slid on a pair of granny panties, moaning with pleasure. She dressed quickly and met Knox back on her porch.

"I'll meet you at my office," she told him as she locked her front door.

When she turned he was smiling sheepishly, again fidgeting with the oxygen tubing. "About that," he said. "Could you—do you think you could give me a ride?"

"You don't drive?"

He fanned his hands out in front of him. "Well, sure, I drive. I just—I lost my car, and seeing as I'm dying and all, I didn't see much point in getting another one."

"How did you get here?"

"SEPTA. The 9 bus drops me right up the street," he explained. SEPTA or the Southeastern Pennsylvania Transportation Authority was Philadelphia's public transportation system.

"Fine," Jocelyn said. "Let's go."

He was silent in the car; the only sound was the hum of his oxygen. She could feel him staring, and when she looked over, she realized he was focused on her hands. "It's the left one," she said, lifting her left hand from the steering wheel and turning it back and forth so he could see the scars on either side. "Yes, it hurt like hell. Still does sometimes. Yes, I was scared shitless. Yes, I still get nightmares, and no, I don't have any desire to discuss it."

Knox nodded. "Didn't think you would."

On her last assignment as a Philadelphia police detective, Jocelyn and Caleb had solved what the press had dubbed the Schoolteacher Attackers case, involving three men who had raped and crucified high-class prostitutes, one of whom had worked as a schoolteacher by day. The scar was from a nail that had been driven into her hand by one of the attackers.

"How much did Kevin tell you?" Jocelyn asked.

Knox stared straight ahead. "Enough," he said. "Hey, this isn't the way to your office."

Jocelyn turned from Pechin Street onto Green Lane, where Olivia's preschool was located. "I know. I have to drive past my daughter's school."

She expected a quip or sarcastic comment like, "What? To make sure it's still there?" but all Knox said was, "Okay."

A moment passed, Jocelyn growing twitchier in her seat. She slowed in front of the school. The kids were inside, locked up securely. Sometimes she could spot Olivia if the children were out playing in the fenced-in area. She relaxed slightly and turned left onto Ridge Avenue. Although she owed Knox no explanation, she said, "It's been hard for me. Since what happened last year. Sometimes I need to check that she's okay."

She chanced a look at him. His hands were folded in his lap, a small, pained smile on his face. "When my daughter was little, I wasn't at ease unless she was with me. The only thing that might have made me feel better while she was at school would have been a Secret Service detail."

"Puh," Jocelyn said. "I wouldn't even trust them."

They both laughed. Relief coursed through her. He understood her special brand of crazy, borne of violence and years on the job bearing witness to the very worst things human beings could do to one another.

◡◠◠◡◠

Jocelyn and Anita had chosen an office on Ridge Pike, just outside of the city. They'd both had enough of Philadelphia's inner city to last a lifetime. The women had met a decade earlier when Jocelyn was still a patrol cop and Anita was a prostitute in one of

Philadelphia's most dangerous areas. Over the years, they'd struck up an unlikely friendship. Eventually, Anita had gotten clean and gone straight, holding down a job as a receptionist. When her mother got cancer, she went back to prostitution, this time as an escort, finding her johns online rather than on the street. That was how the men, The Schoolteacher Attackers, had targeted and assaulted her. Jocelyn had helped crack Anita's case—but at great cost. After the case closed, Jocelyn retired early from the Philadelphia Police Department, and the two women opened a private investigation firm.

Rush & Grant Investigations was run out of a squat, flat-roofed building that Jocelyn was sure used to be a butcher shop, although the realtor had assured them it was previously occupied by an insurance broker. Behind it, to the rear of their small parking lot, was a vacant two-story home that Jocelyn had hoped to move into, but her daughter was adamantly opposed to moving out of their Roxborough row house. So many things had changed for Olivia in the past year that Jocelyn had given up on moving—at least for now.

Olivia had been locked in her bedroom the year before when Jocelyn was attacked. She understood that Jocelyn had been hurt, but she had no idea what had really happened and thus, had no negative associations with their home. Their tiny row house was the only home Olivia had ever known, and Jocelyn had filled it with great memories for her daughter. She was grateful for that, grateful beyond measure. She would just have to find a renter for the new house.

Knox ambled into the office behind her. From behind her desk, Anita smiled at him, one brow raised. "So," she said. "You found her anyway."

Knox tilted his head, almost apologetically. Anita sighed and pointed to a box beside her desk. "That's his," she told Jocelyn.

Jocelyn picked it up. It had some weight to it. "You carried this?"

Knox looked at his feet. "Uh, no."

"He had it Fed Ex'ed," Anita put in. "It came about an hour before he did."

"I didn't mean to be presumptuous," Knox said. "I just—I have enough trouble carting around this damn oxygen tank."

Jocelyn smiled. "It's fine. Let's go back to the conference room."

Anita and Knox took seats at their large conference table while Jocelyn remained standing, rifling through the box. She pulled a few photos from the files inside. They showed a black female lying facedown in grass, beneath a tree. She wore a dark purple sports bra, but she was naked below the waist. Her head was covered by what looked like a small pair of blue running shorts. Bullet holes in the back of her right thigh and her lower and middle back oozed blood. Her right arm extended over her head, as though she were reaching for something or someone. Perhaps she had tried to pull herself up.

Jocelyn glanced up at Knox. "This looks like official police evidence."

He folded his hands over his stomach. He didn't quite meet her eyes. "I made copies of everything. I know, I know, it's against policy and all that, but . . . let's just say that I—well, I just didn't give a damn."

"How long were you on homicide?" Jocelyn asked.

"Twenty-seven years." He met her eyes and motioned to the box. "It was my case."

Jocelyn held his gaze as she passed the photos across the table to Anita. Anita studied them stone-faced, in spite of the horrific nature of the photos. Although the two of them had started out on opposite sides of the law, just like Jocelyn, Anita had seen and experienced enough gruesome crimes that few things shocked her.

Jocelyn saw Knox's eyes wander to Anita's hands and linger there. Everyone stared at the damn scars. "Yeah, her too," Jocelyn said, drawing a sheepish look from Knox. "Both hands."

"I'm sorry," Knox said to Anita. "I didn't mean to stare."

Anita shrugged. "Everybody stares."

"So tell me," Jocelyn said to Knox. "About your case."

Knox cleared his throat as if he were about to address a room full of people. "The victim was Sydney Adams. She was seventeen years old, a track and field star for Franklin West High School. She was a senior there."

"The charter school over by Drexel University?" Anita asked. "The one where they had that shooting in 2006?"

"Yeah, that one," Knox answered. "Sydney was only a month or so from graduating. She left her grandmother's house around seven in the evening for her nightly run through Fairmount Park. She always ran the same route. She didn't get very far that night, so I think she was killed close to seven-thirty, although I was never able to get the medical examiner to say so. He would only give us a four-hour range. He said Syd died sometime between seven and eleven."

"Where in the park?" Jocelyn asked. Fairmount Park was really a collection of outdoor parks that covered over 9,000 acres in the city.

"She started her run around the athletic field on Boxer's Trail. Not too far from her house."

"She lived in Strawberry Mansion?"

"Yeah, over by 31st and Dauphin. Anyway, she was shot in the back three times at close range. There was a bullet lodged in the tree, so there were four shots in all. .22s. There were no shell casings, so we think the killer picked them up and took them."

"Or the killer used a revolver," Jocelyn offered.

"I thought of that," he said, his voice sounding hoarse. "But I still think the shooter was someone she knew."

Knox braced his hands against the edge of the table as he fought for the next few breaths. Anita and Jocelyn exchanged a look. Anita pulled her cell phone out of her pocket, ready to call 911, Jocelyn assumed. But Knox regained his composure. Slowly, he folded his hands in his lap and gave them a tight smile.

"Take your time," Jocelyn said.

For a few moments, there was only the hiss of his oxygen feeding the air into his nose. Finally, he spoke again, "She was in a grassy area, beneath the tree. No mud, so we don't have any footprints. Of course, because so many people frequent that area, it would have been hard to tell if any footprints belonged to the killer. She wasn't found until after midnight when her sister, grandmother, and a few of their neighbors went looking for her.

It was a neighbor who found her and called it in."

"Robbed?"

"Yeah. They took a gold necklace with a charm on it that bore her name, her class ring, and two small gold hoop earrings."

"Raped?"

"No. But the killer pulled her shorts and underwear off and put them over her head."

"They took her pants off but didn't rape her?" Anita said.

Knox fidgeted with the cannula, pushing the tubing deeper into his nostrils. "Yeah. The ME said there was no evidence of sexual assault."

Anita piled the photos neatly atop one another, their edges lined up perfectly, and pushed the pile to the center of the table.

Jocelyn chewed her lower lip. "That sounds a lot like a random," she remarked. "Someone looking for a quick buck. Sees an opportunity, acts impulsively. Maybe he was going to rape her but got interrupted. They *were* in a public park."

"Well, yeah," Knox said. "That's how it's always been treated. We got nothing forensically. No trace evidence. No semen. Not one goddamn piece of evidence except the bullets, which we were never able to match to a gun. I know this is the kind of case most people give up on and Sydney being a black kid? I had no resources for this case." He pointed toward the crime scene photos. "You'd better believe if that was a young white blonde girl, there would have been a goddamn hotline for tips. Maybe if I'd had a hotline, or more news coverage or more manpower, I could have turned something up."

Jocelyn frowned. She looked at Anita, but the other woman's eyes were locked on Knox. He looked at his lap and then back at Jocelyn. "You know it's true."

She did know. The year before, when Anita was viciously attacked and mutilated, no one cared. Only after a white schoolteacher was assaulted by the very same men did the case get the attention it deserved — the kind of attention that often meant the difference between a cleared case and a cold case. The press named the assailants the Schoolteacher Attackers, but Anita was a victim before the teacher. The men should have been called the Receptionist Attackers. Of course, Jocelyn could never prove that the disparity was due to the fact that Anita was black and the other victim was white, but the disparity was there, and she couldn't deny that Knox had a point. He very well may have been given more resources had Sydney been white. But that didn't change anything about the case as it stood now.

Jocelyn said, "I know what you're saying, Knox, and I think you're right, but this is what we've got to work with right now, and what we've got points to an impulsive, random type."

He pointed a finger in the air. "But impulsive random types don't pick up their shell casings and take them with them — I mean assuming he didn't use a revolver."

"Which is why you think it's someone she knew."

Knox reached into his back pocket and pulled out three color photographs, which he pushed across the table to Jocelyn. They were small, three by five inches maybe, and old, as if they had been developed back when people actually used rolls of film. Jocelyn studied them while Knox talked and then handed them to Anita. There wasn't much to them. It was three flirty pictures of the girl.

"She was ambushed. Shot in the back. If it was a robbery, why not just threaten her with the gun and demand her valuables? This guy shot first. The few pieces of jewelry she had on weren't that valuable — although I've routinely checked every pawn shop in the city for the last fourteen years, and none of it ever turned up. Anyway, if the killer's intention was to rape her, why shoot her first?"

"People get shot in this city every day for no good reason at all," Jocelyn pointed out.

"Yeah," Knox said with a grimace. "I remember."

"Who took these photos?" Jocelyn asked, tapping a finger on Sydney Adams' bare midriff.

"I think her track and field coach, Cash Rigo, took them at his home. Based on how broken up he was after her death, I have always suspected him. I couldn't prove it, but these photos show they had a relationship. Sydney hid these photos under her carpet, beneath her nightstand. They obviously had some kind of inappropriate relationship. She tried to keep it hidden."

Jocelyn sighed and rubbed a hand over her eyes, suddenly feeling tired. She needed coffee. "Before we go any further with your Cash Rigo theory, does he have an alibi? I assume he does if you were never able to pin this on him."

Knox pinched his oxygen tubing between a thumb and forefinger. "He left the school at five in the afternoon that day. He was home by himself until nine-thirty that night. His wife, who was the school nurse, was at a Home and School meeting, which started at six-thirty. It went a few hours. Apparently, there had been some ongoing vandalism in the school that parents were up in arms about. There was a lot of damage. Someone had even broken into the nurse's office and stolen some things."

"What about the wife?" Anita interjected. "Any chance she knew about her husband's relationship with this girl and went off the deep end?"

Knox glanced at Anita and shook his head. "I don't think she knew, but even if she did, her alibi is airtight. The Home and School meeting was taped. I've got her on video from six-thirty that night till just after nine. She never even got up to use the bathroom. Anyway, she got home around nine-thirty and found her husband violently ill. She took him to Chestnut Hill Hospital." He pointed at the box. "The records are in there. But he was home alone for hours before his wife came home. He had plenty of time to go to the park, shoot Sydney and get home, assuming that she was killed shortly after seven. She ran the same route every night for two years. Everyone who knew her knew that. The Rigos lived in Mt. Airy, which as you know, is a lot closer to the athletic field than Franklin West."

Anita pulled the box over to her. She handed a set of Emergency Room records to Jocelyn and kept rifling through its contents. She pulled out another pile of photos that looked like they had come from the same roll of film as the flirty photos. She pulled one out and held it up for them both to see. "Is this him?" she asked Knox.

He nodded. Anita caught Jocelyn's eye and handed her the photo. "A pretty boy," both women said in unison. Jocelyn studied the photo more closely, ignoring the quizzical look that Knox directed at Anita and then her. Cash sat at a desk, and judging by the student desks and chalkboard in the background, it was his classroom. He looked young and fresh-faced, not much older than a high school student. He had broad shoulders, kind brown eyes, an angular jaw and curly brown hair cut just short enough to look stylish. Long enough for a woman to want to run her fingers through it, but not so long that it would make him look dorky or effeminate. He wasn't smoking hot, but he would definitely get second looks from most women he encountered.

"I really am going to need some coffee," Jocelyn said, although her mind was abuzz with the news of Rigo's shaky alibi. It was something.

She flipped the pages of the ER records until she came to the discharge summary. Food poisoning. "What did he have for dinner?" she asked.

Knox answered, "Chinese food from a local place that no longer exists. He picked it up on his way home, at about five forty-five, which still gives him plenty of time to shoot Sydney and get home. None of the other patrons that ate there that night got sick."

"How about a gun? Either of the Rigos ever own a gun?"

"Not that I could prove. Nothing registered in either of their names. I went to the house several times, but I could never get a search warrant."

Jocelyn looked into his jaundiced eyes. "I assume you leaned on this guy."

He smiled, his cheeks reddening slightly. "Until I was formally reprimanded, and his wife threatened to file a lawsuit against the police department."

Anita gave a low whistle. "Well," she said.

Knox glanced at her. "I couldn't break him."

Jocelyn pulled out a chair and sat down. "This is not new evidence. I mean we'll call it that to get things moving again, but it's not. This is not a smoking gun. You know that, right?"

Knox frowned, the cannula on his upper lip bobbing. "I know Cash Rigo did this."

"These pictures don't prove that, Knox. You can't even prove that Cash Rigo took these."

"I know Cash Rigo killed Sydney," Knox said. "He did it."

Jocelyn exchanged another look with Anita. She knew her partner was on board, in spite of the fact that Knox had brought them next to nothing to work with. "You have no physical evidence. You have a suspect with something of an alibi. You barely have a motive."

Knox opened his mouth to speak, but Jocelyn leaned forward and held up one of the flirty photos. "Even with these, you've got nothing, Knox. Which means you'll need a confession."

Knox's expression morphed from crestfallen to the kind of earnest, hopeful expression dogs get when their owners pull out a leash. Anita clucked her tongue. "It's been fourteen years, Rush. Fourteen years this piece of shit has gotten away with it. Why in the hell would he confess now?"

Jocelyn smiled. "Because we're about to put the pressure on. First, I need a homicide detective. One who's still on the payroll."

CHAPTER
6

June 8, 2000

It was hot in the house. Stifling. Sweat poured down his face and neck in rivulets, but Cash Rigo made no move to turn on the ancient AC window units throughout the house. Instead, he stood stock-still in the darkness gathering all around him, twilight sinking into the house. It was so quiet. He used to love this time of day, when he got home before his wife, and there was nothing but silence. Blessed silence, occasionally broken up by the muffled sounds of the outside world, like a car passing, a dog barking, and the children at the end of the block shouting and playing. The soft, silent dark time. It was all his, all peace, or what passed for peace in Cash's world.

Today he'd gotten caught up by the table at the end of the foyer hall. The one under Francine's painting with its ridiculously oversized faux teak frame. The table that was more the size of a stool—tall, narrow and good for nothing but holding decorative items, like the photo of the two of them that Francine had placed there the week before. Its gaudy eight by ten frame seemed to mock him. There used to be a candle there. One of those fancy, large candles that cost more than a Thanksgiving turkey and that you could smell throughout the entire house without even lighting it. It had been some kind of tropical scent. It had been there so long, untouched, that a thick film of dust clung to it. He remembered the fruity scent mingling with Sydney's own smell — shampoo, sweat, and freshly cut grass. She had smelled like spring, he thought wistfully.

He heard her voice in his head. *God, you're so lame.*

She used to say that to him all the time. It was a flirtation. She always smiled when she said it, her gaze lingering on him till his face flamed red. It was almost a compliment. She'd said it that night.

That night.

That's what he called it. It stood out from all the other nights of his life. He tried to remember how he'd ended up behind her, his hands on her, their fused bodies rocking the ill-conceived little table until it left a small, thin gouge in the wall behind it. Had it really happened? Of course it had. He'd thought of nothing else for almost a month. Until she was gone.

He clenched and unclenched his fists. The sound of his wife's key in the lock of the front door barely registered. He had to move, but he couldn't. She'd be angry that he hadn't turned the AC on.

You never consider me or my feelings, she would say.

That was what his wife always said. She was right in some ways. He hadn't considered her at all when he'd fucked a seventeen-year-old student at this very table.

Sweat pasted his polo shirt to his body and poured from his crotch, dampening his khakis. He could smell his own foul stink. Francine wouldn't like that either. She didn't like a lot of things. Then again, he was a shitty husband. Even before they married, he'd been a shitty boyfriend.

Since Sydney's death, Cash had told himself he would be better. He had to be better. They were *trying* again. His wife wanted a baby.

Her cool fingers curled around the back of his neck, startling him, as if she'd materialized out of thin air. She stood just behind him, looking over his shoulder. "I always liked that picture of us," she said quietly, fingers kneading the back of his neck.

"What?" he mumbled. He tried to tear his gaze away from the table to look at her, but he couldn't. He could still see Sydney there, feel her in his hands.

Francine moved around his body, filling up the space between Cash and the table. She looked up at him, trying to catch his eyes. She put her hands on his chest. "That photo of us. Don't you remember? The wine festival in Vermont? We hadn't married yet."

"Yeah," he said finally, looking at her. "I remember."

A small smile lit on her round moon face. Her brown hair was pulled back in a ponytail. "Do you remember what we did in the woods that day?" she asked as her hands slid down to his belt buckle.

"Don't," he said as she undid his belt.

The smile tightened on her face. "You're my husband," she said, her voice cracking on the last syllable.

He pushed her hands away. "It's—it's too hot."

She didn't move. Instead, she stood there, her hands poised halfway between their bodies, the corners of her smile failing. He smiled, trying to salvage the moment. But he could already sense her disappointment. "It's hot," he said again, awkwardly. "I'll turn the AC on and make you something to eat."

He left her there, by the table, in the close, hot dark.

CHAPTER 7

October 16, 2014

Caleb's tongue trailed between Jocelyn's breasts, moving lower and lower, circling her navel and then—she gasped and grabbed clumps of his thick brown hair in both her hands. She squirmed against her bedsheets and glanced at her nightstand where the video monitor of Olivia sat. Her four-year-old slept peacefully. She had always been a good sleeper. She didn't usually try sneaking into Jocelyn's bed until three or four in the morning. They'd been lucky in the year they'd been sneaking around. Olivia had never woken up while Caleb was there.

They had already done it once in a frenzy of roaming hands; hot, hungry mouths; and half-removed clothes. Now they were just lounging naked in her bed, enjoying their stolen, secret moments together. She had always loved the feel of his skin against hers. She had never truly enjoyed sex before Caleb. They'd been instantly and inexplicably drawn to each other. Lust at first sight.

Almost a year later, she still couldn't get enough of him. His hands crept beneath her, palming her ass cheeks, bringing her closer to his mouth. "I can't believe I missed the thong," he said, his words muffled against her inner thighs.

"Me either," Jocelyn said. "That may never happen again."

His head shot up, a purple sheet monster. He peeled it back, staring at her with an alarmed look. Tufts of his brown hair shot out from the sides of his head. She eyed his broad chest with its black hair, his muscular arms and the knots at the top of each shoulder. He was lean and well-muscled for his age.

Single dads have to stay in shape, he had told her once, even though his son was nearly nineteen now. She had never met his son.

"Don't take away the thong," he implored. "You would look so hot in a thong."

She laughed and pulled him up beside her, smoothing down one side of his hair. He nibbled her ear. "I'm sorry about today. You know I've been waiting to nail this guy for months. I wouldn't normally ditch you —"

"Stop. Don't apologize for work."

It was a rule. She'd been a detective for many years. Until Olivia came along, her job was her biggest priority. She lived and breathed it. Caleb was every bit as serious and driven as she had been, and Jocelyn respected that. It was one of the things that had first attracted her to him. She would never begrudge him the time he spent taking down people who hurt children — as many of his cases revolved around children. She knew how hard he and his squad had worked the last several months and how badly he had wanted to arrest the Powell suspect.

She touched his cheek. "I'm glad you guys got that piece of shit off the street."

Caleb smiled. He caught her hand and kissed it. "One down, one billion to go."

There was no shortage of perverts or criminals; that was for sure. It was maddening and demoralizing if you let yourself think about it too long. To change the subject, she asked, "Do you know Trent Razmus? In Homicide?"

He sidled closer to her, pressing the length of his naked body against her side, and kissed her shoulder. "You mean Raz?"

Men and their nicknames. She turned into him, face to face,

their lips nearly touching. "Yeah, I guess. Is there more than one Trent Razmus in Homicide?"

Caleb caught her lips, his hands roaming again. "No, there's only one," he breathed as he moved his mouth to her neck. "He's a good guy, but do we have to talk about another man right now?"

She laughed. "We were talking about thongs. They're very uncomfortable."

It was his turn to laugh. His hand closed over one of her breasts, his mouth not far behind. "It won't stay on for long. I promise."

This was what she loved about Caleb—that, post-coitus, he didn't leave or roll over or go unconscious. He kept worshiping her with his mouth and hands. "Please don't deprive me of the thong," he said again. He looked up at her, eyes twinkling. "What color was it?"

She smiled. "Black."

The noise he made was something between a growl and a moan. His head disappeared beneath the sheet again. Jocelyn closed her eyes and concentrated on the light kisses he left along her stomach. After a moment, he said, "Jocelyn."

"Yeah," she breathed.

"I want more."

"Already?" Not that they hadn't done it multiple times before. The record was four. The Night of the Grand Slam they called it. Her best friend, Inez, had taken Olivia overnight and part of the next day. They'd spent a full sixteen hours naked, sleeping little and giving each other a workout. Still, they weren't exactly college kids. She hadn't expected Caleb to be physically ready so soon.

He laughed, his head inching back to the top of the sheet. "No, not that," he said. "I mean I do, but that's not what I meant." He rolled off her and sat on the edge of the bed, his back to her. He pointed at the video monitor, which showed Olivia sleeping peacefully. "It's been nearly a year, Jocelyn. In less than two weeks, it will be one year since we met."

He looked at her over his shoulder, his eyes serious, the lines at the corners crinkling. He let the words hang.

A year.

A year since they'd met in the lobby of the Special Victims Unit, the electricity between them palpable. A year since they'd worked together on the case that had nearly killed her and damn near everyone around her. A year since her sister had been clean. A year since the last of the Schoolteacher Attackers had broken into her home and—

"Joc," Caleb said, his voice firm and loud, calling her back to the present. He turned toward her and touched her cheek, brushing her hair back from her forehead. "Don't," he said. He smiled tenderly at her and lay back down on his side, his elbow bent and head propped on his fist. "Stay with me."

She smiled back at him weakly, pushing the memories away. Still, she shuddered. Caleb pulled her into his arms and she let him, resting her head on his chest, listening to his heartbeat. It was reassuring. "What I meant to say was that I would like to meet Olivia."

Jocelyn reached up and traced his collarbone. "Okay."

He pulled back and looked into her face. "What?"

"I said 'okay.'"

"Just like that?"

She laughed again and punched his chest lightly. "Yeah, just like that. You passed the 365 day screening process, so now you may meet my daughter. In an appropriately sanctioned environment."

Before he could get through his eye roll, she punched him again. He squeezed her and kissed the top of her head. "Will said meeting take place within the next year?" he asked.

"We'll see."

CHAPTER
8

October 17, 2014

"The girls are asleep finally," Inez said, padding barefoot down Jocelyn's steps. She wore pink sweatpants and an oversized Marine Corps T-shirt. She plopped down beside Jocelyn on the couch. Leaning forward, she picked up the bottle of Barefoot Moscato they'd been sharing and filled both their glasses.

Inez and Jocelyn had been friends for over a decade. Inez's youngest daughter, Raquel was only a year older than Olivia, and the two of them were just as close as their mothers. Inez worked patrol in the thirty-fifth district. Over the summer, her husband had returned from his second tour in Afghanistan, but two weeks earlier, he'd been deployed again, this time to West Africa to help contain the Ebola outbreak.

"I don't know what's worse," Inez had said. "Worrying about him getting blown to pieces or worrying about him catching a deadly virus."

Jocelyn's friend was taking this deployment hard. Inez's mother, Martina, had told Jocelyn that Inez wasn't sleeping well—pacing their living room at night and watching QVC until three in the morning. *If I get another set of Wonder Knives delivered*

41

to my house, I'm going to wring her neck, Martina had said.

Which was why Jocelyn had insisted on a slumber party. It was their long-standing ritual.

Inez tucked her legs up beneath her, sipped her wine, and motioned to the television. "This is really fascinating shit, Rush, but I thought we were going to watch the new Denzel Washington movie. Holy shit. Is that a VCR?"

Jocelyn paused the tape she'd been watching of Knox interrogating Cash Rigo on June 27, 2000. She shifted the legal pad she'd been jotting notes on and picked up her wine glass. She smiled at Inez and sipped the Moscato, savoring its sweet taste on her tongue. "It sure is," she told Inez. "Three guesses where I got it from."

It only took one. "Kevin Sullivan is the only person I know who would still have a damn VCR." Jocelyn laughed, nodding as Inez went on. "When did you finally convince him to get rid of his flip phone?"

"Two years ago," Jocelyn supplied. "Yeah, he loaned me the VCR so I could watch all the tapes on this Sydney Adams case."

"Your first major case as a PI, huh?"

Jocelyn nodded again and ran it down for Inez. Then she rewound the tape to where Rigo first started sobbing like a baby. "Look at the time stamp," Jocelyn said, fast-forwarding again. The clock in the upper right-hand corner sped up. "This son of a bitch weeps for fourteen minutes straight."

On the television, Rigo's shoulders quaked like he was doing some kind of funky chair dance. During the last minute, Jocelyn pressed play and turned the volume up so Inez could hear him howl with grief.

"What the hell?" Inez said. "You said this is the coach?"

"Yes! It's weird, right?"

"Last time I saw a man crying like that was that guy over in Olney who backed up over his kid out in front of his house."

"Exactly," Jocelyn said. She took another sip of wine and got up to change the videotape. "Watch," she said. "The boyfriend doesn't even take it that hard."

Thin wiry Lonnie Burgess fidgeted in the metal chair Knox

offered him, his fingers tapping against his thighs. He wore a plain white T-shirt and drab green cargo pants. He looked impossibly young—his face fresh and unlined, and, except for the sadness that sat on his shoulders like a yoke, he seemed confident and hopeful in the way only a child can. The video wasn't the greatest quality, but it was good enough to see him hastily wiping tears from the corners of his eyes when he thought Knox wasn't looking. It was clear that he was distraught but trying to maintain his composure.

"I assume this kid has an alibi," Inez said.

"Yeah," Jocelyn replied. She got up and changed the tape again. This time, the video wasn't from inside of one of the Homicide Unit's dank, cigarette-scarred interrogation rooms. It was a Channel 10 evening newscast from May 9, 2000. The lower, left-hand side of the screen showed a time-stamp of six twenty-five. On the other side, it said LIVE. The reporter was interviewing Lonnie Burgess about the vandalism at Franklin West. He stood outside of the school, talking in earnest about the need for security cameras on the premises while people milled about behind him. Some gathered in knots on Franklin West's steps, talking and smoking, while others went in and out of the building.

"Good God, look at those clothes," Inez said. "Do you think we looked that dated back then?"

"Please, the only thing we were wearing then were our uniforms. I worked so much overtime, I slept in that damn thing sometimes."

"I still do," Inez quipped.

Jocelyn got up and put in the last tape—the one of Francine Rigo. She was small and plump with a round face, her brown hair pulled back in a French braid. She sat primly in her chair across from Knox, her hands folded on the table. Knox was mostly concerned with what time she had gotten home from Franklin West to find her husband ill. He zig-zagged in his questioning. It was a technique used to throw people off, to keep them off balance.

"You arrived home at nine-thirty. Did you go right home from

Franklin West, or did you stop somewhere?"

Francine's voice was soft and had a musical quality to it. "Right home," she answered. With a wan smile, she added, "It had been a long day."

"Did you know Sydney Adams well?"

If Francine was put off by the sudden change of topic, she didn't show it. "As well as a school nurse gets to know any student, I suppose. She came to my office now and then for a headache, or you know, other things."

"Other things?"

Francine unlaced her fingers and spread her palms in a sort of helpless gesture. "Female things," she clarified. "Menstrual cramps, or if she needed a pad or tampon."

"Oh, okay." Knox jotted something down on the pad in front of him.

"I went with Cash and the team to some track and field meets, and Sydney was there. She was very . . ." she trailed off and leaned out of the frame. When she returned, she had a tissue in her hand. She dabbed her eyes as she continued. "Sydney was a sweet girl. Very smart, very kind."

"Was she close with your husband?"

Francine nodded. "Yes. He helped her with her college applications and wrote her a glowing recommendation letter." The tears came faster than Francine could dab them. "Such a bright future ahead of her. It's just so sad."

"What route did you take home that night?" Knox asked, going back to the night of Sydney's murder.

Francine sniffled and fisted her tissue. "Same as always. I took Kelly Drive to Lincoln Drive into Mount Airy."

"And where was your husband when you got home?"

"Where? In the bathroom vomiting."

"Did he ask you to take him to the hospital?"

"I really can't recall whose idea it was, I just know he was in very poor shape—badly dehydrated. It's not like I had an IV and anti-nausea meds on hand."

She frowned then, finally seeming to figure out that Knox might be after something, like her husband. "Why are you asking me about Cash? It's Sydney who was murdered."

Knox gave her a tight smile. "Yes," he said. "You're right. We are just trying to rule people out at this point."

Francine's head reared back. "Rule people out?" Her voice lost its musical quality and took on an edge. "For what?"

Knox stared at her with a hangdog expression. "Mrs. Rigo," was all he said.

The hand with the tissue in it flew up to her chest. "You think my husband had something to do with Sydney's murder."

It wasn't a question. Knox said nothing, letting her stew in the realization. Finally, she said, "My husband would never do anything like that."

Jocelyn stopped the tape as Inez hummed a few bars of *Stand By Your Man.*

"What about her?" Inez asked.

Jocelyn pointed to a file box on the floor near her feet. "I already checked. She's on video at the Home and School meeting from six-thirty until just after nine. No way she could have done it. Knox was right. Rigo is the only person who can't account for all of his time that night. He would have had plenty of time to shoot Sydney and be home in time for his wife to find him ill. Yet, everyone Knox talked to said Rigo was a good guy, a nice guy," Jocelyn said. "Students said he was 'cool.'"

"So he was the Friend Teacher," Inez said.

"Yeah. Looks that way. He probably never enforced a rule in his life."

"Well, that's a slippery slope."

Jocelyn downed the rest of her wine. "Yes," she said. "Yes, it is."

CHAPTER
9

October 18, 2014

Jocelyn took the bridge at the bottom of Wises Mill Road at a snail's pace. It was the entry to the Wissahickon Creek trail closest to her home and had the nearest access to parking, but the bridge itself was only one lane. The bend ahead of it curved in a way that made it damn near impossible to see if there was any oncoming traffic.

"You can go a little faster," Kevin Sullivan said.

She shot him a glare. "You want to drive?"

She and Kevin had been partners at the Philadelphia Police Department's Northwest Detectives before she retired. He was still on the job, in spite of his residual health problems that were courtesy of a major head injury inflicted by none other than one of the Schoolteacher Attackers.

In the passenger seat, Kevin grinned, the corners of his hazel eyes crinkling. "I miss you, Rush. Irritability and all." As she came to the bottom of the other side of the stone bridge and onto the Wissahickon trail, Kevin pointed to their right. "There's a parking lot right there."

She pulled onto the trail slowly, avoiding several joggers, two bicyclists and a mother pushing a double stroller. Motor vehicles were prohibited on the trail except for this tiny stretch between the Wises Mill entrance and the parking lots. The dirt trail was rutted and full of holes. They bounced mercilessly in her SUV.

She parked and they got out, Kevin walking with his cane. He said that he still had muscle weakness in his right side from the year before, but Jocelyn had seen him get around just fine without the cane when needed. She wondered if it had just become a crutch.

They walked south on the trail, passing Valley Green, the restaurant where she and Caleb had had their first date.

"You sure this guy is down here?" Kevin asked. As they moved away from the restaurant and main parking area, the fall foliage closed in on them. Although the trail was wide enough to accommodate two motor vehicles, the area on either side of it was heavily wooded, even on the creek side.

"He said he would be here, about a quarter mile from Valley Green." Jocelyn pointed to the trail before them. "In this direction. He said it would be a lot easier for me to meet him here than to go all the way down to the Roundhouse."

The Roundhouse was Philadelphia's nickname for its police headquarters, a squat four-story building shaped like the double barrels of a shotgun. It sat at 8th and Arch Streets and housed, among other things, the Homicide Unit.

Jocelyn glanced down toward the creek. The bank rose steeply away from it the further they walked. She tried not to jump every time a jogger or a bicyclist flew past them. She and Kevin weren't dressed for the trail, both of them in tailored suits — his brown and hers charcoal gray — looking every bit the detectives they were.

"You know you didn't have to come with me, Kev," she said. A jogger pounded past her, nearly touching her sleeve. In spite of herself, she startled, bumping shoulders with Kevin. She laughed, her nervousness receding as he steadied her with one hand on her elbow. "But I'm glad you did."

"Happy to do it," he said with a smile. "I don't get to see enough of you anymore. Besides, I just arrested four teenage assholes for beating the piss out of a sixty-year-old man right back there." He let go of her elbow and hooked a thumb over his shoulder.

Jocelyn sighed. "It never ends, does it?"

He shook his head. After a beat, he cleared his throat, and Jocelyn knew something difficult was coming. "Besides, Rush," he said. "I feel guilty. I never got to tell you, I'm sorry about . . . about last year. I'm sorry that I didn't get to you in time."

Jocelyn stopped in her tracks, a thick knot forming in her throat. He took a few steps before realizing she had stopped, then turned back and met her eyes, a puzzled look on his face. "Rush?"

Tears stung the backs of her eyes, although she fought them. "Stop," she said. "That wasn't your fault. He was coming after me no matter what. You couldn't have stopped him."

Kevin brushed a hand through his thinning salt and pepper hair — more salt than pepper these days. He squinted at her, even though the trees overhead blocked the sunlight. "You came to me with your theory. I blew you off, and then he attacked you. I should have had your back, that's all I'm saying."

She had never even considered that Kevin might harbor guilt over what had happened the year before. She had never believed that anything that happened was his fault. They couldn't have known what was going to happen that night, no matter what theories Jocelyn was tossing around — or how accurate she had been. Jocelyn smiled, swallowing hard and blinking back her tears. She closed the distance between them in two steps, reached out, and touched his hand. "Kev, I know you've got my back."

He didn't look satisfied. His gaze drifted to the ground. He drew tiny lines in the dirt with his cane. "I just want you to know — that won't happen again."

"Okay," she said. Two bicyclists breezed past them, followed by a woman wearing yoga pants and an oversized sweatshirt, running beside her Siberian husky. "Can we just find Razmus now?"

"Sure."

It wasn't hard to find Trent Razmus. He had driven his unmarked, police-issued Chevrolet Cruze down the trail and parked it alongside a break in the fence that demarcated the creek bank from the trail. People walked, jogged, and biked around it, shooting the car dirty looks and mumbling words like "asshole" and "douchebag." Jocelyn and Kevin squeezed between the black vehicle and the opening in the wooden fence. An overgrown set of stone steps led to the creek bank, but even from the top, they could see a black man in a light gray suit standing on the narrow concrete wall that spanned the width of the creek. He had taken his shoes off and left them on a rock near the shore. His slacks were rolled neatly above his knees. Water rushed over the wall and up over his ankles.

As they reached the bottom of the steps, Jocelyn spotted Trent's suit jacket hanging from a tree limb.

"What the hell is he doing?" Kevin asked.

Jocelyn shrugged. "Beats me."

Trent glanced over at them and waved.

"That's not Trent Razmus," Kevin said. "It's Jimmy Rollins."

Jocelyn laughed. Jimmy Rollins was the Philadelphia Phillies' short stop—although there was talk he would be traded in the coming months. She moved closer to the water and took another look at Trent. He did bear a striking resemblance to the city's beloved baseball player. A shaved head, round face, flat nose, thick brows over kind brown eyes, and a thin, neatly trimmed moustache and goatee.

"That has to be cold," Kevin said.

Jocelyn reached down and dipped a finger into the water. It wasn't freezing, but it wasn't cozy warm either. She could do without the fishy, fetid smell though.

"Rush?" Trent called.

She nodded as she stood back up.

Trent beckoned her. She looked over at Kevin. He waved his cane. "No way am I going in that water, Rush."

She exhaled noisily. Looking back at Trent, she pointed to her chest. "You want me out there?"

He smiled. "I need help."

She didn't smile back. Although the water wasn't moving very quickly, wading barefoot into the Wissahickon Creek was not on her list of things to do that day—or any day. "You lose something?" she asked, stalling.

"Murder weapon."

"Good fucking lord," she muttered under her breath. She sat on a nearby rock and pulled off her shoes and socks. She was glad that she had been shaving her legs regularly these days. "I'm charging Knox double my hourly rate for this bullshit."

Kevin laughed. She'd done weirder things in the name of clearing a case, but she cringed at the thought of putting her bare feet into the creek water. It churned, thick and brown, rushing and gurgling over the wall. Its murky depths gave nothing away. She rolled up her pant legs, stood and shrugged off her jacket, handing it to Kevin, together with her shoulder holster and gun. He didn't even bother to contain his smirk. As she set one bare foot onto the wall, Trent rolled up his shirtsleeves as far as they'd go, revealing thick, muscular forearms with tattoos she couldn't make out.

The water wasn't as cold as she'd expected, but she winced as she felt the slimy coating of sludge that lived on the wall. It was easily a foot wide, so she was able to keep her balance without much trouble. Standing next to Trent, she realized he wasn't much taller than she. He was short and stocky, but given his thick arms and broad chest, he took care of himself.

He smiled at her and extended a hand. Close up, she could see that one of his tattoos was a large dragon, its tail wrapping around his forearm. His other arm was tattooed with a pattern of spiked lines and what looked like thorns. "Trent Razmus," he said.

Jocelyn shook his hand and tried to muster a return smile. "Jocelyn Rush."

"Sorry about this," he said, indicating the creek all around them. "I didn't actually expect to find it."

Jocelyn looked over the wall. Below it was a small outcropping of rocks jutting out from the rushing water. Trent pointed to a crease between two jagged peaks. The gleaming black handle of a pistol protruded from the leaves, sticks, and other debris that had collected between the wall and the rocks.

"Road rage case," Trent explained. "You heard about that guy who got shot on the expressway last week?"

"Sure, it was all over the news. Heard you got the shooter."

"Got a confession too. Guy used to fish back here. Said he tossed the gun into the creek. Right by this wall. First I thought he was bullshitting me, but here I am and there it is."

Jocelyn nodded. "You know you're not getting that without getting wet, right?"

Trent laughed heartily. "Yeah, I know. I just need you to anchor me. Hold onto my belt while I reach down there, so I don't fall and crack my head open."

"I'll try."

He pulled a pair of vinyl gloves from his pocket and pulled them on. Then he turned his back to her and knelt carefully on the wall. Jocelyn wished she had something to hold onto, but they were smack in the middle of the creek. If they tumbled off the wall, it wouldn't kill them, but landing on the rocks below would definitely cause a fracture or two. She planted her feet shoulder-width apart, bent her knees slightly, and held tight to Trent's belt as he reached into the crevice.

It took several tries, but he came up with the gun. He held it gingerly with his thumb and forefinger. She helped him to his feet. The front of his shirt and pants were completely soaked. "Your clothes are ruined," Jocelyn said.

Trent grinned, holding the gun up as though he'd just caught a prize trout. "You know this guy who got killed had a ten-year-old son?"

Jocelyn swallowed. "Yeah, they said that on the news."

He took his eyes off the gun to meet hers. "Worth it."

Jocelyn couldn't argue with that. They made their way carefully back to the shore. Trent grabbed his jacket from the tree limb, pulled a small brown paper bag out of the pocket and dropped the gun into it. After tucking the bag back into his jacket pocket and removing his gloves, he sat beside Jocelyn on a large stone, and they started putting their socks and shoes back on. Trent glanced up at Kevin. After they made introductions, Trent turned back to Jocelyn. "Knox didn't come?"

Jocelyn struggled to pull her socks over her wet feet. She thought of how Olivia always complained that her pajamas were too tight whenever she tried pulling them on after bath time without properly drying her skin. Jocelyn swallowed the smile that instantly came to her face and looked at Trent. "He wasn't feeling so hot. Did he tell you about his . . . illness?"

Trent nodded. "He told me he was dying."

"You and Knox go back aways?" Kevin asked.

"You could say that."

Jocelyn got both socks and shoes on. She'd have to stop at home to wash her feet later. "Are you familiar with the Sydney Adams case?" she asked Trent.

"The Adams case is Knox's baby. He's never given up on that one. Yeah, I know all about it. He told me about the new photos they found in Syd's old room. Nothing I can do with them though."

"Do you think that Cash Rigo did it?"

Trent stood and brushed off his pants. "Knox was a good cop and a great detective. I've never known him to be wrong. So if he thinks Cash Rigo did it, then I'm sure he did."

An awkward silence ensued. Jocelyn stood up and took her jacket back from Kevin. Trent said, "You're not convinced."

"No," Jocelyn admitted. "I'm not one hundred percent on this one. It looks too much like a random shooting."

"Okay, okay. That's fair, but if I'm advocating for Knox, I have to tell you that my man, Knox, sees things other people don't. He's all about the details."

Jocelyn exchanged a look with Kevin. She could practically hear his thoughts: *Is this guy going to tell us how Knox sees dead people next?*

She looked back at Trent, and her mind flashed on the crime scene photos. "The shorts and underwear over Sydney's head."

Trent smiled again. "You got it. Knox thinks that shows remorse or even guilt. The killer shot her from behind. She never saw him. Why go to the trouble of taking off her panties and shorts and staging the scene if you're trying to make it look like a random shooting? Rigo felt guilty. Even in death he didn't want her to see him, so he covered her head and face. That's a public place, and there's a high risk of being seen committing the crime.

Why would Rigo take such a risk? His guilt was eating him alive. I'll get you all the interview transcripts we have—if you want. I mean I'll work with you if you think you can do something with this. You can read the transcripts. You'll see that every person we talked to who knew Sydney and Rigo said he was a broken man after her murder."

Jocelyn blew out a breath. "He could have just been broken up because he lost a great student who he'd been fucking around with. I mean any misogynist psychopath with a gun could have shot this girl in the back and placed her undergarments on her head as a form of humiliation. Maybe the killer was going to rape her but didn't have time. Maybe the panties over the head is part of his ritual."

She stopped talking when she realized that both men were staring at her hands. She looked down to see that she'd been unconsciously stroking the scar on her left hand with the fingers of her right. She jammed her hands into her jacket pockets. "These sickos have rituals sometimes, that's all I'm saying. Did you check for sexual assaults or murders before Sydney's where the victims' heads were covered?"

Trent was looking at her as if she was a spooked rabbit. She hated that look. "Yes," he said softly. "Knox did. He didn't come up with anything. Come on up to my car. There's something I want to show you."

CHAPTER 10

October 18, 2014

They followed him up the stone steps. A few people had gathered along the fence at the top, probably to watch her and Trent tumble into the creek. As the three of them reached the car, the onlookers dispersed. Trent unlocked the door and fished his wallet out from under the driver's seat. From it, he pulled an old photo. It looked even older than the ones Knox had found in Sydney's room. On closer inspection, Jocelyn realized it was a color copy of an old photo that Trent had laminated. It showed a room with mustard yellow walls and a heavy wooden dining room table with four chairs pushed up against it. In front of the table, an ironing board lay on its side. Next to that was a drinking glass, also on its side, its contents making a darkened blotch on the pea green carpet. A crumpled garment lay next to it. On the table was a pile of folded clothes, a floral centerpiece, a bottle of spray starch, what looked like a pile of unopened mail, and an empty drinking glass.

"That's an old crime scene photo," Kevin said, looking at it over Jocelyn's shoulder.

Trent explained, "That was taken the day of my mother's murder in 1981. While my brothers and I were at school and my dad was at work, someone entered the house where my mother was ironing my dad's clothes. The killer beat her in the head with the iron and strangled her to death with the cord. The case was unsolved until 2002. Knox was still on the force then, still sober most days."

Trent talked about it in a detached way. Clinical. Like it was just another case—one of the hundreds the Homicide Unit saw every year. Jocelyn wondered how long it had taken him to get to that point. "I'm sorry," she said.

"Thanks." He pointed to the table in the photo. "Knox solved this case on this photo."

Jocelyn bit her lip and studied the photo again. She felt like she was playing Spot the Difference. Her eyes kept coming back to the empty glass on the table. "The drinking glass," she said. "She knew the killer. Invited him in—offered him a drink."

Trent nodded.

"Did they print the glass?"

"Wiped clean, like everything else. There was never any sign of forced entry, so we knew she let the killer in, but no one could figure out who it was. Knox said she would only offer a drink to someone she knew well. Someone she had business with."

"Business?"

"Yeah. Whoever it was came to talk. Otherwise, they would never have had drinks. Whatever they talked about didn't go so well."

Jocelyn gave a slow nod. "So what kind of drama was your mom dealing with in her life at that time?"

Trent raised his index finger in the air as if he'd just had a brilliant idea. "Right!" he exclaimed. "My mom's best friend lived three doors down. Her husband used to beat the shit out of her. Two weeks before her murder, my mom called 911 after one of their disputes made its way into the street."

"But the wife wouldn't press charges," Kevin put in.

"Exactly. The husband paid my mom a visit. Told her to butt out. My mom—she wasn't the type to be pushed around." His eyes shone with equal measures of pride and grief.

"So the husband killed her, but how did he get away with it for so long?" Kevin asked.

"The wife was his alibi. Said he came home for lunch that day and that he was with her the whole time. She killed herself a few months after my mom died. Took her secret to the grave."

"So how'd you find out who it was?" Jocelyn asked.

"The husband was in prison for something else. Life without parole."

"LWOP," Jocelyn said. "How about that?"

Trent couldn't help but smile. "Yep. Knox took me in, got a full confession from the guy."

"That's one hell of a story," Kevin said.

"Sure is," Trent agreed. "So, you see, if Knox says Cash Rigo did it, then I believe him."

Jocelyn folded her arms across her chest. "Okay. Fair enough. But I've been over the file, and there's nothing in it that's going to put Rigo away."

"True."

"And those photos — the flirty ones — they will not get him off the street."

"Also true."

"We need a confession."

He remained still, appraising her, a smile in his eyes, one part appreciation, one part incredulity. Kevin's face remained impassive.

Jocelyn forged ahead. "I need you to go on television and tell the world that you've come across new evidence, that the case is active again and that the Philadelphia Homicide Unit is pursuing this new, promising lead."

Trent burst into laughter. She could see him trying to hold it in as she spoke, but once she had finished, he lost it. He had a good belly laugh, his body curling slightly. Finally, he composed himself, folding his photo carefully and putting it back into his wallet. "Are you out of your mind?"

She put her hands on her hips. "Do you want to close this case?" He didn't respond so she said, "Do you want to help Knox?"

The last vestiges of laughter left his face. "Okay," he said. "I'll go on TV and lie."

"It won't be a lie," Jocelyn said. "We're going to put the pressure on this fucker and get a confession. Just like your mom's killer."

Trent frowned. "Rush, you're not getting a confession from this guy. He has shit to lose. He doesn't have an LWOP."

Kevin scoffed, pushing his way between Trent and Jocelyn to lean against the car. "He's married, isn't he?"

Jocelyn laughed. "We can do it," she assured Trent.

He gave her a skeptical look. "We?"

She smiled. "I need you there as a figurehead. The threat of actual police and all that."

"Okay, assuming I can get approval from my captain to re-open this case, where do we start?"

"Do you know any reporters?"

CHAPTER 11

October 20, 2014

When Jocelyn got to work on Monday, Knox was already there. He sat at the conference room table, which made him look small and frail, like a child sitting at the big people's table. His skin seemed sallower than when she had seen him the week before. Anita moved around him, unpacking the rest of the materials he had brought them concerning Sydney Adams' case and tacking up various items along their "case wall," which was the area that Jocelyn had designated for posting important documents or photos, timelines or theories on their big cases.

It had never been used.

This was their first big case, their first real case that didn't involve serving someone with a civil complaint or subpoena, or surveilling cheating spouses and workers' compensation claimants. Even though cheating spouses and workers' compensation claimants had kept them in business so far, Jocelyn was happy to have something else to do.

Knox didn't look up when Jocelyn entered the room. As she got closer, she realized that he was asleep. His chin was bent to his chest. The portable oxygen tank beside him hummed steadily.

Jocelyn tapped him lightly on the shoulder. He startled awake, looking around wild-eyed, his hands flying up in front of him, curled into fists like a boxer ready for the first round. Jocelyn could smell the booze on him. She leaned down and peered into his eyes, a smile on her face. "If you hit me — even by accident — I will hit you back."

He blinked several times, his jaundiced eyes coming into focus. He smiled back sheepishly, a flush coloring his cheeks. "I — I'm sorry," he stammered. "Sometimes I wake up swinging, especially when I'm — " he trailed off, looking down at the table.

Anita breezed past him and set a steaming cup of coffee in front of him. "When you're drunk?" she supplied. Her tone held no malice. Anita herself had struggled mightily with addiction in the past. "Black, right? One sugar?"

Knox curled a tremulous hand around the mug. "Yes, to both. Thanks."

"So," Anita said, addressing them both. "I thought about the whole getting Sydney Adams' name back in the press thing. We can start a scholarship program — the Sydney Adams Scholarship Fund for female track stars with excellent grades. We can work out the particulars."

"Dorothy would have loved that," Knox said.

"That's a great idea," Jocelyn agreed. "But how do you propose to fund it?"

Anita smiled, and Jocelyn knew she had something good up her sleeve. "Swartz Camp & Bell has agreed to fund it and match whatever we get through fundraising, up to five thousand dollars per year."

Jocelyn's eyes widened. "Holy shit. We're in business! Swartz Camp & Bell is . . . ?"

"A law firm downtown," Knox said. "Dorothy was a secretary there for years."

"So we plan a fundraiser," Jocelyn said, excitement making her feel all tingly inside. God, she missed this. "And we will get speakers to talk about Sydney." She turned and panned the case wall until she found the list of people Knox had interviewed on the original case. She walked over and skimmed a finger down the list. "First her sister, then her boyfriend, Lonnie Burgess, and then, Cash Rigo. We can have a dinner. Charge per plate."

"You're going to ask the man you think killed her to speak at a fundraiser in her honor?" Anita asked. "You think he'll do it?"

"If he wants to look innocent, he will," Jocelyn replied. "Think about it. If he was close to Sydney, if he was her mentor, what reason could he possibly give for not speaking? If he says no, that will make him even more suspect. It's worth a try."

Anita didn't look convinced but said, "Okay. I'll set it up."

Knox raised a hand to get their attention. "There's a place in Roxborough. PTG Caterers. It will fit plenty of people, but it's cozy enough for us to make Rigo uncomfortable. Dorothy's funeral luncheon was there. It's a nice place."

Jocelyn turned to Anita, but the other woman was already out the door, headed back to her desk, calling, "I'm on it" over her shoulder.

Jocelyn turned back to Knox, who was twisting the knobs on his oxygen tank. She sat down next to him and softened her voice. "You know," she said. "You don't have to be here. I mean if you're not feeling well. Anita and I can handle this. It's fine if you want to go home and rest."

Knox smiled, the corners of his mouth tightening. "There's no home for me anymore," he said, his voice raspy. "Just this case. I'd like to be here."

"Okay," Jocelyn said. "But how about you stop taking the bus. I'll drive you wherever you need to go. Until you find your car."

He laughed, lapsing into a coughing fit. Pounding his chest with a closed fist, he said, "I might die before that happens."

Before Jocelyn could respond, her cell phone chirped. She pulled it out of her pocket and saw a text message from Trent Razmus.

> Got clearance from my captain. Watch the 12:00 news. Channel 6. Again at 4, 5, 6 and 11.

"That didn't take long," Jocelyn said.

"What's that?" Knox asked.

"Razmus came through for us. We've got our newscast."

She went over to the corner of the room to a flat screen television they'd had mounted on the wall and turned it on, flipping to Channel 6. The twelve o'clock news was underway. They sat through several "top stories" which entailed coverage of the Ebola scare and various shootings throughout the city. Then traffic. Finally, a rectangular graphic with the words COLD CASE superimposed over an image of yellow crime scene tape appeared next to the anchor's head. The woman spoke, her voice clear and loud. "Police are looking at the cold case of a murdered teenager after new evidence was brought to light last week." She launched into a recap of the details of Sydney's murder and concluded with, "Police are not discussing the nature of the new evidence, but they are hopeful that they'll bring Sydney Adams' killer to justice very soon."

They cut to Trent Razmus standing in front of the police headquarters sign at 8th and Arch Streets. His mouth was set, brow drawn down in seriousness. "We're not at liberty to discuss the new developments. This is an active investigation again. We hope to have a suspect in custody soon."

Once the broadcast returned to other news, Jocelyn turned the television off and shot Trent a quick text thanking him. Anita appeared in the doorway with a pen and pad of paper in hand. "PTG has availability within the next month. How soon do you want to do this?"

Jocelyn glanced at Knox, but he shrugged. She pursed her lips momentarily. "Well, our client is dying, so as soon as we can. I guess it will depend on how quickly we can amass some people to attend."

"Okay, I'll make some calls then, see what kind of interest there is, how many people we can get on short notice. Old classmates and teachers, family members, old friends. Let's see if we can pin this down in two to three weeks." She made a notation on her pad. "So, we get a few people to talk about what kind of person Sydney was, and then what?"

"We'll need photos. We'll pick three good ones and have them blown up," Jocelyn said. She walked over to where Anita had hung the flirty photos. She tapped a finger on the one of Sydney laughing and reaching for the camera. "This one," she said. "We blow up this one."

Knox sat up straighter, his eyes bulging. "Are you out of your mind?"

Anita smiled. "She is, a little."

Jocelyn said, "Nobody knows the photos are the 'new evidence.' We'll start bringing out the blow-ups while Rigo gives his speech. See if we can spook him, and we'll need someone to collect drinking glasses and put them into paper bags. Not in a place where everyone will see, but in a place Cash Rigo will."

"Drinking glasses?" Anita asked.

"So it looks like we're collecting prints and DNA," Knox said, shooting a look of admiration in Jocelyn's direction.

Anita's face brightened. "So it will make him think we've either got his prints or DNA to make comparisons. Brilliant."

"I want this guy rattled," Jocelyn said. "I'll go to his house and ask him to give a speech about Sydney."

"What are you going to tell Rigo—about who you are?" Knox asked.

"I'm going to tell him that Jynx hired us to track down Sydney's old classmates and friends to invite to the fundraiser."

"That's kind of lame," Knox said bluntly.

"Exactly," Jocelyn agreed. "I want him to know I'm lying. I want him to think I'm in league with the police. We've got to make him nervous."

CHAPTER 12

October 22, 2014

Lonnie Burgess had become a lawyer specializing in estate and family law. He was a solo practitioner with a small office in the Germantown section of the city. It was housed in a three-story, semi-detached brick home. The upper floors each had three windows in front, and the first floor was a windowfront framed by ornately carved wood that had been painted a golden yellow. Dirt clung to the creases in the wood. White curtains obscured the view inside but served to make the words Attorney at Law, which were stenciled in gold, stand out. Jocelyn let herself in, setting off a bell as she opened the door. Inside, the walls were painted a bland taupe, punctuated by large oil paintings of mountain landscapes. A crack in the plaster snaked down behind one of the paintings. On the ceiling above it was a small water stain. Jocelyn's feet sunk into the plush, beige carpet. The secretary, a black woman who looked twice Jocelyn's age, sat behind a desk, typing away at a computer.

Jocelyn had called ahead. Once she introduced herself, the secretary waved Jocelyn into Lonnie's office through a doorway to her left. Lonnie stood up from behind his massive oak desk and came around it to shake her hand. He had a kind, easy smile. He was tall, like Caleb but huskier, carrying more weight in his torso. The rangy teenager she had seen in Knox's interrogation video was gone. The man before her had obviously filled out, resembling a football player rather than a lawyer, although the wire-rimmed glasses resting on his face made him look more erudite. His hair was cut close to the sides of his head but was longer and curly on the top.

"Ms. Rush," he said, motioning to the two chairs in front of his desk. "Nice to meet you. Have a seat."

She sat in the nearest chair, and he took the one across from her, instead of retreating behind his desk. She liked him already.

"I saw on the news that Syd's case has been re-opened," he said. "Do they really have a suspect this time?"

Jocelyn nodded. "I think so, Mr. Burgess."

"Call me Lonnie."

Jocelyn smiled. "Lonnie, I've been asked to assist in trying to bring some attention to Sydney's case—try to help bolster the police efforts. I could use your help."

He spread his hands in his lap. "Anything."

"One of the things we had in mind was a scholarship in Sydney's name." She explained about the fundraiser, and he eagerly agreed to speak about Sydney.

"What else can I do to help?"

"It would be great if you could tell me a little bit about Sydney," Jocelyn said.

Lonnie's smile faded for a moment, his eyes taking on a glassy, pained look. "Sydney was an amazing girl. She was gorgeous, smart, and funny as hell. She had a real dry wit about her, a great sense of humor. I know people tend to romanticize the dead, but Sydney really was a great person. Always kind to people. Always had a smile on her face."

"When did you start dating?"

"We were in the tenth grade."

"You were both students at Franklin West?"

He nodded. "Yeah. We had geometry together as sophomores. It wasn't easy for me. Syd helped me out. Like I said, she was smart."

Jocelyn motioned toward the law degree on the wall behind him. "I see you went to Temple, here in Philadelphia. Sydney had planned to go to Georgetown. Had you planned on staying together?"

"Do the long distance thing? Sure, we talked about it. D.C. is only a short train ride from here. We were going to try to make it work." He scratched behind his ear and shifted in his seat.

"But?" Jocelyn prompted, sensing something unsaid. "Did something change?"

His forehead crinkled. "About a month before she died, Sydney became . . . I don't know . . . distant. I didn't see as much of her. Even when we were together, she seemed distracted. I just thought it was the specter of graduation, of college, of the fact that everything about our lives was about to change."

Jocelyn crossed one leg over the other and leaned forward. "Lonnie," she said. "I need to ask a very personal question."

He smiled. "Can't say I'll answer it, but go ahead."

"How were things between you and Sydney sexually?"

Lonnie frowned. He didn't look as shocked or put-off as she had expected. He considered his words for a long moment before speaking. His tone was a statement, not a question. "You think there was someone else."

"There is a theory that has come up in the investigation — then and now — that Sydney might have been seeing someone in secret, so yes."

He looked away. His shoulders slumped a bit. When he looked back at her, the glassy look was back. He sighed. "I always wondered. I mean we were teenagers, you know? Filled with raging hormones. We had sex a lot — as much as we could. You know how it is when you're teenagers. You want to do it all the time. You sneak around so you don't get caught by your parents. It's all new and exciting, but there's nowhere to actually do it."

He laughed, and she laughed with him — she and her first-and-only boyfriend in high school had had the same problem. Now she was sneaking around with Caleb and hiding it from her four-year-old.

"Then," Lonnie said, "about two weeks before she died, she kind of pulled away. She didn't want to do it. Said she needed time to think about things. I pressed her on it—what things? But she wouldn't say. I just thought it was the college thing—that we were about to be separated, that everything was going to change. I suppose, in the back of my mind, I worried there was another guy. I mean now, fourteen years later, as a grown, more experienced man, it seems pretty obvious that she needed time to think because she'd met someone else."

"When was the last time you talked to her before she died?"

"That day at school," he said. "I waited with her at the bus stop. She kissed me before she got on the bus, like, really kissed me. I thought—" again, he spread his hands in his lap. "I thought it was a good sign. Like maybe she had thought about things and decided they were fine as they were."

"I'm sorry," Jocelyn said.

Lonnie waved a hand dismissively even though tears glistened in his eyes. "We were teenagers. Who knows what would have become of us. I'm sure Syd would have met someone else away at school. Or maybe we might have made it."

"Are you married?"

Lonnie laughed, the tone bitter. "Twice divorced," he said. He reached over to his desk and turned a photo frame so that she could see its front. A tall, pudgy boy with a gap-toothed smile lay in a pile of fall leaves. He looked seven or eight, maybe. "But my second wife gave me a beautiful son," Lonnie said. "He is all that matters now."

"He's cute," Jocelyn said, meaning it. Lonnie's face shone with obvious pride. Jocelyn could relate. Her entire world revolved around her own daughter. Right now, if anyone checked her phone, they'd find 661 photos of Olivia taken just in the last year, and in her jacket pocket were two pictures Olivia had drawn for her on Post-it notes the last time she'd gone to work with Jocelyn.

"So," Lonnie said. "You haven't said why you think there was someone else."

"I can't tell you why. Not yet. But let me ask you, looking back on things, do you have any idea who she might have been seeing?"

He looked at his lap, lips pursed, thinking. He shook his head slowly. "No," he said. "I really can't. I mean I've thought about it over the years—from time to time—but I could never come up with anyone. Syd had a full life, a busy schedule. We had trouble fitting each other in. I'm not sure where she would have found the time to meet someone else and develop a relationship. Although I suppose things happen."

"What about someone she already had a relationship with? Someone older, perhaps?" Jocelyn suggested.

"Like who?"

"I don't know. A teacher, maybe? A coach?"

Lonnie was completely still for a long moment. He stared at her, a strange, half-puzzled look on his face. Disbelief warring with something else. It was as if he'd just figured out the answer to a riddle, but the answer was wholly unexpected. Jocelyn waited. The moment stretched on. Lonnie licked his lips but said nothing. Finally, Jocelyn said, "You have someone in mind?"

"You think Sydney was having a sexual relationship with Cash Rigo?"

"There is a possibility," she admitted. "They were close, weren't they?"

Lonnie blinked as if bringing himself back from a reverie. "Yes, they were. He was our coach and history teacher. He was cool. I mean, to us. Sydney used to say he was lame, but I know she genuinely liked him. She was always hanging around him. He was one of those teachers who tried to be your buddy, you know? Hard to believe he would do something like that, but . . ." he trailed off.

Jocelyn uncrossed her legs. It suddenly felt overly hot in the office. She resisted the urge to pull off her jacket. "But what?" she prompted.

Lonnie leaned closer to her, their heads nearly touching. They'd lowered their voices unconsciously, even though they were completely alone in his office. "I've never told anyone this story," he began. "You know Cash Rigo was married to the school nurse, right?"

Jocelyn nodded. "Francine."

"Yeah. We called her Mrs. Rigo. She came to school once . . ." he hesitated. He looked at his hands, picking at a cuticle on his left thumb. "Busted up."

Jocelyn sat up straighter. "In what way?"

Lonnie looked back up at her. He pointed to his face. "Black eye. She told people she ran into a door or something ridiculous like that, and that, of course, sparked up some rumors."

"When was that?"

Lonnie's eyebrows drew together. "It was senior year, I remember that much. It was before Syd died."

"Weeks before she died? Months?"

"A couple of months. It had to be sometime in March of that year because it was still cold. I twisted my ankle." He snapped his fingers. "Yeah, March. It was right before a big meet we had with Roxborough High School. I remember I was pretty bummed out that I couldn't run that night. Anyway, I went to her office for my ankle, and she had a pretty nasty black eye."

Jocelyn frowned. "There was nothing in the case files about domestic violence."

Lonnie said, "Like I said, they were just rumors. I totally forgot about the whole thing. I mean Syd died two months later, and the way she was murdered—"

He broke off and looked away from Jocelyn, his eyes finding a spot on the floor next to her chair. He took a deep breath, his chest rising and falling slowly, a slight tremble in his frame.

"Did Mrs. Rigo say anything about her black eye?" Jocelyn asked. "Offer any explanation for it?"

He took another breath, this one less shaky, and met her gaze again. "While I was there, in her office, she asked me if I could keep a secret. I said sure I could, even though I didn't really care about her secrets. I mean, I was seventeen. I cared about sports and Syd and getting laid. She told me that she had had a fight with Cash—that things weren't good between them, and she was afraid of him."

"She just told you all this? Just blurted it out?"

"Yeah."

"But why?" Jocelyn asked. "Why would she tell all that stuff to a seventeen-year-old student?"

Lonnie smiled, a sardonic twist to his lips. "Because she wanted a gun."

Jocelyn couldn't keep the surprise from her face. "She asked you to get her a gun?"

Lonnie nodded slowly, chuckling. "I was so mad. I mean I felt badly for her, no doubt, but here's this white woman asking a black teenage boy to get her a gun."

Jocelyn leaned back in her seat, stunned. "That is wrong on so many levels."

"I know it," Lonnie agreed.

"What did you tell her?"

"I told her I couldn't help her. I asked why she'd assume that just because I was black and lived in North Philly that I could get her a gun. She got upset, said it wasn't like that. I said that's exactly what it's like. She begged me not to tell on her. She said Cash would kill her."

"And you never told?"

He shook his head. "She was so . . . pathetic. I really did feel badly for her. I mean, I was angry, but I wasn't about to get in the middle of anyone's domestic drama. A few more months, and I was out of that school. I didn't want to get caught up in anything that might derail my future." He looked at his hands again. "Selfish, I suppose."

"No," Jocelyn said firmly. "Not selfish at all. Francine Rigo was a grown woman. No matter how bad her situation was at home, she had no business asking a seventeen-year-old kid for help, much less asking you to do something illegal."

"True," Lonnie said noncommittally.

"And, from what my partner and I have gathered thus far, they're still married, so maybe she didn't need that gun after all."

"I guess she didn't. It was weird though. Coach Rigo never struck me as a wife-beater — or a murderer."

Jocelyn thought of all the people she had arrested during her time as a police officer. Many looked and acted the part of criminal, but there were a large number of her collars who didn't seem all that bad—and they were often the ones who had committed the most heinous crimes. She gave Lonnie a pained smile. As if of its own free will, her right hand moved to cover the scar on her other hand. "You never know what people are like behind closed doors."

CHAPTER
13

October 23, 2014

Jocelyn purposely waited for Cash Rigo to drive away before she knocked on the Rigos' front door. She wanted to talk to Francine Rigo alone and she wanted to catch them both off-balance. They lived in a large two-story Tudor-style home in Mount Airy. It was a neighborhood nestled between the Chestnut Hill and Germantown neighborhoods in the city, touching both affluence and poverty, relative safety on one side and a strong likelihood of violence on the other. It had been rejuvenated in recent years, its large Victorian and Tudor-style homes rehabbed, and inhabited by young professionals like the Rigos, who kept their homes with loving precision—fresh paint, neatly mowed lawns, and perfectly pruned gardens. Nothing in disrepair.

Francine opened the front door with a confused smile on her face. She wasn't what Jocelyn had expected, although Jocelyn wasn't sure what she'd been expecting, having only seen Francine before on grainy police footage. The woman before her was short and plump. She wore a billowing red blouse over black leggings with brown soft-leather boots that came up to her knees. Her round face was framed by shoulder length brown hair that looked fresh from a salon — the ends cut to curl under, her locks shiny and soft-looking. She had big blue eyes, a small straight nose, and a thin mouth. She was plain, her attractiveness understated. Jocelyn would bet that she spent a lot of time to look as casually attractive as she did now. Not a knock-out, Kevin would say, but worth a look.

"Can I help you?" Francine said.

Jocelyn took a decisive step forward as she extended her hand in greeting, nearly putting one foot inside the house. "Jocelyn Rush. I've been hired by the family of one of your husband's former students. We're holding a scholarship fundraiser, and we were hoping he'd speak. Is he home?"

Jocelyn craned her neck to look behind Francine, even though she knew Cash wasn't there. Another step put her over the threshold.

Francine backed up slightly. "Do you have a business card or something?" She still had a smile plastered on her face, although it faltered slightly.

"Of course," Jocelyn said, smiling back. She handed Francine a business card. "You can keep that."

"Thank you," Francine said tightly, studying Jocelyn's card. "My husband just went to the store. You're welcome to come in and wait. Which student did you say this was about?"

Jocelyn took another step into the foyer. Francine closed the door. Jocelyn made sure to look into her eyes when she replied, "Sydney Adams."

Something passed over Francine's face, like a ripple in still waters. Something haunted, something pained. She smiled a mirthless smile. "Oh," she said softly. "Sydney. She was a very special girl."

"Yes, she was," Jocelyn agreed. "I understand that she and your husband were close."

The corners of Francine's mouth stiffened. "They were." She motioned to her left where Jocelyn could see a sitting room. "Please. Come sit."

The room was beautifully decorated in muted blue tones. A couch, love seat, and a recliner were centered around a glass-topped coffee table that held a tall vase with an artificial floral arrangement in it and several large, hardback coffee table books. Along one wall was a credenza topped with framed photos of Cash and Francine. Above it hung a sign that read: *Welcome to Our Happily Ever After*. The other walls were decorated with a series of paintings of exotic flowers done in mesmerizing pastel swirls. It looked like something out of a high-end catalog.

Jocelyn took a seat on the cushy blue couch, which nearly swallowed her. She braced both hands on the edge, trying to steady herself. Across from her, on the other side of the coffee table, Francine perched on the very edge of an equally plush love seat. So that was the trick, Jocelyn thought. She struggled to get her ass onto the very edge of the couch. Finally, she looked at Francine. The woman had placed both hands over her stomach, almost protectively.

Kevin used to say, "Never ask a woman if she's pregnant unless you see a baby's head crowning." But Jocelyn was certain of what she saw. This was her opening. "How far along are you?"

Francine's face flushed—a happy glow, her face breaking into a huge smile. "Fourteen weeks," she said. "We've been trying a long time."

"This is your first child?"

The smile wavered. "Yeah. I hope so. I mean I've had miscarriages. This is as far as I've ever gotten, so we're very hopeful." She raised both hands, her index and middle fingers crossed.

"I'm sorry to hear that," Jocelyn said. She placed her hands flat on her knees.

"Do you have children?"

Jocelyn smiled. "A daughter. Olivia. She's four."

Francine's eyes flitted to Jocelyn's hand, her brow furrowing when she saw Jocelyn's scar. "What happened to your hand?"

Jocelyn looked down at her left hand.

Quickly, Francine added, "I'm sorry. That was so rude of me. Forget I asked."

Jocelyn continued to stare at the scar. She'd never used it before to help her with an interview or interrogation. She had a strange relationship with it. The mere sight of it brought back the worst night of her life, yet it represented an end to the secrecy that had destroyed her family and a new chance at a relationship with her sister. But it was there every day, every minute, forever visible, and always provoking questions. Jocelyn stroked the gnarled skin on top of her hand. She turned her palm over and showed Francine the matching scar on the inside. Francine's hand flew to her mouth.

"A man did this," Jocelyn said.

"Dear God, I'm sorry."

Jocelyn met her eyes. "It's okay. I'm fine."

Francine's hand slid down to her chest. She leaned forward to get a better look at the scar, a look of guarded fascination on her face.

"You can come closer," Jocelyn told her. "It's okay. I know people . . . well, they can't help but look at it."

Francine moved around the coffee table and perched beside Jocelyn. "Does it hurt?"

"No. Not anymore." She didn't tell the woman about the phantom pain. At least that's what she thought it was when pain pierced the wound out of nowhere like the nail was being driven in all over again. The doctor said it was likely nerve pain. She was grateful it didn't happen often.

Francine continued staring. Then she reached for Jocelyn's hand but stopped herself. "I'm sorry," she said. "I'm a school nurse. I never get to see anything . . ." She didn't finish the sentence, and Jocelyn wondered what she was going to say. Gruesome? Interesting? Instead, Francine said, "May I?"

It was an odd request, but Jocelyn was about to ask the woman some tough questions. She was going to need Francine's cooperation if at all possible. "Sure," Jocelyn said, offering up her palm.

Hesitantly, Francine traced the circumference of the scar with her index finger. Her touch was light and gentle, like a butterfly's wings.

"Francine," Jocelyn said as the woman pulled back. "Before your husband gets home, there's something I need to ask you."

74

The woman's eyes flitted to Jocelyn's face. "Is that from a . . ."

"A nail, yes," Jocelyn said, curling her hand into a fist and pulling it closer to her body. "Francine," she tried again. "I talked to Lonnie Burgess the other day. Do you remember him? He was Sydney Adams' boyfriend."

Francine's attention finally left Jocelyn's scar. "Yes, I remember him," she said. "He was a sweet boy. Very smart."

"Lonnie was also asked to speak at the scholarship fundraiser. I talked with him at length about Sydney and, well, it came up that in his senior year, you asked him to get you a gun because you were afraid of your husband."

Francine drew back, away from Jocelyn as she spoke. Her expression closed off. Her hands circled her belly once more.

"I hate to bring this up," Jocelyn said. "But it is important to Sydney's case for us to know if you had a gun in this house at the time Sydney was murdered."

"Well, if you spoke with Lonnie, then he would have told you that he did not get me a gun."

"He said that, yes."

"It was a very stupid thing that I did — asking a teenage boy to get me a gun. I was — I was very distraught at the time. I wasn't thinking straight."

"Did your husband hit you, Francine?"

Francine smiled, and Jocelyn was struck by how forced and fake it seemed. "There was a time, before Sydney Adams was murdered, that I felt afraid of my husband. I had just had a miscarriage. I wanted to try again. He didn't. I may have . . . pushed a little too hard. We argued a lot. Things were very tense. But my husband has never hit me."

Jocelyn tried her best to keep the skepticism out of her voice. She'd dealt with thousands of domestic violence cases during her tenure with the Philadelphia Police Department. Many women lied about being abused, even as they stood before her with battered faces and bodies. But Jocelyn knew that they lied because their lives often depended on convincing others that their husbands were not abusing them.

"Francine," Jocelyn said. "This is just between us. You don't have to cover for him with me. I'm not going to arrest him or make any kind of trouble for you. I know what men are capable of." She raised her scarred hand in the air for emphasis.

Francine's smile loosened somewhat. Either she had a ton of practice lying, or she was telling the truth—that her husband frightened her, but he had never actually hit her. "Cash is not like that," Francine said. "He has never hit me, and he never would. I never needed that gun, and I realized that after I calmed down. It was a very emotional time. I had just lost a child."

"I understand," Jocelyn said. "I'm sorry. I didn't mean to pry."

"You're a private investigator," Francine said, pointing to Jocelyn's business card on the coffee table. "That's your job. You know, we filed a grievance with the police department years ago. We thought this matter—Sydney's case—was closed."

"I'm not with the police, Mrs. Rigo. Sydney's family hired me. I'm a neutral party."

Jocelyn heard the lock in the front door turn. A cold blast of air sailed through the room as the door opened and closed.

"Fran," a male voice called. "They didn't have escarole, so I just got fresh spinach."

Jocelyn heard the sounds of plastic bags rustling from what she assumed was the kitchen.

"Francine?"

Cash Rigo pulled up short when he entered the living room. He looked at Jocelyn, then his wife. He had definitely aged and put on about twenty pounds. His cheeks were fuller, his skin beginning to wrinkle. His brown hair showed strands of gray here and there. He didn't look as fresh as he had in the photo Sydney had taken of him. He was still an attractive man, but he seemed to have lost the shine of youth. He looked tired and insubstantial. Not what Jocelyn expected of a murder suspect. But that was just the thing, wasn't it? Murderers hardly ever looked murderous.

Francine stood quickly when she saw him, hands still covering her belly. "Honey," she said. "This is Jocelyn Rush."

He stepped forward, an uncertain smile on his face, and extended a hand. "Cash Rigo."

Jocelyn stood and shook his hand.

"She's here about Sydney Adams," Francine explained.

Cash's hand went limp in Jocelyn's. He pulled it away, face ashen. He swallowed, his Adam's apple bobbing in his throat.

"She's not with the police," Francine assured him quickly.

Jocelyn smiled and told him about the scholarship program and fundraiser. "We were hoping you could speak," she finished. "Talk about the kind of person Sydney was, that sort of thing."

Cash swallowed again as the color returned to his face. Francine moved closer to him and touched his hand. He looked at her face, a genuine smile breaking across his own.

"It's in a few weeks. Plenty of time to come up with something. What do you think?" Francine asked.

He looked back at Jocelyn. "Uh sure, I could do that."

"You remember Sydney, right?" Francine added, her tone bland.

His gaze flickered to his wife momentarily, his face paling again. Jocelyn couldn't tell if it was panic or incredulity, but he quickly regained his composure. He managed a tight smile for Jocelyn's sake. "Of course I do."

CHAPTER
14

March 5, 2000

Cash Rigo had never been so angry. Not even when he was a teenager, and his little brother totaled the brand new car he'd spent three summers saving for—working for a landscaping business with a shitty boss who was as stupid as he was tyrannical. Or when his best friend made a pass at his wife two weeks before their wedding.

But today his wife had crossed a line.

"Calm down," she told him as they stood arguing in their living room. It was like telling a tsunami not to crash onto shore. He couldn't stop himself. His whole body burned and shook with rage. His face was on fire.

Francine put her hands up, a tiny worry line creasing the skin above her nose. "Cash, please."

But he was a category five hurricane, an F-5 tornado bearing down on their home. He could not be slowed, mollified or reasoned with. A guttural cry issued from his throat as he upended the coffee table, shattering the glass vase with multi-colored marbles in its base and fake flowers in its neck. Francine's heavy, hardcover coffee table books—a book of Picasso's art, a book of historical sites in and around Philadelphia, and a photography collection of natural disasters—flew through the air, tumbling in a blur of pages. The sharp corner of one of them landed on top of Francine's left foot. She was wearing black flats, the delicate skin atop her instep exposed. She let out a yowl and leaped onto the couch, as though escaping a mouse. She clasped her foot with both hands.

"Cash!" she cried.

He kicked the debris scattered on the floor. He didn't look at his wife. He couldn't. If he looked at her face, he didn't know what he'd do.

"How could you?" he hollered, pacing before her. Glass shards from the vase crunched beneath his sneakers. "Why? Why would you bring our personal lives to work like that?"

It wasn't the first time she'd done it, but it was certainly the worst thing she'd ever shared at their place of employment.

"I was confiding in a friend," Francine offered.

"A friend?" Cash spat. "Since when is Terri Marvin a friend?"

"Since her husband has trouble getting it up too." Her words were the sound of the first crack of thunder shattering the pregnant stillness after a lightning strike.

He went after her, jumping like a large feral cat pouncing on its prey. He knocked her backward, curling both hands around her throat and squeezing for all he was worth. The couch back couldn't hold their combined weight. It flipped, throwing them across the room. He was vaguely aware of the strangled gasp as Francine's head and back slammed against the living room wall. His hands had come away from her throat in the fall, and now they searched blindly for the soft flesh, raking over her waist, her breasts, tearing at her clothes.

She kicked at him, trying to crawl away, her breath wheezy. Their struggle dislodged the large, wooden decorative sign on the wall above them. The one that said *Welcome to Our Happily Ever After*. It crashed down on his head, and he threw his arms up to shield himself. The sign bounced off him and tumbled toward his wife, the corner of it hitting her square in the right eye.

Her hands flew to her face, covering her eye. She screamed—

an otherworldly howl of pain that instantly brought to mind images of his wife disfigured, with a pulpy, ruined eye, the soft orb pierced by a piece of wood from the sign. The stuff of B-grade horror movies.

"Oh my God, Francine!" he cried. The rage inside him dissipated like a puff of steam, gone instantly. "Francine! Oh my God, Fran. I'm sorry. Let me see your eye. Oh my God, Fran."

He pulled at her wrists, but she jerked away from him as though he were a live wire, shocking her and sending a scorching current through her whole body. "Don't touch me," she shrieked.

She pressed her back into the wall, her legs moving like pistons against the carpet, trying in vain to put some distance between them.

"Fran," he implored. "Please. Please let me help you. I am so sorry. I don't know—I wasn't thinking. I—I—"

Gently this time, he touched her wrists, but she pulled away again. She turned her face, staring at him with her good eye, that eye wide with terror and wet with tears.

Instantly, he felt like the biggest piece of shit on the planet. Just like always. He had failed her again. He had sinned again. He had once more cemented a place for himself in the annals of shitty husbandry. Like when they were seniors in college, and he'd left her alone in their apartment so he could study for finals with the hot girl from his Medieval History class. Now he couldn't even remember the girl's goddamn name. Francine had begged him to stay in that night. She hadn't felt well, was coming down with the flu, and had even offered to help him study. But he didn't want to stay. So while he was getting a blow job from the hot girl in the library stairwell, someone broke into their apartment and raped Francine.

He had arrived back at their apartment to find police officers and EMTs crowding their small living room. The EMTs took Francine to the hospital, where the doctors did a rape kit. Then she gave a lengthy statement to police. Unfortunately, it had been so dark she was unable to give a good description of the guy. Even with DNA, the police had never found the guy. For months, Francine lived in terror that her attacker would return. Cash had found them another apartment, and even though she felt safer there, she was still plagued with anxiety. The entire ordeal had taken them over a year to recover from. He hadn't been able to take it anymore—her brooding, her anger, her frigidity. When he told her that he wanted to end things, she took thirty Percocet tablets and locked herself in their bathroom.

Their mutual friends had castigated him, saying that he had abandoned her in her darkest hour, tossing her aside like garbage when she could no longer fulfill his every need, reinforcing every horrible thing she suspected about herself after the rape: that she was dirty, used up, damaged goods. Unwanted.

Cash did not want to be that guy.

So he had stayed, and they worked through it. Things had slowly gotten better. There was an incident with her niece just before their wedding, but she seemed to get past that quickly. They never even talked about it after the wedding. Then she got pregnant. He wasn't thrilled about the pregnancy. He wasn't ready for kids. He could barely manage himself, barely keep Francine happy, which was a full-time job. How would he deal with a child? But Francine was happier than he had seen her in years. Finally. And the sex. It was the dirtiest, kinkiest sex Cash had ever had.

Then one Sunday, when Francine was almost ten weeks along, he had gone to the Eagles game with a group of friends, tailgating at nine in the morning, drunk off his ass by the time the game started. He had arrived home late that night, thoroughly hammered, to an empty house. While he'd been out partying, his wife had miscarried. She'd taken a cab to the hospital.

It was after that that his dick stopped working. For the last several months, he had been hopelessly unable to fuck his wife. It was as if his penis was afraid of her. Afraid of hurting her—or worse—fulfilling her. Giving her another baby and sending her back onto that high, only to disappoint her again. Only to have it all come crashing back down again. Only to have to start all over—like after the rape, the suicide attempt, and the miscarriage. Cash wasn't sure how much more of the roller coaster ride he could take. Now that she had told the biggest gossip at school that he couldn't get it up, he'd never be able to perform.

"You're going to leave me," Francine wailed, bringing him back from his memories.

He shook his head, still tugging at her hands, which were clamped firmly over her right eye. "No, Fran. I'm not going to leave you. Please, just let me see your eye. I think we may need to go to the hospital."

More tears from her other eye. "And tell them what? That you tried to kill me?"

His stomach felt hollow. He sat back on his haunches and rubbed his eyes with both hands, suppressing a sigh. *Great*, he thought. *Wait until Terri Marvin hears about this. Now I'll be known as the impotent wife beater.*

"I'm sorry, Fran. I didn't mean it. I would never hurt you."

"But you did," she sobbed, shoulders quaking. It was her ugly cry — her face knotted and beet red, snot and tears pouring down to her chin. He hated her ugly cry. Dreaded it. Would do anything to make it stop.

"I'm so sorry, Fran. Please believe me. That will never happen again. I'll make this up to you. I will. But please let me see your eye. We need to take care of that first."

Finally, she pulled her hands away. Cash's whole body went loose with relief. Her eyelid and socket had already purpled and swollen, but her actual eyeball looked uninjured. No splinters, no skewers. "Oh, thank God," he breathed. "Let me get you some ice."

She stayed there while he ran to the kitchen and dumped a tray of ice into a towel. He sat beside her, back against the wall, as she held it to her face. He was trying to think of the best way to word his apology when she asked, "Why can't you have sex with me?" Her tone wasn't caustic or accusatory. It was a genuine question.

"Francine, I don't think now is the time—"

"No," she cut in. "I want to know what—what's wrong with me?"

He turned and touched her cheek, trying to smile. "Oh, Fran, there's nothing wrong with you. Nothing. All that stuff we were doing when you got pregnant—I mean, wow. That was mind-blowing. Believe me, it's not you."

Her lower lip quivered. "Is it because I'm not young anymore? Is it because I don't look like those girls, those young track girls with their perfect bodies in their skimpy outfits?"

His head reared back as if she had slapped him. "What? No. Absolutely not. Fran, those girls are my students. I don't think of them like that."

"None of them? There's not even one that you, you know, notice like that?"

Immediately, Sydney Adams sprang to mind. He pushed thoughts of her away. "No," he lied. "Not even one. You're my wife. There's only you. I know I've fucked up in the past, but I'm telling you—since our wedding there has only been you. I'm not going to leave. I'm sorry I hurt you. I'm sorry I haven't been able to . . . you know, perform. I can be better. Maybe it's like a vascular thing. I'll go see the doctor. Please. Give me another chance."

She looked away from him. He noticed that her body was trembling. He wanted to pull her into his arms, but he didn't think she would let him.

"You strangled me," she whispered.

He closed his eyes and rested the back of his head against the wall. "I'm so sorry, Francine. It was a mistake. I would never hurt you—again. I mean that will never happen again. I promise. I swear to you."

She didn't respond. He opened his eyes and moved around to face her, sitting with his legs crossed. He stared into her face, trying to look as sincere as he could. Slowly, he placed a hand on her thigh. "Please, Fran. We've been through so much. Don't leave me now. Let's work on this. Give me one more chance."

It seemed like hours. His lower body felt completely numb. Finally, she lowered the towel from her face, the skin around her eye an ugly, bloated mess. "Okay," she whispered. "One more chance."

CHAPTER 15

October 28, 2014

The smell of whiskey was overpowering. As Jocelyn and Kevin approached the front entrance of Knox's three-story apartment building made of faded brick, they found the source behind a large bougainvillea. Knox lay in a heap, his cheek pressed to the concrete, nasal cannula up around his forehead. Jocelyn and Kevin stood over him, staring blankly for a long moment. They'd dealt with their share of drunks over the years, but they were unprepared to find Knox in this state.

Kevin checked his watch. "How long ago did he call?"

Jocelyn put her hands on her hips. "It wasn't that long. Maybe fifteen minutes."

They'd been having lunch when Knox called her and asked her to pick him up on her way back to the office. She planned to meet with Anita and Trent to hammer out the final details of Sydney Adams' fundraiser. Knox wanted to be there, and she had told him if he needed a ride he should call her.

She scratched her temple. "Well, I guess I should have known he was drunk. He did butt-dial me three times before he finally got on the phone. I just figured it was because he had a new phone."

Kevin squatted down, keeping one palm on the top of his cane to steady himself. He checked for a pulse. "Still alive." He jumped back quickly when Knox stirred, moaning and rolling from his stomach onto his side. His white hair stuck out every which way. He curled his body around his oxygen tank, a dying man's teddy bear. Kevin stood up. "He usually wakes up swinging."

"I know."

Kevin looked down at Knox. He brushed a hand through his thinning hair. "I think he's just drunk."

Jocelyn sighed. She pulled out her phone and checked the time. She was due to meet Trent in fifteen minutes. "All right," she said. "Help me get him into the car."

"You want to take him to a hospital?"

Jocelyn frowned at her former partner. She knew she should be disgusted or, at the very least, annoyed with Knox's drunkenness and his total inability to control it. She could do without the smell, and her job would be easier if he wasn't falling down drunk. But she liked Knox. She understood his need to clear this case on a deeply personal level. "He's dying, Kev. What are they going to do for him at the hospital? He wanted to be involved in this case. Let's take him to my office."

Kevin shook his head and sighed. "If you say so." He wrinkled his nose. "It's your car."

It took five solid minutes of shouting and careful nudging to wake Knox. People passing in cars slowed to see what was going on. A few pedestrians stopped to watch them try to rouse him, one woman offering to call 911. Kevin flashed his credentials, thanked her for her concern, and sent her on her way. Knox rolled onto his back and sat up slowly, blinking at them and looking very much like a man who had no idea where he was or how he had gotten there.

Kevin watched the good Samaritan lady disappear down the block. "Nice to know there are still decent people."

"Yep," Jocelyn agreed. "It's shocking but a nice surprise. Now help me get him up."

They each took an arm, lifting Knox to his feet. His oxygen

tubing was wrapped around his torso. Kevin propped him up while Jocelyn untangled it. "Nice shirt," she told him as she put the cannula back over his ears, tucking the nasal tubes along his upper lip.

Knox blinked again and glanced down at his bright blue, button-down Hawaiian shirt. Its red and yellow flowers were like bursts of fireworks. "I like this shirt," he said. "This is my shirt, right?"

Jocelyn picked up the oxygen canister. It felt twice as heavy as Knox himself. "I wouldn't know," she said, smiling grimly. "You got a coat or what?"

He looked around as if seeing the outside world for the first time after many years. His rheumy eyes widened. "Do I have a coat?"

"All right," Kevin groused. "This whole twenty questions thing is pointless. Let's just put him in the car."

They hobbled over to Jocelyn's Ford Explorer. It was old, but it had served her well. Kevin held Knox up while Jocelyn transferred Olivia's car seat from the backseat to the very rear of the vehicle. Then she helped him stuff Knox inside. He curled up on the backseat, hugging his canister once more.

As she drove, Knox snored loudly, his booze-laced breath filling up the car, hot and thick. She and Kevin both cracked their windows. She was feeling queasy. To keep her mind off the smell, she asked Kevin, "How long have you known Knox?"

He gazed out the window, watching houses, stores and apartment complexes fly past. "Most of my career," he said. "I ran into him a lot when I was with Center City Detectives. We kept in touch, would grab a beer now and then."

Jocelyn glanced at Kevin. "What happened to him?"

Kevin shrugged. "The Sydney Adams case wrecked him. I mean he worked homicide a lot of years. Saw a lot of shit, but he was fine. Then the Adams case came along. He couldn't clear it. He went from being a regular old depressed detective to being a raging alcoholic at a hundred miles an hour. He just fell apart. Couldn't stop drinking. His wife left him, brass tried getting him to go to rehab, but it didn't take. The story goes that one day he showed up for work drunk off his ass, covered in vomit, and then he whipped out his dick and took a piss all over the water cooler. That was his last day."

"Jesus," Jocelyn said.

In the back, Knox stirred. They waited to see if he would wake, but he simply rolled over onto his other side and resumed snoring.

"That's nothing," Kevin said. "You remember that drunk dad wedding video? It was on YouTube a few years ago?"

"Which one?"

"Guy walking his daughter down the aisle, stumbling, passes out—"

"Oh God," Jocelyn cut him off. She knew exactly the video he was talking about. It had gone viral four or five years ago. It was on all the major television networks after it caught fire on the internet. "He passed out at the altar and when the groom tried to help him up, he woke up swinging. Oh my God." She palmed her forehead. "He was the drunken father of the bride who cold-cocked the groom?"

Kevin nodded. "Yep. That was Knox. Knocked the groom out—gave him a nice gash that bled all over his daughter's wedding dress."

"Holy shit." Jocelyn looked in her rearview mirror at Knox's back. She hadn't known him long, and she certainly didn't know him well, but the man she knew was frail and desperate to do this one last thing before he passed. It was hard to imagine him as the drunken father of the bride from that video. Then again, he was practically black-out drunk in the back of her car.

"They went through with the wedding?" Jocelyn asked.

"They had to. Weddings are expensive. They couldn't do it twice."

Jocelyn had never been a fancy wedding type of woman. In fact, she'd never even dated anyone she might actually consider marrying. Until Caleb. She had a sudden flash of standing at some kind of altar with him, wearing a dress that was like a thong for her whole body—uncomfortable. She pushed the image away. It was too soon. He hadn't even met Olivia yet and that was a crucial step in the evolution of their relationship.

"His daughter has never forgiven him," Kevin added.

"I guess not."

From the back came the sound of retching, then the smell of hot vomit wafted up to the front seat. Jocelyn's heart sank. She had hoped to get to her office vomit-free. "Son of a bitch," she said.

Kevin snickered. "I told you — it's your car."

She punched him hard in his arm. "Yeah, but I'm driving, so you can climb back there and make sure he doesn't choke to death on his own vomit."

Kevin sat perfectly still, staring at her. "Are you serious?"

She shot him a deadly look. "What do you think?"

He sighed and unbuckled his seat belt. "Fuck," he said. He leaned between the seats, wrestling Knox into a seated position. Jocelyn heard the click of a seat belt as Kevin latched the man in. Kevin sat back in the passenger's seat, a look of disgust on his face. "I don't know," he said. "You might need a new car."

✧

Kevin was due at Northwest Detectives for the evening shift, so after he helped her and Trent get Knox into the bathroom, he left. Anita helped Jocelyn gather what cleaning products they had on hand so she could clean out the backseat of her Explorer. An hour later, both Jocelyn and her vehicle smelled like Lysol. Knox was awake, though not fully alert, and propped up in a chair at the conference room table. He and Trent both smelled like the floral-scented hand soap they kept in their bathroom. Anything was better than the vomit. Anita was midway through her presentation — they had the date, location, menu, silent auction items that Knox had agreed to purchase, photos, and speakers — when Knox spoke.

"You got Rigo?" he asked, head swiveling around the room until his gaze landed on Jocelyn.

She frowned at him. "I told you that last week."

"You're drunk," Anita told him. "You don't remember."

His head snapped back, his chin becoming one with the loose, yellow skin beneath it. "I'm not drunk."

"And I'm not black," Anita shot back. She gave him the kind of severely arched eyebrow that she usually only reserved for her teenage son when he tried lying to her.

Trent snickered. Knox stared at Anita with his wide eyes. Then he turned back to Jocelyn. "You think he'll really come?"

"I think if he doesn't come, that makes him look even more suspicious," she said. "If he was that close to Sydney, and he didn't kill her, he should want to do this. I called his house yesterday, and his wife says they're still coming. By the way, what do you even know about the Rigos? They've got a pretty nice house for a teacher and a school nurse."

Knox waved a hand in the air. "Some kind of inheritance she got from a relative. It was enough for them to buy that house."

"She comes from money?" Jocelyn asked.

"Her mother's mother had a little bit of money. Got it in a personal injury settlement and willed it to Francine and her brother. He's older, lives in California. Other than that, they were a regular, working-class family. Her mom was an office manager for a hand surgeon, and her dad worked for an insurance company. They did okay, but they didn't have a ton of money. Francine went to Temple University. That's where she met Rigo. His family is in South Jersey. He has a younger brother. Dad was a plumber. Mom was a schoolteacher. Rigo's parents are divorced; Francine's are still together." Knox struggled to catch his breath by the time he had finished, again twisting the dials on his oxygen canister.

"No indication that he had an abusive childhood, anything like that?"

"No," he wheezed. They gave him a moment. He pressed the tubing deeper into his nose and took several shallow breaths before continuing. "I mean I looked into him pretty thoroughly when Sydney was first murdered. Couldn't come up with anything other than his parents are divorced."

"Lots of people's parents get divorced," Trent put in. "They don't all go around murdering seventeen-year-old girls."

"What about domestic calls?" Jocelyn asked. "At the Rigos' house?"

Knox stared at her blankly until Trent said, "I looked. Nothing. They've never called the police for anything, the entire time they've lived there."

"That doesn't mean a damn thing," Anita said. "Just because a wife doesn't call the police every time her dick of a husband hits her doesn't mean he isn't doing it."

"That's true," Jocelyn agreed. "But if he had a history of violence or at least the hint of one, it might make this whole case easier to work with."

Knox pointed a finger at his chest. "You're telling me," he said loudly.

Jocelyn sighed. "Well, let's hope my plan works, because otherwise, we've got shit."

CHAPTER
16

November 11, 2014

"So let me get this straight," Jynx said. "You think that this man had a sexual relationship with my underage sister, then stalked her and shot her in the back in cold blood, but you asked him to speak at a fundraiser in her honor."

Jocelyn held the other woman's gaze for a long moment, taking in her words. Their whole plan boiled down to one absurd sentence. There was no way around it. "Yeah," Jocelyn replied. "Basically."

Although Knox had assured her that Jynx would go along with whatever plan they concocted, Jocelyn braced herself for the woman's protest. Instead, Jynx shook her head, clucked her tongue and waddled away. "Well," she called over her shoulder. "I hope you get your man."

Jocelyn watched as she seated herself at a table near the podium Anita had set up. Knox had been right about PTG Caterers. It managed to be both spacious and intimate at the same time. It was perfect for what they had planned.

They had set up the area for the speakers along the wall opposite the front door. PTG would serve dinner, then coffee and dessert. Anita had managed to garner far more interest than any of them had anticipated. As seven o'clock approached, the place filled up quickly with family, friends, and a few neighbors. There was a handful of Sydney's classmates, some faculty from her high school, and also a few people who had worked with Dorothy Adams at Swartz Camp & Bell.

It had been Anita's idea to charge per plate and then have a silent auction on items Knox had provided. Judging by the pricey electronics he had chosen, he didn't plan on paying his bills in the last few months of his life.

Knox wouldn't be there. They had all agreed, given the Rigos' complaints about him during the initial investigation, it would be best that they not run into him. Jocelyn had enough planned for them.

Trent was there. He stood, chatting with Anita at the entrance to the alcove between the main dining area and the kitchen. It was directly across from the bathrooms. As the tables filled up, Inez sidled over. Jocelyn had enlisted her help for the evening, tasking her with selling tickets at the door. Olivia and Inez's daughter, Raquel, were with Inez's mother for the evening. Inez looked nothing like a cop tonight, with her black hair flowing down her back, her A-line gray dress, belted at the waist, hugging her slender frame, and a pair of black heels on her feet.

"You ready to do this?" Inez asked.

Jocelyn wiped her sweaty palms on her slacks. "I think so."

Inez motioned toward Jynx. "She okay with this?"

"Seems that way."

"Even with the coach speaking? I mean if he really killed this girl, that's pretty creepy—asking him to give a speech about her."

Jocelyn grimaced. "I know, but it's been fourteen years. Knox said she'd be open to just about anything if it meant finding Sydney's killer. Although, apparently, she isn't sold on the coach as the killer, so maybe that's why it doesn't seem to be bothering her."

"Well, regardless, the scholarship is a good thing."

Car doors slammed outside. Jocelyn peeked out the front door. She saw Francine Rigo first, tottering in a pair of high-heeled, leather boots. She wore a black dress that clung to her back but billowed in the front to allow room for her burgeoning belly. It was a sheer lace material that hung over the stretchy black fabric beneath it. It was pretty, elegant and understated. Cash hurried behind her, catching one of her hands in his and wrapping his other arm around her waist as if to steady her.

Jocelyn sighed. She almost felt bad about the fact that she was about to take Francine's husband and the father of her child away from her at what should be the happiest time of their lives.

Almost.

She still didn't buy Francine's assertion that Cash had never hit her. Maybe he had only hit her once. Maybe he hit her all the time, but Jocelyn had no doubt that he had hit her before Sydney Adams' death.

"Thank you for coming," Jocelyn said.

Francine smiled warmly. "Good to see you again."

Cash nodded at her, looking very much like a man who hadn't shit for a month. Inez led them over to Jynx's table where she sat with her husband, two of her cousins and Lonnie. Jocelyn watched them greet one another. Only Cash looked stiff and uncomfortable, his movements stilted and jerky, his face bloodless, lips pressed into a thin line. Even when he smiled, the corners of his mouth seemed pinched, as if smiling was a great strain on him.

Inez handed her a thick, white envelope. "Sold out," she said.

Jocelyn took it and smiled. "Thanks. Thanks for coming."

Inez winked and looked over at the table where the Rigos sat. She laughed. "Look at this fucking guy. He looks like he's about to get a proctology consult—at a teaching hospital."

"Well," Jocelyn replied. "Let's get this party started."

They let the crowd eat first—salad followed by chicken cordon bleu and filet mignon with grilled mixed vegetables and roasted potatoes. The food smelled delicious and elicited a hearty growl from Jocelyn's stomach, but she was too nervous to eat. When the wait staff began serving dessert and coffee, she went to the podium. She greeted the crowd and introduced Jynx, who spoke for about ten minutes, explaining the scholarship. Anita had prepped the woman earlier that evening. Jynx went on to talk about Sydney—telling personal stories that made the crowd laugh but brought tears to Jynx's eyes. They streamed down her face, and she dabbed them gracefully with a folded napkin. She finished by introducing Lonnie.

Jocelyn felt her phone vibrate in her jacket pocket. She pulled it out, saw Knox's name and hit answer. She heard rustling. "Knox," she hissed into the phone. No answer. She heard the whir of his oxygen machine, the wheeze of his breath and the sound of liquid sloshing in a glass. "Knox," she tried again. Nothing. She waited several seconds, but he didn't speak into the phone. Another butt dial. She'd have to get him to sober up long enough to teach him how to use his new cell phone. She hung up, put her phone away and turned her attention back to Lonnie.

He spoke a bit longer than Jynx, with a wistfulness that only a first love could leave behind. It was while he talked that Cash stood to use the restroom. Jocelyn breathed a sigh of relief. Their plan rested on him seeing what Anita and Trent had staged in the alcove across from the restrooms. She saw Cash turn first toward the alcove where Trent was bagging glasses and labeling each bag with a guest's name. She knew that two brown paper bags labeled Rigo, C. and Rigo, F. were right on the edge of the counter, in plain sight.

Jocelyn couldn't see the look on his face, but she noted how slowly he moved away from the alcove and into the restroom as if he were in great pain. He emerged five minutes later, even paler than he'd been before. His brow glistened with sweat. He barely had time to sit back down before Lonnie introduced him.

The crowd clapped politely as Cash made his way to the podium. He pulled a crumpled piece of paper from his suit jacket pocket. Jocelyn noticed that his hands trembled as he smoothed it out. He looked at the crowd with a nervous smile and cleared his throat.

"I've, uh, been teaching history and coaching track and field at Franklin West for sixteen years. It was my first and only teaching job after college. I've been lucky to be able to work with some really bright and incredible young people, like Mr. Burgess, here."

He motioned to Lonnie, who smiled what looked like a very sincere smile. Although Jocelyn knew Lonnie had great affection for his and Sydney's old coach, surely, after what they had discussed in his office a few weeks earlier, the sight of Cash made him uncomfortable. If it did, he wasn't showing it. She sighed. Lawyers made great liars. She liked Lonnie a whole lot more than most lawyers she knew, but it always astounded her how easily they could act one way all while feeling the exact opposite.

"And of course, Sydney Adams," Cash went on. "When I came to Franklin West, Sydney was a junior. She'd already been running track for two years. She was strong, dedicated, a hard worker. I always tell the kids, 'go out hard and finish harder, leave it all out on the track.' Well, that was Syd. She left it all on the track every time. She always strove to beat her personal record. There wasn't much I could coach her on. She was . . ." he wiped his brow.

Discreetly, from her spot near the front door, Jocelyn signaled Anita and Inez to move on with the next phase of the plan. They went back to the kitchen and emerged with the first blown up photo of Sydney—her senior picture. In it, she wore a white graduation cap and gown and held a flower in an artificial pose. Her smile was serene, the soft touch glow of the photo making her image jump from the two by three foot glossy cork foam board, as if she were a physical presence in the room. She was gorgeous. All these years later, so many people had shown up to honor her. It hurt Jocelyn's heart a little knowing she would never light up a room again.

As Inez and Anita set it on one of the three collapsible easels they'd placed opposite the podium earlier that evening, Cash's eyes were drawn to it. It was as though he saw an apparition. He stumbled over his words, his voice disappearing momentarily. He wiped at his brow again, tearing his gaze from the photo, focusing instead on his sweat-dampened notes.

"Sydney was every teacher's dream student," he went on. "Bright, inquisitive, studious." As his litany of adjectives continued, Inez and Anita carried out the second photo. This one was a candid shot of Sydney and Dorothy. Dorothy sat at what looked like a dinner table. Sydney stood behind her, arms wrapped around her grandmother's neck, her cheek pressed to the other woman's face. Dorothy's aged hands curled over Sydney's forearm. Both women smiled brightly—their faces happy and free somehow—like they had no cares or worries. Like they had everything they needed already.

Jocelyn had a sudden, sharp pang for her own mother who had died three years earlier. The mother she and her sister had known in junior high—before their family went all to hell. She pushed those thoughts aside and looked back at Cash as Inez and Anita brought out the third and final blown-up photo, the most innocent of the three flirty photos. The one of Sydney laughing and reaching for the camera—reaching for Cash from the grave.

It had its intended effect.

Cash stopped in mid-sentence, looking stricken, like a man who'd just witnessed a heinous crime. He tried to speak again but choked on his words, lapsing into a coughing fit so bad that his wife and several others rose to assist him. He latched onto Francine's arm, positioning her with her back to the photo as he waved the others away. He pounded on his chest to no avail. Jocelyn couldn't hear what Francine was saying, but Cash shook his head vigorously and pulled her toward the front door, still managing to keep her back to the photographs. Francine scooped up her purse and let her husband drag her out the door, his coughing slowing considerably.

Anita moved to the podium to remind everyone about the silent auction and distract them from the awkward spectacle. Jocelyn followed the Rigos outside. They had snagged a parking spot near the entrance to PTG, one building over in front of a local dentist's office. Cars whizzed past on Ridge Avenue. The street lights cast a golden glow over the parking lot. Across the street, smokers stood outside a local bar.

Cash had stopped coughing. He helped Francine into the passenger's side of their Ford Focus, pushing her a little too forcefully for Jocelyn's taste. She heard Francine's voice, "Ow, honey, watch my—"

He slammed the door and hurried around the back of the car. He froze when he saw Jocelyn, his right hand in his jacket pocket.

His eyes were wide and frantic.

"You okay?" Jocelyn asked, approaching him slowly.

Quickly, he looked toward the passenger's side of the car, then back at Jocelyn. He shook his head and threaded his fingers through his hair, rubbing the top of his head until his hair stood straight up. When he spoke, his voice was high-pitched. "How could you?" He motioned toward PTG, his voice cracking on the word you. He cleared his throat. "My wife."

As if the words had conjured her, Francine opened her door and stepped out of the car. She smoothed her dress over her belly and adjusted the strap of her purse, which rested on her right shoulder. "Cash," she said. "I don't know what's going on right now, but I—"

He cut her off, his tone suddenly hard and firm. Commanding. "Get back in the car, Francine."

She bristled, but said nothing, staring at him. He didn't even look at her. From the side of his mouth, he growled, "Get back in the car, Francine. Now."

His words were like a knife's edge and right then, Jocelyn wanted to punch him in the face. Francine's brow furrowed. She looked from him to Jocelyn. Jocelyn smiled and acknowledged her as though Cash had not spoken. "You okay, Mrs. Rigo?"

Francine raised her chin. "Fine," she said. "I just have to go to the bathroom."

She took a step toward Cash and halted as if waiting for him to stop her. When he said nothing and made no move toward her, she stepped around him and walked back to the restaurant, her boot heels clacking on the pavement.

Cash waited until the door closed behind her before stepping toward Jocelyn. Her heart rate ticked up a beat. She made a conscious effort not to back away from him. She'd killed more formidable foes than him, she reminded herself. Plus Inez, Anita, and Trent were right inside.

"How could you do that?" he asked.

Jocelyn kept her face blank. She stood perfectly still. Calm. "I'm sorry?"

He paced before her, gesturing wildly toward the restaurant.

"The photo," he spat. "My wife is here with me. My wife!"

"Mr. Rigo, I'm not sure I understand what's going on here."

He threw his arms in the air, still pacing rapidly. He glanced behind her as if to make sure Francine wasn't approaching. "My wife," he said. "She doesn't know. Sydney and I—we—" He broke off.

"Your wife doesn't know what, Mr. Rigo?"

He froze and looked down at the ground as if considering something. When he looked back up at her, he seemed calmer somehow.

"You're not with the police, right? I mean I know the police are here. Don't try lying. I saw that man back there by the bathrooms. He's a detective, I bet. Here from the police. But you, you're not with the police, right?"

"I'm a private investigator," Jocelyn answered.

He drew closer, his voice quieter. "If I tell you something, you can't—you can't, like, do anything about it, right?"

"I'm not a priest, Mr. Rigo."

Maybe she should have said nothing or lied and risked being accused of entrapping him later. If he was going to confess to a murder after getting away with it for fourteen years, in the parking lot of a dentist, he was going to do it no matter what she said or didn't say. But he didn't ask her for any further explanation. He motioned back toward the entrance of PTG. "My wife," he began, his eyes darting all around. "She doesn't know."

Jocelyn stared hard at him. "Doesn't know what, Mr. Rigo?"

He glanced at his feet again. "Sydney and I, we had—she came to my house and we—"

They heard Francine's boots before they saw her. Jocelyn turned to look at her and was stunned by the change in her demeanor. Two bright circles of pink colored her cheeks. She narrowed her eyes at her husband, her mouth set in an angry line. She no longer had trouble walking in her high-heeled boots. She strode toward them, both hands curled around her belly.

"Are you okay?" Jocelyn asked, but Francine didn't even acknowledge her. She walked up to her husband, pointed at the driver's side of their car and said, "Get in the fucking car, Cash."

"Francine," he began.

"Now," she shrieked, clomping past him and getting into the car on the passenger's side.

Like a child who'd been acting up at a party and now had to leave, Cash scurried to the driver's side and got in. He didn't give Jocelyn another glance. As they backed out of the parking lot and onto Ridge Avenue, Jocelyn swore she heard shouting coming from the inside of the car.

CHAPTER 17

November 11, 2014

"You lying bastard," Francine roared, her voice so high that it hurt his ears. Cash hated it when she got like this. It was very rare. His wife was sweet. That's what everyone loved about her. They fought like any other couple, and in private, she could occasionally get angry enough to raise her voice at him, but for the most part, she was the kind of person everyone loved. He hated it when she got *mean* angry, when she was fully enraged. It made the hair on the back of his neck stand up. It had really only happened one other time in their relationship—right before they got married. He wished she would cry. Even her ugly cry would be better than this.

"Francine," he said and stopped. The truth was that he had no idea what to say to her. Not about this. Not about Sydney. He'd been hiding this from her for fourteen years. He hadn't been prepared to discuss Sydney back then, and he was no more prepared with the passage of time.

"You humiliated me," Francine said. "You took me there in front of all those people and talked about that—that whore like she was some kind of saint."

"Francine," he said, his tone a caution.

She ignored him. "You said nothing ever happened between you two. But that photo, everyone saw that photo, Cash. Everyone!"

"They don't know what it—" he broke off. He had almost said *what it means.*

Francine's voice went up an octave. "You said she was never in our house. That's what you said."

He was at a loss. "I—"

"Shut up," she screamed suddenly, her voice piercing and shrill. She covered her ears. "I can't believe anything you say. You lie. That's all you do. You're a lying pedophile!"

"She was seventeen!" Cash snapped.

Francine took her hands away from her ears and glared at him. "She was a teenage girl, Cash. Do you understand? Seventeen. You were an adult, her teacher. Why don't you see how wrong it was? Do you have any idea how close you came to destroying our lives? Again? You would have been on the six o'clock news. We would have lost everything, and even if you got away with it, our lives would have been destroyed. You'd never work again. I would be one of those dumb wives everyone would hate because they'd wonder, *How could she not know?* I thought you learned your lesson with Elise." She stroked her belly as she spoke. Without warning, tears spilled down her cheeks. An odd sense of relief flooded through him. The crying was familiar territory. It was safe. "She was a teenage girl, Cash. A student. In our home!"

He scoffed. "Like you never had a student over."

He felt her eyes burning holes into his face. "What are you talking about?"

He glanced at her. More tears. That was good. "I'm talking about Davey Pantalone. Remember him? He was a student. I came home from practice and found him at my dinner table."

Francine rolled her eyes and swiped at her ruddy cheeks. "Oh, please. His mother had just died. I felt badly for him. I invited him over for dinner, one time. *One time.* On the day he buried his mother. That was it. I know that Sydney wasn't over for dinner, you piece of shit. At least I'm not some kind of fucking pervert.

How many times did you fuck her in our home, Cash?"

They stopped at a red light. He squeezed his eyes closed, feeling sick to his stomach. "Francine, please," he murmured. "Can we not talk about this right now?"

"Oh, you don't want to do this now?" she spat, her anger rising again like the head of a snake. "Okay, well, when is a good time for us to talk about Sydney Adams, Cash? When? I thought this whole thing with Sydney's murder was over, but here we are, fourteen years later. No wonder the police won't let it go. You're a fucking liar. "

"I thought it was over too, Fran," he said. "I thought the whole thing was taken care of fourteen years ago." He glanced over at her, but she stared straight ahead. Her tears had slowed. He waited for her to say something, but she didn't.

"I'm sorry," he said quietly. "I really am. I'm afraid — I'm afraid they're never going to let it go, Francine." Her silence was like a thousand wasps buzzing angrily between them. "Didn't you see the glasses they were collecting? Across from the bathrooms in that little area? They were putting our drinking glasses into paper bags."

She stared out the window. "I saw," she said. "So what?"

He banged a palm on the steering wheel. "So what? It's evidence. Fingerprints or whatever. You saw the news the other night, obviously this new evidence they've got is pretty serious. They're not going to stop."

"Where did they get this evidence?"

"How the fuck should I know? They manufactured it for all I know. You know they've wanted to pin this on me from the beginning. They're the police, Fran. They do whatever they want, and they want to put me away for Syd's murder."

"That woman," Francine said. "The nice one with the scar on her hand. She said she wasn't with the police."

Cash rolled his eyes. "Don't be naïve. She's helping them." *And I almost told her everything.* Anger roiled inside of him. He didn't know who he was more furious with — the police or himself for being so stupid.

"But I didn't see the detective — you know, the one I filed that grievance against."

"He's probably retired. Jesus Christ. Are you listening to me? Do you understand how serious this is?"

He pulled into their driveway and turned the car off. Francine stared straight ahead, making no move to get out of the car. "Why are you saying these things?" she asked.

He made a noise of exasperation in his throat. "I need your help, Francine. I need you to . . . to fix this, like you did with Elise."

Still, she refused to look at him. She laughed, the sound acerbic and mirthless. "Even if I could, how would I do that, Cash? I can't fix everything for you, you stupid shit. You should have learned your lesson back then, but you didn't. Instead, you betrayed me, you lied to me, you violated the sanctity of our home, of our marriage, and you got yourself in trouble with that whore."

He knew the things she was saying were important, that she was right. He was a liar, a bad husband, a cheater. He had betrayed her in the worst possible way. But all he really heard was his wife disparaging a dead girl. "Syd was not a whore," he shouted.

Francine turned her head in time for him to see her roll her eyes. "Please. What kind of a girl fucks her married coach in his home, where he lives with his wife? How long was it going on, Cash? How many times did you fuck that whore?"

A hot flash of rage consumed Cash. He gritted his teeth. "Don't call her that."

Francine sneered, but a fresh round of tears filled her eyes. "She almost destroyed our lives fourteen years ago, and she may still destroy us now. I'll call her whatever I want. She was a whore."

He white-knuckled the steering wheel. "Francine, I'm warning you."

She laughed again, sharply, and wiped a tear from her cheek. "Fuck you," she said, her voice almost a whisper. "And your little whore."

His vision narrowed. His chest felt tight, and his heartbeat thundered in his ears. He reached for her, but she scrambled out of the car and ran for their front door. He went after her, shouting her name. She couldn't run very well in the boots she wore. He caught up with her quickly. His hand shot out to grab her arm, but before he could clamp down on it, she fell, facedown, sprawled on her stomach.

Cash felt like someone had punched him in the solar plexus. He stood over her, paralyzed. He knew he should help her, but he couldn't get his limbs to move. She got to her knees and let out a wail that cut to his bones. The spell broken, he reached for her again, but she slapped his hand away. She stumbled to her feet and sprinted for the door, legs wobbly like a drunk person.

He went after her.

CHAPTER 18

November 12, 2014

It was after midnight by the time they left PTG. Jocelyn, Anita, and Inez drove back to Jocelyn and Anita's office in one vehicle, with Trent following in his own car. Jocelyn had two of the blow-ups in her arms and was almost to the door when she saw what looked like a heap of clothes in front of the door. Her heartbeat ticked up slightly. They had an outdoor light, but in the dark, it cast strange shadows, making it hard to see the oxygen tank a few feet away from the collapsed figure. Jocelyn tossed the blow-ups and ran for the door. She dropped to her knees and saw that the person was Knox. She should have known. Who else would be lying outside her office doors? He had curled up on his side, knees pulled to his chest. She smelled vomit. As she rolled him over, she saw the source of the smell beneath him. Definitely whiskey again. Lots of it. The scene was becoming familiar.

Behind her, she heard shouting and then feet pounding the asphalt. Anita, Trent, and Inez stood over them. "What the hell is this?" Inez said.

"Is he . . . is he okay?" Trent asked, kneeling beside Jocelyn.

She pressed her fingers to the side of his throat and felt his

105

pulse. "He's alive."

"He's drunk," Anita announced. She gently nudged Trent out of the way. He and Jocelyn stood up and backed away. "Knox," Anita said loudly. She leaned down and shook Knox's shoulder hard. Then she stepped back quickly as if he were a bomb that might go off. "Knox," she yelled again.

He stirred, slowly at first, rolling completely onto his back and groaning. His nasal cannula hung from his left ear. Anita leaned down again, this time gently prodding his shoulder. She jumped back as his upper body sprung up, fists flailing. He hollered unintelligible words, some of which were most definitely expletives. His wrist clanged off the oxygen tank, which only seemed to infuriate him more. The four of them stood there watching for a long moment. Trent moved toward Knox, but Anita placed a hand on his forearm, stopping him.

"Give him a minute," she said.

It wasn't long before he wore himself out. His arms fell to his side. His chest heaved, a high-pitched wheeze sounding with each breath. He fumbled for his cannula. Trent looked at Anita and she nodded. He bent and put the cannula back onto Knox's face. He lifted the man, and Inez stepped forward to help. They managed to get Knox, his oxygen tank, and all the stuff from the benefit they'd dropped in the parking lot inside in a few minutes.

The smell of vomit and booze clung to Knox, hanging like a cloud in the conference room, in spite of both Anita and Inez's attempts to clean him up. He mumbled apologies, threw up in the trash can, and finally settled into some semblance of alertness after Anita gave him two cups of coffee. Jocelyn set one of the blow-ups of Sydney—her graduation photo—in the chair across the table from him. He blinked several times, the photo seeming to sober him more than the caffeine.

He licked his lips, his eyes finding Jocelyn's. "How did it go?"

She stood across the table from him, one hand on her hip. "How did you get here?"

"The bus."

"I told you to call me if you needed a ride. You butt-dialed me earlier. Was that you trying to get in touch with me for a ride?"

He looked puzzled. "Butt-dialed you?"

"Accidentally dialed me without meaning to, like when your phone is in your back pocket, and you sit down, and buttons get pressed. Pocket-dialing, butt-dialing. It's an expression."

Knox laughed. "Oh, no. I didn't mean to, I wasn't calling. I'm sure you would have loved me throwing up in your car again."

Jocelyn smiled tightly. "Yeah, that would have been a blast."

Knox repeated. "How did it go?"

"I'd say pretty damn good," Inez interjected, sailing into the room, her hands full of creamers, sugar packets, and wooden stirrers. Behind her were Anita and Trent, both carrying ceramic mugs filled with steaming coffee. They took a moment to settle into seats and fix their coffees. Jocelyn glanced at the clock on the wall. Coffee after midnight. She felt like she was back on the job. She had even missed the window of time to call Olivia at Martina's house and wish her a goodnight. She felt part guilt and part exhilaration.

She recapped the night for Knox, up to the part where Cash flipped out and dragged his wife outside.

"So the wife didn't see the photo?" Knox asked. His trembling fingers fidgeted with the dials on his oxygen tank.

"Not on the way out," Anita put in. "He kept her back to it and got out of there like his ass was on fire."

"But she went back in," Jocelyn said.

"Oh, she definitely saw it on the way back in," Inez said.

Trent sipped from his cup and nodded. "Spent quite a few minutes studying it."

"Yeah, and when she came back outside, she was different," Jocelyn said. "Angry, upset. They high-tailed it out of there."

Knox nodded. "How about Cash?"

Jocelyn recapped the conversation at his car.

Trent stroked the goatee on his chin. "Well, you definitely got his panties in a bunch."

"You think he was going to confess?" Anita asked Jocelyn.

She stifled a yawn. "I think he was definitely about to tell me about the affair. The murder? I don't know. It's hard to say. I'd love another crack at him though."

Nods all around. "So how do we do that?" Anita asked.

Jocelyn's cell phone rang. "I don't know yet," she said as she pulled the phone from her pocket and answered it.

"Rush," Kevin said. "I'm at Einstein. I think you might want to get down here. Your boy, Cash Rigo, just brought his wife into the ER."

CHAPTER 19

November 12, 2014

Jocelyn hadn't been to Einstein Medical Center in over a year—not since she was attacked in her home. Although Einstein wasn't the closest hospital to her home, it was the closest with a trauma team. She had hoped to never set foot in the place again.

But here she was.

She stood just inside the ER, the sliding glass doors behind her whooshing open and closed as people flowed in and out—more in than out. As always, it was a full house, the waiting area standing room only. Children cried. Grown men moaned in pain. There were a few drunks with police escorts—likely DUI arrests waiting to get blood tests. As usual, the security guards ignored her.

Jocelyn's body felt as though it was made of stone. She couldn't move. She told herself to reach into her pocket and get her phone. At least call Kevin and let him know she was there but that she was losing her mind. But her arms wouldn't move either.

A nurse in navy blue scrubs, who had bustled past her about three times already, stopped in front of her and peered into her face. "Hey, lady, you okay?"

Jocelyn's eyes shifted to the woman. She appeared to be in her fifties, her face lined and leathery, her thin brown hair curled and teased out into a kind of helmet. She wore a gold chain around her neck with a cross on it. "Hon," the nurse said, more loudly this time as if Jocelyn was hard of hearing. "You okay?"

Jocelyn opened her mouth to speak, wishing her legs would move when she felt a warm hand curl around her tricep, squeezing. "I've got this one," Nurse Kim Bottinger said, dismissing the other woman.

Jocelyn looked over. Kim smiled reassuringly. "Tough being back," she said softly. It wasn't a question. Kim's dirty blonde hair was pulled back into a loose pony tail. Wisps had escaped and floated around her head. Backlit by the light from the waiting area, she looked like an angel. Jocelyn felt her own body relax— almost too much. Her legs felt like Jell-O. Kim linked her arm with Jocelyn's, holding her up. "Breathe," Kim reminded her. "It's not you this time."

Jocelyn and Kevin had met Kim in this very ER a year ago. Kevin had been happily dating the woman ever since. Jocelyn had to admit, of all the women Kevin had ever dated or married, she liked Kim the best. Kim patted her arm. "Come on, then. I'll take you to Kevin."

"Thanks," Jocelyn said weakly.

As they weaved through the crowded ER, Jocelyn tried to regain her composure. The bad things were over, she reminded herself. She and everyone she loved were okay.

Kevin leaned against a wall opposite several curtained areas, one foot folded behind him, flat against the wall. He held his phone in one hand, using his other index finger to scroll down the screen. He looked up as they approached, a huge smile breaking across his face. He didn't have a cane, Jocelyn noted.

"Look who I found," Kim said.

"Rush," he said, dropping his phone into his jacket pocket. "That was quick."

He exchanged a meaningful look with Kim, who squeezed Jocelyn's arm before going back to work.

The sight of Kevin seemed to ground her. She began to feel

solid again, in control. "What's going on?" she asked, her voice strong and firm.

"I wouldn't normally get a call on this," he said, lowering his voice. "But Kim called. Said a guy brought his pregnant wife in, saying she fell. When Kim asked her the domestic questions, she didn't answer."

The domestic violence questions. Jocelyn knew them. Hospital staff were required to ask you: Do you feel safe in your home? Is anyone abusing you? If your significant other refused to leave the room, the nurse would discreetly point to it while asking you to sign the consent for treatment forms and indicate for you to circle yes or no.

"Francine Rigo," Jocelyn said.

Kevin nodded. "She says she fell. I had a tough time getting the husband out of the room. He got upset when I showed up. Said it was a private matter, and they needed to know if their baby was okay."

Jocelyn sucked in a breath. "The baby."

Kevin shook his head and looked at the floor. "The baby didn't make it," he said. "The doctor ran all kinds of tests. There's no heartbeat."

Jocelyn closed her eyes, a lump forming in her throat. She hardly knew Francine. Maybe her husband was a killer or a wife-beater. Or both. But Jocelyn wouldn't wish a miscarriage on any woman. She had provoked Cash the evening before. She had meant to provoke him. Put the pressure on, make him believe he would soon be arrested for Sydney Adams' murder. Was it simply a coincidence that a short time later, his wife mysteriously fell and lost her baby? Jocelyn opened her eyes and looked at her former partner. His hazel eyes were dark with sympathy. "Shit, Kev."

She turned away from him, looking at the wall of closed curtains. She rubbed her temples, thinking about how excited Francine had seemed, how her hands had been perpetually curled around her small baby bump. "Fuck," Jocelyn said. "Fuck, fuck, fuck!"

"I know," Kevin said. "So, look . . . her husband went home to get some things for her. They have to admit her—do a procedure.

You want to talk to her?"

Jocelyn tried to think past the little well of guilt filling up the pit of her stomach. "I'm not on the job, Kev. There are all kinds of privacy violations going on right now."

"Fuck that. You want to put the pressure on this guy? You get to his wife. If you get him off the street, it'll be the best fucking thing that ever happened to her."

Jocelyn sighed. Maybe it would be. Maybe it would be good for Francine to be rid of her murdering asshole of a husband while she still had a few child-bearing years left. Not that it was Jocelyn's place to judge or to meddle. But maybe she could just talk to Francine. The woman had seemed receptive to her when they'd met at the Rigos' home.

She and Kevin quickly put together a ruse where she would walk past Francine's partially pulled curtain talking loudly on her phone about just having spoken with a client in the ER. They hardly needed to bother.

Francine was near catatonic when Jocelyn happened by her bed. She didn't look at Jocelyn or even acknowledge her presence. She lay curled on her side, staring sightlessly in front of her. She wore two hospital gowns, one open facing front and the other open facing back. Jocelyn had done the same thing when she'd been admitted the year before. It was the only way to cover all the important parts, and you couldn't be chastised for not wearing a gown.

Jocelyn stepped tentatively into the room. She was a decent interrogator, but she'd never been a great actor. She was having a hard enough time bullshitting Olivia about Santa Claus. Approaching Francine, she couldn't keep her surprise from sounding insincere, but the sympathy in her tone was real. She wouldn't wish the loss of a child on anyone. The creeping, nagging sense that she was somehow responsible made her feet feel heavy, like blocks of concrete. She reminded herself that the only person responsible for the actions of an abusive spouse was the abusive spouse himself.

"Mrs. Rigo? Is that you? What are you doing here? Are you okay?"

Francine didn't respond, staring past Jocelyn, seeing something in her own mind that her reality couldn't compete with. Jocelyn stood there awkwardly fidgeting with her phone. A long, excruciating moment passed. Every sound in the place seemed amplified. Jocelyn glanced at the floor. "I'm sorry. I'm being rude. We barely know one another. I'll go."

When she turned her back, Francine said, "I lost the baby." Her tone was flat, matter-of-fact, betraying the numbness she must have felt.

Again, Jocelyn tried not to feel heartbroken for the woman. She was actively trying to put Francine's husband in prison, with good reason. She turned back. Francine still would not meet her eyes. "I'm so sorry," Jocelyn said. "What happened?"

"I fell."

Jocelyn knelt beside the bed so she could get face to face with Francine. She avoided Jocelyn's gaze but made no effort to move away or turn over. "Francine, is that really what happened?"

She didn't answer. Jocelyn studied her face, but there was nothing there, just a pallid, worn-out woman whose mind had shut down in the face of trauma. Jocelyn's heart ached for her. "Francine," Jocelyn tried again. "You can tell me the truth. I can help you. Did your husband hurt you? Is that how you lost the baby?"

A single tear escaped Francine's right eye, sliding down her cheek and onto the pillow beneath her head. In the same monotone, she said, "I told you, Miss Rush. My husband has never hit me."

With that, she rolled over to her other side, turning her back on Jocelyn.

CHAPTER 20

November 13, 2014

Jocelyn stood at her dining room table, stirring Betty Crocker cake mix and various other ingredients in a large blue plastic bowl. It looked like chocolate sludge. She could have sworn the last time she made cupcakes, the batter wasn't so soupy. She scooped some of it with her big, plastic spoon and let it pour back into the bowl. She looked at Anita, who sat at the other end of the table, completely engrossed in her laptop. Beyond her, in the living room, Anita's eleven-year-old daughter, Pia, sat with Olivia on the couch. They each had an iPad in their hands. Pia appeared to be showing Olivia how to play a game, using her own iPad as a guide. Jocelyn turned her gaze back to Anita.

Anita looked up from her laptop. Jocelyn scooped another spoonful of batter and let it fall back into the bowl. "I don't think I'm doing this right," she said.

"Rush, you're not making it from scratch. Just follow the directions on the box. You can't possibly screw it up."

Jocelyn stirred it some more. "You might think that, but I am actually quite skilled at destroying cupcakes by following the recipe on the box. The last time Olivia needed cupcakes for school,

114

they turned out so badly she wouldn't even let me take them in, and when I tried to go store-bought she was even more upset."

Jocelyn threw the spoon into the bowl, sloshing the soupy batter. She leaned over the table, placing both palms flat on the table. "Do you know what she said to me?"

Jocelyn didn't wait for Anita to answer. She lowered her voice so Olivia wouldn't overhear her. "She said all the other mommies made the bestest cupcakes except for me."

Anita rolled her eyes. "Rush, you're over-thinking this."

Jocelyn took the spoon up again and waved it at Anita, drops of chocolate batter arcing across the table. "Am I?" she said, eyes wide. "Why can't I make cupcakes that look like Minions or a goddamn Disney Princess? You should see what the other moms came up with. Those other moms—"

"Fuck those other moms," Anita said abruptly.

They glanced back toward the living room, but their daughters were fully engrossed in whatever was on their iPads. Looking at one another across the table again, Anita said, "There's more to being a good mother than making perfect cupcakes. We both know that."

Jocelyn took that in, silent and grateful for a new perspective. She'd stressed more over these stupid cupcakes than she had about opening her own business.

"Besides," Anita added, lowering her voice. "Can those other moms kill a man?"

Jocelyn looked down at her scar. "Not sure I'd get credit for that with my four-year-old. She still thinks I cut my hand on a window."

"Well, one day she'll know the truth, and she will appreciate it," Anita said. "In the meantime, I'll help you decorate the cupcakes."

The laptop emitted a low ding. Anita focused on the screen. Jocelyn could hear the click of the mouse as Anita navigated whatever had stolen her attention. "Finally," Anita murmured under her breath.

Abandoning the batter, Jocelyn moved around to where Anita sat. "What've you got?"

Anita pointed to the screen where she'd pulled up a photo of a young, Asian girl. Jocelyn estimated her age at sixteen or seventeen. It was an outdoor shot from the waist up. She stood in a field, bleachers fanned out behind her. She had long beautiful black hair and a radiant smile. The black and purple tank top she wore had the initials FW on it.

"Franklin West," Jocelyn said.

"Meet Becky Wu," Anita said. "She was a senior at Franklin West in 2005."

"Let me guess. She ran track and field."

Anita nodded. She clicked a few more times, bringing up an article on philly.com from June 2005. *Tragic Death of Teen Track Star Prompts Change in School Policy.*

CHAPTER 21

November 13, 2014

According to the article that Anita had found, Becky Wu's best friend was a girl named Jordan McMaisch. It took a simple Google search for Anita to find out that McMaisch still lived and worked in Philadelphia. She was the co-owner of an online magazine called *Philly on the Real,* and their offices were located in Center City in a high-rise near 17th and JFK Boulevard. Anita shot off an email to the woman, explaining that they were private investigators looking into accidental deaths at area high schools and asking if she'd be willing to talk to them about Becky Wu. Either *Philly on the Real* wasn't very busy, or McMaisch was an obsessive email-checker because within the hour, Anita and Jocelyn had an invitation to meet with her in her office that same day. They had just enough time to bake the cupcakes. When they were finished, Jocelyn set them on the counter to cool, and she and Anita loaded the girls into Jocelyn's car.

Evening was setting in, but luckily, they had missed most of the rush hour traffic. Jocelyn was grateful that both girls were still enthralled by whatever game they played on their iPads. They didn't complain once about the forty-minute drive into Center

City. *Philly on the Real* occupied a small suite of rooms on the tenth floor, its floor-to-ceiling windows overlooking the bustling streets below. The main room looked more like the community area of a college dorm than the office of an online magazine. Low couches and bean bag chairs were scattered throughout. Each one was a different color—all of them loud and bright. Pinks, purples, oranges, and fluorescent greens. Small white cubes dotted the room, some with actual magazines left haphazardly atop them. Jocelyn spotted a *Cosmo* and a copy of *Atlantic Monthly*. Eclectic tastes. Vending machines lined one wall, and open doors to what appeared to be individual offices stretched the length of the other. These were more traditional, with desks and filing cabinets. From one of them, a woman emerged.

Jocelyn expected her to look like a starving college student, to greet them wearing bunny slippers and sweats that said JUICY across her ass, with her hair tossed up into a lazy woman's bun, but she was dressed professionally. Business casual. Jordan McMaisch looked older than the one photo that Anita had been able to find of her online. She wore knee-high brown leather boots over charcoal tights. Her clingy black dress was broken up by a wide brown belt and a multi-colored scarf that wrapped around her neck and hung down over her breasts. Her black hair cascaded down her back in shiny waves, and her silver, dangly earrings caught the fluorescent lights above, glinting whenever she turned her head. She was attractive, with striking blue eyes and a smattering of freckles across her nose.

McMaisch greeted each of them with firm handshakes and led them to her office. Pia and Olivia had already claimed a couple of bean bag chairs and were back on their iPads. Jocelyn positioned herself inside McMaisch's office so that she could still see the girls from where she sat. The office was furnished with what looked like IKEA furniture. There were few personal items. McMaisch's desk was clear except for her laptop, phone, and a tablet. Everything was online these days.

"So," McMaisch said, taking a seat behind her desk. "You said in your email you're private investigators. You're here about Becky. Who hired you?"

Jocelyn caught her gaze. "Well, we've been hired by the family of another former Franklin West student who also passed away. We were looking into student deaths at Franklin West—there certainly weren't many before the shooting in 2006."

McMaisch shuddered. "That happened the year after I graduated. I can't even imagine. So is this, like, for a civil suit against Franklin West?"

"No, nothing that juicy, I'm afraid. We're really not at liberty to discuss the details of my client's case. We really don't think that Becky's death has any correlation to it. I am here mostly to satisfy my own personal curiosity about the circumstances of Becky's death."

McMaisch raised a brow. She didn't look convinced, but she seemed to understand that pushing Jocelyn wouldn't get her very far. She fidgeted with her phone, turning it over and over. "Okay," she said. "What do you want to know?"

"You were there the day Becky died," Jocelyn said.

McMaisch bowed her head. "Yes, I was. It was—it was horrible. We ran track and field. We practiced all the time. We were constantly outside. Becky knew she was allergic to bees—her mom was insane about it—but we never really thought about it, you know? We were teenagers."

"She'd never gotten stung before?" Anita asked.

"No. Not since she was really young, I think. Her mother was always on her about that EpiPen, but Becky thought she was just being overprotective. She didn't remember getting stung—I think she was too young to remember it. If you think about it, it's pretty amazing that she never got stung when she got older, seeing how we were outdoors all the time. Anyway, Becky never worried about it. She had an EpiPen, but she always left it in her locker. You know how it is when you're a teenager. You think you're invincible." She smiled weakly. "Maybe that's the trick though. Not to worry about things so much?"

Jocelyn returned the smile. "Shit happens whether you worry or not."

McMaisch laughed. She pushed her phone away from her, toward the edge of the desk but then pulled it back. "I guess it does, doesn't it? Well, I never gave the bee allergy a thought until that day. Becky swelled up so fast. So fast. I never saw anything like that. Her airway closed right up. The coach scooped her up, ran her inside to the nurse's office. The school required the nurse to keep an EpiPen in the office. They used the EpiPen, but it was too late. I guess if coach had been required to carry one, she might still be alive. I mean, like I said, Becky never would have carried hers every single time she went on the field. She never did. That was Becky."

Jocelyn frowned. "What do you mean, 'that was Becky'?"

McMaisch took her hand away from the phone and let it rest on the table. "Becky was very . . . defiant. She hated, more than anything, to be told what to do. Well, except maybe being told no. She never, ever took no for an answer. She was like a force of nature that way. It always seemed so insane to me that something as simple as a bee sting killed her."

"How did the coach take her death?" Jocelyn asked.

McMaisch leaned back in her chair and rolled her eyes, looking instantly like a seventeen-year-old girl. "Oh my God, Coach Rigo. He was never the same after that. I mean she practically died in his arms, and if what Becky said was true—" she stopped abruptly, as if she just remembered who she was talking to.

Jocelyn and Anita exchanged a look.

Pay dirt, Jocelyn thought. "What did Becky say, Ms. McMaisch?"

The woman shifted in her chair and folded her arms across her chest. Her cheeks turned pink. "Look, I don't think—I mean I don't know—it was just talk."

"You can tell us, Jordan," Anita said softly. "It's just us girls here."

McMaisch hesitated, her eyes cast downward. "Becky said that she and Coach Rigo were . . . involved."

"Like having an affair?" Jocelyn asked.

"Well, she never said that. She just—well, she had a crush on him. We all did. I mean he was young and hot and the nicest teacher we had. Becky was into him, but I'm really not sure if she liked him, or if he was just something for her to . . ." she trailed off, searching for the right word. Then she said, "Conquer."

"He was a conquest?" Jocelyn prompted.

McMaisch nodded. "Becky was like that. Plus, we had this really popular friend who was seeing an older guy—like, a married guy—and it kind of became a competition to see who could get an older guy. Becky decided to go after Coach Rigo."

"Did she succeed?" Jocelyn asked.

"I really don't know. She never said for sure. She just hinted at it."

"In what way?"

McMaisch blushed again. "Well, there were rumors that Coach couldn't, you know, get it up. One of our friends overheard one of the English teachers telling the school secretary that he was impotent. So one day we were all talking about boys and men and Becky said the rumors about Coach weren't true. I asked her if she'd slept with him, and she said something like, 'a girl doesn't kiss and tell.' That's what made me think she hadn't been with him because if she had, I think she would've bragged about it. She was like that. But then she died right in front of our eyes."

She wiped away a tear before it slid down her cheek.

"How about the EpiPen that was used?" Jocelyn asked. "Did it fail?"

"No," McMaisch said emphatically. "The EpiPen was fine. There was nothing wrong with it. Believe me, they checked all that."

"They?" Anita said.

"School administration. Even the police were brought in. It was a huge deal. But the pen wasn't expired or faulty or anything. The nurse gave it the right way. The reason Becky died was because it took too long for her to get to it. She went into cardiac arrest from the anaphylaxis, and her airway was closed. Did you know that it only takes six minutes for an adult to suffocate? Coach ran as fast as he could, but she was a goner even before he made it to the nurse's office. If she hadn't left her EpiPen in her locker, or if they required Coach to carry one onto the field, she would have lived. They changed school policy after that. They stopped keeping them locked up in the nurse's office and made the coaches keep them on the field."

"That must have been tough on the coach," Jocelyn said.

McMaisch wiped away another tear. Her fingers returned to her phone, pushing it from side to side on the surface of the desk. "Oh my God, he was wrecked after that. Just totally wrecked. He couldn't even coach the rest of the year. They had one of the other teachers do it. Our whole class was devastated. The whole school."

"I'm sorry for your loss, Miss McMaisch," Jocelyn said. She stood, smoothed her slacks, and offered the young woman a sympathetic smile. "Thank you for taking the time to speak with us."

McMaisch's tears were coming faster now. She wiped them away as quickly as she could. Jocelyn felt a pang of guilt for having made her relive the whole thing. The woman stood and smiled bravely, ready to walk them out. "It's no problem, really. Was I any help?"

Jocelyn glanced at Anita, who wore a grim smile. She nodded almost imperceptibly.

"Yes," both women said in unison.

CHAPTER 22

November 14, 2014

From where she was parked, three houses down from the Rigos,' Jocelyn watched Trent approach her car. He strolled right past the Rigos' house, hands in his jacket pockets, lips pursed like he was whistling. His breath came out in a cloud of white. The temperature had dropped suddenly and significantly in the last day or two. Jocelyn toggled the heat knob in her Explorer, turning it up another notch. The vehicle still smelled faintly of Knox's vomit, in spite of the mass quantities of air fresheners she'd stashed beneath the seats. She unlocked the doors as Trent drew closer.

He climbed in, blew on his cupped hands, put them up to the air vent and said, "Tell me about Becky Wu."

No greetings, no pleasantries. It was a cop thing. Get right to the point. Discard everything not important and get to the crux of a matter. It had taken Jocelyn a while after her retirement to break the habit. No wonder she didn't make fast friends with any of those damn pre-K moms.

"In 2005, she was a senior at Franklin West. She was a star on Cash Rigo's track team. Anita and I spoke with an old classmate.

Evidently, Wu had a crush on Rigo. The classmate says Wu hinted that there might have been a sexual relationship between her and Rigo. Anyway, Wu was out on the field one day, warming up, and she was stung by a couple of bees."

Trent turned and looked at her, an incredulous look on his face. "Bees, Rush? You're coming at me with bees?"

Jocelyn rolled her eyes. "I know, I know. Just listen. She was allergic to them. Started swelling up right away. Her airway closed, and she went into cardiac arrest. Rigo carried her to the nurse's office. Francine gave Wu the EpiPen, but it was too late. Becky Wu died in Cash's arms."

Trent bit the inside of his cheek. "Okay," he said slowly. "Any chance Rigo sicced a bunch of killer bees on this girl?"

"No. It was legit. An accident. Twenty people saw the bees sting her. The EpiPen was not faulty and hadn't been tampered with. The school changed its policy on EpiPens after that. Made the coaches carry them, keep them on the field."

"What's this got to do with Sydney Adams?"

Jocelyn made a sound of frustration, something between a heavy sigh and a growl. Trent raised a brow at her. She motioned to the Rigos' house as she spoke. "It's got nothing to do with Sydney Adams' murder, but it's something. Something we can use to get under this guy's skin while he's still vulnerable."

Trent shook his head. "I don't follow."

"The idea was to put pressure on this asshole. Make him feel like the walls are closing in, like he might as well get it over with and confess because it's only a matter of time before we—well, you—come for him."

"Okay."

"The newscast, the charity benefit, the photo—that rattled him. He was about to confess something to me outside PTG that night."

"I thought you said he was probably only confessing to the affair."

"Right," Jocelyn said. "And confessing to his inappropriate relationship with Sydney would have been a step in the right direction. Clearly, we threw him off his game. Plus, now he is probably more stressed out because Francine had a miscarriage.

Now is the time to apply more pressure, put him on the defensive. What better way than to bring up Becky Wu, another student he was close to who died in his arms?"

Trent smiled. "Okay, okay," he said. "I got you now. So this is a surprise visit then."

Jocelyn grinned. "Shock and awe."

CHAPTER 23

November 14, 2014

Cash Rigo looked like he hadn't bathed in a week. He answered his front door wearing red sweatpants and a white V-neck T-shirt with coffee and pit stains on it. His face registered surprise when he saw Jocelyn, his brows shooting upward, and fear when he saw Trent behind her. His facial muscles slackened, and his eyes widened. He kept one half of his body behind the door. "Can I help you?"

He must not have brushed his teeth in a few days either. Jocelyn couldn't help but wrinkle her nose when she caught a whiff of his foul breath. He didn't notice. He was too busy staring at Trent. Jocelyn put on a fake smile. "Mr. Rigo, we need to talk."

He ignored her and stepped back even further, retreating into his foyer. Jocelyn took that opportunity to muscle her way inside, just as she had with Francine a few weeks earlier.

"My wife is very sick," he said. "You can't come in."

Jocelyn was in the foyer, but Trent stayed on the steps. He flashed his badge. When he spoke, his tone was calm but firm. Jocelyn could tell he was one of those people—you did what he said. "Mr. Rigo, maybe you can come downtown and talk with us there so we don't disturb your wife."

Cash stared at Trent. "You're with the police," he said dumbly.

Trent dropped his credentials back into his pocket and smiled. He stepped inside so he was shoulder to shoulder with Jocelyn. "That's correct."

Cash looked back at Jocelyn. "I thought you were a private investigator."

Cold air flowed in around them. Jocelyn smiled and made a point of shivering. Cash caught on and closed the door slowly, cutting off the frigid air outside. He stared at her expectantly.

"Oh I am," she assured him. "I'm here as a courtesy to my client."

Cash's face paled. "The family?"

Jocelyn kept the amiable smile on her face. She felt like a flight attendant. "Yes, Sydney's family."

Trent rolled his eyes and hooked a thumb toward Jocelyn. "Yeah," he joked. "Now I got two bosses."

Cash looked mildly confused, a line creasing his brow. But their humor seemed to tamp down some of his anxiety. Jocelyn noticed his shoulders relax, a bit of color returning to his face. "Uh, sure, okay," he stammered. "Come on in."

He pushed the hair around on his head as he led them to the living room.

"Sit on the edge," Jocelyn whispered to Trent. He gave her a puzzled look until he watched her perch herself on the edge of the cushy couch. She patted the space beside her, and he sat. Cash sat across from them. Jocelyn noticed the coffee table books hadn't moved since she'd met with Francine.

Cash's left knee bobbed up and down at machine gun speed. His eyes were everywhere at once—on her, on Trent, on the doorway to the foyer, on the archway to Jocelyn's left that led into the kitchen. He looked exactly like every guilty suspect she'd ever interrogated. Right before they broke.

Trent said, "Mr. Rigo, what was the nature of your relationship with Sydney Adams?"

"My what?"

"Your relationship," Trent repeated. "What was the nature of your relationship with Sydney Adams?"

Cash looked at each of them, incredulous. "My relationship? She was my student. I was her coach. I—"

Jocelyn didn't let him finish. "Was that all?"

"I'm not sure what you're getting at."

Trent tried again. "You and Sydney, did you spend a lot of time alone together?"

Cash shook his head slowly from side to side, looking shell-shocked. Jocelyn heard a creek from the hall—probably the steps. She kept her gaze on Cash.

"She was my student," Cash said again. "I was her coach."

"What about when she came here? To your house?" Jocelyn asked. "Was that to study? Or were you coaching her privately?"

Another creek, closer this time. Cash looked like he might vomit. His mouth hung open.

"Mr. Rigo?" Jocelyn coaxed.

"What about Becky Wu?" Trent asked. Cash's head snapped in Trent's direction so fast, Jocelyn was surprised he didn't have whiplash. "You ever coach her privately?"

Jocelyn could sense Francine's presence lurking in the shadowy archway by the steps.

"Becky? She was—I don't—what does Becky Wu—"

Trent didn't give him a chance to finish stumbling over his words. "Becky Wu," Trent said. "She died in 2005. She was a student. You were her coach."

Cash's voice had a squeaky quality to it, like a mouse caught in a trap—still alive but badly hurt. "Becky had an allergic reaction to a bee sting. I had nothing to do—"

"Cash," Francine's voice rang out across the living room, a little too loudly.

All three of them turned toward the sound. She stood in the archway in a fuzzy, blue robe and teal and white plaid pajama bottoms. Her hair was pulled back in a messy pony tail. Her skin was ghostly white except for the dark circles under her eyes. She rested one hand against the archway and the other over her stomach. She stared at her husband, smiling weakly. "I was calling you," she complained. A lie. She'd been standing on the steps almost the entire time they'd been there. She made an unconvincing attempt to act as if she'd just noticed Jocelyn and Trent. "Oh, hello," she said, her voice strained, as though she was in pain.

Jocelyn imagined she was — the thought of the physical trauma of the miscarriage and D&C alone made Jocelyn cringe inside. Again, Jocelyn felt the stinging slap of guilt. She pushed it aside.

"I didn't know we had company. I'll make coffee." Francine smiled at Jocelyn. "Would you like some?"

"Please, don't trouble yourself," Jocelyn said. "You look like you need your rest."

But Francine had already turned, shuffling off to the kitchen. They all sat frozen, listening to the sounds of Francine moving around the kitchen — cabinets opening and closing, dishes clinking, and water running. Cash stood abruptly, as if it had just dawned on him that he should help his wife. "Give me a minute," he said.

Jocelyn stood too and motioned to the stairs. "Can I use your restroom?"

Cash sighed and nodded. "Top of the steps, to your right."

The second-floor hall was painted in periwinkle blue, paintings of flowers dotting the walls. Jocelyn turned right at the top of the steps, peeking quietly into each room as she went. One room held a home office with a treadmill and ironing board taking up most of it. Men's shirts hung from the frame of the treadmill. There was a smattering of paper beside a powered-down laptop on the desk. Bookshelves were lined with history books. Framed photographs of Cash and Francine graced the shelves. None looked recent. The door to the next room was slightly ajar. Jocelyn poked her head inside. It was an unfinished nursery. It had been decorated in light greens and yellows with baby animals dancing along the border of the wall. The crib was partially assembled, the bedding folded in a pile on the floor. Parts of the crib along with some power tools lay in the center of the floor. A dresser sat against one wall, wrapped tightly in plastic. An unopened video monitor — much like the one Jocelyn still used for her own daughter — sat atop it. The thought that Francine would never know the unique anxiety of wondering whether her baby was still breathing or not a dozen times a night made Jocelyn immeasurably sad.

She moved on to the next door which was the bathroom. It was bright, large and airy with a tile floor and a freestanding cast-iron, clawfoot tub. Like the rest of the house, it was neatly kept, decorated with blue accents. She relieved herself and then took a look around. A closet held cleaning supplies, extra towels, washcloths, and tampons. The medicine cabinet was crowded with men's shaving tools, toothpaste and lots of over-the-counter drugs, like Aleve, Motrin, Benadryl, and Sudafed. Others were prescription drugs. For Francine there was Prilosec and a large bottle of prenatal vitamins. On the shelf below those were bottles with Cash's name on them: Lisinopril and Imitrex.

Jocelyn took photos of the bottles with her phone. She wasn't sure what she'd be able to do with the information, but one never knew what would end up being useful in an investigation. There were two bottles whose labels had been peeled off. They were on the very top shelf behind a box of Band-Aids and two rolls of gauze. Jocelyn opened the first and peeked inside. She recognized the oblong shape of the Percocet tablets immediately. She'd taken the drug for a few weeks after being attacked the year before. The bottle was half full. The other bottle held two types of pills. The first was white and hexagonal with the word Searle and 1461 printed on one side and what looked like an image of some sort of internal organ on the other side. A stomach maybe. The other pill was blue and diamond shaped with Pfizer printed on one side and VGR 50 on the other. Jocelyn pocketed one of each and made her way back downstairs.

The scent of freshly brewed coffee wafted up toward her, as did the sounds of hushed, angry voices. Jocelyn stepped onto the landing as quietly as she could, keeping out of sight of the doorway leading to the kitchen but leaning toward it so she could hear the Rigos.

"I just washed those, Cash," Francine said.

"Do you think I give a rat's ass which cups these assholes drink from? I'm using these," he answered.

A heavy sigh. "If you don't care, then just use the ones I put out. They're nicer—and clean."

"No," Cash said firmly. "We're not giving them the fancy mugs, Fran. Can't you see they're out to get us?"

There was a beat of heavy silence. Then Francine hissed, "Us?"

Another tense moment of silence, this one longer. Jocelyn heard two mugs clanging against one another. Then Cash barked, "Go back to goddamn bed, Fran."

Quickly, Jocelyn returned to the couch, where Trent was thumbing through the coffee table book on natural disasters. He opened his mouth to speak, but Jocelyn stopped him with a finger over her lips.

A moment later, Cash followed behind Jocelyn with two cups of coffee. Evidently, he had won the coffee cup argument, because he gave them both old faded Temple University mugs. Trent's was chipped along the rim and Jocelyn's handle had previously broken off and been glued back on. Cash left and came back with a spoon, a bowl of sugar, and a small carton of half and half. He watched them fix their coffee. Trent took his time, and Jocelyn was sure he moved slowly just to piss Cash off.

Cash sat on the arm of the love seat across from them, arms folded over his chest, eyes cast down at them. Jocelyn and Trent sipped their coffee at the same time. It was surprisingly tepid and unusually bitter. Must be dark roast, she thought. But as Kevin had always said, even bad coffee is good coffee. She kept drinking while Cash and Trent stared one another down.

Finally, Cash looked away. He stood up. "You people have some nerve," he said, so quietly that Jocelyn strained to hear him. "Coming to my home, insinuating—"

Trent said, "We know about you and Sydney, Mr. Rigo."

Jocelyn tried to hide her reaction. They hadn't even discussed putting all their cards on the table yet. Cash's gaze returned to Trent's face. Trent stood, facing off with the other man. Cash made a half-hearted attempt at a scoff. "I don't know what you're talking about."

Trent downed his coffee and slammed his cup on the table. When he stepped into Cash, Jocelyn stood quickly, ready to get between them if necessary. But Trent just smiled like the cat that ate the canary. Like he knew something Cash didn't. "You know exactly what I'm talking about, you piece of shit."

"Trent," Jocelyn cautioned, clamping a hand down on his arm.

The two men's faces were inches apart.

"Get out of my house," Cash said.

"You think these kids are expendable?" Trent continued, his tone low and menacing, like a dog's growl. "Becky Wu. Sydney Adams. You think you can just use them up and discard them when you're finished with them?"

"Get out of my house."

"Trent," Jocelyn urged, tugging now on his arm. She pulled him toward the front door, but he kept staring at Cash, who followed them, keeping his distance, his steps tentative.

Trent pointed his index finger at Cash's chest. "I'm comin' for you," he promised.

Jocelyn pushed him out onto the front stoop as Cash reached the doorway. He threw his arms into the air, as if in surrender, and kept walking toward the street. Jocelyn stood just outside the Rigos' front door, between the two men.

"You got nothing on me," Cash yelled after Trent, but again, his tone was lame and unconvincing.

At that moment, Jocelyn saw what Trent had been attempting by confronting Cash with his relationships with Sydney and Becky Wu. He'd set her up nicely in there, all she had to do was tighten the noose and hope Rigo never called their bluff.

She caught Cash's eye, her face a mask of sympathy. "They'll have everything they need soon, Mr. Rigo," she warned. "Evidence doesn't lie."

CHAPTER
24

April 21, 2005

Becky Wu waited for Coach Rigo outside the boys' locker room. He was always the last one out. He said it was so that none of the boys would linger there and get into trouble. Becky had always wondered what kind of trouble Coach meant—until last week. She'd waited for him like she always did so they could walk out to the field together. But they'd ended up back in the locker room.

She'd been flirting with him for weeks. She knew it was wrong, but all the girls had crushes on him. She was the only one with enough balls to do something about it. Once she put the pressure on, once she went for it with him, she was surprised how easily he gave in. Of course, the whole time she was giving him the blow job, he was saying "no" and "stop," but not in a real way. Not in the kind of way he really meant it. It was more of a breathy, gasping expression of pleasure. He'd let her do it.

Twice the week before, he'd let her give him a blow job in the boys' locker room before practice. He never pushed her away or walked off. In fact, Becky remembered being a little shocked at how rock hard he was in her mouth. There'd been rumors for years that Coach Rigo couldn't get it up. But that clearly wasn't a problem where Becky was concerned. Now that she had his full attention, she was hoping to take things to the next level. She wondered what sex would be like with an older man. A couple of her friends had done it. They always said older men were better at sex. They'd been at it longer, had had more partners, more practice.

Becky was going to find out.

After the last boy on the track team left the locker room, she waited five minutes. Then she swept in, surprising Coach Rigo, who was packing a small duffel bag with his teacher clothes. He wore loose-fitting track shorts and a Franklin West tank top. His mouth hung open as she drew closer to him, dropping her own bag on the floor. He was standing by one of the benches between two rows of lockers. When she got close to him, he moved—putting the bench between their bodies.

Becky frowned.

"Miss Wu," Cash began.

Her frown deepened.

"I've been meaning to talk to you about . . ." he hesitated, as if trying to find the right word for what they'd been doing. He finally settled on, "Things. I've been meaning to talk to you about certain things that happened between us last week."

She raised her eyebrows and wiggled them suggestively. "You mean the kissing, the heavy petting, or the blow jobs?"

His face went instantly red, glowing like a burner on an electric stove. "Oh God," he groaned. "All of it, Beck—Miss Wu. It was completely inappropriate, and it cannot happen again."

Becky stepped over the bench, but he moved away from her until his back was against the lockers.

"Because you don't want it to?" she asked, pressing the length of her body against his. She immediately felt his erection against her stomach.

He slid away, to the side, along the row of lockers. Putting more distance between them. He held up both hands as if to ward her off. "Miss Wu," he said. "I am a married man. You are my student, and you're underage. I should never have let you . . ." he trailed off, like he couldn't bring himself to say out loud what they had done. Which was laughable, considering the size of the erection tenting his shorts. "I'm sorry," he added. He licked his lips and cleared his throat. "Nothing can ever happen between us again."

She waited for the punchline, but it didn't come. "You're kidding me, right?" she said, stepping back and putting a hand on her hip.

He shook his head. "No, I'm not kidding. I'm sorry. What happened between us was a mistake."

She gave it one last effort, stepping in front of him again and placing her hand on his dick. He jumped as if she'd shocked him. "It didn't *feel* like a mistake," she whispered, drawing out the word feel.

This time, he forcefully pushed her away. The backs of her legs hit the bench and threw her off-balance. She half fell, half sat on the bench. She felt her shock as a real, physical thing, as if she'd touched a live wire.

Becky was not used to being rejected.

She planted her feet and sprung up, pushing his chest with both hands. The sound of him smashing into the lockers was explosive, loud and reverberating. His shock mirrored hers, but now hers morphed into anger. She poked her finger at his chest. "How dare you?" she shrieked.

He looked around, as if someone might happen by them at any second. "Keep your voice down."

Before she could speak, the creak of the locker room door froze them in place. Becky took a step toward the door and poked her head around the row of lockers. The door was still and closed. No one was there. She turned back toward Rigo, arms akimbo. Her chest heaved; her whole body abuzz.

"Don't you get it? I can ruin your life. I can go to the principal or to the police right now and tell them you made me do those things."

A muscle in his jaw twitched. His eyes darkened. "Becky, please."

She sneered. "Oh, it's Becky now, is it? Not Miss Wu? So, what? Are you not dumping me after all?"

"I wasn't dumping you. You're a great girl, but we cannot be together. I'm married."

She drew closer, ran a finger down the center of his chest, hooking it into his waistband. He stared at it, his face frozen in horror, as if it were a deadly spider crawling on him.

"I've heard the rumors," she said. "That you can't get it up for your wife. But obviously, you can for me. What if I told your wife? Yes, let's tell your wife about us. I'm guessing then you won't be married anymore."

"Becky," he said in a slightly begging tone, "Please don't."

"Please don't," she parroted, her voice high-pitched and mocking.

She turned, picked up her bag, and walked toward the door. Glancing back at him, she mimicked him again. "'Please don't.' That's what I'll tell everyone I said when you came onto me."

~∞∞~

She let him sweat it out for a few days. She avoided him at school, cutting his class and steering clear of him in the halls so he couldn't get her alone. Every time she saw him, he looked more and more like a man standing before a time bomb that he didn't know how to diffuse. She had no intention of telling his wife or the principal or the police. What she wanted was him, and she had him in the palm of her hand. In another day or two, he'd be willing to do anything she asked.

Until then, she wouldn't be waiting for him outside of the boys' locker room. She grabbed her duffel bag out of her locker and headed toward the track behind Franklin West. The sun was high in the sky, but cool air glided over her bare legs. She'd worn the shortest pair of track shorts she owned, for Coach's benefit. Besides, in a half hour, she'd be sweating.

She smiled at her teammates, dropped her bag on the grassy area at the center of the track, and started loosening up. A few minutes later, Cash emerged. She felt his eyes on her as she stretched and almost laughed. This was going to be fun. She peeled off her jacket and knelt by her bag, unzipping it and stuffing her jacket inside.

She felt a prick on her hand before she heard the buzzing or saw the bees. One by one, they alighted from inside her bag, buzzing angrily and attacking her. How the hell did they get into her bag? Becky tried to scream, but her throat was already closing. Her skin felt hot and tight. She looked at her hand. It was beginning to swell. So was her tongue. She stumbled to her feet, unsteady, clawing at her throat as more bees stung her arms and legs.

She looked around, panic setting every cell in her body on fire. No one even noticed her distress. Most of her teammates were already doing laps around the track. A handful were still stretching only a few feet away. Becky swatted at the bees and ran toward Coach Rigo. He would know what to do. She'd left her EpiPen in her locker, but the school nurse would have one, too. Her mother had always insisted that she have it on her person at all times, but Becky hadn't been stung by a bee since she was two years old. She had no memory of it and had always thought her mother was just exaggerating the severity of her allergic reaction. Her mother exaggerated a lot of things.

Except this.

Becky fell three times before she reached Coach Rigo. Her teammates finally noticed her flailing her swollen limbs as she stumbled toward him. She heard them screaming, felt their hands gripping her, trying to keep her upright.

"Oh my God!"

"Becky!"

"What the hell?"

"What happened?"

"Someone help!"

Her lungs screamed. Her skin seared, and her body ached. She fell again. Her teammates tried to lift her, but she couldn't move. Her cheek lay on the grass. Her airway was completely closed. There was no time left. She thrashed and clawed at her throat. Then she felt strong arms scoop her up. Rigo's face floated above hers. He carried her, running as fast as he could go, jostling her burning form. He shouted something, but she could no longer hear his words. Her vision grayed at the edges.

Please God, she prayed. *Please help me.*

CHAPTER
25

November 14, 2014

Jocelyn pressed her cell phone tightly to her ear. With her free hand, she used her index finger to plug her other ear. She stood on the second floor of Dirk's Gameplex, the floor without the giant arcade, but she still had trouble hearing Anita.

"What did you say?"

"How did it go with Rigo?" Anita said.

"Great, I think. I mean we've almost got him. Problem is I'm holding imaginary evidence over his head. That's only going to work for another week or two before he gets wise and calls our bluff. I'm going to need more."

Jocelyn couldn't be sure, but she thought she heard a sigh. Then, "What happens if you can't find more?"

"I don't know. I guess Trent brings him in and gives it his last, best shot, all or nothing. By the way, I might be able to help with the 'more.'"

"Meaning what?"

"I went through the Rigos' medicine cabinet. I found some pills I couldn't identify. Could be nothing, but I'd like to take them to a pharmacy and see if we can find out what they are. I put them in my top, left desk drawer in an envelope."

Anita let out a low whistle. "Damn, Rush. You're ruthless."

"Yeah, well, my client is dying so I have to do what I can to move things along. Speaking of Knox, have you heard from him?"

"No. I called, but no answer and no return call."

"Same here. I'll text Trent and ask him to go check on Knox."

"How's it going there?"

Jocelyn couldn't suppress her smile. "Fantastic, actually. They're hitting it off so well I doubt they've even noticed I'm gone."

Anita laughed. "That's great. Now get back in there and try not to think about work for a few hours."

"Okay."

"I mean it, Rush."

"You'll work on the pills?"

"Don't make me come out there, Rush. I will kick your ass."

Jocelyn chuckled. "Yeah, yeah."

She ended the call, shot off a quick text to Trent, and slipped her phone into the back pocket of her jeans. She made her way down the steps to the cavernous lower level of Dirk's Gameplex. It was bigger than her high school auditorium, filled with arcade games, and low lit in blue tones, with a bar and a few tables tucked along the far wall.

It had been shockingly easy to convince Olivia to meet Caleb. Jocelyn had feared she would reject even the idea of a man in her mother's life, but on the contrary, her interest in him was feverish and endless. The entire drive to the Plymouth Meeting Mall, Olivia had peppered Jocelyn with questions about Caleb.

"Where did you meet him? Where did he come from? Is he old like Uncle Kevin? Is he a daddy? Does he have a gun? Does he like chicken nuggets?"

Jocelyn had done her best to keep up with the rapid-fire interrogation. Of course, once Olivia came face to face with Caleb, she clammed up, spending twenty minutes hiding behind Jocelyn's leg, sneaking peeks at him, and giggling convulsively when he made silly faces at her. They sat in a booth and ordered burgers and chicken strips for Olivia. All it took was one trick with his straw wrapper, and Olivia was talking non-stop to Caleb. Forty-five minutes later, they were bonding over an extremely competitive game of Ninja Fruit while Jocelyn took Anita's call.

Jocelyn searched the massive arcade and spotted Caleb and Olivia at a crane machine. Olivia's arms were already filled with poor quality stuffed animals. She jumped up and down beside Caleb. Jocelyn was willing to bet he'd already dropped forty bucks in the arcade. Her stomach gave a rumble as she made her way across the floor to them. She felt the very beginnings of nausea and hoped it would go away. As she passed a knot of teenage boys gathered around the basketball games, her insides gurgled. Grateful that the din of the arcade games drowned out the sound, she covered her stomach with one hand and moved past them as quickly as she could.

"Mommy! Mommy!" Olivia called as Jocelyn walked up to them. "Look at all the prizes Caleb got!"

"Wow." Jocelyn smiled. "That's great, honey."

Olivia's brown eyes were wide as saucers. She squeezed the stuffed animals to her belly and bobbed her head in Caleb's direction, her straight, light brown hair swishing over her shoulders. "And look! Look at Caleb's butt."

Jocelyn smiled uncertainly, suddenly feeling very hot. She tugged at the collar of her long-sleeved shirt. "Caleb's butt?"

"It's not what you think," Caleb said. He winked and turned, revealing a bunch of arcade tickets stuffed into the back pockets of his jeans, trailing almost to the floor.

"Wow," Jocelyn said again. She put a hand on the crane machine to steady herself. Heat spread over her body like a fast-moving rash. Beads of sweat popped up along her upper lip.

Caleb frowned at her. "You okay?"

Olivia asked, "Mommy, can we play some more?"

Jocelyn did her best to smile. "Sure," she said. "Mommy might need to use the restroom anyway."

Caleb reached out and touched her chin tenderly. "Joc, you look really pale."

The nausea intensified. She wondered if she could make it to the bathroom before she vomited all over the place. "My stomach is upset," she said. "I'm going to use the bathroom. You okay with Olivia?"

"Of course," he said. He smiled at her, but concern darkened his visage.

She tried not to sprint to the ladies' bathroom.

"If you're not back in fifteen minutes, I'm coming after you," Caleb called.

She didn't make it to a stall. Projectile vomit exploded from her body as soon as she crossed the threshold. She sprayed the doors of several stalls before crashing through one of them. She was only vaguely aware enough of being alone in the bathroom to be thankful for it. But she pitied the restaurant employee who would be tasked with cleaning up after her. She folded her body over the toilet, fitting her face into the hole. Every limb felt hot and weak. Sweat poured from every pore of her body, wicking her clothes to her skin, matting her hair against her cheeks and the back of her neck.

"Oh God," she moaned.

She hadn't been this sick since her first year as a detective when she and Kevin had gotten food poisoning from a steak shop in North Philadelphia. She was simultaneously horrified and relieved that she was out with Caleb at the moment. Horrified because she really didn't want another human being to see her like this, but relieved because there was no way she could take care of Olivia as sick as she was, much less get home.

Her abdomen clenched viciously. She cried out and her body spasmed, spraying more vomit into the toilet and across the back of the stall.

How much had she eaten today?

She pulled her cell phone out of her back pocket to call Caleb. She needed to go home. She needed her own bathroom. She needed privacy. The phone slipped out of her sweaty fingers and clattered to the tile floor. Her body convulsed again, bringing up more. Time became an endless, ever-looping vomit train with no destination in sight. She had no idea how long she was there before she saw Caleb's black shoes and Olivia's little Hello Kitty sneakers.

"Mommy! Mommy!" Olivia cried, panic making her voice high-pitched.

"I'm okay, honey," Jocelyn said, her voice hoarse.

She tried to stand but her legs were too wobbly. Caleb lifted her easily, holding her around the waist. "Jocelyn," he said. "You should have called. Come on, we're going to the hospital."

Olivia held a large plastic bag in one hand, likely with all of her loot. With her other hand, she picked up Jocelyn's phone. "Mommy, your phone."

Jocelyn took it and tried to smile at her daughter. She could tell by the slight quiver in Olivia's bottom lip that the girl was scared. Jocelyn had to stay calm. "Thank you, sweetie," she said.

She fumbled to put it back in her pocket until Caleb took it and put it in his own. With his other arm, he scooped Olivia up, bag and all. "Let's go," he said.

Jocelyn let him guide her, stumbling over her own feet, gripping his waist tightly to stay upright. "Not to the hospital," Jocelyn said. "Please just take me home."

"Will my mommy be okay?" Olivia asked as they reached the parking lot. The cold air was a balm to Jocelyn's burning skin.

"She'll be fine," Caleb assured Olivia. "She just has a really bad belly ache."

Caleb loaded both of them into her car since she had Olivia's booster seat. He strapped Olivia in and then buckled Jocelyn into the passenger's seat. She'd put a yellow Shop Rite bag on the floor for trash, which she used to vomit into during the ride home. It took fifteen minutes, and Caleb drove like he was being pursued by men with guns, but it still felt like the longest car ride of Jocelyn's life.

"We're almost there," Caleb assured her over and over. He kept one palm on the back of her neck.

"Is my mommy okay?" Olivia kept asking.

Between heaves, Jocelyn tried to steady her voice. "I'm fine, honey."

Caleb tried too. "She's just a little bit sick, Olivia. We'll get her home and take care of her."

"I know what she needs," Olivia said.

It turned out to be a Disney Princess ice pack and Olivia's stuffed bear, Snowflake Bearington of the Bearingtons, which she always gave Jocelyn to sleep with when Jocelyn didn't feel well. Once at home, Olivia set both items next to Jocelyn on the bathroom floor, where her mother had taken up position, dry-heaving into the toilet every few minutes.

At least it was *her* toilet.

Caleb knelt beside her, smoothing hair out of her face and grimacing at what he saw. As Olivia went to get Jocelyn's fuzzy robe, Caleb whispered, "You're scaring me a little, Rush. What's going on here?"

Her body felt so weak, like a pile of trash light enough to blow away in the wind.

"You're burning up," Caleb added, pressing a cool palm to her forehead.

She closed her eyes. The nausea was unbearable. She'd brought up everything she'd consumed that day, and still she felt like she was being batted to and fro in the bottom of a shoddy boat on choppy seas. The S.S. Vomit.

"I'm just sick," she said. "Can you stay? Watch Olivia?"

"Of course," he said.

"Thank you."

"What can I get you right now?"

Jocelyn tried a smile. "Privacy," she said. "I just need to be close to the toilet awhile longer."

He looked as though he wanted very badly to ignore her request, but he didn't. He left her there, mercifully, and went in search of Olivia. He left the bathroom door ajar and convinced Olivia to play in her room, which was just down the hall from the bathroom. Jocelyn knew he was doing it so he'd be able to hear her if she called for him.

She dry-heaved a few more times, then began bringing up bile. Mostly, she lay on the floor, curled around the toilet with her sweaty cheek pressed against the tile. Her body was cushioned by her fuzzy robe, which Olivia had insisted would make her feel better. She was too hot to put it on, so she'd spread it out and lay on top of it. She knew her four-year-old daughter was trying to take care of her in her own way. Jocelyn had no idea how long she was on the floor. Her exhausted body drifted in and out of sleep. She listened to Caleb and Olivia talking down the hall.

"This one is Princess Anna," Olivia explained in a voice patient parents use on unruly children. Jocelyn knew at once that Olivia had broken out her Disney dolls. Right now, *Frozen* was all the rage among the pre-K set. Jocelyn almost felt bad—Caleb had a college-age son, but he had never had the girl experience as a parent. "You can be Anna, and I'll be Elsa."

"You don't have any boy dolls? An Army guy? A policeman?" Caleb asked.

Olivia giggled. "No," she said. "I'm a girl, silly." A pause. "There is a boy doll named Kristoff, but I don't have him because Mommy says you don't need a man to complete your life."

Caleb's guffaw masked Jocelyn's groan. Olivia really was at an age where Jocelyn needed to watch what she said in front of her. The kid was like a sponge—or an elephant. She remembered everything.

"You can be the reindeer if you want," Olivia offered. There was a longer silence. Then Olivia asked him, "Do you love my mommy?"

Jocelyn's breath hitched in her throat. She prayed her gurgling, nauseated stomach would stay calm long enough for her to hear the answer. She and Caleb had never said the L-word, never discussed it. Jocelyn rolled away from the toilet, closer to the door, covering her cramping abdomen with both hands as she strained to hear.

"Yes," Caleb told Olivia. "I love your mommy very much. Do you know who your mommy loves more than anyone in the world?"

"Me," Olivia answered easily.

Good girl.

"Exactly," Caleb said. "Since you are the most important person in your mommy's life, I wanted to meet you and spend time with you."

Heart. Melting.

Jocelyn hoped she'd remember this later. She hoped it was real

144

and not a result of illness-induced delirium.

"You could be my mommy's boyfriend," Olivia offered.

"Really?" Caleb said. "That would be okay with you?"

"Sure. My mommy never goes on dates. She never had a boyfriend before."

"Well, I would like that very much," Caleb told her.

"You'll have to hold her hand though," Olivia said, her tone grave. "And you might have to see her naked and rub butts with her."

Jocelyn gasped. From Caleb, there was perfect silence.

Olivia explained, "My friend Raquel told me that's what grown-ups do when they're in love." She lowered her voice to a whisper that Jocelyn could barely make out. "It's called sex."

This time, Caleb laughed loudly, the kind of free and unfettered laughter he let loose when something struck him as deeply and unexpectedly funny. Finally, he said, "I don't know. That sounds pretty gross, but I'll talk to your mommy about it."

"So, do you want to be the reindeer?"

Jocelyn turned back toward the toilet as the stabbing pains in her abdomen increased in frequency and intensity. She pulled herself up and brought up more bile. When she finished, she lay back down on the floor, drifting to sleep once more. It didn't last long. She woke again soon after, dry heaving. This time, Caleb was there next to her, rubbing her back. He wore a tiara and he said, "That's it, I'm calling Inez to come take Olivia, and then I'm taking you to the hospital."

CHAPTER 26

November 14, 2014

After Inez picked up Olivia for the night, Caleb brought Jocelyn to Roxborough Memorial Hospital. It was only a few blocks away from her house. They didn't have a large trauma bay like Einstein, but they were well-equipped to deal with her emergency. Lucky for her, she'd been one of only three people waiting to be seen when she arrived, and they got her registered and hooked up to an IV pretty quickly. It had gotten crowded since then. She could tell by the number of voices she heard in the hallway and the sound of people walking rapidly back and forth past her room. And by how long it was taking Caleb to find a blanket.

She was in a room with two gurneys and a curtain separating them. Evidently, they'd filled the other gurney, because the curtain had been pulled since the last time she'd woken. The man on the other side moaned and heaved. He sounded like she had only a short time ago.

Initially, she had fallen into a deep, dreamless sleep as the IV pumped sweet relief into her veins. Her body had been too exhausted to stay awake a moment longer. Now she drifted in and out, basking in the drowsy calm that had fallen over her since the

146

anti-nausea medication began to take effect. She was grateful to be free from the spasms, abdominal cramps, vomiting, and dry heaves. The profuse sweating had finally stopped, but now she was freezing, even though she'd flat out refused to change into a gown. She had a hard enough time with hospitals after last year's attack. She'd shoot someone before she put a damn gown on again.

Now, her eyes struggled to stay open. Finally, she felt the blessed heavy warmth of a blanket. She opened her eyes to see Caleb leaning over her, tucking the edges of the blanket under her body. She smiled. "You don't have to mummify me," she said.

He kissed her forehead. "It will keep the heat in."

He worked his way down to her feet while she studied his profile. The strong jaw covered in stubble, his straight, narrow nose, thick brown hair. She was definitely feeling better if she was envisioning him naked.

"Where's your tiara?" she asked. "That was a good look for you."

He laughed. "Funny thing about that. When you're not a little girl or an actual princess, people don't take you too seriously wearing those things."

Jocelyn smirked. "Inez let you wear it to the hospital, did she?"

He scrunched his face up. "Pretty much, yeah."

Laughter made her abs ache, but she couldn't help it.

"That's all right. I'll get her back," Caleb said from the foot of the gurney. "You know, you could at least take your shoes off."

"No," Jocelyn said firmly. "No gowns and no taking off my shoes."

He laughed and worked his way up the other side of the gurney, tucking, tucking, tucking. She did feel warmer. He took up position near her head, gently stroking her hair away from her face and staring down at her with a tenderness that nearly brought tears to her eyes. She thought about his confession to Olivia.

"You look better," he said.

From the other side of the curtain, another moan sounded. Jocelyn glanced in that direction. "I'm better than that guy," she said.

"Yeah," Caleb said and hesitated. "About that—"

Before he could finish, as if on cue, the curtain pulled back. Kevin stood in the middle of the room and beyond him, on the gurney opposite hers, lay Trent Razmus.

He lay on his side, wearing a gown and gripping the metal rail of the gurney, an IV drip dangling from his left hand. His brown skin had taken on a grayish hue. He made a half-hearted attempt to point at Jocelyn. "You," he said.

Behind him, in a chair, Knox snored, his chin on his chest, one hand resting on top of his portable O$_2$ tank.

Kevin grimaced, looking from Jocelyn to Trent and back. "Just look at you two."

"What the fuck?" Jocelyn blurted.

Trent closed his eyes, taking measured breaths through his nose. Caleb motioned to him. "He came in after you. You were sleeping. He got sick just like you. About an hour after you."

Trent didn't open his eyes but hooked a thumb over his shoulder toward Knox. "I was checking on Knox like you asked. He's alive by the way. Drunk, I think, but alive."

"Do I want to know which one of you drove?" Kevin asked.

"No." Trent opened one eye and looked at Kevin. "No, you do not."

Jocelyn had barely been able to stand up, let alone drive. She couldn't blame Trent for allowing Knox to take the wheel. Desperate times. But she was grateful they'd both made it there in one piece without harming anyone else.

"I'm going to need a new car though. The inside of mine is covered in vomit."

Jocelyn thought about the way she'd sprayed the ladies' room at the restaurant. "Oh shit," she said.

"Anyway," Kevin cut in. "Caleb thought it was suspicious that both of you got violently ill at the same time."

"It obviously wasn't dinner," Caleb added. "Olivia and I are fine."

"I called the restaurant," Kevin said. "No other patrons got sick."

148

Trent opened both eyes a slit, regarding the three of them. "Knox wasn't sick either."

"So," Kevin said. "Where'd you guys eat lunch?"

"We didn't have lunch together," Trent said.

Jocelyn sat up straight, her body like a spring. "That no good piece of shit," she said. She tried to free her legs so she could get up until she realized she wasn't yet fit to go anywhere. She was dizzy, dehydrated, and she smelled of vomit. "Son of a bitch," she added. Her head dropped back onto the pillow. "It was Rigo. He poisoned us."

Kevin raised a skeptical brow. "You guys had lunch with the Rigos?"

"Just coffee," Trent said, his voice still weak.

"It was the mugs," Jocelyn said. "He did something to our coffee mugs." She told them about the argument the Rigos had had in the kitchen. "He was so insistent on using the old mugs."

"Those were some beat-looking cups," Trent said. "I thought mine was going to disintegrate in my hand."

"You really think Rigo poisoned you?" Caleb asked.

Jocelyn scowled and gestured toward Trent. "You really think he didn't?"

Caleb shrugged. "That's pretty ballsy."

"We'll get blood tests," Kevin said. "I'll fill out a report. No sense in getting the mugs though. If he's got half a brain, I'm sure he cleaned them out by now. Depending on what the blood tests turn up, we'll go from there."

Rage fought its way up from Jocelyn's core. She clenched both fists. She hadn't felt this kind of anger since before her attack and that had been nearly twenty years' worth of anger. "I'm going to kill him," she said.

Trent laughed wearily. "I know you didn't say that in a room full of cops."

"Fuck off," she shot back. "That motherfucker is going down. I'll strangle him with my own damn hands."

"Rush," Kevin cautioned.

"Don't," she snapped.

The three men stared at her, none of them willing to provoke her any further. Then a raspy voice came from the other side of the room. "I'll kill him — I'll be dead anyway by the time my trial comes," Knox said. "But I'd like to get a confession out of him first."

CHAPTER 27

November 14–17, 2014

The hospital kept both Jocelyn and Trent well into the next morning. Inez kept Olivia for the night, assuring Jocelyn that if she needed more time to recover, Inez could take the girls to the Poconos for the weekend. Inez was literally the only person Jocelyn would trust to take Olivia on a trip without her. Jocelyn went home with Caleb. She talked to Olivia by phone to reassure her that everything was just fine. She had to use Caleb's phone. Hers was only working intermittently since she dropped it onto the bathroom floor at Dirk's Gameplex. She suspected some vomit had gotten into its inner parts. She'd have to get a new one soon.

Caleb drew her a bath and gave her one of his shirts to sleep in. He threw her vomit-soaked clothes in the wash. Jocelyn felt a thousand times better once she cleaned the vomit smell from her body and hair. Still, she felt weak and bone-tired. Caleb perched on the edge of his bed and tucked her in. The bed smelled like him — like some kind of mountain-fresh scented soap and his own musk. She breathed it in as her head sank into his pillow.

"Hey," he said, smiling and stroking her hair away from her face. "We'll actually get to sleep together tonight. First time ever."

Jocelyn smiled back. "No—there was the Night of the Grand Slam."

Caleb laughed. "That doesn't count. We didn't actually sleep that night."

Jocelyn felt a flush darken her cheeks, amazed that he still had that effect on her after a year. "Well," she said. "This isn't how I imagined our first night."

Caleb stood and stripped to his boxers. He moved around to the other side of the bed and slid under the covers with her. He pulled her to him, spooning her, so she could feel the warmth of his skin and the beat of his heart against her back.

"I'm glad you're okay," he murmured, his breath in her ear. "I know you're angry."

"I'm not angry," she said. "I'm homicidal."

He chuckled and squeezed her tighter. "You need to rest."

But she was already drifting off, lulled by his warmth and his breath on her skin. "Caleb," she said, just before sleep claimed her, "I love you too."

ꙮ

She slept. Caleb went to work in her vehicle the next day, and Jocelyn slept through his entire shift. When he came home, they ate soup and crackers. Caleb loaded her up with water and ginger ale. Then Jocelyn slept some more. They stayed in bed Sunday, making love and eating the blandest food Caleb could find in his cupboards. Jocelyn spoke with Olivia on the phone as often as she could. Olivia regaled her with tales of her and Raquel's mountain adventures. Jocelyn was glad her daughter, at least, was having a great weekend.

Early Monday morning, Jocelyn felt well enough to get out of bed, although she was still weak and not ready for a real meal. She picked Olivia up from Inez and dropped her off at school. Afterward, she took Caleb back to the mall to get his vehicle. Then she spent nearly two hours getting a replacement phone before driving home, intent on spending the rest of the day cleaning her bathroom. The thought of driving to the Rigos' instead, to drag Cash out of the house by his balls so she could beat the piss out of him, did cross her mind.

But she restrained herself.

She was seriously considering spending the day on her couch watching daytime television as she let herself into the house. It only took a second for her to realize that something was off. She closed the door quietly and stood perfectly still, listening. Definite noises in her kitchen. Cabinets opening and closing, and the water running.

Son of a bitch.

She didn't have her gun. She hadn't taken it with her to Dirk's Gameplex on Friday night. It was upstairs in the lock box in her underwear drawer. Her heart pounded. Sweat popped out along her brow. She looked around the living room for something to use as a weapon. Then she remembered the aluminum baseball bat she'd hidden under the love seat just for such an occasion. Squatting down, she slid a hand under the love seat and swept it back and forth until she found the handle.

She had it up and ready, both palms choked around its handle, her legs planted apart in a batter's stance when her sister, Camille, walked out of the kitchen, a bowl of salad in her hand. They shrieked at the same time. Camille's salad flew everywhere. One of her hands went to her chest. Jocelyn dropped the bat. Like a mirror image, she too stood with her hand on her chest. Their mother would have found this hilarious. The two of them scaring the shit out of each other.

"What are you doing here?" Jocelyn said, catching her breath.

Chest heaving, Camille bent to pick up the remnants of her salad. "Didn't you get my messages?"

Jocelyn closed the distance between them and knelt beside her sister. They threw the chopped vegetables into the bowl, and Camille took it into the kitchen and dumped it in the trash.

"My phone broke," Jocelyn explained. "I had to get a new one. I've been using Caleb's phone. I really haven't looked at mine all weekend."

Camille returned with handfuls of paper towels and blotted the globs of dressing that remained on the carpet.

"Don't worry about it," Jocelyn said, climbing to her feet. Her legs felt wobbly. She sat on the couch.

Camille stood before her, crumpled paper towels clutched in her hands, her frown matching Jocelyn's own. They weren't twins—Camille was two years younger than Jocelyn—but their resemblance was remarkable, especially now that Camille was clean. She had gained weight and with it, curves. Her brown hair was cut sharply in a chic, sophisticated bob, the front longer than the back. Even in jeans and a cream-colored peasant blouse she managed to look elegant. Only the scars on her hands marred her stylish look. But Jocelyn knew that the scars Camille bore on her soul were far worse than those on her hands.

"You know," Camille said. "The last time I was here, you gave me a key and told me to stop in whenever I wanted to."

Jocelyn stood and waved Camille over. She folded her little sister into a hug. "You scared me," she said into Camille's hair. It smelled like coconut. "I wasn't expecting you. Of course you're welcome here any time. Olivia will be thrilled to see you."

As Jocelyn released her, Camille wadded the paper towels into a tight ball and looked around the living room. "Where is Olivia?"

Jocelyn plopped back onto the couch. "At school."

She patted the couch cushion beside her, and Camille sat. "You don't look so good," Camille noted.

Jocelyn smiled wanly. She gave Camille a brief recap of the Adams case and how she and Trent had been poisoned.

"Holy shit," Camille said. "You must want to kill this guy."

Jocelyn laughed. She opened and closed her fists, imagining using them on Cash, even though at the moment, she felt weak and ineffectual. "Oh, I do."

"How'd it go with Olivia and Caleb?"

Jocelyn relaxed her hands. "Great. Hey, you didn't tell me what you're doing in Philadelphia."

Camille had gone to an inpatient rehab in California the year before. She'd stayed out there and started talking about going to college. She wanted to become a psychologist. Jocelyn missed her like crazy, but California had done Camille well. She'd been drug-free and sober for a year—the longest she'd been clean since she was sixteen years old.

Camille gave a tight smile, one corner of her mouth dimpling. "Well, there's Thanksgiving . . ."

She trailed off, looking away. Sensing something more, Jocelyn said, "What else?"

Camille fisted the ball of paper towels. "I agreed to testify at Uncle Simon's trial."

Jocelyn had known it was coming up. When Camille was in high school, she had been gang-raped by five boys from their school. Their father had brushed it under the carpet, buying off doctors and law enforcement personnel until it was as though the rape had never even happened. Their mother had gone along with it, but she, like her children, had never recovered from the trauma. Before she died, she had asked Simon—her brother—to frame Camille's rapists for child pornography. When she and Bruce Rush died in a car accident three years earlier, Simon put the plan into action.

He and Bruce had run the biggest criminal defense law firm in the city for decades, Rush and Wilde. Simon's client list afforded him access to every type of criminal imaginable. Criminals who could break into the homes of Camille's rapists, hack into their personal computers and plant child pornography. Three of the rapists were charged with possession of child pornography. The other two were dead and in prison, respectively. Ironically, it was Caleb and his team at Special Victims who had helped exonerate the remaining rapists of the child pornography charges. He was able to track down the man who had broken into their homes and the hacker who had planted the evidence on their PCs—both of whom were going to testify that Simon had hired them to do so.

Jocelyn knew that the District Attorney's office salivated at the chance to fell the man who had bested them in court for the last forty years, gaining acquittal after acquittal. What the DA didn't have was motivation, and that was where Camille came in. She was the connection between the men who had been framed and Simon—but she was also Simon's niece. She and Simon had always been close. He had come to her rescue during her years on the street more times than Jocelyn could count. It was Simon who had helped Camille find the rehab facility in California and arranged for her to be admitted there. He was, and always had been, a tremendous support for Camille.

Jocelyn said, "You're testifying on Uncle Simon's behalf?"

Camille fidgeted with the ball of paper towels, tearing off small pieces and rolling those into spit-ball sized wads. Jocelyn reached over and took the paper towels from Camille's hands, placing them onto the coffee table.

"Not on anyone's behalf," Camille said. She pointed to her chest. "For me. I'm testifying as to what happened to me. That's all." She hesitated, a rosy hue infusing her cheeks with color. Jocelyn knew she wasn't going to like what came next. "I'm going to ask Zachary Whitman if he'll testify too."

Jocelyn groaned. Whitman had been the lookout the night Camille was raped. Jocelyn never could decide if that made him the most detestable or the least detestable of the five. Either way, he made her skin crawl. She leaned back against the couch and looked up at the ceiling. "Oh my God, Camille—"

Her sister stood and paced in front of Jocelyn, folding her arms across her chest. "I need this," she explained. "He can corroborate my story."

Jocelyn put a hand to her chest. "I can corroborate your story," she said. "Me."

Camille sighed. "You weren't actually there, remember? Whitman saw the whole thing. It has to be him."

It was true. Although Jocelyn had been in the house that night, she had no real memories of what happened. After their father covered up the rape and silenced his daughters, Jocelyn had driven her car into a tree, giving herself a grievous head injury. Whether she had done so on purpose or not, she would never know. Her memories from the weeks just before the accident were gone. Although the doctors had said there was a slim possibility of her recovering them, she never had. The night of Camille's rape was lost to her forever.

Jocelyn watched her sister walk back and forth. Her chin was thrust out in a look of determination. There would be no changing her mind. Camille wanted Whitman to testify. She wanted her story told and validated in a public forum. What better place than a court of law? She had probably come all this way to confront Whitman and ask him to testify. Jocelyn reached out a hand and caught one of Camille's wrists as she passed. Camille stopped moving and looked down at her.

"Okay," Jocelyn agreed. She looked at the scar on Camille's hand—it matched her own except, like Anita, Camille had one on each hand. "Okay to Whitman testifying, but I'll ask him, all right? I've already been in a room with him once. Let me do it."

Camille bit her lower lip and nodded. Some of the tension leaked from her body.

Jocelyn released her wrist. "Simon is okay with this?"

"You know how he is," Camille replied, smiling. "He always says, 'just let the legal process play out.' He's fine with it."

"Do you think you're ready for this?"

Camille sat back down, resting her elbows on her thighs, head in hands. "The trial's not for another nine months. I'll meet with the prosecutors now while I'm here, spend some time with you and Olivia—and Uncle Simon."

Jocelyn bristled but kept silent. She had barely spoken to Simon in the last year after she'd been inadvertently sucked into the initial child pornography investigation. She had read recently in the newspaper that after his indictment, Simon sold his practice, finally retiring at the age of seventy-five. She had let him see Olivia only twice in the last year. Both times he had taken her to the zoo, and both times, Jocelyn had trailed them the entire day without revealing herself.

She had trust issues.

A high-pitched noise issued from her jacket pocket—tinny-sounding music. It took her a moment to realize it was her new cell phone. She'd have to change the ring tone. She pulled it out, saw it was the office number, and answered.

"Rush," Anita said. "You need to come in right now. All of you. I already called Kevin, and he's on his way."

"All of us?"

"Yeah, you, Knox, and Raz. Call them and get over here."

CHAPTER 28

November 17, 2014

They were a weary bunch, gathered around the conference room table at Jocelyn's office. Trent slumped in a chair across from her. He wouldn't take his coat off, like he was freezing. Stubble grew unevenly on his cheeks, and there were large bags under his eyes. He had obviously had a much rougher weekend than Jocelyn. Knox sat next to him, reeking of booze—tequila this time, Jocelyn suspected, based on the smell—and fidgeting with his nasal cannula. He looked as though he hadn't slept in a week. Only Anita looked healthy and well-rested as she distributed cups of coffee in disposable, foam cups.

Trent and Jocelyn exchanged a look. "These your fancy cups, Rush?"

Jocelyn laughed drily. "Top of the line for you, Raz."

Both Trent and Jocelyn left their coffees untouched.

"Kevin's here," Anita announced. She took up position at the head of the table and sipped her own coffee. Kevin sailed in and stood beside Anita. Whatever news the two of them had, they'd already discussed it.

Kevin looked around and let out a low whistle. "Just look at you sad sacks. Gettin' the business from a borderline pedophile high school track and field coach."

A chorus of fuck-yous erupted from around the table. Knox picked up a pen and threw it at Kevin, who dodged it easily. Kevin pulled his cell phone from his jacket pocket, swiping, scrolling, swiping and scrolling once more until he found what he was looking for. He squinted and held the screen at arm's length. Jocelyn knew he had reading glasses. She also knew they were in his top, right desk drawer at Northwest Detectives. Men were so stubborn.

"Listeria," he proclaimed. "Both your blood tests came up positive for Listeria. It is a foodborne bacteria that causes, among other things, nausea, vomiting, and abdominal cramps."

"Food poisoning?" Knox said.

Kevin nodded. "Right. It's found in water and soil, so you can get it from raw vegetables, meat, soft cheeses."

"It's not found in coffee," Trent pointed out.

"True," Kevin said. "But you can grow it in a lab."

Jocelyn zeroed in on Trent. "You think we both just happened to get food poisoning — the same kind — at exactly the same time?"

Trent said, "How'd he do it? Where does he get it from? Where does he keep it? Does he have a bottle of listeria in his fridge? It sounds absurd."

Jocelyn felt anger heat her stomach again. She stood and pointed an accusing finger at Trent. "You don't think he did it."

Anita cleared her throat, drawing their attention. "Before you two start brawling, you're going to want to hear what I have to say."

Jocelyn resumed her seat. All eyes went to Anita. She pulled a baggie from her pocket and held it up. Jocelyn recognized the two pills she'd stolen from the Rigos' medicine cabinet.

"These are the pills Rush got from the Rigos' medicine cabinet. This one," Anita said, pointing to the blue diamond-shaped pill, "is Viagra."

Knox did a little half cough, half chuckle. "Son of a bitch."

"And this," Anita continued, pointing to the other pill, "Is Cytotec."

They all stared at her blankly. "Cytotec is used to bring about miscarriages in women," she explained.

One by one, their jaws lowered until they were all staring at her in open-mouthed shock. The silence in the room was so complete that the hiss of Knox's oxygen tank was a roar.

Then Trent said, "That sick son of a bitch. He takes Viagra so he can have sex with his wife, and after he knocks her up, he poisons her so she has a miscarriage?"

"That bastard," Jocelyn said. "Francine said she had had miscarriages before. I wonder if he's been doing this their entire marriage." She smacked her palm against her forehead and looked at Knox. "Do you think he poisoned himself the night of Sydney's murder to give himself something of an alibi?"

Knox shifted in his seat. "Don't know. Guess it's possible. I memorized those ER records. They didn't take blood. But if he did, then he's a lot more calculating than I've been giving him credit for."

It was sick and disturbing.

My husband has never hit me.

Jocelyn heard Francine's words in her mind. She wondered if the woman suspected that Cash poisoned her. But how could she? How could she suspect her husband of such a thing and stay with him? Jocelyn sighed. She wasn't that naïve. People did all kinds of abhorrent and unbelievable things to keep their families intact or in the name of what they thought was love. Just look at her own fucked up family.

"Rush?" Kevin said. He waved a hand in front of her face.

She blinked and gave her head a shake. "Sorry."

"What's your next move?" Kevin asked.

She looked at each of them. They watched her, looking to her to make a decision, to tell them what would come next. The words "I don't know" were on the tip of her tongue when a loud ping sounded from outside the conference room.

"Someone's here," Anita said. She slipped out of the room, closing the door behind her.

Knox said, "Can we go to the DA with the poisonings?"

Trent shook his head. "I don't see how we can even prove it.

The guy's a history teacher. Where's he getting listeria from?"

"You can ask him when you get him to confess to Sydney Adams' murder," Jocelyn said.

Trent shot her a dirty look. "What the fuck do you think this is, Rush? Confessions 'R' Us? You have some kind of plan for getting a confession out of this fucker? Because so far, all I've got to show for my trouble is a goddamn night in the hospital. I have other cases, you know, cases with leads and shit."

Jocelyn's cheeks blazed. She pointed a finger at him. "Maybe if you stopped complaining for five seconds, you could develop some leads in *this* case. This asshole poisoned us, Trent, whether you fucking believe it or not. I don't give a rat's ass where he got the listeria from. I care about making him pay, and you should too. Stop being a fucking pussy."

Eyes flashing, Trent stood up so fast, his chair flew out from under him and fell on its side. They stared hard at one another from across the table. Jocelyn genuinely liked Trent, but at that moment, she wanted more than anything to punch him right in his smug face.

"Raz," Knox wheezed, putting a yellowed hand on Trent's forearm.

Kevin waved both hands in the air. "All right, kids, settle down. We can—and should—take this to the DA, even if we don't get very far. I didn't say this earlier because I know Rush would blow a gasket, but listeria poisoning can be fatal."

Both Jocelyn and Trent's heads swiveled in Kevin's direction. Immediately, Olivia's smiling face flashed across the screen of Jocelyn's mind. Fear joined the congealed rage inside her, heating it, renewing its urgency. She and Trent started speaking at the same time, but then Anita reappeared in the doorway. Her eyes were wide. Her fingers drummed against the edge of the doorframe. "You're not going to believe this," she said in a hushed tone. "Francine Rigo is here."

CHAPTER 29

November 17, 2014

They were all completely silent until Anita said, "Did you guys hear me? Francine Rigo is here."

Jocelyn stepped back from the table. She wiped sweaty palms on her jeans. "Okay," she said. "Bring her to my office."

She waited until Anita had shown Francine into her office before she walked in. Francine sat in one of the guest chairs, her back straight, legs pressed together and crossed primly at the ankles. She'd set her black Coach purse beside her feet. Her hands rested on the arms of the chair. She had made an effort to look nice, wearing a gray Cashmere poncho sweater over a lacy camisole with black slacks. On her feet were a shiny pair of black flats. Her hair was pulled back into a tight bun. She wore light makeup, but Jocelyn could still see the pallor beneath it. She still looked sick and exhausted.

Jocelyn perched on the edge of her desk and smiled. "What can I do for you, Mrs. Rigo?"

Francine gave a weak smile. "I just wanted to thank you."

"Thank me? For what?"

"Well, last week, when you came to the hospital—you were the

162

only person who really asked me how I was. I just—I appreciated that."

"I'm still concerned about you, Francine. You've been through a lot. How are you feeling?"

Francine shrugged. She looked at the floor. When she looked back up, her eyes were brimming with tears. She bit her lower lip. "Oh, you know, I'm fine." She looked to the side, her next words slipping out quietly, on the edge of a sigh. "I'm always fine."

Jocelyn shifted and folded her arms across her chest. "You know," she said. "You don't always have to be fine."

Francine looked momentarily confused, her smile quavering. "I'm not sure what you mean."

Jocelyn's voice was gentle but firm. "Come on, Francine. You're a smart woman. Tell me what happened Tuesday night."

"The night of the benefit?"

"The night you lost your baby. What really happened?"

Francine's voice was barely audible. "I fell."

Jocelyn's tone took on a slight edge, like a teacher talking to a student claiming a lame excuse. *The dog ate my homework.* "Francine."

This time, Francine sounded more convincing. She touched her forehead. "I did. I fell outside of the house. We were arguing in the car—"

"About what?"

Francine gave another weak smile, a wry twist to her mouth. "Please, Miss Rush. I think we both know what my husband and I were fighting about."

"Your husband had an affair with Sydney Adams."

For a split second, Francine's face fell, but she gathered her composure quickly. "There was something between them, yes. I knew when I saw the photo of her at the benefit. It was taken at my home. Sydney never came to our house. At least, I didn't think she had ever been there. But clearly she was, and my husband lied about it, so I drew the obvious conclusion."

"He never admitted it to you?"

Francine shook her head. "He never came out and said the words."

"But you had a fight over Sydney?"

"Well, yeah. My husband had an affair with a seventeen-year-old student and kept it from me for fourteen years. Of course we had a fight."

"Did he push you? Is that why you fell?"

Another shake of her head. "No. I tripped. I got back up and went inside. He came in after me. I told him to leave me alone. I went to bed and a couple hours later, I woke up with horrible cramps. I started bleeding."

"Did he leave you alone?"

"Of course," Francine said. "Miss Rush, you seem hell-bent on making me into a victim of domestic violence. I'm not. My husband has a lot of flaws, but he does not beat me."

"Do you know what Cytotec is?" Jocelyn asked.

Francine's eyelids fluttered. "I don't know. I mean it sounds like a medication. I'm a nurse, not a pharmacist. Is that what it is?"

Jocelyn nodded. "You're right. It's a medication. It's used to end a pregnancy."

Francine's mouth opened as if in shock, but she quickly clamped it shut. Jocelyn stood and took the chair next to her. She turned it so that she faced the woman.

"Why are you telling me this?" Francine asked. Her hands went to her belly, as if her baby was still there.

Jocelyn felt a pang. "There are other ways that a man can hurt his wife. There are many forms of domestic abuse."

"What are you saying?"

Jocelyn took a page from Francine's book. "I think we both know that your husband's so-called flaws are much worse than him being a cheater. I think there are a lot of things about your husband that you prefer not to discuss. That's your prerogative, your business, but I've got to tell you, Francine, I'm worried about you. I think you're in danger."

Francine put a hand to her chest. "From my husband?"

Jocelyn held her gaze for a long moment. "You tell me, Francine."

She didn't respond right away, looking everywhere but at Jocelyn. Finally, she shook her head. "No, Cash would never hurt me. I mean not like that. He's a shitty husband sometimes, weak, but he isn't violent."

"When I first spoke with you in your home, you told me there was a time you felt afraid of him, enough that you asked a student to help you get a gun."

Francine's eyes widened, her expression earnest. "I told you, that was a mistake. I wasn't thinking straight. I was distraught. Cash would never really hurt me—"

Jocelyn held up a palm to silence her. "Okay, I get it. Cash is your husband. Your loyalty lies with him. I understand that. I won't try to convince you of what I believe. But let me tell you a story.

"Three years ago, I was working as a detective with the Philadelphia Police Department. My partner and I got a call for a disturbance house."

Francine looked puzzled.

"That's cop talk for a domestic violence call. Neighbors had heard screaming, glass breaking, that sort of thing, coming from inside. One of them called it in. Marked units responded first. Inside the house, there was a man and a woman. They'd obviously been fighting. Both had scrapes and bruises on them. House was trashed. Responding officers thought, 'husband and wife,' right? Wrong. They called us because the woman was a nineteen-year-old who'd been missing from her house for a week. The guy was holding her against her will, keeping her in his basement unless his wife went out, then he'd bring her upstairs. When my partner and I got there, we found a body in his basement. Had to turn the case over to homicide. The guy's wife came home while we were processing the scene. Do you know what she said when she came home from work to find the police crawling all over her house?"

Francine stared at her, rapt, waiting for her to go on.

"She said she didn't know. She said she had no idea."

Jocelyn paused for effect. She leaned in closer and repeated, "She didn't know. She claimed she had no idea that her husband had been bringing college-age women into their home, assaulting them and, in at least one case that we know of, killing them. She had no idea that her husband was a rapist and a murderer."

Francine said, "Maybe she didn't."

Jocelyn sat back. "Maybe. Maybe he was that good at keeping his activities secret. We don't know what their relationship was like behind closed doors. But I can tell you that this woman was crucified in the press. No one believed she was that clueless. How do you live with someone for twenty years and never have any inkling that your husband is a murderer? How could she not know? That's what people said. She's either a fucking idiot or worse, a liar. Maybe she did know but said nothing. Or maybe—and this is what I believe—that she didn't know, not really, but subconsciously she knew something was wrong. I think over the years she saw things, had some suspicions, but she pushed them aside, again and again, because it was easier to look the other way and ignore the nagging suspicions that her husband was a criminal of the worst kind than to have to speak up and do something about it.

"In hindsight, she could probably look back and think of a hundred examples where he set off alarm bells, and she chose to ignore them. But when he finally got caught, it was too late. Her life was ruined, and she came off looking complicit. No one believed her. Everyone thought she was just as bad as her raping, murdering husband for not putting it together and doing something about it."

Francine brought her hands to her lap. They trembled and she folded them, lacing her fingers together tightly. "Why are you telling me this?"

Jocelyn leaned in again, talking low as if conveying a secret. "Because I know you can put the pieces together, Francine. I want you to put them together. Maybe I am wrong about the domestic violence, but I know for a fact that your husband is a suspect in Sydney Adams' murder. It's only a matter of time before the police show up on your doorstep and take him away. They're closing in, Francine, and when they come, I'd hate to see you on the eleven o'clock news as the most hated woman in the city. The fucking idiot who had no idea her husband was a killer. Or worse—the liar who knew, or at least saw signs, but turned the

166

other way. The way I see it, Francine, you have two choices. You can be that woman, or you can be the hero in this whole thing. You can be the wife who puts it all together and helps catch a killer."

Jocelyn's mouth was dry from speaking. She wanted very badly to get a drink of water, but she stayed rooted to her seat, eyes unblinking and focused on Francine. A slow shiver started in the woman's shoulders and worked its way down to her legs. Jocelyn felt a pinprick of excitement. She had no idea how much or how little Francine knew about her husband's activities. She'd been taking a risk, dangling her theory like a piece of baited fishing line with no guarantee of a bite.

But she'd obviously hit a nerve.

Francine's cheeks had flushed as Jocelyn spoke, driving away the pallor caused by the recent trauma to her body. Now, as she stood on unsteady legs, her face was aflame. She clutched her purse to her stomach. She wouldn't meet Jocelyn's eyes. She turned and walked to the door. Over her shoulder, she said, "You have no idea what you're talking about." She paused. Jocelyn waited, hoping she'd turn around, sit back down, and tell Jocelyn what she was thinking or what she knew. Instead, Francine said, "I'll let myself out."

CHAPTER 30

November 17, 2014

The conference room was completely silent as Jocelyn went back in. Only the sound of Knox's O_2 tank whirring could be heard. All heads turned toward her, except for Trent, and her friends let out a collective breath.

"Well?" Knox asked.

Jocelyn yawned. She felt drained, as if she had been the one leaned on instead of Francine. She plopped into the chair between Anita and Kevin and shook her head. "I don't know," she said.

"What was she here for?" Trent asked, his voice barely audible. He kept his eyes on the table.

"She wanted to thank me for being nice to her at the hospital."

"That's odd," Anita said.

"You think she knew her husband poisoned you?" Knox asked. "Maybe she came to see how you were?"

Jocelyn shrugged. "Who knows? She's hard to read."

"She knows something," Kevin said. "Why else would she show up here?"

"She knew about the affair," Jocelyn said. She recapped the conversation for them.

"You really think she knows he killed Sydney?" Anita asked.

"I don't know," Jocelyn said honestly.

"Well," Knox said. "You planted the seed. Gave it your best shot. Let her sleep on it. Why don't you and Raz take a day. Maybe you can make up. Tomorrow's another day."

Jocelyn met Trent's eyes. She wasn't good at apologizing, and apparently, neither was he. They settled on a nod. Truce.

"Not for you," Anita said to Knox. "You don't have many days left."

Knox looked from Jocelyn to Trent and smiled. "Oh, I think I've got one more."

CHAPTER 31

November 17, 2014

They didn't need to sleep on it. Jocelyn got the call a few hours later. She was dozing on her couch while Camille and Olivia played dolls on the living room floor, the two of them so alike that it made Jocelyn's throat constrict.

Francine Rigo called her cell phone. Jocelyn didn't know who she was at first, the call was so unexpected. Then she remembered she had given Francine her business card a month earlier when Jocelyn visited her home. On the other line, Francine sobbed. "I found something."

Jocelyn felt like she'd taken an intravenous shot of caffeine. She sprang up from the couch, phone pressed to her ear, searching for her sneakers while Camille and Olivia stared at her, suddenly silent.

"Francine?" Jocelyn went to the kitchen and pulled her holster down from the top of the fridge.

"I found something," Francine blubbered. "Cash isn't here. Can you come?"

"I'll be there in twenty."

She left Camille and Olivia with hurried hugs and kisses and a breathless explanation. She called Trent on the way but got his voicemail. She left a message and dropped her phone onto the passenger's side seat. She drove like a maniac at first, until she realized that no matter what Francine had found, the case was still fourteen years old. The answers to the mystery of who shot Sydney Adams could wait another fifteen minutes. There was no point in Jocelyn getting into an accident over it. She slowed the vehicle and her breath. By the time she pulled up in front of the Rigos' house, her heart rate had returned to normal as well. She took a breath and called Knox. She got his voicemail too and left a message.

She knocked softly on the door and listened to footsteps inside. Francine pulled the door open and regarded Jocelyn with red-rimmed eyes. Her hair was in a messy ponytail, brown wisps hanging down the sides of her face. Gone was the outfit she'd worn to Jocelyn's office. In its place was a black pair of yoga pants and an oversized maroon Temple University sweatshirt, the sleeves rolled up to her elbows. She didn't speak. Instead, she turned and walked deeper into the foyer, down the narrow hall that ran alongside the steps. A chandelier cast a harsh yellow glow over the area.

Jocelyn closed the front door and followed Francine. She almost didn't hear the woman when she said, "Cash is still at school."

Where the hallway terminated near what Jocelyn assumed was a closet door, a tall, narrow table lay on its side. Beside it was an eight by ten photo frame that had been placed face down on the carpet. Beyond that was a much larger, thick wooden frame that had been mangled. Shards of glass lay everywhere. The painting that had been inside the wooden frame was bent and discarded. Jocelyn recognized it at once. She'd seen the corner of it in the flirty photos of Sydney. Knox had described it to her. The Tree of Death, he called it. It was every bit as creepy and odd as he had described. It was a barren tree in a snowy landscape. Its branches were painted in black with a series of striking red lines going from each branch to the ground. The lines were straight, forming what looked like a red cage around the bottom of the tree. They stood out like streaks of blood. On the floor next to the painting was a hammer.

A tremor ran down Jocelyn's spine. A wave of dizziness passed over her. Unconsciously, the fingers of her right hand found her scar and stroked it.

She looked away from the hammer to the frame itself, which was a thick, dark faux teak. Francine had pulled it apart at the corners and used the hammer to smash the frame into several pieces. Francine stood over them, staring at the glass and wood debris at her feet. She motioned to the overturned table. Her voice was low and flat. "He stands in front of the table and just stares — I mean not recently, but he used to do it all the time. He'd go on staring for a good half hour if I didn't stop him. At first I thought he was studying my painting. I was flattered. I took one of those art classes where you drink wine while you paint. It was his idea to have the stupid thing framed and hung. I wanted it back here so it wouldn't be so visible to our visitors. I mean it's not that good. It doesn't go with anything else in the house."

Jocelyn didn't know whether she should say something or not to try to move things along, or if she should just let the woman talk. Francine seemed almost in a trance. It was as if she were talking to herself. "I always wondered why he spent so much time right here, staring. Then today, after I saw you —" she broke off and met Jocelyn's eyes.

Jocelyn nodded, a small, slight movement to indicate that Francine should keep talking.

"I thought it was the table at first, maybe he hid something there — taped under or behind it. Then I looked behind the frame but there was nothing there. I opened the back of the frame, took the painting out. Then I . . . I don't know what came over me. I just knew there was something here. I wasn't sure what but I knew. Why does he spend so much time in this tiny space just staring? There had to be something here."

"Francine," Jocelyn said, placing a hand on her shoulder.

Francine stiffened.

"What did you find?"

The woman swallowed, her throat quivering. She pointed to

the floor. "He hollowed out a piece of the frame." She nudged a jagged piece of the frame with the toe of her sneaker. In the light, something glinted. Something shiny and gold. Jocelyn squatted down for a closer look. On the inside of the wooden frame, the side that would have faced the wall, a wide groove had been cut. From the looks of it, a flat, smooth piece of wood had been glued atop the hole, making a secret compartment, and Francine had used the claw of the hammer to pry it off. Inside was a small pair of gold hoop earrings, what looked like a girls' class ring, and a delicate gold chain with a charm on it. Jocelyn bent her fingers and, using the middle knuckle of her index finger, turned the piece of wood slightly so that she could clearly read what the charm said.

Her head spun. A hollow feeling descended into her stomach. She blinked once, read it again. She wasn't seeing things.

The charm read: *Sydney.*

CHAPTER 32

November 17, 2014

"He did it, didn't he?" Francine said, her voice quavering.

Jocelyn stood. She couldn't tear her eyes away from the jewelry. She realized in that moment that, in spite of her efforts to break Cash Rigo, she had never really believed in his guilt. She'd taken the case for Knox, because he was dying. Because she wanted to work on a real case again. Something that mattered. Something that would put a bad guy in prison. Something that would give a family peace. But here it was. The smoking gun.

The mythical smoking gun, as Knox called it.

Holy shit.

Francine's hand wrapped around Jocelyn's wrist, clammy and moist. "He did it, didn't he? Didn't he? I remember when Sydney died, all the news reports said that the murderer took her jewelry. My husband murdered Sydney Adams, didn't he? Why else would he have this stuff? Why would he keep it? Hide it?"

"Mrs. Rigo," Jocelyn said, her voice a croak. Her mouth was dry. She licked her lips, pulled her wrist from Francine's grasp, and motioned in the direction of the kitchen. "I think we should go sit down."

Francine met her eyes. She looked wild now, like a frightened animal. "In my house," she said. "He hid her jewelry in my house all this time."

Jocelyn gripped her shoulders and peered hard into her wide, wild eyes. "Francine, listen to me. You understand that I need to make some phone calls now, right? You understand that I need to call the police—you understand what happens now, don't you?"

Francine's eyes seemed to come into focus again. She nodded very slowly. "Yes," she murmured.

Jocelyn led her to the kitchen and seated her in a chair at the table. Jocelyn made several phone calls while Francine stared straight ahead, her eyes blank, unseeing. When Jocelyn finally put her cell phone on the table, Francine asked, "Would you like some coffee?"

Jocelyn stared at the woman, swallowing the first three sarcastic replies that came to mind. It was Cash who had given them the tainted coffee, after all. "No thanks," Jocelyn said.

When her phone rang again, she picked it up immediately. As she put it to her ear, she heard Francine whisper, "My God. What else has he done?"

CHAPTER
33

November 17, 2014

"Holy fucking shit, Rush," Trent said. He lowered his voice to a whisper. "I mean holy shit." It had been a half hour since Jocelyn arrived at the Rigos' house. She stood with Trent on the front steps. She had already given him the run down and shown him the jewelry. A crime scene unit was inside processing the scene while uniformed officers babysat Francine. Not that she needed monitoring. She'd been nearly catatonic since Jocelyn seated her in the kitchen.

"I know," Jocelyn said. "It's insane."

Their breath came out in great white clouds. Trent tugged at the collar of his jacket, pulling it up toward his ears. Jocelyn hadn't even had time to put on her coat before she left the house, but she barely felt the cold. Her adrenaline was pumping so hard and fast, she felt like she'd be awake for a month.

Trent pulled his cell phone out and looked at it. "I'm trying to get an arrest warrant now, before he comes home."

"Send a marked unit to the school," Jocelyn suggested.

Trent shook his head. "Nah. I don't want to spook him. We'll be ready for him when he gets here. I'll have the uniforms park

176

down the street so he doesn't see the car right away."

From the corner of her eye, Jocelyn saw Knox ambling up the street, bundled in a large, brown coat that had seen better days and dragging his O₂ tank behind him. His skin was flushed bright red. As she approached him, she could hear his wheezing.

"Jesus, Knox. I could have had someone pick you up."

His frame shook. Jocelyn couldn't tell if it was from the cold or exertion or something else. His voice was scratchy. "Tell me," he said.

As she told him what Francine had found, he seemed to deflate, his legs buckling, his body falling straight down. Jocelyn grabbed his shoulders quickly. Trent ran over and they took up position on either side of Knox, half dragging and half carrying him. For the first time in weeks, he didn't reek of alcohol.

"My car," Jocelyn said. "I'm right here, in the front of the house."

Together, she and Trent stuffed Knox and his O₂ tank into her backseat. Jocelyn used her keys to start the car and blast the heat. She went back to the passenger's side rear where Trent stood, looking into the backseat at Knox. He pulled his phone back out. "Should we call 911?" he asked Jocelyn. More quietly, he added, "He doesn't seem drunk."

Jocelyn climbed into the car and pulled Knox toward her so that he was sitting upright. She looked back at Trent. "Give him a minute. I'll stay with him."

Trent went back to the house, his stride brisk, cell phone pressed to his ear. Jocelyn sat next to Knox while he came to, blinking like a baby animal and adjusting the settings on his O₂ tank with shaky hands. "I'm okay," he said. "I'm okay. Let me stay. I need to stay."

Jocelyn touched his forearm. "Knox," she said. "You can sit here. You can't come inside the house, but you can be here. I'll leave it running so you don't freeze your ass off. They're waiting for him to come home. Then they'll take him in."

"I just want to see," he said. "I want to see him in handcuffs."

She smiled. "I know. You will."

Once she was sure Knox wasn't going to drop over, she went

back to the house. Trent was in the kitchen with the two uniformed officers, interviewing Francine, his voice soft and soothing. Francine gave mostly monosyllabic answers, her gaze still vacant.

Trent had staged the scene for maximum effect. They all stood around the kitchen table—him, Jocelyn, a crime scene technician, and the two uniformed officers. The jewelry was in three separate bags, spread on the table where Cash would be able to see them.

They heard him come in—the opening and closing of the front door, the blast of cold air, and the rustling of his coat. He must have noticed the debris on the floor when he went to hang his coat in the foyer closet because there was a hint of panic in his voice when he yelled, "Fran!"

His footsteps sounded in the entryway. Trent gave Francine a look and she called, "In the kitchen," her voice reedy and high-pitched.

"Jesus Christ, Fran, what the hell happ—"

He pulled up short at the entrance to the kitchen, the soles of his sneakers squeaking on the tile. He stared at them, his eyes taking in each one of them, and his face growing whiter by the second. "What the hell is going on? Why are you people in my house?"

You people.

Jocelyn wanted to punch him in the face.

"They found Sydney's jewelry," Francine blurted.

Trent held up a hand to silence her. At the same time, Jocelyn said, "Mrs. Rigo."

Cash looked baffled. His eyes flicked to the tabletop. They were all gathered around it like onlookers at the scene of a horrific accident. He took a step closer, then another. He pointed. "Is that . . . ? Oh my God."

His eyes locked on his wife's face. "Oh my God," he cried. "Oh my God, Francine." He looked on the verge of hysteria, his skin gray, eyes bulging, his entire body starting to wobble.

With a nod from Trent, the two uniformed officers moved in, flanking Cash and taking hold of his arms. He didn't resist. He didn't even look away from his wife. His voice was quieter when he spoke next, tinged with sadness, and what sounded to Jocelyn like resignation. "Oh my God, Fran."

Her name was a question and a plea. She didn't blink. As Trent read Cash his rights in a loud, clear voice, Francine told her husband, "Do the right thing."

CHAPTER
34

November 17, 2014

Cash looked exactly like a man whose whole life had just disappeared before his eyes. Once at the Roundhouse, Trent placed him in an interrogation room. The Homicide Unit's interrogation rooms were small and equipped with a table and chairs that had seen better days. Every surface inside the room was scarred by cigarette burns and graffiti. They didn't have a fancy two-way mirror. Inset into the wall was a large glassed-in video camera, its unapologetic eye pointed right at the center of the room.

From another, more comfortable room down the hall, Jocelyn and Knox watched Cash on a small closed-circuit television. It wasn't the best picture, but it was good enough for Jocelyn to see that the color still hadn't come back into Cash's face. His expression was pinched, tortured, like someone was jamming bamboo shoots under his fingernails. But he was alone in the room.

Trent left him there for a long time. It was a technique cops used sometimes. Let the suspect get all worked up, give them time for their imagination to conjure the worst case scenario. By the time the detective came in, they were so relieved to see another person, someone in authority, someone with the power to get them out of the tiny room, that they were more inclined to tell investigators anything they wanted to know. It didn't work on all suspects, and depending on the person, it could backfire, but in this case, the Trent-imposed alone time seemed to be having the desired effect.

Cash paced, then sat down, his heels bobbing, tapping out a staccato beat on the tile floor. Then he paced some more. He kept running both hands through his hair, then raising his face to the ceiling, a gesture of helplessness. A couple of times, he looked close to tears.

Knox sat in a chair, eyes fixed on the screen, a strange, satisfied smile on his face. Jocelyn alternated between watching Cash slowly lose his shit and watching Knox watch Cash. She had already called Camille to make sure she was okay with feeding Olivia dinner and getting her to bed. She had Camille put Olivia on the phone so she could apologize and explain why she wasn't home, but Olivia didn't seem to notice Jocelyn's absence at all as she was so thrilled to have her Aunt Camille all to herself for a whole night. Jocelyn had also updated Anita and sent brief texts to Caleb, Kevin, and Inez.

She was still digesting what Francine had unearthed. She couldn't remember a time in her nearly twenty-year career that evidence had been dropped in her lap in such a way. Handed to her on the proverbial silver platter. She had expected to feel more jubilant about it. She and Knox should have been high-fiving their asses off on the way to the nearest bar, but all Jocelyn felt was uncomfortable.

"Knox?" she said finally.

"Yeah." He looked up at her, his eyes twinkling.

She'd given him what he wanted, fulfilled his dying wish. She'd closed Sydney Adams' cold case. Gotten a murderer—and a molester of teenage girls—off the street. She smiled uneasily. "Nothing," she said. "Never mind." She squeezed his shoulder. "You need anything? I'm going to go get a soda."

"No," he said, turning his eyes back to the television. "I don't need anything at all."

Jocelyn had been to the vending machine twice and the restroom three times by the time Trent graced Cash with his presence. Jocelyn's empty coke bottles were lined up on the table beside the television. Cash's whole body slackened with relief once Trent entered.

"Have a seat, Mr. Rigo," Trent said. Under one arm, he carried a file folder and legal pad. He had a cup of coffee in one hand and a water bottle in the other. When Cash wasn't looking, Trent looked directly at the camera and nodded, his signal to them that he'd gotten confirmation from Jynx that the jewelry found in Cash Rigo's home belonged to her late sister.

Cash plopped into the nearest chair and waited for Trent to take his place at the table. Trent placed the coffee and the water in front of the other man. "I didn't know what you'd prefer, but I figured you'd be thirsty."

"Thank you," Cash said, reaching for the water. He slugged down half of it while Trent sat down, arranging his legal pad and pen in front of him and pushing the file folder off to the side. Trent read Cash his Miranda rights for the second time that day. Jocelyn held her breath when he finished, expecting Cash to immediately demand a lawyer, but he didn't.

"Can I get you anything else?" Trent asked. The friendliness was calculated. Jocelyn knew that Trent wanted to punch Cash in the throat just as much as she did. Neither one of them was fully recovered from the coffee incident.

Cash shook his head. "No, no. I'm fine."

Trent took him through some baseline questions, things they knew to be true like his name, age, address, and occupation. Finally, Trent said, "I want to talk to you about Sydney Adams."

Cash leaned toward Trent, his face brightening, almost hopeful. "Listen," he said. "That stuff you found in my house, you don't understand. It's not what it looks like."

Trent put his pen behind one ear and regarded Cash steadily. "Really?" he said. "Because it looks like you were in possession of the jewelry that Sydney Adams was wearing on the night she died. That's what it looks like."

Cash shook his head and spread his hands in a plaintive gesture. "But that's not—I didn't put it there."

Trent let his gaze linger on the man, let the moment stretch out. "Oh, you didn't put it there? Where did it come from, Mr. Rigo?"

"I don't know."

"You don't know how a dead girl's jewelry got into your house?"

Cash shook his head again, the movement more frantic this time. "No, I don't. I'm telling you, this is all a big mistake."

Trent gave a curt shake of his head, as if trying to shake off something perplexing. "Okay," he said. "Let's talk about Sydney Adams. You were close to Sydney, weren't you?"

"Well, yes, but—"

"How close? Did you have a physical relationship with her?"

Cash dropped his gaze and squeezed the bridge of his nose with his thumb and forefinger. "We didn't—it wasn't like that."

"Like what?" Trent asked. "Because I have photos of Sydney posing suggestively in your home."

"Oh my God," Cash said. "This is a nightmare."

"Oh, it is," Trent agreed. "It is a nightmare that the Adams family has been living for fourteen years. Now, before you lie to me again, I want you to think long and hard about what they're going through."

Again, Cash looked close to tears. "I did. I *have* thought about it. I can't—I don't—what do you want me to say?"

Trent leaned in closer toward the man, his face serious but sympathetic. "I want you to tell me the truth, Mr. Rigo."

"I am!"

"No. I don't think you are."

Trent reached into the file folder and pulled out a photo. From the angle of the camera, it was difficult to see clearly, but Jocelyn was pretty sure it was one of the flirty photos. Trent tapped his index finger on the photo. "Look at this face, Mr. Rigo."

Cash did, his face slowly falling to pieces, drooping, every line that age and stress had etched there now more visible. "Sydney," he said, the note of longing in his voice palpable. He reached out to touch the photo but apparently thought better of it and rested his hand in his lap. He looked down. "I cared for her," he said. "I know none of you will believe me, but I did."

"If you really cared about Sydney Adams, then you will give her family peace, Cash. Just tell me what happened between you and Sydney. The truth."

The moment stretched out, heavy and silent. Cash's shoulders quaked. Silent tears slid down his cheeks. Then, in a broken voice, he said, "A few weeks before Syd died, we were at my house."

"Why was Sydney at your house?"

"We had a meet in Cheltenham that afternoon. We were supposed to take pictures for the yearbook. Of course, I forgot my camera. Syd had one but it wasn't—it wasn't very good quality. She only had a few pictures left on her roll of film." He laughed nervously, wiping his tears. "Roll of film. Remember those days?"

Trent gave a brief smile and nod. Cash continued. "So I was going to drive to my house, get my camera, and meet the team at Cheltenham. They were going on the bus. Syd offered to ride with me. She wanted to talk to me about the colleges she'd been accepted to."

"And did she?"

"Yeah. That's not a line. She was my student. I had helped her with her applications. Sydney was smart and accomplished. She was going places. I just wanted to help."

"So what happened when you got to your house?"

"I made her wait in the car," Cash said, as if he were defending himself. "I did. I made her wait, but I couldn't find the damn camera. I thought it was in the foyer closet, but I couldn't find it. Syd got tired of waiting. She came in. She had her camera. She said if I could at least find some film, we could see if her camera would take it. I couldn't find any film either. Then she was teasing me because I was so disorganized, and then she said I was a bad photographer anyway."

"Why would she say that?"

Cash sighed. "Because the year before I'd taken photos of the championship meet, and they all came out blurry."

"So what happened next?"

"I took her camera from her, as a joke, and said I would prove her wrong. That I could take perfect photos. I started to take pictures. Of course, I couldn't work her camera. She laughed. She said, 'you're so lame.' That's what she always said to me, but she wasn't being mean. It was like this joke between us. Anyway, she reached for the camera and the flash went off. So I went to take more pictures and she posed for me. She posed for *me*." He repeated, as if to emphasize that he hadn't done anything wrong.

"Then what happened?" Trent asked quietly.

"Then the film ran out. I thought I broke the camera. She took it from me. She was standing there, by that table in my foyer hall, fiddling with it. She took the film out and put it on the table. She was just standing there and I felt . . ." he trailed off. His eyes glazed over, like he was back in the foyer along with Sydney. "I felt . . ."

Trent waited but when Cash didn't speak, he coaxed him. "You felt what, Mr. Rigo?"

Cash blinked, whatever visions he'd been indulging in gone. He looked all around the room, wiping his palms repeatedly on his pants. "I wanted her," he said finally. "Sydney had been flirting with me for a long time. You've seen her photos. She was gorgeous. I wanted . . . I wanted to touch her. She didn't stop me. She didn't say no."

Jocelyn felt sick to her stomach. Beside her, Knox made a *hmph* noise.

"What did you do, Mr. Rigo?" Trent asked.

Cash hung his head. "I—I grabbed her. From behind. I—I grabbed her hips, and I pushed her against the table. She didn't say no."

"What happened then?"

"We had—we had sex."

"You had sexual intercourse with Sydney Adams?"

"Yes."

"In your home?"

"Yes."

"What happened after that?"

"What?"

"After you had intercourse with Miss Adams, what did you

do?"

Cash said, "I—I apologized to her."

Jocelyn saw red. Her reaction was instantaneous. Her face burned, and her fists clenched, her heartrate increasing rapidly as if she'd just sprinted once around the building. "If you have to apologize to a woman after you have sex with her, that's a real problem," she muttered.

"That piece of shit," Knox agreed.

"Why did you apologize?" Trent went on, calm and collected.

"I was her teacher," Cash explained. "She was a student."

"You thought you did something wrong?"

Cash looked up. "I thought I confused things."

"What things?"

"Things between Sydney and me."

"What did Miss Adams say?"

"She said, 'don't worry about it.'"

"Oh my God," Jocelyn groaned.

"She told you not to worry about it?" Trent said, a note of incredulity working its way into his tone. "You had intercourse with a seventeen-year-old student in the home you share with your wife, and this girl told you not to worry about it?"

Cash shifted in his chair. "I mean, she wasn't mad or anything. She liked it."

"Did she tell you that?"

"No, but she didn't stop it."

"I hate to break it to you," Trent said, fingers raised in a pair of air quotes. "But 'not stopping it' doesn't mean it was consensual."

"You think I raped her?" Cash said, his voice rising an octave. "You don't understand. It wasn't like that. Sydney and I were close. She was mature for her age."

Trent went back to the story. "Did you both go to the meet after that?"

"Of course," Cash said.

"Did the two of you discuss what happened?"

"No. I mean right after it happened, I said I was sorry, and she said don't worry about it, but we didn't talk about it again. I—I didn't see much of her after that, at least, not alone."

"Do you think she was avoiding you?"

"No. I don't know. She came to practices and meets. She always had a smile. She seemed fine."

"But she didn't talk to you?"

Cash hung his head again, as if realizing for the first time that his encounter with Sydney wasn't as two-sided as he'd always believed.

"Did you try to talk to her?" Trent asked.

"I wanted to, but there was never a good time. And then she was dead."

"Then she was dead," Trent repeated in a low voice. "That's an interesting choice of words."

Cash's expression tightened, the lines around his mouth deepening. "You people," he said. "You're obsessed. You've been trying to pin Sydney's murder on me for fourteen years. I didn't do it!"

Trent leaned back in his chair, a practiced look of surprise on his face. "Pin it on you? Is that what you think?"

"That's what I know."

"Okay, well let me tell you what I know. I know that you, an older, married man, a teacher, a coach, a trusted mentor, had sex with seventeen-year-old Sydney Adams in your home. I know that there's a good probability that it wasn't consensual. I know that a few weeks later, Sydney Adams was murdered while out for her nightly jog. I know that everyone close to her, present company included, knew the jogging path she took six days a week. I know that after the two of you had sex, Sydney stopped talking to you. I know that you have no alibi for the night of Sydney's murder. I know that a few hours ago, your wife found hidden in your home the jewelry that Sydney Adams was wearing the night she was killed. That's what I know."

"It wasn't me," Cash insisted.

Beside Jocelyn, Knox said, "That's what all the killers say."

"How'd the jewelry get into your house, Cash?" Trent asked.

"I don't know!"

"How do you explain it?"

"I can't, okay? I can't."

"There's only one explanation, Mr. Rigo. You know it and I know it."

"My wife —" Cash began but faltered.

Trent laughed. "Your wife? You think your wife put it there? You think your wife hollowed out a compartment in the back of the frame and hid it there for fourteen years? Is your wife a good carpenter? Does she do a little light carpentry on the side? How'd your wife get the jewelry?" He wiggled his eyebrows at Cash and went on without letting the man speak. "Unlike you, she has an alibi for the night Sydney died. Ninety people saw her at the Home and School meeting, at the exact same time that Sydney was gunned down in Fairmount Park. We have her on tape at that meeting."

Cash shook his head back and forth like a metronome as Trent spoke. "You don't understand."

Trent stood up and rifled through the file he'd brought in. He pulled out color crime scene photos and tossed them onto the table. They fanned out before Cash, eclipsing the flirty photo from earlier. "You think your wife would do this?"

"Oh my God," Cash said, his voice so high it sounded like a woman's. He seemed genuinely shocked. "Sydney!"

Jocelyn felt a tickle at the back of her neck, like fingers walking over her skin. "Knox," she said. "What if —"

Trent's voice cut her off. "What is it that your wife said to you before you left today? Huh? What did she say?"

"She said to do the right thing," Cash responded, his voice suddenly flat, devoid of emotion. Resigned.

"Do the right thing!" Trent boomed. "Tell the truth, Cash. Or are you gonna put her through it too? You gonna bring her into this nightmare too? Don't you think she's been through enough?"

Cash's shoulders rounded. "Yeah," he said. "She has." He looked up at Trent. The two men stared at each other for a long moment. Jocelyn could hear the tick of a clock, the whir of Knox's O_2 tank, and the wheeze of his breath. Then Cash said, "What do I have to do? How do I do this?"

"Just tell the truth," Trent said.

Cash sat up straighter. He placed his palms on his knees. His voice was strong and firm as he said, "I killed Sydney Adams."

It was like all the air was sucked out of the room. For several seconds, she didn't hear Knox wheezing. She looked over at him. He was still alive, staring at the screen. Then, as Trent began taking Cash through the particulars of Sydney's murder, Knox stood up and, without a word, left the room.

CHAPTER
35

1996

Cash didn't know that Francine's niece was a virgin until it was too late. Afterward, the girl bled all over Francine's parents' couch. It was all over him, too. On his shorts and in his pubic hair. He stood over her, swearing. "What the fuck?"

Elise lay there in her skin-tight, hot pink tank top, naked from the waist down, her eyes huge, her mouth shaped like an O, staring in horror at the mess between her legs. It was at that exact moment that Francine walked in. She was supposed to be out at a pre-wedding brunch with her family. They were getting married in three days. They were staying with her folks until after the wedding. Francine's brother, his wife, and their fourteen-year-old daughter had flown in from California for the ceremony.

Cash had worked early that morning for his old landscaping company. He was trying to come up with some extra cash for their honeymoon. He'd come back and found Elise sprawled on the couch, watching *SpongeBob*. She told him she'd feigned illness to get out of going to "that stupid brunch." They'd talked and joked like they always did. She flirted with him like she always did — making him coffee and prancing around in shorts so short and tight that he could see the outline of the cleft between her legs. He never understood why her parents let her dress that way. He knew she did it on purpose. He'd been watching her all week. How could he not? That morning they'd been alone for the first time with no chance of being interrupted, and things had gotten out of hand. She felt twice as good as he thought she would, but he wasn't prepared for the blood.

Then there was Francine.

She stood in the living room doorway, purse dangling from her shoulder, her face hardening into angry lines.

"Fran," he said.

"What have you done?" she shrieked.

"Fran, I'm sorry," he said, reaching down for his shorts so he could pull them up and cover himself.

She strode over to him and slapped him hard across the face, whipping his head to the side. His brain felt rattled. He put a hand to his cheek and stared at her, paralyzed. He'd never seen her like this.

"You piece of shit," she said. "Get upstairs right now. Go to our room and wait for me there."

He kept staring at her dumbly. She wasn't usually so take-charge. He'd expected her to be angry, but then he'd expected her to dissolve into tears like she always did when he did something to upset or offend her.

But she didn't.

Instead, when he made no move to go upstairs, she pointed toward the steps and screeched, "Now!" startling the hell out of him.

As he ambled toward the steps, pulling his shorts up, he heard her tell Elise in a much calmer, nicer voice, "Oh sweetie, don't worry. Everyone bleeds the first time. It's perfectly normal. Why don't you go to the bathroom and clean yourself up. I'll meet you in your bedroom."

Cash sat on Francine's bed, his crotch itching, waiting for her to come. He wondered what she was doing. Later, he realized she was cleaning the couch cushion, although he would never figure out how she got the blood out of it. He heard the shower come on in the bathroom down the hall. He listened for what seemed like an eternity. Finally, he heard Francine's footsteps. He stood when she walked in. "Fran," he began. "I am so sorry. It's not what you think. I mean — I — "

Her voice was low but hostile. She poked his chest. "Shut up," she hissed. "Just shut the fuck up. You're disgusting. You are a weak, disgusting, sorry excuse for a man. Do you have any idea what you've done?"

He stared at her, the hairs on the back of his neck standing up. This was not his fiancée. This angry woman who used the F-word was not the woman he'd known the last six years. Her eyes were ablaze with rage and hatred. She seemed to grow taller with each exhortation. "It is three days before our wedding, and you rape my niece in my parents' house?"

Cash put his hands out, palms up. "No, no, no. I didn't rape her, Fran. I swear to God, I didn't rape her. She was flirting with me. All week she's been coming on to me. Today we were alone and it just — things just happened. I swear, Fran, you've seen the way she dresses."

She slapped him again, harder this time. He tasted blood on the inside of his mouth.

"She's fucking crying, Cash. When you fuck a girl and she cries, that's not a good sign. You fucking idiot. That girl is fourteen years old."

"Fran, I swear to God, I didn't hurt her. She was into it."

She put her hands on her hips. "Stop talking before I rip your fucking balls off and stuff them down your throat. Do you understand that you've just ruined our lives? Our entire life! Elise is going to tell my brother that you raped her. If you're lucky, he'll beat you to death. If you're not, he'll call the police. You're going to go to prison for being a child rapist. Let's not even talk about the fact that you fucking cheated on me."

She came at him, striking with a flurry of closed-fist punches. He put his arms up to shield his face from the blows. She was surprisingly strong. "I'm sorry," he cried. "I'm sorry, Fran."

"Three fucking days," she panted once she exhausted herself. "You just had to hold out for three fucking days. Then I would have gotten my inheritance from my grandmother's estate. We were supposed to buy a house with it, remember? I don't get it unless I get married, remember, you piece of shit? You think I want to stay in this house after you go to prison for raping a fourteen-year-old girl?"

"What?" Cash said.

She stared at him, looking maniacal, fists still clenched at her sides. "You ruined everything."

"You're thinking about your inheritance right now?"

She moved closer to him, her face inches from his. "It's not my inheritance anymore, is it, you fucking rapist? Now it's your defense fund."

"My defense fund? We're still getting married?"

"Fucking right, we are." She pointed at the door. "I'm going to fix this. When I tell you, you're going to apologize to Elise. Then you're going to go get a hotel room and stay in it till the wedding. While you're there, you're going to keep your fucking dick in your pants—that means no raping anyone. You think you can restrain yourself for three days?"

"I didn't rape her."

She slapped him again. His cheek was on fire. The coppery taste of blood filled his mouth. "You don't fucking talk anymore. In three days, you're going to marry me. I'm going to get my money, and hopefully by then, Elise will be back in California recovering from her ordeal. You just better pray that she doesn't get knocked up."

He flinched even as he opened his mouth to speak, expecting another slap. "What makes you think she won't tell even after she's back in California?"

Francine rolled her eyes at him. "I said I'd fix it, didn't I?"

CHAPTER 36

1996

Francine spun on her heel and stalked off, out the door and down the hall. He peeked around the doorway in time to see her and Elise emerging from the bathroom, Elise cloaked in a towel and Francine's arm wrapped around her shoulders. He watched them cross the hall to one of the guest bedrooms where Elise had been sleeping.

Cash crept down the hall, pressing his back against the wall until he could make out their voices. He heard sniffling. Then shushing. Then a voice he knew to be his future wife's but was so radically different in tone from the woman who'd just slapped him around that he questioned his very sanity.

"It's okay, sweetie. Don't cry. Really, it will be okay. Shhh," Francine soothed.

Elise's voice was more tortured, high-pitched, and thick with tears. "Oh my God, Aunt Fran, I didn't mean for that to happen. He just wouldn't stop."

Cash heard a loud sob, then more shushing. Then Francine's voice, consoling and oh-so-reasonable, "Well, as upsetting and disappointing as this is, I can't say I'm surprised."

Another sniffle. "You're not?"

"Oh Elise, I've seen the way you and Cash flirt—"

"Oh, but I didn't mean anything by it."

"Shhh, it's okay. You're a stunning young woman. You've got gorgeous hair and beautiful, glowing skin, a perfect body that's firm in all the right places still . . . and the way you dress, well, I've always said flaunt it if you've got it but sometimes . . ."

There was silence as Francine drifted off. Then Elise's voice, "What? What is it?"

Cash heard some rustling, like one or both of them shifting their weight on the bed. "Oh honey," Francine said. "You're already so upset. I don't want to make it worse."

"Just tell me."

"Well, sometimes the way you dress leaves very little to the imagination, Elise. A man like Cash, well, really. What do you expect?"

Two creaks, the bedframe and the floor. Cash guessed Elise had stood. "What?" she gasped. "How can you say that? My mom says women should be able to dress however they want, and that men need to learn to control themselves."

Francine sighed. "But that's not the world we live in, is it?"

Silence.

"Is it?" Francine repeated.

Three more creaks. Likely Francine standing and advancing on Elise. Cash could picture the girl, arms crossed under her perky little breasts, chin thrust forward, lower lip puffed out, sulky and stubborn. He'd watched her do it to her parents and grandparents at least a dozen times. It always worked.

Except this time.

"Your mother," Francine told her. "Is a lovely, well-meaning person, and she is right. We should get to do whatever we damn well please, and men should learn to restrain themselves. But they don't, Elise. I was raped in college. Did you know that?"

"N-no," Elise stammered.

"Yes, I was, by a filthy, disgusting beast of a man who broke into my apartment while I was sleeping and fucked me raw."

Cash winced. He'd never heard her talk about it like that. The rape had always been a touchy subject. A landmine.

"That's the real world, Elise. You cannot count on men to have self-control, and when you prance around in front of them for a week with your tight little ass hanging out and your tits in their face, and you flirt with them constantly, what do you expect, Elise? Really. What did you think would happen?"

"But I—I—"

"You were alone with my fiancé for what? An hour? My fiancé has been alone with tons of women, and I've never walked in on him humping anyone before. So you can't tell me that this was all him. I've sat in silence since you came, watching this flirtation between you two, trusting that it would go no further than that."

"Aunt Fran, I said I was sorry."

"I know you like him, Elise. I can see why. Most women do."

"Well, yeah, I liked him. I mean I had a crush on him."

"I trusted you, Elise."

"Wh—what?" Shock.

"Like I said, the attraction between you two was obvious. Cash is a man. A young, virile man. I expect him to have little to no self-control, but you're my family. You're a woman, too. I would have expected more loyalty, more restraint on your part."

Elise's voice was high-pitched. "My part? Aunt Fran, what he just did to me was—"

Francine didn't let her finish. "Did you tell him to stop?"

"No, I—not at first—I didn't think—"

"Did you tell him no?"

"I don't know. I mean maybe, yeah. I don't know. It all happened so fast."

"Did you push him away?"

"Well, not at first. I—"

Francine's questions were like machine gun bursts. "Did you scream? Did you yell for help?"

"No, I—"

"Did you hit him? Scratch him? Kick him?"

"I didn't—I couldn't—"

"Did you think for one second how I would feel?"

Elise's voice went up another octave. Cash could hear the tears in her voice again. "Aunt Fran, I said I was sorry."

"Did you like it?"

Incredulity. "What?"

"Even for a little bit, did you like it? Did you enjoy having this attractive older man not be able to keep his hands off you? Did any of it feel good?"

"Well, sure at first, but—"

"I'm so disappointed in you, Elise. What will your parents think? Your dad?"

"Oh my God, my dad will freak."

"Yes, he will. You realize what you've done here, don't you? All these people have traveled here for my wedding, which is only three days from now. Grandma and Pop-pop have spent tens of thousands of dollars on this wedding—all of which will be lost now. It's way too close to the wedding for refunds. But never mind the money, Elise. This is a true scandal you've embroiled us all in. Cash will go to jail. It will likely be on the news. Everyone in the whole family will know what you did. And Grandma— well, she just started feeling better from her last round of chemo. The doctors told us not to stress her out, but this . . . well, I don't even want to think about what something like this would do to her."

Elise sniffled again. Francine let her cry it out for a few minutes. Cash had no idea how she had done it—spun the entire situation so that it seemed like Elise's fault. He'd never heard her talk that way before or be in total control of a situation. Staring at the hallway paneling, he could almost believe it wasn't his fiancée speaking at all. He was tempted to peek into the room to make sure it was really her, but he couldn't risk breaking the spell Francine was weaving around young Elise.

Finally, Francine spoke again. "Sometimes, things happen and we feel . . . conflicted about them. Sometimes we need to put those things behind us and move on because not doing that would hurt more people than it's worth."

"What are you saying?" Elise said.

"I'm saying, right now, both you and Cash have a choice. This little thing between you two, this indiscretion, the two of you can drag the whole sordid thing into the light, tell the whole world, ruin my wedding, disappoint your parents, scandalize the entire family, and put Grandma's health at risk. Or you can keep quiet about it, and all of us can move on with our lives. I know Cash will apologize, and I am sure I can get him on board. Really, it's for the greater good. Why hurt more people than you have to? This way it will only be me that the two of you destroyed."

"Are you telling me to lie?"

"Of course not," Francine said. "I'm telling you to do the right thing."

With that, Francine left the girl alone. As she passed Cash in the hall, she clutched his elbow and dragged him into the bathroom. She pushed him until he hit his head against the top of the cabinet where Francine's mother kept the towels. Then she opened the cabinet door roughly, hitting him in the face with it. He reached for his nose, eyes watering as Francine rifled through the inside of the cabinet. She pulled out a towel and threw it at him.

"Clean yourself up," she snapped.

Before she left him alone, she said, "I hope you're happy, you piece of shit."

The fucked-up thing was that he was happy. Elise didn't get pregnant, and she never told anyone what happened. Francine married him, they got her inheritance, and she bought her dream house. Most importantly, Francine kept him out of prison, in spite of his infidelity and its unfortunate proximity to their wedding.

They never spoke of it after that. He never saw that side of his wife again. Oddly, she never really punished him for what happened with Elise. Once they exchanged vows, she acted as if it had never happened. They danced the night away at their reception and fucked like bunnies on their honeymoon in Punta Cana. Everything went forward exactly as Francine had wanted.

But Cash always suspected that, someday, she would make him pay for that day.

CHAPTER 37

November 17, 2014

Camille had fallen asleep curled up next to Olivia in Olivia's new twin bed. Her "big girl" bed Jocelyn called it. It was just big enough for a four-year-old and a grown woman. Jocelyn watched them sleep for several minutes, the two of them on their sides, their brown hair fanned out on the pillow. A year ago, Jocelyn had told Camille that she could be part of Olivia's life. She had no way of knowing how Camille would handle it—if she would be the kind of aunt who sent cards on Olivia's birthday and at Christmas, or if she'd make a real attempt to know the daughter she'd given up. Jocelyn was pleasantly surprised by Camille's efforts. She had made several trips home to visit, and she skyped with them regularly. Most importantly, when Camille was with Olivia, her attention was truly focused on the girl.

This is what Jocelyn had hoped for, and yet, the sight of the two of them snuggled up, side by side, started a small niggling anxiety in the pit of her stomach. A voice in the back of her head asked, *what if she wants Olivia for her own one day?* The rational part of her mind answered that that was impossible. Camille had signed her parental rights away when Olivia was less than a month old. Last year, when Camille talked about getting clean, Jocelyn had made it very clear that Olivia was her daughter, not Camille's, and that was not going to change. *What if Olivia wants to go with Camille?* The voice asked. But Jocelyn was the only mother Olivia had ever known. This was her home. Living with Camille, having Camille for a mother, would never enter the young girl's mind. At least not for a very long time.

Jocelyn pushed her fears aside and tried to focus on the miracle right in front of her. Her sister was clean, finally, and she was here. She was making a real effort. She wanted to be a part of their lives. Jocelyn wanted to take a photograph of the two of them but worried the flash would wake Olivia. Instead, she kissed them both on their foreheads and went back to her room, where Caleb waited. They'd have an hour together before he had to go to work. He lay on her bed, fully clothed, an arm bent behind his head. He smiled as she climbed onto the bed and curled up beside him. The tension in her body dissipated as he pulled her to him, enveloping her into his arms. She closed her eyes, inhaled his scent and sighed. She wished like crazy that he didn't have to work. She wanted nothing more than to sleep the entire night in his arms.

"So," he said. "Raz got a confession."

"Mmmmm, yeah," she murmured.

"I thought you'd be more excited."

She opened her eyes, which were level with his chest. She traced the hollow of his throat with her fingers. "I did too," she admitted. "I don't know. I was listening to Cash Rigo talk about killing Sydney, and he just seemed so . . . insincere."

Caleb shifted so he could look at her face. "What do you mean?"

"I don't know. It was almost like he was making it up as he went along. Raz asked him why he kept the jewelry but not the gun. He said he didn't know, that he wasn't thinking straight so he buried the gun in Fairmount Park near Sydney's body."

"Why would you bury the murder weapon near the body?" Caleb said. "That makes no sense."

"I know he's not the brightest bulb on the tree," Jocelyn agreed. "But really, I expected more from him."

"Where'd he get the gun?"

"He said he doesn't remember. He can't even remember the type of gun he used."

Caleb snorted. "He doesn't remember?" Skepticism dripped from every word.

Jocelyn laughed. "I know. It's absurd. I just don't get him. He showed so much emotion when he talked about her, about what happened between them, but when he confessed to murdering her, it was like he was reading from cue cards."

"You've never thought he did it," Caleb pointed out. "Maybe that's coloring your perception."

"Maybe," she yawned. "It doesn't matter, does it? Knox finally got his man. The case is closed."

"Where is Knox, anyway? I thought for sure you two would be out celebrating."

"I don't know. Home, I guess. I was at the office earlier to talk to Anita, and I tried calling him a few times, but he didn't answer." She closed her eyes again and nestled closer to Caleb. "I'll try him again in the morning."

She must have fallen asleep, the exhaustion of the last few days catching up to her. She woke up thrashing against the hands gripping her shoulders.

"Joc, Joc! Calm down. It's okay. You're safe."

It was Camille's voice, and Jocelyn followed it from the dark chaos of her dreams to her dimly lit bedroom. Caleb was gone. Her beside lamp was still on, its small circle of light illuminating a piece of paper on her nightstand. Camille snatched it up and handed it to her. "He left a note," she explained.

You were snoring.
Didn't want to wake you.
Call you tomorrow. Love you.
Caleb.

As she read it, Jocelyn wiped the sweat from her brow.

"You were screaming," Camille said.

Jocelyn winced. She looked toward the door. "Olivia?"

"She slept through it."

"She sleeps through a lot, thank God."

"You were dreaming," Camille said. A statement, not a question.

"Yeah. I still have nightmares about last year. When I was at that house today — the wife used a hammer to find evidence her husband hid in a picture frame. I think seeing the hammer brought it back."

Camille gave her a pained smile. She sat beside Jocelyn and slung an arm across her sister's shoulders. "Yeah," she said. "I have a hard time with hammers too."

In the dream, Jocelyn was being pursued by her attacker. When he finally caught up to her, she looked at his face, but it wasn't the man who'd assaulted her. It was Francine Rigo.

Jocelyn patted Camille's knee. "Do you remember when we were kids and mom took that pottery class?"

Camille laughed. "How could I forget? Remember she made that hideous vase and insisted on displaying it in the living room?"

Jocelyn smiled at the memory. In spite of everything, sometimes she missed their mother very much. "I remember," Jocelyn said. "Dad always wanted to move it — "

"But mom wouldn't let him touch it under any circumstances."

Jocelyn nodded. "Right," she said. "Mom could have hidden something in that vase for decades, and dad would never know."

"What?" Camille said, her face puzzled.

Jocelyn shook her head. "Nothing. Never mind." She stood and went to her dresser, looking for her phone. "I was just thinking about the frame this lady had."

Her phone wasn't on her dresser, or her nightstand, or in her coat pocket. It wasn't in the living room or kitchen. Camille called it three times, but it was nowhere to be found. Jocelyn searched her car but didn't find it. "Shit," she said. "I must have left it at the office."

"Well, that doesn't surprise me." Camille stood outside of Jocelyn's vehicle in her pajamas and bare feet, hugging herself. "You were just poisoned, and you've had a non-stop day. You've been going a million miles an hour since I got here. You need to take a rest."

Fully aware that she was about to do the exact opposite of what Camille was getting at, Jocelyn said, "I'm just going to run up to the office and see if it's there."

Camille rolled her eyes but smiled. "Of course you are."

The truth was—and she realized it while she was driving to her office—that she didn't want to be out of contact with Caleb that long. He always texted her when he worked overnight. Sometimes she couldn't sleep, and his texts got her through the difficult parts of the night. Sometimes she loved waking up to two dozen messages from him, some silly, some sweet, and some overtly sexual. Besides, he would worry if she didn't respond when she woke up, which was usually the same time he was headed home to sleep.

The phone wasn't in her office either. She tore the place apart, growing more and more frustrated with each moment that passed, but it was nowhere to be found. Back in the car, her blood pressure up ten points, she finally heard it. She was sitting at the red light at Ridge Pike and Cathedral Road, heading back into Roxborough when she heard the weird, tinny ring of her new phone.

There was no one on the road, so she put the car in park and got out, sticking her head under the driver's seat, where the screen glowed. By the time she fished it out and righted herself in the driver's seat again, the ringing had died. There were six missed calls from Knox in the last hour, but no voicemails. She was about to hit the tiny green telephone icon next to his number to call him back when the phone rang again.

She swiped answer and pressed the phone to her ear. "Knox," she said. "You okay?" No answer came. She heard breathing, rustling, then footsteps. "Knox," she said. "You butt-dialed me again."

She was about to hang up when she heard something else. A female voice. "Did you find it okay?"

The voice was familiar, but Jocelyn couldn't place it. The light in front of her had cycled back to red again. A vehicle pulled up on her left, the young woman in it singing along to the music blasting from her speakers.

"Yes," Knox answered. "Thank you."

"Sit," the woman told him.

Jocelyn heard the sound of a chair scraping over tiles, Knox's signature wheezing and then the clink of dishes.

"So," the woman said. "Did you just come to tell me that my husband confessed? Are you here to gloat?"

CHAPTER
38

November 17, 2014

Francine didn't sound angry or bitter. She didn't sound at all like a woman whose husband had just confessed to killing a seventeen-year-old girl.

There was a strange gurgling sound. It took Jocelyn a moment to figure out that it was coffee brewing. The traffic light turned green. Singing Girl surged forward, her taillights disappearing down Henry Avenue in seconds. Jocelyn bore left and followed.

Knox's voice. "Not to gloat."

"Well," Francine said. "Seeing as you're here so late, would you like some coffee?"

"I hate to trouble you."

"Oh, it's no trouble," Francine said. "I'll even let you use the fancy mugs."

Jocelyn came to the next light, which was red. Singing Girl was long gone. Headlights glowed in Jocelyn's rearview mirror. Two cars pulled up behind her. On the phone, she heard Knox laugh. "I don't think your husband would approve of your letting me drink from the good china."

Jocelyn heard the sound of liquid pouring, what sounded like something being pushed across the table, the fridge opening and closing and finally, the sound of a spoon clinking against the inside of a mug. "Thank you," Knox said.

Behind Jocelyn, one of the vehicles beeped. She glanced up to see the green light and hit the gas, again using one hand to steer while the other kept the phone pressed against her ear. She heard the sound of another chair scraping tile. A sigh. Then Francine said, "Well, neither of us needs to be concerned with what my husband thinks anymore."

Jocelyn had a sinking feeling in her stomach. Knox hadn't been with them that day. He only knew about the mugs because Jocelyn and Trent had told him. Jocelyn hadn't told Francine that she and Trent had been sick, much less that they suspected Cash of poisoning them using the mugs. But Francine didn't seem to find Knox's comment puzzling at all. She continued, "So, Mr. Knox, why are you here?"

Jocelyn sped up, but she still seemed to be hitting every red light.

"I'm here to ask you why your husband would confess to a crime he didn't commit—especially one that's going to put him in prison for life."

Jocelyn gasped. She inched forward into the intersection, searching for vehicles coming from her right and left. When she saw none, she went through the red light.

"You people," Francine said, her tone derisive. "You've worked for fourteen years to pin this on my husband, and now that you have, you're not happy. Really, I don't know what more I can do for you. You're destined to die unsatisfied."

Jocelyn's throat constricted. Knox was calm as ever. "Me?" he said. "No. I won't die unsatisfied. Not now. I know the truth."

"Oh? What truth is that?"

Jocelyn heard a sound like Knox shifting in his chair. "Tell me, Mrs. Rigo, doesn't it bother you, even a little bit, that no one will ever know how truly brilliant you are? All these years you've been pulling the strings, orchestrating all of this. How did you get your husband to take the fall for Sydney Adams' murder?"

Jocelyn pulled up to another red light. This time, there were three cars in front of her. Her fingers drummed against the steering wheel. "Come on."

"What makes you think Cash didn't kill Sydney?" Francine asked.

A creak, Knox shifting again. "My friend Raz, he went at Cash for a good, long while. The evidence against him is pretty solid, even without a confession. Almost too solid. But Cash wouldn't confess. Even in the face of a smoking gun, he wouldn't confess. It wasn't until Raz reminded him of something his lovely wife said that he confessed. 'Do the right thing.'"

The light changed. The cars inched forward. Jocelyn gave a light beep, but it only made them go slower. She struck the steering wheel with her palm. "Come the fuck on," she growled.

"So I told my husband to do the right thing. You don't think he should?"

Knox gave a wheezy laugh. "Depends on what you think the right thing is, I guess. Opinions might differ. Your husband, he's not a good actor. Not as good as you. When he saw the crime scene photos, I knew. He wasn't there that night."

Jocelyn beeped her horn until all the cars in front of her got out of the way. She sped around them, not even acknowledging the middle fingers and the expletives being shouted her way.

"You," Knox went on. "You're an exceptional actor, aren't you? I'll bet you've been giving Oscar-worthy performances your entire life, haven't you? So tell me, how did you do it? How did you pull it all off?"

Silence. Knox waited. There was the sound of swallowing. *The coffee.*

Jocelyn hit another red light, crept through the intersection and, when she determined that it was clear, went through it. She had already missed the turn off Henry Avenue that would lead her to her house. She was headed for the Rigos.' Francine didn't respond, so Knox took another tack. "Let's talk about Becky Wu then."

"Oh please," Francine scoffed.

Jocelyn turned off Henry Avenue onto Roxborough Avenue, snaking along the edge of the Walnut Lane Golf Course. She'd have to cross the Wissahickon Creek to get to the Rigos' neighborhood. As she raced across the bridge on Walnut Lane, her heart was in her throat. She pressed the phone ever harder against her ear. Its screen was hot against her skin.

"How'd you do it?" Knox asked.

More silence. Then, "Do you really think I'm stupid enough to tell you all my secrets, old man?"

"I don't think you're stupid at all. But I do think it's killing you inside to have to keep all those secrets. I know you would never take a risk like that. So I'm going to drink this coffee—all of it—and then you're going to tell me everything."

"Knox, no!" Jocelyn cried even though she knew he wouldn't hear her. She was relieved that she had put the phone on mute a few lights back so she could listen and not worry about Francine hearing any of her outbursts. Jocelyn wanted to call 911, but if she hung up, she'd lose her connection to Knox. Instead, she blew another red light, making her way onto West Cliveden Street and deeper into Mt. Airy.

Jocelyn heard a metallic thump. "See this?" Knox said. "I'm sick. I've only got a few months to live, so whether I die tonight or I die a few months from now, it's all the same to me. But I'd really like to hear your side of the story, Francine."

"No!" Jocelyn shouted.

She sped up, blowing through two more stop signs and swerving around a double-parked taxi.

"And what will I tell the police when you turn up dead in my kitchen? Don't you think it will be suspicious?" Francine asked.

"You'll tell them I came to gloat. I have a long history of harassing you and your husband. I'm a drunk. You'll tell them I showed up intoxicated to harass you. Maybe I fell, maybe I had a heart attack. Either way, you'll say I dropped dead in your kitchen. I lost credibility a long time ago, Francine. No one will question you. My prognosis is well-documented. There won't be an autopsy. Now, I'm halfway through this cup, so you better start talking."

"What do you want to know?"

"How'd you frame Cash?"

She laughed. "Oh, my husband is so easy. He's weak and very stupid. It wasn't hard. Of course, the food poisoning went a bit further than I intended. I had to take him to the ER. The good thing was that it was late enough to where he still could have gone and killed her."

Jocelyn came to a dead stop where the gas company had opened up the street. They hadn't set up any signs, just a cone, a Philadelphia Gas Works truck and a gaping hole in the middle of the street. The stream of expletives that shot out of Jocelyn's mouth would have made a sailor blush.

"The food poisoning," Knox said. "You give him the same thing you gave Rush and Razmus?"

"The detective and the PI?"

"Yeah."

"Oh, yes, the very same. Listeria. Yucky stuff."

"Why poison them, by the way?"

Jocelyn tried backing up one-handed, but a car had already pulled up behind her.

"Why not?" she heard Francine say.

She clutched the phone tighter and gritted her teeth. "You fucking bitch," she said. Behind her, the other driver began making a three point turn.

"Where'd you get listeria?" Knox asked.

"The eleventh grade biology teacher."

"He grows it in his lab? He just gives it to you to poison people with?"

Francine scoffed. "Don't be naïve. Everything has a price. He has eight children. His wife only allows him to fuck her once a month with the lights out in the missionary position."

"So you sleep with him?"

"When I need something, yes. Or sometimes just to watch him flagellate himself for weeks afterward."

Finally, the other driver completed the turn and pulled away. Jocelyn backed up and turned as fast as she could, heading in the direction she had come.

"That what you do for fun? Watch people suffer?" Knox asked. His wheezing was getting worse.

"People are no fun if you can't watch them sweat it out every now and then."

"You've been watching Cash sweat it out for years."

Francine snickered. "Oh yes. My husband is most entertaining. As I said, he is weak. The opportunities for provoking his guilt were nearly endless."

"What do you mean?"

Jocelyn weaved her way through a seemingly endless network of narrow, one-way side streets, having to turn around twice because of people who had double-parked their vehicles dead center in the street and left them there. They didn't even put their blinkers on.

"Fuckers," she said.

Francine went on, her tone conversational, as if she were having brunch with a girlfriend. "In case you hadn't noticed, my husband can't keep his dick in his pants, especially around young girls. He tries, or he thinks he does, but he is just not capable of controlling himself. He did it in college, then three days before our wedding, then he did it with Sydney, and with Becky Wu. Those are just the ones I know about."

"So he cheats?"

"Incessantly."

Knox coughed, a wretched-sounding wet cough. On a great wheezing exhale, he said, "You married him anyway."

"He serves a purpose."

"The cheating doesn't bother you?"

"Of course it bothers me, but marriage would be no fun without something to punish him for."

"How do you punish him?"

"It depends."

"Frame him for murder? Spread rumors to your colleagues that he's impotent?"

"You catch on quick, although he really does have trouble getting it up."

Jocelyn heard Knox swallow again. Then what sounded like his mug hitting the table hard. His voice was getting weaker, his breathing more labored. She could envision him toggling the dials on his oxygen tank. "Did you put the bees in Becky Wu's bag?"

"In a manner of speaking."

"Biology teacher?"

"No. One of my most sickly students—her mother was a beekeeper. I befriended her for a time. Learned a lot about bees. Did you know all it takes is a little bit of smoke to make bees sluggish? Burn a little bit of newspaper in a bucket, and you've got a homemade bee smoker. Sedates them quite well. Back then, I had a young man, a former student, who was willing to do anything at all for me, so I had him plant them in her bag."

Another wet cough. "What happened to him?"

"Who knows? He's probably in prison. Really, he was always quite troubled."

Jocelyn was almost there. She got stuck behind a food delivery driver. He'd left his car in the middle of the street, the driver's side door ajar. She watched him make his way up to one of the row houses lining the street. He jogged, but he still seemed to be moving in slow motion.

"Did you tamper with the EpiPen?" Knox wheezed.

Francine laughed. "Of course not. That would be far too suspicious. I really didn't intend for that little twit to die. That idiot was supposed to have an EpiPen with her, but she left it in her locker. Teenagers. They think they're invincible. Her death was a bonus. The allergic reaction would have been sufficient. Not so easy to suck your coach's dick when your tongue is swollen, is it?"

"I wouldn't know," Knox said.

Francine's laugh was positively giddy.

Jocelyn beeped. The delivery driver ran back to his car. He waved at her and got in. It was an eternity before he finally pulled away.

"Were there others?" Knox asked.

"Others that my husband cheated with? There was a girl in college, but I didn't do anything to her. I was far more concerned with punishing Cash. So one night while he was out supposedly studying with her, I staged my own rape. It wasn't hard to do. Meet a stranger at a bar, have some rough vehicular sex, go home, break a window, throw the house into disarray. It was quite fun, really. I tortured him with that for years. The best part was that I didn't have to fuck him, but he felt so sorry for me, he was at my beck and call twenty-four-seven. Of course, he did tire of it. He threatened to leave."

"I'm not sure I want to know, but how did you get him to stay?"

"I tried suicide, of course. Overdose."

Jocelyn heard rustling again. The sound of two taps. Knox checking to see if his phone was still there? "Weren't you worried you'd actually die?"

"One has to take risks."

"Cash must have felt really terrible after that."

"It was glorious. He was twice as attentive as he was after the rape. Every second of his life was consumed with pleasing me. The only thing that puts him in that state now is a good miscarriage."

Jocelyn gasped. Her stomach felt light and hollow.

Knox's voice revealed no surprise or shock though surely he was every bit as sickened as Jocelyn. Then again, every breath had become a loud, heavy huff with an underlying high-pitched wheeze. "The Cytotec?"

"Very clever of your P.I. by the way. How did she know?"

"She . . . went through your medicine cabinet."

"I admire her ruthlessness. She thought Cash did it, but he's not that smart. Even if he were, he doesn't have it in him to hurt someone else — not like that."

"So you say." He paused for breath. "Didn't it hurt? Inducing miscarriages?"

"Of course. But that pain was temporary. The effect on Cash lasted months. He became my servant, my slave, my whipping boy. Have you ever had someone like that in your life? Someone who feels so badly for you that they will do anything you ask? They'll wait on you, lavish you with gifts, be nice to you even when you're cruel to them. Even when they hate you, they'll still fawn all over you. It is the best feeling."

"Can't say I've experienced that."

No normal person would even want that experience, Jocelyn thought. No normal person would harm themselves, kill their own future children, and manipulate others for a few months of extra attention and sympathy. For a split second, Jocelyn wondered if Francine had Munchausen's, a syndrome where a person made themselves ill for attention. But it couldn't be that. Francine's issues were far more wide-reaching. She talked about Becky Wu's death with the same degree of emotion she might express if a restaurant got her order wrong.

She was monstrous.

"Is that . . . is that why Cash confessed to killing Sydney? He feels sorry for you?"

Every side street seemed suddenly clogged with slow drivers. Jocelyn drove as aggressively as she could, but there was simply no fighting Philadelphia's crowded, impossibly narrow streets. Even after eleven in the evening, the traffic was just as heavy as it was during the morning rush hour. Or maybe it just seemed that way because she was in such a hurry.

"Cash owes me," Francine said, sounding almost bored. "He's been a supremely shitty and inadequate husband."

"But you . . . you set it up that way," Knox countered.

"Oh please. Unchecked, he would have been on the sex offender registry eighteen years ago."

"You've been grooming him," Knox said. "All these years. Fucking . . . with his head. In — indoctrinating him."

"Puh. Call it what you will. He's in jail and I'm not."

"How did you . . ." He paused and took several short breaths. "How did you know he wouldn't throw you under the bus once he got downtown?"

She laughed again. "Oh, please. Even if he tried, who would believe him?"

We would, Jocelyn thought. She and Knox had both suspected.

"How would he prove it? I'm just the poor, sad wife whose cheating, murderous husband duped her. Now that I found the evidence he hid in our home and turned him in, I'll be a hero. No one would believe I did it. There's no evidence that I did. I couldn't possibly have killed her. I was at the Home and School meeting the entire night."

Francine was right. There was no physical evidence to tie her to the crime. Her alibi was airtight.

"How . . . then?" Knox asked.

"Really, must I tell you everything? Where is the fun in that? You can't figure some of it out on your own?"

"You kept . . . the jewelry," Knox gasped. "What about . . . the gun?"

"Wait here." There was the screech of a chair on the tile, footsteps, silence, then more footsteps. "See?" she said. "I keep it in my closet with my wedding dress. Cash would never search there."

The sound coming from Knox's scourged lungs was a death rattle. His voice was a croak. "So you . . . poison your husband to keep him home so he has no . . . no alibi. You have Sydney k-killed and k-keep the jewelry to plant later."

Finally, Jocelyn was there. She pulled all the way up onto the Rigos' perfectly manicured front lawn and threw the Explorer into park. She leapt out of the vehicle and took off in a dead run toward the door, phone still pressed to her ear.

"You make it sound so simple," Francine said. "I assure you it was not."

"Your g-g-gun, it's n-n-not—"

Jocelyn had her hand on the doorknob when she heard the clatter. She jammed her phone into her jeans pocket, pulled her gun from its holster, and burst through the door. "Knox!"

CHAPTER 39

November 17, 2014

Jocelyn rushed into the kitchen and trained her gun on Francine. For a moment, it was as though Francine didn't even see Jocelyn. Her eyes were glued to Knox, who lay on the floor next to an overturned chair, faceup and unmoving. His oxygen cart was undisturbed, but his nasal cannula hung from one cheek. His eyes were glazed, his breathing shallow. All the color had leached from his skin.

"Knox!" Jocelyn cried. She kept her gun pointed at Francine as she knelt beside him, trying to fix his cannula with her free hand.

Francine snapped out of her trance. "What are you doing here?"

Jocelyn took a second to take in the woman's face. She was smiling, cheeks bright red. She was having trouble looking away from Knox's crumpled form. She had the look of exhilaration children get after sledding in the snow—or the look adults get after sex. Pleasure, excitement, thrill.

She's enjoying this.

With her free hand, Jocelyn pulled out her cell phone and held it up. "Knox called me."

Confusion creased Francine's face, but her smile didn't diminish. "What? How? We were here the whole time, talking. When did he call you?"

Jocelyn stared at her. She watched Francine's glowing smile fall apart, replaced by a look of bafflement. "How long were you listening?"

"Long enough. I'm calling 911."

"No," Francine said. She walked slowly toward Jocelyn, a gun in her hand. She pointed it at Jocelyn, but her finger wasn't on the trigger.

Jocelyn put her cell phone down next to Knox and stood, wrapping both palms around the handgrip of her Glock. She sighted in on Francine's chest. "Put the gun down," Jocelyn ordered.

Francine's grin returned. "Oh, I don't think so."

Jocelyn's hands and arms were steady. So steady. She felt a strange sense of calm descend on her. She was surprised by it. On the inside, her anxiety raged. An image of Olivia's face appeared, front and center, in her mind. She thought of the times she'd almost been stabbed or had her throat slashed while she was on the job. Not to mention last year's attack. She had left all of that behind so she could be there for Olivia.

Yet here she was facing off with a monster who had a gun pointed at her head.

Olivia.

"You don't want to do this with me," Jocelyn told Francine.

The look on Francine's face could only be described as delight. "Why? Because you used to be a cop?"

No, because I have a kid.

"Because, Francine, if only one of us is walking out of this house, it's going to be me."

"You broke into my house uninvited. I have every right to shoot you, but if you shoot me, you'll go to prison. While I'm sure you'd survive just fine—you seem pretty tough—I don't think your daughter would like that very much, would she? You did say you have a daughter, didn't you?"

Jocelyn clenched her jaw. Her arms ached. Francine

mentioning Olivia made her want to vomit, but no way was she giving Francine the satisfaction of showing it. "You left the door unlocked," she said quietly. Francine didn't respond, so Jocelyn asked, "What did you give Knox?"

"Does it matter?"

"It matters to me. Tell me."

"Let's just say it was something far more potent than Listeria — it's amazing what you can get from the internet these days. Anyway, he'll be dead in a few minutes. Even if you could get him to a hospital, there's nothing they'd do. If he's terminally ill as he claims, he's probably a DNR." She must have seen the confusion on Jocelyn's face because she said, "Do Not Resuscitate."

Francine's arms shook with the effort of holding her weapon aloft, pointed at Jocelyn. She lowered it slightly. Jocelyn kept her own gun in position.

"So," Francine said. "Here we are. You evidently know my secrets. I have an interest in keeping them. Because I like you, I'm going to make you an offer."

At Jocelyn's feet, Knox groaned and coughed. It took everything she had to keep her focus on Francine and not drop to her knees to try to comfort Knox in his last moments.

"Put your gun down, Francine," Jocelyn said.

Francine laughed. "I'll put mine down when you put yours down."

"Not a chance."

A smile snaked across Francine's face. "Do you want to hear my offer?"

"I don't make deals with Satan."

"Not even for your daughter? Don't you want to go home tonight?"

"Put your fucking gun down, Francine," Jocelyn shouted in what Olivia called her 'Scary Mommy' voice. "Now."

Francine's smile flattened out. Bewilderment or disappointment, maybe. It was impossible for Jocelyn to know. The woman had spent a lifetime fooling people, acting the part of a warm, kind, oftentimes pitiful human being. None of it was real.

"You're being completely unreasonable, Miss Rush." She

shook her head. "I'm very disappointed in you."

Francine raised her gun, and this time, Jocelyn's eyes were drawn to her index finger as it curled around the trigger. In that instant, Jocelyn fired her own gun. The shot was deafening in the confines of the kitchen, its echo reverberating off the walls. The bullet hit Francine square in the chest. Her body jumped, and the gun in her hand clattered to the floor. She stumbled backward, crashing into the kitchen cabinets and sinking to the floor. She looked down and watched blood spread across her sternum, staining her white shirt, a slow-blooming flower.

Jocelyn kicked Francine's gun away from her and kept the Glock trained on the woman. She stepped closer. Francine looked up, her face the perfect picture of complete and utter shock. Her eyes followed Jocelyn as she rushed over to Knox, but she didn't try to move.

Jocelyn pulled Knox's head into her lap and slapped his cheeks lightly. Tears streamed down her face. He opened his eyes. It took a few seconds for them to focus on her.

"Knox," she said. "I'm sorry. I'm sorry I didn't get here in time."

He smiled. He reached up and clamped a hand over her forearm. "You did good," he said. "You did good."

There was a heavy silence. She could only tell he was still alive by the occasional jerk of his body fighting for every breath. "Thank you," he told her.

Then his eyes went glassy, staring upward. A smile spread across his face. He lifted his hand from her arm and reached for the ceiling. "She's there," he gasped. "She's there this time."

"Who's there, Knox?"

Stillness claimed his body. She felt him relax, his struggle over. His eyes remained fixed upward, a beatific smile on his face. On his last exhale, he said, "Sydney."

CHAPTER 40

November 17, 2014

Jocelyn didn't know which of them died first. Sometime while she was holding Knox in his final moments, Francine passed as well. A wide-eyed look of shock was carved into her face. Blood pooled around her. The house was disturbingly silent. Jocelyn sat on the floor, Knox's head in her lap, tears falling faster than she could wipe them away. She stared across the kitchen at Francine's body. She almost expected the woman to move or to break out into the creepy grin she'd given Jocelyn during their standoff. But there was no movement, no noise. No sirens in the distance. It didn't surprise her that the gunshot had gone unnoticed or unacknowledged by Francine's neighbors. This was Philadelphia, after all.

She reached across Knox's body to where she had put her phone down. With quaking fingers, she found Kevin's smiling face in her contacts and pressed the little green phone next to it. He picked up after three rings. "Rush?"

"Kev," Jocelyn sobbed.

"Rush? You okay?"

"Kev? Something bad happened."

It only took Kevin fifteen minutes to get to the Rigos' house, but it felt like an eternity. She couldn't stop crying. Her body shook so hard that her teeth chattered. Finally, Kevin was there, lifting her, pulling her away from Knox, sitting her down in one of the kitchen chairs. He knelt in front of her and gently gripped her shoulders.

"Rush," he said, trying to capture her gaze. "Tell me what happened here."

A tissue appeared in his hand and she took it, wiping the tears and snot from her face. "I fucked up, Kev. I fucked up. I should have just called 911. I couldn't have saved Knox anyway. I should have just hung up and called 911. Oh my God, Olivia. All I could think of was her face—what if I go to prison for this just like Francine said?"

She was on the verge of hysteria. Kevin took one of her hands and squeezed. "Rush," he said. "Look at me. Look. At. Me. I need you to take a breath. Start at the beginning. How did you get here?"

She looked into his hazel eyes and did as he said, sucking in a deep breath and exhaling slowly. Then she told him what had happened beginning with Knox walking out of the confession and ending with her shooting Francine. "Then I was sitting here and I realized how this would look. She was right. I shot her in her own kitchen. I'm not a cop anymore, Kev. I wasn't responding to a call."

"But you thought she was going to shoot."

Jocelyn sniffled. "She raised the gun. Her finger was on the trigger."

"Okay," Kevin said, looking all around the room. He stood and walked over to Francine's gun. He peered down at it. "I think the shooting was clean," he said. "You thought she was going to shoot you first."

"Kev, we're in her house."

He turned. "Knox called you. He was poisoned. You kept him on the line. The door was open. You're a former detective. You're credible, and you're the last one standing. Rush, no way is this bitch worth going to prison over. It's not gonna happen." Kevin pulled out his phone. "I'm calling it in. I'll get Trent and Inez down here."

Her best friend as the first responder and Trent to investigate the homicides. Trent wouldn't recommend pressing charges against her, not once he heard the whole story. Not once he found out that Francine had killed Knox. Jocelyn was lucky, even though that was the very last thing she felt. She'd been careless, reckless even. Now Knox and Francine were dead, and a man was staring down the barrel of a life sentence for a murder he didn't commit. How had everything gotten so fucked up so quickly?

It didn't take long for the cavalry to show up. With an intense look of disapproval, Trent listened to her story and then moved her to the living room while the crime scene unit processed the scene. Inez stood guard beside her, silent. Jocelyn sank into the couch. She tried to close her eyes but every time she did, the scene in the kitchen replayed itself over and over. Francine's face, all aglow, and her consternation when she realized that Jocelyn wouldn't be manipulated. Then her arm coming up, the barrel of the gun like a dead eye staring right at Jocelyn's face.

Jocelyn opened her eyes. She blinked a few times. "The gun," she said.

"What's that?" Inez asked.

"The fucking gun," Jocelyn said. She tried to get up from the couch, but she was like a turtle on its back. Inez watched her with a befuddled expression.

"Goddamn this couch!" Jocelyn blurted. She stuck out a hand but Inez didn't take it. Instead, she put her hands on her hips and arched a brow. "Oh no," Inez said. "I see how you're getting—all angry and agitated. I think it's best if you just stay down."

Jocelyn stopped struggling and glared at her friend.

"Where you going to go, Rush?" Inez asked, her voice gentler. "They're processing a crime scene in there."

Jocelyn folded her arms over her chest. She knew it was Inez's way of controlling the situation. She was doing her job and being nice about it. Jocelyn was a witness.

"The gun," Jocelyn said again. "The one Francine threatened

me with—it's a .45 cal isn't it?"

"Yeah, a Ruger P90. I don't even think they make those anymore."

"I need to talk to Trent."

"Oh, you'll be talking to Trent into the wee hours of the night down at the Roundhouse," Inez said. "Don't you worry about that."

CHAPTER
41

November 18, 2014

Jocelyn had been in plenty of interrogation rooms before, but never as the person being questioned. Inez had driven her to the Roundhouse and delivered her to the Homicide Unit, where she waited at Trent's desk until one of the other detectives ushered her into a small, foul-smelling room with assurances that Trent would be right with her.

She paced for fifteen minutes before pulling out her phone and sending him a text. They hadn't taken her phone — that was a good sign. She could see why some suspects went bat-shit crazy waiting in the tiny rooms, why some would say anything to get out of them. It wasn't exactly a spa.

Trent came in five minutes later. He handed her a coke. "No coffee, right?" he smiled but it didn't reach his eyes. He looked awful. Stubble covered his cheeks, and bags hung beneath his eyes.

"Not ready for coffee yet," Jocelyn said.

"Me either." Trent sat in a chair, legal pad and pen in his hand. "So, you're left to your own devices for a few hours, and all hell breaks loose."

"Trent," Jocelyn said, touching his forearm. "I'm sorry about Knox."

He looked down and away from her, clearing his throat. "Yeah, thanks."

She gave him a moment to rein in whatever emotions he felt. She knew he had been close to Knox. Trent was one of the few people who still cared whether Knox lived or died. She hadn't known Knox long, but she was still in shock herself. The man had died in her arms, and she still had trouble believing he was really gone.

After another series of throat-clearings, Trent finally said, "Okay, I know you told me everything that went down when we were at the scene, but I have two dead bodies on my hands so I gotta try to unfuck this clusterfuck. I need a formal statement." He tapped his pen against the legal pad.

"Fine," Jocelyn said. "But before we do that, you have to listen to me—Sydney Adams' killer is still out there."

"According to the confession I took from Cash Rigo just a few hours ago, Sydney Adams' killer is in custody right now."

Jocelyn shook her head vehemently, leaning in toward Trent. "No, no, no. Francine basically admitted to Knox that she framed Cash for the murder. It wasn't him. There's someone else."

"Rush, I've got Sydney Adams' jewelry in the Rigo home. I've got a confession and now, I've got a gun in the Rigo home. You said that Francine and Knox were discussing Sydney's murder, Knox asked her if she kept the gun, and she went upstairs and got it. Jewelry. Confession. Gun. It's a done deal."

Jocelyn threw her hands in the air. "Haven't you heard anything I've said all night? She framed him. And the gun? Yes, Knox asked her about it. Then yes, she went and got it, but listen to me— the confession is false. And the gun Francine had tonight was a Ruger P90, which shoots .45s, not .22s."

Trent's eyes widened as he put together what Jocelyn had earlier. He had likely been too overwhelmed by the scene and the bizarre scenario to make the connection, although Jocelyn was sure he would have once the dust settled. "The bullets they pulled out of Sydney were .22s."

"Right, it's not the same gun."

"So she had two guns, and her husband used the other one to kill Sydney, and then he buried it in the park like he said."

"No, someone else did the shooting. She orchestrated it, but someone else shot Sydney."

"Yeah, her husband. Maybe they were both in on it, and she let him take the fall."

"No, Trent. Come on. Cash didn't know where he got the gun or even what caliber it was. He didn't know how many times Sydney was shot. He was covering for his wife, but he didn't do it. Francine even said he was weak and stupid. She said the food poisoning went wrong but still left enough time that he *could* have gone and killed Sydney. Could have. Meaning he didn't. You saw Cash's face when you showed him the crime scene photos. He didn't do it."

"How can we believe anything that crazy bitch said?" Trent asked. "I've got a confession, Rush."

"Because she wanted us to know. That's how Knox got her to talk—he knew she couldn't stand nobody knowing how brilliant she was. The fun of it for her was in setting up her idiot husband."

He rubbed a hand over his face. "Oh my God. Jesus H. This gives new meaning to the word clusterfuck."

"Trent," Jocelyn said. "Sydney Adams' killer is still out there."

"I have a confession," he said again.

Jocelyn grabbed his forearm. "You know as well as I do that that confession is bogus. Even without Francine confirming it, it was a weak confession. A good defense lawyer could have it thrown out faster than you can say acquittal. My father would have had a field day with that joke of a confession. Trent, the killer is still out there."

He swiped a hand over his eyes. He wouldn't look at her. She had a bad feeling that he was about to stand up and walk out, leaving her there in the tiny interrogation room. "Trent," she tried again. "Knox knew. He knew Cash was lying. That's why he went to see Francine. Think about it. Up until yesterday, no one was more convinced of Cash's guilt than Knox. For fourteen years, Knox believed that Cash killed Sydney. Within a few hours that all changed. You said it yourself, Knox was a great detective. The shooter is still out there. Cash didn't kill Sydney. We have to find the shooter. The real shooter."

Seconds, then minutes passed. Jocelyn could tell because she could hear the ticking of the wall clock above the table. She thought about how in the last month, the ambient noise she usually heard was Knox's oxygen tank. Now he was gone.

Trent pushed his legal pad over to her. "First, your statement," he said. "Then I'll get Cash up here and tell him you killed his wife."

CHAPTER 42

November 18, 2014

Trent had Cash brought back up from the holding area. He'd been processed but not transferred. He would be arraigned in the morning and transferred to one of the city prisons. He still had on the khakis, sneakers, and blue polo shirt he'd worn the day before. A hint of stubble covered his cheeks. His hair was in disarray, his cheeks puffy. He looked as though he'd been sleeping. This time, Trent was waiting for him in the interrogation room.

Confusion lined Cash's face. "It's the middle of the night. What's going on?"

Trent motioned to a chair. "Please. Sit."

Cash rubbed his wrists as he took a seat. Trent didn't wait any longer. He launched right into the news. "Mr. Rigo, I'm afraid I have some very bad news."

Cash laughed drily. "Worse than me going to prison for the rest of my life?"

Trent didn't respond right away. He squeezed the bridge of his nose before facing Cash again. "Your wife is dead."

The smile froze on Cash's face, almost as if he was operated by remote control and someone had hit pause.

"Mr. Rigo?" Trent said. "Did you hear me? Your wife, Francine, is dead. I'm very sorry."

It was the approach Jocelyn favored, ripping off the bandage quickly. Dragging out bad news never changed the nature of it.

Finally, Cash said, "What? What are you talking about?"

"Late last night, a man—a former homicide detective—went to your home. His name was Augustus Knox. He worked Sydney's original case."

"I remember him," Cash said. "Why are you telling me this? Did he kill my wife?"

Jocelyn's stomach clenched. Up to that point, she had felt nothing, no guilt whatsoever about having ended Francine's life. Francine was a monster. She had orchestrated the deaths of two young, smart, vibrant women. Who knows what they might have contributed to the world if given a chance. Two families had been destroyed. And that was the tip of the iceberg. She had faked her own rape, intentionally brought on the miscarriages of her own children, and poisoned people. She had killed Knox. The things Francine had done were unforgiveable, and Jocelyn wasn't the forgiving type to begin with. She accepted that bad things— terrible, horrific things—happened in the world but in her mind, certain things could simply not be forgiven. Ever. Certain people, like Francine, were so devoid of humanity that they didn't deserve forgiveness, or sympathy, or whatever you wanted to call it. Jocelyn had no feelings of warmth for a person like Francine.

But here was her husband. Jocelyn didn't have a high opinion of Cash either, but in some ways, he'd been duped just as grandly as everyone else Francine had come across in her lifetime. Jocelyn felt a kernel of sympathy for the man until she remembered him confessing to his inappropriate sexual encounter with Sydney. She waited for the guilt to hit her or creep up on her, but there was nothing.

"No," Trent said. "Knox did not kill her. Your wife invited him in for coffee. She poisoned him. We're not sure what she used, but we know it was in the coffee—or on the mug that she gave him. Toxicology will take several weeks. He called Ms. Rush, who came to his aid. Your wife attempted to shoot Ms. Rush, at which point Ms. Rush shot her. She was shot in the chest. She died on the scene."

For a long, pregnant moment, Cash stared at Trent, his expression morphing from puzzled shock to disbelief. Then he burst into laughter. Great, loud belly laughter. He doubled over, holding his stomach, laughing until tears ran down his cheeks. Trent put a hand on Rigo's shoulder. "Mr. Rigo, this is serious. Your wife was shot and killed in your home last night."

Cash sat up and wiped the tears from his face. He shook his head. "I don't believe you. My wife hated guns. You said she shot at someone? She would never have a gun in our house."

"But she did, Mr. Rigo. She'd been keeping it with her wedding dress."

Cash shook his head, incredulous. "I don't know what you're trying to do here—if you want me to confess to something else I didn't—I mean to something else, but you've gotten everything out of me that you're going to get. In fact, I think I probably should get a lawyer now that you're making such outlandish claims."

"You do need a lawyer, Mr. Rigo. You've been charged with first degree murder. Your wife suggested to Mr. Knox that your confession was false. If that's true, you will need a good lawyer to get the charges dropped."

"Get them dropped? You just said that my wife told you my confession was bullshit. If I say it is too, you can just drop them, right?"

"It's not that simple. You confessed. Your wife, before she died, didn't say you were innocent. She implied it. She gave us nothing to go on before she was killed. This doesn't exonerate you."

Cash ran a hand through his hair and laughed again. "Why are we even having this conversation? What are you trying to pull? My wife is not dead."

Trent squeezed the bridge of his nose again. He sighed heavily and picked his phone up from the table. His movements were slow, as though his body was weighed down with exhaustion and grief. She knew he hadn't yet had time to process Knox's death. He scrolled and then handed Cash the phone. In the transfer, Jocelyn saw that it was a photo of Francine's body from the neck up taken at the scene. "Is this your wife?"

Cash stared at the photo for a long time. His hands trembled. The shaking made its way from his hands to his shoulders until his chair creaked beneath him. Gently, Trent reached over and took the phone from Cash's hands. The man kept staring at his hands, at the empty space where the phone had been. "Oh my God, Francine. Francine!"

He howled her name over and over, holding his empty palms upward as though he was waiting for something. Trent left him there. A moment later, he met Jocelyn in the room she'd been watching from, the same room she and Knox had been in just hours earlier.

"Well, that didn't go well," Trent said.

"He's in shock." She pointed at the television screen where they could see Cash rocking back and forth in his chair, weeping into his open hands, his howls piercing in the confines of the tiny room.

Trent nodded. "I'm going to have to get him some medical attention if he doesn't calm down."

"She's controlled nearly all of his adult life. He confessed to murder for her. Her being killed is not something he's prepared to deal with." Jocelyn said. "You could make the charges go away, you know. We both know he didn't kill Sydney."

"He confessed, Rush. Besides, when he comes out of this we might need his help identifying Francine's associates. We may need leverage in the future. This guy fucked around with underage girls, students. He admitted to it, but I can't do dick about it because the statute has run on any rape charges we could have slapped him with. Fuck him. I'm not doing him any favors."

Jocelyn wasn't the only person who had trouble with forgiveness.

CHAPTER 43

November 18, 2014

It was past dawn when Jocelyn finally got home. The sun broke over the horizon, flooding the city with what seemed to her like an unforgiving light. Trent had given her a ride from the Roundhouse back to the Rigos' so she could get her car. They drove in silence, both too exhausted, too shocked, and too numb to speak. He left her at her vehicle with no more than a nod and drove off. She blasted the heater. The Rigos' home had been cordoned off with crime scene tape. A few neighbors stood outside talking, likely discussing what they thought had happened. Gawkers, Inez called them.

She had never been so grateful to be home. Camille and Olivia sat across from one another at the dining room table eating waffles slathered with whipped cream.

"Mommy!" Olivia exclaimed.

Jocelyn lifted the girl out of her chair, hugging her until she said, "Mommy, you're squeezing me too much."

Jocelyn kissed her and inhaled the fruity scent of her shampoo, the smell instantly easing some of her anxiety. She set Olivia back down and fingered the girl's ponytail. "Aunt Camille did a good job," she said. Olivia was dressed and ready for school, her hair in a neater ponytail than Jocelyn had ever been able to give her.

Olivia shook her head, swishing the ponytail back and forth. "Can Aunt Camille pick me up from school today?"

"Not today, honey," Jocelyn said. "She's not on the pick-up list, but you'll see her after school, I'm sure."

Olivia pouted. A vertical line appeared over the bridge of her nose. "Can't we put her on the list?"

Jocelyn suppressed a sigh and smiled tightly. She had neither the time nor the energy for this conversation. Olivia had a point. It seemed so simple. Put Camille on the pick-up list. Why not? Camille had come a long way from the junkie who'd put her infant to bed in the bathroom sink of a meth lab. But Jocelyn wasn't ready for this. She hadn't really been prepared to see the two of them gel so perfectly. Sure, Camille had visited before and often skyped with Olivia, but this visit was different. Camille was now a year clean, and she seemed more clear-headed and focused. The milestone had made her stronger, more self-assured. She was more attentive to Olivia; she showed more interest in the girl. Jocelyn's stomach knotted. How could she say no without confusing Olivia and hurting Camille's feelings?

"Honey, I'm only going to be here for a couple of weeks. I think the pick-up list is for people who live here all the time," Camille said, smiling warmly at Olivia. She reached across the table and squeezed the girl's hand gently. "We can spend time together when you come home from school, okay?"

Olivia beamed, her annoyance with her mother forgotten. "Okay. Want to watch Disney Junior with me before I go to school?"

"Tell you what, I'll do these dishes, and then I'll be right in."

Olivia bounded off into the living room where the Disney channel was already playing.

As Camille started clearing their plates, Jocelyn said, "Camille, I'm sorry. I—"

Camille stopped her, the warm and genuine smile directed toward Jocelyn this time. "There was a time when it never even would have occurred to you to try to spare my feelings. That you tried just now — that you even wanted to — means a lot to me. It's fine. You're her mother. You've done an amazing job. I don't need to be on the pick-up list."

"Thank you," Jocelyn said.

Camille paused, halfway to the kitchen, and winked at Jocelyn. "And I'm not going to try to take her from you."

"I didn't—"

"Yeah, you did. I can see it all over you every time you watch us together."

Jocelyn followed her sister into the kitchen as Camille started washing the breakfast dishes. "You're different this time."

"I'm starting my life, Joc. Really starting it. *My* life. I haven't been in a position to do a damn thing about my life since I was fifteen. It's liberating. I'm clean, I have resources. I have you and Olivia, friends in California. Real friends who understand what I've been through and care for me anyway. I feel . . . hope."

Tears stung the backs of Jocelyn's eyes. This was what their mother had fought so hard for. Year after year after year. Rehab facility after rehab facility.

"It's not over," Camille added. "I still struggle. All the time. But my life is different now. I'm different."

"I'm glad," Jocelyn said.

Camille met Jocelyn's eyes, staring hard at her older sister with a fierce intensity. "But I know that Olivia is yours. I accept that."

Jocelyn swallowed over the lump in her throat. "Okay."

"I got your texts," Camille said, changing the subject. She put the clean dishes in the drain board and dried her hands on a kitchen towel. "I'm sorry about Knox."

Jocelyn sighed, blinking back the Knox-related tears that threatened to come atop the Camille-related tears. "Thanks."

Camille walked over and took Jocelyn's hands, squeezing gently. "Are you okay?"

"No," Jocelyn said. "I don't think I am."

"Is there anything I can do? Take Olivia to school? I don't have to be on a list to drop her off."

Jocelyn shook her head. "No, thank you, but I want to do it. I want normal right now."

"Okay," Camille said, releasing her sister's hands. "So what happens now? With your case, I mean?"

"Trent will run a search on the gun Francine had to see who it's registered to, if it's even legal, and go from there, I guess."

"You killed that woman."

"Yes," Jocelyn said.

"Does it bother you?"

"No. Maybe it should, but it doesn't. She was going to kill me. She was a truly deranged person." Jocelyn's body quaked involuntarily. Whispering, in case Olivia came into the kitchen, she recounted most of the things Francine had told Knox.

Camille listened with rapt attention, her frown deepening with each one of Jocelyn's words. "Wow," she said. "It's hard to believe someone like that could fool so many people for so long."

"I know."

"That's almost scarier than a person who'd just walk up and shoot you. I think I'd take a straight up violent psycho over Francine's brand of psycho any day."

Jocelyn nodded. She suddenly felt very sleepy, and she knew she was going to crash soon. "I need to get Olivia to school."

"I'm meeting with the DA today," Camille said.

"Okay," Jocelyn said. Even though she knew she'd never be able to stay awake, she offered, "Do you want me to go with you?"

Camille smiled. "Thank you but no. I can handle it. But I am going to need you to talk to Whitman for me and soon. Not today, but soon."

Jocelyn nodded. "I'll do it. I'll call him before I crash and see if he can meet me tomorrow or the next day."

Camille went into the dining room, where her purse sat on the table, and returned with a computer printout. She handed it to Jocelyn. "All his information is there."

"I thought he was a Criminology professor at the University of Pennsylvania."

Camille said, "Evidently, the child porn charges took a toll on his career."

Jocelyn stared at the phone number for Whitman's office at the Community College of Philadelphia. She felt a measure of satisfaction, which she tried to tamp down. From the very beginning, he was the only one of Camille's rapists who had ever shown any signs of remorse. He hadn't participated, he had been the lookout, but that had always struck Jocelyn as equally horrific. What kind of person watched something like that and did nothing to stop it? Immediately afterward, it was Whitman who ratted the other boys out to Bruce Rush. It was Whitman who had finally acknowledged the crime and apologized for his part in it when he came face to face with Jocelyn the year before. It was Whitman who had helped her crack the Schoolteacher case. As contemptible as he was as a human being, he was a brilliant criminologist. As disgusting and despicable as what he'd done to Camille was, he was now being punished for something he hadn't done. It was undeniable that Jocelyn felt joy at the prospect of Whitman suffering after what he'd done to her sister, but she generally didn't believe that people should be crucified for things they hadn't done.

"Joc?" Camille said, drawing her out of her reverie.

Jocelyn looked at her sister. "I'll take care of it."

Camille grabbed Jocelyn and hugged her tightly, whispering a thank you into Jocelyn's hair.

Jocelyn took Olivia to school, grateful for the normalcy of the act. Olivia kept her grounded, tethered to sanity. It was on the way home that Jocelyn started to crack. Tears streaked her cheeks. Her whole body hiccupped with sobs. She had to blink away the tears blurring her vision repeatedly. Of course she hit every red light on the way home. She willed the pedestrians on Ridge Avenue not to look at her.

At home, Camille was gone, but Caleb was there. He had come for her after working all night. She walked straight into his arms and cried until she had no tears left. They fell asleep on her bed in a tangle of limbs, fully clothed. Camille woke them in time for Jocelyn to pick up Olivia from school. She left Caleb passed out in her bed and took a shower, hoping to clear the fog from her head. She checked her phone before she left the house. She had a return call from Zachary Whitman. He had an open appointment Thursday morning.

They ordered pizza for dinner, and Camille and Jocelyn watched Olivia and Caleb play Just Dance on her Wii, laughing till their sides hurt. Caleb had a lot of things going for him, but dancing wasn't one of them. Trent called her around six that evening. "Guess who the P90 is registered to?" he asked without preamble.

"The eleventh grade biology teacher."

Trent sounded disappointed. "How did you know?"

"It was a guess."

"Hmph. Well, a damn good one. Guy's name is Craig Hubbard. His Ruger P90 was stolen from his truck two months before Sydney's murder."

"Interesting," Jocelyn said.

"Guess what other kind of gun he has registered in his name?"

Jocelyn sat up straight, excitement stirring butterflies in her stomach. "Tell me."

"A Smith and Wesson Model 48. Takes .22 cal."

CHAPTER
44

November 19, 2014

Craig Hubbard was every bit the weak, sniveling loser that Francine had described. Watching him weep in fear behind his desk at Franklin West, Jocelyn couldn't believe Francine had ever let Hubbard touch her. He was thin and slight, mostly bald with a bad comb-over and what Inez would have called a perv mustache. But it was his uncontrollable sobbing the moment he saw Trent's badge that really made him unattractive.

"Oh God," he cried. "Please don't tell my wife."

Jocelyn and Trent stood side by side in front of the large metal desk. They exchanged a raised brow look, and Jocelyn knew they were both thinking the same thing.

What the hell did this guy do?

"That depends on you," Trent said. "If you cooperate with us, we don't need to tell your wife."

Hubbard's sobs lessened, the quaking in his shoulders subsiding. "I couldn't help it," he cried. "Men have needs. I have needs, and Francine—well, she could be very pushy, you know? She had ways of . . . convincing people. I know I'm weak. After the last time, I swore I'd never be with her again. Please don't tell my wife."

Jocelyn and Trent exchanged another look.

Trent leaned over the desk and looked into Hubbard's eyes. "Mr. Hubbard, the police don't show up when you're having an affair. That's your personal business. It's not cool, but it's not a crime. You need to stop lying to me right now, or I'll drag your sorry ass downtown, and we'll have to call your wife."

Hubbard threw up his hands. "Okay, okay," he said. He looked behind them, toward the doorway, as if he expected someone to appear there at any second. He lowered his voice. "Is she really . . . gone?"

They had notified the school staff of Francine's death and Cash's arrest but had asked them to keep it quiet. Trent was trying to keep it out of the press until he sorted the mess out. He looked from Hubbard to Jocelyn and back. Jocelyn leaned in and put both hands on the desk. "I shot her myself. She's dead. Now let's hear what you've got to say."

Hubbard stared at her for a long moment. Jocelyn heard the clock above the man's head tick. He slumped in his chair and brought a hand to his forehead. He breathed in and out in short, rapid breaths. When he looked back up at them, the tension in his face and body loosened. He looked almost droopy. It was relief, Jocelyn realized. Craig Hubbard was relieved to be free of Francine Rigo. How many years had she held him in her sway? How many other people had she manipulated into situations they wished they could get out of? How many people would be relieved to hear of her death?

Jocelyn shivered.

"I didn't know what she was going to do with it," Hubbard said. "I swear to God. She asked me for it—"

"For what?" Trent asked.

"The listeria."

Trent frowned. Jocelyn realized that he thought Hubbard was talking about the gun. He was likely thinking that Hubbard had given it to Francine and then reported it stolen.

"She asked you for something that people get food poisoning from, and you just gave it to her?" Jocelyn asked. Her anger simmered as she thought about the night she'd spent wrapped around the toilet.

Hubbard wouldn't meet her eyes. "You don't understand," he whined. "She threatened to—"

Trent tapped his fingers on the desk to silence the man. "How many times did she ask you for it?"

"Not many. Four or five times."

"How long were you two having an affair?"

Hubbard's cheeks burned red. He continued to look at his lap. "On and off for sixteen years. It wasn't really an affair though. I mean at first it was, but then I wanted to stop and she didn't. That was the first time she asked me for it. That was the agreement. I would grow it and give it to her, and she would leave me alone."

Trent said, "She asked you for listeria?"

"No, no. It wasn't like that. The students were experimenting with Gram stains, and one day she started asking me about different organisms—what you could grow. She was interested in antibiotics actually. I was just talking about different bacteria and brought up the example of food poisoning organisms. She asked me to grow some—to show her—so I did. But it was a weakened strain. Then she wanted the samples. She said there was a neighbor who kept coming over whenever they had a party and making unwanted advances."

"Of course she did," Jocelyn said.

"So you thought Francine poisoning this neighbor was a good solution to her problems?" Trent asked skeptically.

Hubbard threw his hands up again. "No, I didn't, but I just wanted—needed—her to leave me alone." Tears filled the man's eyes again. "I'm sorry. I'm so sorry. Please—"

Jocelyn slapped the desk hard. "Don't," she snapped. "Just answer the questions."

Instantly cowing, Hubbard looked back and forth between them. Trent went on. "Okay, so you gave her the listeria. Then what happened?"

"She left me alone for a long time. Years. I thought it was really over. But every so often, she'd find me. I tried to avoid her, not to give into temptation but she—she did things."

Hubbard said the words "did things" in a tone that was half revulsion, half awe. "I'm sorry," he repeated. "I couldn't say no. God help me, I couldn't say no."

"She asked you for it last week, didn't she?" Jocelyn asked.

He nodded as a sob worked its way up his windpipe. "I'm so sorry."

"She ever ask you for anything else?" Trent asked.

Hubbard hiccupped, looking at Trent in earnest. "Like what?"

Trent folded his arms across his chest. "You know what, Mr. Hubbard. Now, come on."

The man's shoulder blades drew together, his body tensing. "Wh-what? No, no. I don't."

Trent sighed. He pulled the Ruger P90 out of his coat pocket and put it on the desk. It was wrapped in clear plastic, and Hubbard recognized it immediately. He leaned forward. "A P90. I used to have—oh my God, is that mine? Where did you get that?" He stood, pushing his chair out of the way and backing up against the dry-erase board behind the desk. He pointed at the gun, his voice so high it sounded like a creaking door. "Where did you get that?"

"From Francine Rigo," Jocelyn said quietly.

A vein in Hubbard's neck throbbed. "I did not give that to her. I would never—that was stolen from my truck. I filed a police report."

"Are you a firearms enthusiast?" Trent asked.

"I have some handguns that I use for home defense, and I have a concealed carry permit. It's all legal."

"What kinds of guns?" Jocelyn asked.

Hubbard's eyes darted toward her. "What?"

"You said 'some guns.' What kinds?"

"A Smith and Wesson Model 48, a Beretta 92FS and a Glock 23 that I bought after my P90 was stolen."

"So you never discussed firearms with Mrs. Rigo?" Trent asked.

Hubbard shook his head. "She hated guns. She would never let her husband buy one. It was not a topic she ever wanted to discuss."

"Then how did your P90 get into her hands?" Jocelyn asked.

Hubbard's eyes watered. The fear rolling off him was palpable. "I don't know. I swear to you I don't know. It must be some kind of mistake."

"Oh, no mistake, Mr. Hubbard." Trent pointed at the gun. "We got that from inside Francine's home. From her dead body. It's registered to you."

"I swear to you, I didn't give her that gun. It was stolen from my truck fourteen years ago. I'm telling the truth. I swear."

Trent waited a long moment. Hubbard said nothing. He simply stared at them with a desperate, pleading look in his eyes.

"Tell me about Sydney Adams," Trent said.

What appeared to be genuine confusion wrinkled the man's brow. "Who?"

"Sydney Adams," Trent repeated.

He looked back and forth between them, waiting for one of them to give him an explanation. Then he said, "Oh my God, is that the neighbor? Is Sydney Adams the neighbor Francine poisoned?"

"Sydney was a girl," Jocelyn said. "A senior here in 2000."

Again, the man waited, looking at them expectantly. There wasn't even the briefest flicker of recognition in his face. He really had no idea who Sydney was, or at least he didn't remember her. Although he had clearly heard about Francine's death from his colleagues, he obviously had not heard about Cash's arrest.

"She was shot in Fairmount Park," Trent supplied.

Hubbard shook his head, his face scrunched with the effort of searching his memory banks. Then his face lit up as he hit on something. "She ran track, didn't she? Her murder was just in the news recently, wasn't it?"

"That's right," Jocelyn said.

He stared at them with no desire to fill the awkward silence, Jocelyn noted. Either he had no involvement whatsoever in Sydney's murder, or he was just as skilled a liar as Francine had been.

Trent sighed. "We're finished here. Thank you for your time, Mr. Hubbard."

The man looked surprised but smiled at them, obviously relieved that they'd be leaving soon. "Oh, sure, okay."

Jocelyn waited until they were outside of the school before asking Trent, "What about the Smith and Wesson Model 48?"

As they got to the car, Trent opened the passenger's side door for her. "I sent two officers to his house with a warrant for it before we came here. Someone in the crime scene unit owes me a favor. He'll fire it and check the ballistics against the rounds pulled from Sydney's body."

Jocelyn stood by the open door but made no move to get in. "What happened to not telling his wife?"

Trent said, "What happened to not cheating on your wife?"

"Good point."

"Maybe he didn't shoot Sydney Adams—we'll know by tomorrow. But he gave that psychopath the poison. He knew what she was using it for. He's every bit as guilty as she is."

"Right," Jocelyn said, thinking of Zachary Whitman. Like Whitman, Hubbard was a bystander who saw what was going on but made no move to stop it.

Bystanders made her skin crawl.

She sat in the car. Trent closed her door and went around to the driver's side. After he started the car, he took one last look at Franklin West.

"Fuck him," he added.

CHAPTER 45

November 20, 2014

Jocelyn sat in the hall outside of Zachary Whitman's office at the Community College of Philadelphia. She could hear him through the partially closed door discussing an assignment with a student. She looked at the time on her phone. She was ten minutes early. She leaned back against the gray cinderblock wall and closed her eyes. The hall was dimly lit, making it hard for her not to curl up on the bench and take a nap. She'd managed to get a full eight hours of sleep the night before, but she still felt exhausted. She hadn't felt right since the poisoning, no matter how much sleep she got. Her eyes burned, her limbs felt heavy, and her legs ached. She'd had two cokes that morning. She still couldn't drink coffee. The caffeine had helped clear her mental fog, but her body still felt like it needed to sleep for a week.

The squeak of sneakers on the tile floor down the hall startled Jocelyn. She opened her eyes to see a group of students passing by, completely oblivious to her. She blinked several times and pulled her phone back out, re-reading the texts that Trent had sent her earlier that morning. The ballistics tests on Hubbard's Model 48 came back negative. The bullets that killed Sydney were not fired from his gun. Moreover, Jocelyn had checked the news footage of Lonnie from the night Sydney was killed and spotted Hubbard in the background, standing on Franklin West's steps, which gave him an alibi, even though neither Jocelyn nor Trent believed that Hubbard had done it.

Which left them nowhere.

Cash had recanted, but the DA wouldn't drop the charges. Word was he'd gotten himself a high-powered defense attorney to sort the mess out. Still, unless someone found the real shooter, the charges against Cash would stand. Trouble was, they didn't even have any suspects. Jocelyn had no interest in saving Cash's ass, but she had a vested interest in finding Sydney Adams' real killer.

Tears welled behind her eyes as she thought of Knox dying in her lap, telling her she did good. He had brought Jocelyn the case—his last case, the thing that had eclipsed even his family in the remaining years of his life—and she'd failed him. She'd fucked up grandly, killing Francine and, with her, their best chance of finding out the true identity of Sydney's shooter. She kept revisiting the moment Francine raised her gun, kept seeing her finger on the trigger, wondering if she could have done things differently.

Always, the image of Olivia's beautiful face flashed in her mind.

No, she'd handled it the only way that she could. She could take no chances. She had to be there for her daughter. She had come too close the year before. Besides her sister and uncle, both of whom were embattled in their own ways, Jocelyn had no real family to speak of. She knew that Inez would take care of Olivia, and Kevin would help too, but it wouldn't be the same. Jocelyn was Olivia's mother. She needed to be there for the girl, damn the cost.

She'd just have to find Sydney Adams' killer the hard way.

"Detective?"

Zachary Whitman stood before her, smiling that ever-present amiable smile of his, the same one he'd given her a year ago when he was in police custody for possession of child pornography.

Sure, he'd been exonerated of the child porn charges, but the smile still gave her the creeps. He looked the same. Maybe a little thinner, a little grayer, but he had the same brown hair parted in the center and feathered on the sides, the same wire-rimmed glasses over a straight, narrow nose, and the same slight frame.

"Whitman," she said, standing.

He extended a hand, but she didn't take it. He put his hands behind his back and looked briefly at the floor. "Well, come in," he said, gesturing to his open door. Jocelyn passed through and took the first chair she saw. Whitman sat behind his desk, and Jocelyn felt her anxiety ease with the barrier between them. The office was small. Whitman's large, metal desk took up most of it. Like the hallway, the walls were painted gray cinderblocks. There was no window. The muted blue outdoor carpet seemed to add to the gloom. Fluorescent lights hung overhead, but Whitman kept them off in favor of a table lamp he'd obviously brought in himself. It sat atop a tall, black filing cabinet, casting a soft glow over the institutional room. The rest of the walls were lined with overflowing bookcases. He stared at her, watching her take it in.

"It just screams ivy league, doesn't it?" he joked lamely.

She bit back a caustic reply, managing a tight smile instead.

"So," he said. "What can I do for you?"

Jocelyn mouth suddenly felt dry. "My sister would like you to testify at our uncle's trial."

"Your uncle framed me. Obviously, I'm going to testify," he said. "I've already spoken with the DA."

"I mean about what you did to her."

The smile again. "Well, that goes to the heart of the matter, doesn't it? It speaks to your uncle's motive."

"Of the three of you, Pearce is dead and Evans' attorney has advised him against testifying at all. It's important to Camille that you are honest, that you tell what you did to her."

"She's looking for validation."

"Call it whatever you want. We know your attorney is going to want you to go into as little detail as humanly possible. I'm asking you to tell a jury exactly what the five of you did. No censoring, no editing. Camille needs this, and you're going to give it to her."

He chuckled lightly. "Really, Detective Rush, you don't have to strong-arm me. I am happy to do as Camille wishes. This is the only way I can perhaps take some responsibility for her rape. There is no question I'll do it."

Of course he would. The statute of limitations had run out years ago. Whitman could go on the damn *Today Show* and tell the whole world what he and the other boys had done, and nothing would happen to him. Still, Jocelyn felt some relief that he didn't put up a fight. Camille would be glad. She couldn't bring herself to thank him so she just said, "Okay."

She stood to leave but Whitman said, "You seem tired and tense. Is everything okay, Detective?"

The hair on the back of her neck stood at attention. Jocelyn stared at him. "You know we're not friends, right? I mean, you know that the only thing that stops me from shooting you is the threat of prison, right? Some people are of a forgiving nature. I am not one of those people."

He folded his hands in his lap and looked down at them. "Yes, I'm aware. I was simply making an observation. Is it a case that's keeping you up at night?"

She put a hand on one hip. "What the fuck is this? What are you doing?"

He looked up at her and opened his mouth to speak, but she cut him off. "And don't say you can help me."

He smiled again, this time with a sardonic twist to his lips. "Okay," he said. "I was just curious about what you were working on. I . . . I miss it. I miss the work. I used to get requests from police detectives all over the country for consults. Getting to consult on real cases was just as gratifying as teaching. I don't even get to teach advanced courses here." He raised both hands. "Not that I'm complaining. After all that's happened, I'm just grateful to have a job. I just miss the stuff that used to go along with it. I don't get those calls anymore."

"You expect me to feel sorry for you?"

He met her glare head on. "Of course not. I'm only suggesting that we set aside our past associations for a few minutes. I'll be a criminal psychologist and you'll be a detective, and we'll talk about your case. I can hel—I may have insights that would be useful in your investigation."

She held his gaze for several seconds, every nerve in her body on edge. Her impulse was to tell him to go fuck himself, spin on her heel and walk out, leaving him unsatisfied and humiliated. Given their past associations, it must have taken a lot for him to admit to her that it bothered him—what he had been reduced to. Not that she felt badly for him. She couldn't. It wasn't in her. Watching a gang rape and doing nothing to stop it was not forgivable in her book. It would never be.

But she didn't give in to her impulse. Maybe because she was so tired. Maybe because between the two of them, she and Trent had precisely zero leads in the Sydney Adams case. Maybe because she was so desperate.

She sat back down and rubbed the nape of her neck. "This is confidential," she said.

He nodded.

"I'm in private practice," she added. "I've got my own P.I. firm. I've been working with the police on this cold case."

She gave him a run down, starting with what the file had contained when Knox brought it to her, all the way up to the fatal confrontation in the Rigos' kitchen and the interview with Hubbard. Her words came out stilted and awkward at first, but the longer she talked, the more her body relaxed and the easier it was to relate the facts. She didn't relax entirely, but enough for her skin to stop crawling. Mostly. Whitman listened carefully and attentively, fingers steepled beneath his chin. He was silent for a moment when she finished. Then he said, "Francine is as fascinating as she is abhorrent, isn't she?"

"I killed her," Jocelyn said. "You're referring to her in the present tense."

Whitman chuckled again. "Yes, but she makes an intriguing case study in the present, doesn't she?"

"She was a sociopath, wasn't she? Or a psychopath?"

Whitman nodded. "Well, both of those fall under the umbrella of Antisocial Personality Disorder. There are different types of sociopaths and different degrees of anti-social behavior. Some say sociopaths and psychopaths are the same thing. Some make distinctions. Some believe that a psychopath is born with no conscience whereas sociopaths are made the way they are by their life experiences. There are many schools of thought on the subject. Sociopaths can sometimes be more impulsive and act without thinking about the consequences whereas your typical psychopath is more methodical and better capable of planning. The two share several characteristics.

"Without having met Francine, it's hard to say what her true diagnosis would have been, but it sounds like she definitely had an antisocial personality disorder. She showed no remorse for any of the things she did. She was promiscuous—I'm betting the biology teacher is not her only conquest—and clearly, she was a liar. She manipulated people for nothing more than entertainment, it seems. She has all the hallmarks of a psychopath or even a sociopath. I personally would lean more toward psychopath because of the methodical, long-term planning involved in her crimes."

Jocelyn said, "When people think of psychopaths, they think of violence, like serial killers."

"And many violent killers are psychopaths," Whitman said. "But the truth is that many psychopaths live among us, function in society and never physically harm anyone or anything. Many CEOs are psychopaths or sociopaths. Your father was a psychopath."

Jocelyn sat perfectly still. Anger rose up inside her, an immediate defensive response to an attack on her father, but then reason moved up beside it. Although she had never thought about her father's psychological make up, he had done a pretty horrible thing by brushing Camille's gang rape under the carpet, even going so far as to take money from the rapists' families in what he claimed was for reparation. He was driven both at work and at home. Jocelyn had known him to be a ruthless man, especially in business. She had never considered the fact that his ruthlessness was an indicator of psychopathology.

Whitman paused in his explanation, seemingly watching the conflict inside her play out in her facial expressions. Then he continued, "The key distinction here between a psychopath and a normal person is that psychopaths do not have a conscience. That means they feel no guilt, no remorse for anything that they do. Ever. They are great mimics, of course, and will convince people that they feel the same range of emotions as everyone else, but the truth is that they are simply not capable of feeling those emotions. If they are found out, the people around them are often astounded by their acting ability. They can put on quite a show of emotion. They figure out when and where to do it for the maximum effect, and they blend in with the rest of society quite well that way. But all of it is false, a put-on. It's all a show. There is no substance to it."

Jocelyn sighed. "That sounds like Francine." *And my father.*

Again, Whitman nodded. "It is a hard concept for a conscience-bound person to wrap their minds around. Francine was likely never overtly violent toward anyone. It can't be ruled out, obviously, given how far-reaching her manipulations appear to be. Perhaps she didn't enjoy actually carrying out the violence. Perhaps she didn't want to risk being caught, or maybe it was simply more fun, more entertaining, for her to manipulate others. It becomes like a sport for the psychopath, to see how far they can take things, how they can completely manipulate another person, to see what they can get another person to do. I suspect this was the case with Francine. The manipulation was a game she loved to play. I would venture that there was someone in her life at the time Sydney Adams was murdered that she was able to manipulate into killing the girl. You need to look at her contact with people in the year leading up to Sydney's murder to see who she was spending time with. Who would have been around for her to play with?"

"Okay, so we look at friends, colleagues, neighbors, students," Jocelyn said.

"You'll want to take a close look at students," Whitman said. "It would have been much easier for her to manipulate a teenager into killing someone than a grown man. Teenagers haven't yet developed the part of their brains responsible for thinking of long-term consequences. Their hormones are raging. Given the right subject, it might have been quite easy for her to convince a young lover to kill her husband's paramour. You might remember the Pamela Smart case out of New Hampshire in 1990. Schoolteacher manipulates teen lover into killing her husband."

"I've heard of it. So, you're suggesting Francine had an affair with a student like she did with the biology teacher?"

"If I had to speculate, yes. Given the fact that the biology teacher has been cleared as a suspect, I would next be looking at Franklin West students enrolled at that time."

"That would make sense," Jocelyn said. She closed her eyes briefly, flashing back to the conversation between Francine and Knox. "She said she had a male student plant the bees in Becky Wu's bag. That was several years after Sydney's death, but like you're saying, it's a pattern of behavior with her—God knows how many students she manipulated. She said that student was troubled and likely in prison, so that might account for him not ratting her out over the Becky Wu thing. She was the school nurse. Maybe we're talking about students who frequently showed up in her office."

"Yes, an excellent place to start. You'll want to look at student records for male students with a history of disciplinary issues. They would be more likely to be manipulated into committing a crime."

"Kids who were suspended or expelled? Kids with juvenile records, then?"

"Yes, I would bet money that when you find who you're looking for, he will have a history of brushes with the law, mostly likely for vandalism, simple assault, drug charges, theft. Misdemeanor crimes. He will have been suspended from school at some point, if not expelled. There might have been some major stressor in his life around the time Francine targeted him—the death of a family member, a break up, something like that. Something that would have left him more vulnerable to her advances."

"Okay," Jocelyn said, nodding. "What else? Am I looking for a loner? The boy dressed all in black brooding in the corner of the cafeteria?"

Whitman laughed. "Sort of. He likely would have had friends, but not many. He's certainly not star quarterback material. He would have done okay academically, but any failing grades would be a result of him not applying himself. He's smart, whoever he is. He's eluded everyone for fourteen years, probably in large part because of Francine's careful planning, but also because he's been smart enough to keep his mouth shut."

"Okay," Jocelyn said. "But that's what I don't get. He killed someone for Francine, and then he just stopped existing? How? Why would he keep his mouth shut all this time? If they were having an affair, surely he would want more at some point. I mean he killed a girl for her. Or has she carried on the affair all this time, on and off like with Hubbard?"

"Well, there are several scenarios which may have played out," Whitman replied. "And you need to prepare yourself—this person may no longer be alive. Just like whoever helped her with Becky Wu may no longer be alive. We're talking about a very long time period. In Sydney's case, fourteen years. Her killer may be dead. He may be in prison. Perhaps the affair fizzled out, or he wanted to put some distance between them. Perhaps, once Francine got what she wanted, she dumped him. Though, from what you told me, the more likely scenario is that she wanted to keep him around in case she needed something later, in which case, as he grew into a man, he might have tired of her, seen her as a crazy old woman, or he simply tired of doing her bidding. It's more likely he distanced himself as much as he could—just like Hubbard tried to do."

"He could never tell her secret because it was his secret too," Jocelyn mused. "He pulled the trigger. She could never tell on him because he'd tell about her involvement and the affair. Her sleeping with a student would have been career suicide."

"Assured mutual destruction," Whitman agreed.

Jocelyn bit her lower lip. Then she said, "I can't see Francine cowing to a boy or anyone for that matter. She'd simply deny her involvement and the affair. Who wouldn't believe her? You should have seen this woman, Whitman. The face she presented to the world—warm, sweet, wholesome. I felt badly for her. Put her next to a delinquent with a history of bad behavior and no one would believe a troubled kid over her."

"I suspect that was part of the fun for Francine. So you think there is something else in play here?"

Jocelyn nodded. "Maybe a sex tape? Although I can't see her consenting to one. I don't know. Something that would be undeniable and damaging. I think he has something on her that he can prove. Otherwise, he'd never be able to keep her at a distance."

Whitman smiled. "Sounds like you've got some work to do."

"Yes, it's a direction to go in at least. One last thing, how does a person that manipulative fly under the radar for that long, even from her own husband?"

"How did she fly under your radar, Detective?"

"I'm not a detective anymore," Jocelyn reminded him.

"Sure you are, you just haven't got a badge anymore. So tell me, how does she do it? You already know."

It didn't take long for Jocelyn to figure it out. She rubbed her palms over her face. "Oh my God," she moaned. "I felt badly for her. That's how she did it. People would feel so badly for her that they never looked past that. No one ever looked more deeply into her behavior because they were too busy feeling sorry for her."

"Precisely," Whitman said. "One of the things psychopaths do best is evoke pity from the rest of us, those of us with a conscience. It is one of the most useful tools in their arsenal."

"And if there was nothing going on to pity her for, she would manufacture something."

"Yes. Think of her husband. He surely wanted to leave, but you cannot in good conscience leave a rape victim or a woman who's just lost a baby. Confessing to Sydney Adams' murder was probably the most liberating thing he's ever done. It finally gets him out of her sphere of control. Plus, the whole world feels sorry for her—poor clueless Francine, the loyal, loving wife who finds out her husband is a cheating murderer."

Jocelyn bit her bottom lip. "Or Francine the hero who turned her husband in when she found out. Jesus." A shiver worked its way through her body. When she'd said those things to Francine, she was just trying to break the case, not give the woman ideas.

"Exactly," Whitman said. His smile had taken on a more natural quality, one of genuine enjoyment. He liked what he did, and he was good at it. He was in the zone, in his own personal state of flow.

She couldn't bring herself to thank him, even putting aside their "past associations" and trying to view him as nothing more than a criminal psychologist consulting on a case. She simply couldn't do it. She noticed his eyes flick to her lap and back. She was stroking her scar again. It was becoming a nervous habit. She stilled her hands, busied them smoothing her hair back behind her ears. Whitman said nothing.

She stood and straightened her jacket. "Well, I should get going," she said. "You've been—" even the word *helpful* stuck in her throat. Finally, she said, "Of use."

Whitman stood and saw her to the door, his less creepy smile still in place, the corner of his mouth twitching slightly. "Thank you," he said.

CHAPTER 46

November 20, 2014

"How'd it go with Whitman?" Anita asked.

Jocelyn plopped into one of the guest chairs in their reception area and threw her feet up on the coffee table. "It was . . . interesting."

Anita clucked her tongue. She peered at Jocelyn from the doorway to her office. "I bet. Is he going to do what Camille wants?"

"Yeah, he says he will."

"You feel better?"

"After talking to Whitman? I feel like I need a shower, but yes, I'm glad for Camille. It's important to her."

"I talked to Jynx. She's planning the funeral."

"From the hospital?" The morning after Knox's death, Jynx had gone into labor.

"She's home. Apparently Knox's daughter wants nothing to do with any of it. Jynx said probably next week. They're going to try for before Thanksgiving."

Jocelyn nodded. She knew all about fractured families. She hadn't gone to her own parents' funeral, although what her parents had done seemed significantly worse than ruining a wedding or even being a semi-absent parent during the teen years. But who was she to judge? She had no idea what Bianca Knox had gone through, not really.

"You said Jynx is home?"

⌒⦾⦾⦾⌒

Jynx lived in a twin home in the Wynnefield Heights section of the city. Jocelyn and Anita arrived bearing a gift bag filled with clothes and toys for her newborn daughter. Jynx greeted them with a smile, though her eyes were red-rimmed. It was remarkable the way her body had snapped back to a much smaller shape after birth. Although Jocelyn had raised Olivia from one week old, she had no frame of reference for pregnancy or giving birth.

"Myron's upstairs with the baby," Jynx said as she led them into her kitchen. It was small and dated but decorated cheerily in a coffee theme, with steaming coffee mug decals on the cream-colored walls, towels and placemats featuring mugs that said "latte" or "mocha" beneath them, and a distressed sign hanging above the kitchen table that said *This Home Runs on Love and Coffee.* It had a cozy, modern feel to it. The table was retro style Formica with a white-speckled top. They took seats around it.

"I couldn't find Sydney's yearbook, so I called Lonnie. He should be here any minute," Jynx said.

They chatted about Jynx's new baby until Lonnie arrived, carrying a small box of souvenirs from his time at Franklin West. They sat around Jynx's kitchen table, drinking hot tea—Jocelyn still couldn't drink coffee, and Jynx wasn't having any since she was nursing—while Jocelyn delivered the news that she didn't believe that Cash's confession was real. With great discomfort, she relayed all that Francine had revealed in the final minutes of her life. She told the story like a cop, detached, formal, like it had happened to someone else. But beneath the table, Anita reached into her lap and squeezed her hand. Talking about Knox's demise still brought tears to her eyes. Everything about the situation, the case, that night, was still raw and emotional for her.

Both Jynx and Lonnie's mouths hung open. Jynx looked at Lonnie and then back to Jocelyn. "Trent told us Knox passed. He didn't say how. I thought . . . I just thought it was his medical issues. I . . ." she drifted off as tears spilled down her cheeks. She wiped them away.

Lonnie had not moved. He sat, statue-like, his mouth forming an O, his stare fixed on Jocelyn. Then he said, "She really poisoned him?"

Jocelyn nodded. "Knox knew it was the only way to get her to tell the truth. He sacrificed himself to get to the truth."

Her voice had become hoarse, the lump in her throat making it difficult to speak.

Anita picked up the tale. "Unfortunately, Francine died before we could learn the identity of the shooter. Jocelyn spoke with a criminologist who had some ideas in terms of locating a suspect."

Jocelyn cleared her throat. She smiled at Anita, a silent thank you. She told them what she and Whitman had discussed. Lonnie had saved all four of his yearbooks from Franklin West. They pored over them, Lonnie trying to pinpoint which male students had been known troublemakers until they had a list of five names.

"The trouble is," he said. "I didn't know everyone. I knew the people I hung around with. You need school records, if they even go back that far."

"I already tried," Anita replied. "They won't release them to us. That's something Trent will need to get."

"You could go to the next closest source," Jynx suggested.

They stared at her. She sighed, stood up, and retrieved her phone from the kitchen counter. A few taps and scrolls later, she found what she was looking for. She turned the display toward them. It was an article from their local NBC news. The headline read: *Local Coach Released on Bond in Murder of High School Student.* There was a photo of Cash making his way up his front walk amidst news reporters and yellow crime scene tape.

Jocelyn groaned. "So it's out there now. What does it say about Francine?"

Jynx turned the phone back to her and scrolled some more. She read: "In a bizarre twist, just hours after Cash Rigo's arrest in this cold case, investigators hired by the family of Sydney Adams confronted Francine Rigo in her home about her possible involvement in the death of the young student. There was a shootout that left Francine Rigo and one retired Philadelphia homicide detective dead. Police had just finished processing the crime scene about an hour before Cash Rigo arrived home. That is all the information police are providing at this time, but stay with NBC10 for the latest news and developments in this story."

Anita checked the time on her phone. "Well, I expect that our office will be receiving about a thousand calls within the next few hours."

"If they figure out that you're the private investigators," Jynx said.

Jocelyn rubbed her eyes with both hands. "They always find out. We're taking the next few days off. Don't even go back to the office."

"But you could talk to Rigo," Jynx said. "He's home."

"I shot his wife."

Jynx shrugged. "So you apologize, then find out which students his wife was messing around with when Sydney died."

They all laughed nervously until they realized that Jynx was serious. "Do you want to wait for Trent to do it?" she asked pointedly. "That man is messed up, I'm telling you. He was close to Knox. He's not taking this well. If you want a name, the quickest, surest way is to ask Cash Rigo."

CHAPTER
47

November 20, 2014

"You've got balls," Cash said when he opened his front door to find Jocelyn standing there. From the street, cameras whirred and reporters shouted. She'd parked two blocks away, although the walk had weakened her resolve considerably. But now, here she stood.

There was only one way to do this. The matter-of-fact approach. "I need to talk to you."

"Are you fucking kidding me?" Cash said. He tried closing the door, but Jocelyn wedged her foot between the door and its frame.

"I'm calling the police," Cash said.

Jocelyn glanced behind her. "You sure you want to do that?"

He leaned in closer to her. "You killed my wife."

Jocelyn kept her voice controlled and even. "I'm sorry for your loss, Mr. Rigo."

"That's it? You shoot my wife in our home, and that's what you have to say?"

"I need to talk to you. Please. I don't want to be here anymore than you want me here, but I'm trying to find the person who shot Sydney."

At the mention of her name, his face softened. She hoped he'd be willing to talk to her for no other reason than finding the shooter would exonerate him. It was self-preservation.

He let her in.

She followed him into the kitchen, shuddering involuntarily as she entered. She looked to the floor where Knox had died, reliving every agonizing second. She didn't even notice Cash down on his knees beside a bucket of soapy water, pushing a wet scrub brush back and forth across the floor, trying to get Francine's blood out of the tile. "This is where she died, isn't it? They said the other guy was poisoned, so I'm guessing he didn't bleed."

Jocelyn stepped closer. "You should use ammonia. Peroxide on the grout."

He stopped, sat back on his heels and wiped his brow with a forearm. "They teach you that in private eye school?"

"I was a police officer for seventeen years. You pick things up."

"Detective Razmus told me what Francine said. The things she . . . did."

"You don't believe him."

Cash shook his head. "That's the thing. I *do* believe him. Sort of. I mean some things I can believe. There was a side to Francine that was different. Like it wasn't her. It was someone else. But I really only saw it one time."

"When was that?"

"Right before our wedding. I—" he stopped himself. Whatever had happened wasn't something he was willing to share. "It's not important. My point is that she was like a totally different person. It was a shock."

"You married her anyway."

He laughed bitterly. "I had no choice."

"Everyone has a choice, Mr. Rigo."

"Not with Francine around." He went back to scrubbing. "You know she used to watch talk shows? She loved talk shows. She liked to hear about peoples'—oh my God." He stopped moving. Through his T-shirt, Jocelyn could see his shoulder blades draw together. "She liked to hear about other peoples' suffering," he went on, his voice a heavy sigh. "Of course she did," he added, almost to himself. He resumed scrubbing, talking to Jocelyn over his shoulder in a voice laden with bone-weary exhaustion. "The more complicated and sordid the topic, the more interesting the show was to her. There was one host who used this expression all the time – Francine used to repeat it constantly – it was something like, 'When a person shows you their true colors, take notice and don't ever forget it.' I don't know, something like that."

He looked back at her, a strained smile on his stubbled face. "Maybe she was talking about herself. I always assumed that the Francine I went to college with, the Francine I married, the Francine who lived with me here in this house all these years was the real Francine. I assumed *those* were her true colors. I guess I was wrong. The woman I met three days before our wedding – that was the true Francine. That's what she was trying to tell me, I guess. You know, she used that expression about my best friend."

Again, he swiped his brow with the back of his hand, leaving a streak of rust-colored soapsuds on his forehead. The things she and Whitman had discussed flew round and round in Jocelyn's head. Part of her wanted to tell Cash everything she had learned about psychopaths and how neatly Francine seemed to fit the mold, but she figured shooting his wife had forfeited her right to posit any theories about Francine's psychological make up. So she kept her mouth shut and let him talk.

"About two weeks before my wedding, we were out with the wedding party at this Irish bar, partying hard. We were all drunk. The place was packed. There was a live band. It was really chaotic in there. Francine and I got separated. I didn't think too much of it. We finally caught up after an hour or so in the hall to the bathrooms. She told me my best friend – my best man – had felt her up on the dance floor, tried to kiss her and grabbed her tits. I confronted him. He swore it was the other way around, but naturally I didn't believe him. We never spoke again. She said she never liked him, that I was blind to who he really was, and then she said that bullshit about people showing their true colors. Now I wonder. I mean, I guess now I know my friend was telling the truth, not Francine. I don't know why I never made the connection. I mean just a couple of weeks later, she showed me *her* true colors."

Jocelyn stood frozen in place, arms crossed over her chest, listening. Cash swished the scrub brush around in the bucket and moved over a foot so he could work on a new set of blood-stained tiles. "How many times do you think she did that? How many people do you think she threw under the bus like that, to cut them out of my life? Cause that's what happened. I lost my best friend. I keep thinking of different people in my life that I dropped over the years because they did something to offend or upset Francine. It was all her."

He stopped scrubbing and drew a finger along the grout between two of the tiles. He looked back at her. "You said peroxide?"

Jocelyn nodded. "Yeah, it's your best bet."

"Okay." He threw his scrub brush into the bucket. It splashed bloody suds up and into the air, landing in an arced pattern on the kitchen cabinets. Cash laughed drily. "Fuck this." He stood, walked to his kitchen table and sat down. Jocelyn remained standing.

He looked her in the eye as he wiped his palms on his already soaked sweatpants. "When I woke up this morning, do you know what I felt?"

Jocelyn didn't answer. She didn't think he expected her to. He didn't wait for an answer. "I woke up in jail. I felt disoriented. Took a minute for everything to come rushing back and when it did, I felt relief. Relief." He laughed again, harsher this time. "Francine always said I was a shitty husband."

"Mr. Rigo," Jocelyn said. "The person who shot Sydney is still out there. I believe whoever killed her was also a student at Franklin West."

"What about her boyfriend?"

"He has an alibi, you know that. No, we're talking about someone your wife was close to, someone she may have cultivated a relationship with. Perhaps a troubled boy, someone with a history of disciplinary problems, suspensions."

Cash shook his head. "Francine didn't have relationships with the students. She wasn't even a teacher."

"But students came to her office when they were sick. She had access." Jocelyn reached into her pocket and pulled out the list Lonnie had helped her compile. "Can you look at these names? Maybe one of them will ring a bell."

He stood slowly, the chair beneath him creaking. Immediately, it brought to mind the sounds she had heard over the phone during Knox and Francine's conversation. Knox had shifted in his chair several times before he collapsed. Jocelyn held the list out to Cash. He took it from her and studied it, his face paling. He pointed to the third name on it. "Oh my God," he said. "This kid. He was here. She had him here for dinner once after his mom died. He's the one who vandalized the school — her office, in fact."

"Do you know what happened to him?"

Cash shook his head. "No, I never heard — wait, wait. I know he worked for a contractor after he was expelled. They were doing renovations on the school in 2005, and he was a worker. I remember because it was right around the time that Becky died."

"Really?"

"Yeah, I was surprised they let him back into the building, but Francine thought it was poetic, him repairing the school he had once vandalized. It almost became a controversy, but then Becky died, and no one cared about the contractors."

"Do you remember the name of the company?" Jocelyn asked.

"No, sorry. You think he was the shooter?"

Jocelyn took the list back and slipped it into her pocket. "I don't know, but I'm going to find out."

CHAPTER 48

November 20, 2014

She found Trent at Knox's apartment. He wore jeans and a faded, drab olive-green Marine Corps T-shirt. He held a trash bag in his hand, picking his way through the living room, throwing beer cans and old food containers into it as he went. He'd left the apartment door ajar, and when Jocelyn stepped over the threshold, she realized why. It smelled like the floor of a crowded bar — old food, stale beer, the hint of cigarette smoke, and the faint scent of spoiled garbage. She covered her nose with a shirt sleeve and waded in. Only the coffee table remained pristine, with Sydney's school picture framed atop it. A large, bulky manila envelope sat beside the frame. In his shaky handwriting, Knox had used a black Sharpie to write his daughter's name on the envelope.

Trent glanced over his shoulder at her. "Rush, you ever think about going home? Getting some damn rest? Don't you have a kid you gotta pick up or something?" His voice held no malice or even annoyance. He sounded worn out, and Jocelyn couldn't figure out if he was joking or not, so she said, "Olivia's with her aunt. Look, I found something."

He didn't stop and didn't look back at her. He chucked a stack of old newspapers into the trash bag, some Chinese takeout containers, and a man's loafer, its sole peeled away from the shoe. Jocelyn followed him as he neared the darkened kitchen. "Did you hear me?" she said. "I think I know who shot Sydney and where you can find him."

Trent paused. He turned to face her, clutching the garbage bag in one hand. "My friend died," he said. "No one cared when my mom was killed. No one. Until Knox. He cared. He cleared the case. Maybe he was a drunk and a shitty father, but he was my friend, and now he's dead. I took the day off because some crazy-ass psycho bitch killed my friend, and I need—" he faltered, his voice cracking. He looked at the floor, but not before she saw the tears in his eyes. "I need to take a minute."

"My client died," Jocelyn responded. "My client died thinking that I solved his case, but I didn't. I haven't caught the shooter, and I damn well can't go to Knox's funeral knowing I didn't do that. I need your help, Trent."

He said nothing, staring at the floor where he had unearthed a square of the threadbare brown carpet.

"Sydney's case was the only thing he cared about, Trent. I mean, look at this shithole. The whole place is trashed. Except for that." She pointed at the coffee table. "He cleared the most important case of your life. I'm asking you to clear the most important case of his. Right now. Today. Please."

He drew in a deep breath, his posture straightening, his broad chest puffing out. He clenched his jaw and dropped the garbage bag onto the floor. He met her eyes. "Okay," he said. "Let's see what you got."

CHAPTER 49

November 20, 2014

"Anita looked it up. Davey Pantalone was a senior in 2000. Same as Sydney and Lonnie. He was, by all accounts, a loner. At least Lonnie remembered him as always being by himself, smoking pot behind the bleachers during lunch periods, that sort of thing. We couldn't get his juvenile record, but Anita sweet-talked the school secretary and found out that he'd been suspended twice in his junior year for drug violations. She says at some point, he actually was charged with possession. In his senior year, he was linked to the ongoing vandalism. He was charged, convicted, and expelled."

Trent said, "Wait. The vandalism they had the big Home and School meeting about? The meeting Francine, Lonnie and Hubbard were at the night that Sydney was murdered?"

Jocelyn nodded. "The very same. Before the vandalism started, Pantalone had been going to the school nurse—Francine—for headaches, dizziness, fatigue, and occasional GI distress. It went on for months. Sydney was murdered in May. Pantalone had been spending the better part of his school day in Francine's office, starting back in October, *before* Sydney's murder. Then his mother died of a drug overdose. Cash says Francine had him over for dinner right after she passed."

Trent held up a hand. "Hold up a minute. You talked to Cash Rigo?"

"Yeah."

He pointed at her. "You? You, personally?"

Jocelyn shifted her weight from foot to foot. "Yes, me personally. Listen, Trent—"

He laughed, shaking his head. "You shot the man's wife in his home, and you went back to talk to him. You've got balls, lady. I'll give you that. Big, hairy balls."

Jocelyn put a hand on her hip. "Hairy balls, yes. Are you listening to me or not?"

"This kid had dinner at the Rigos.'"

"Francine invited him. It was a couple months before Sydney's murder. About the same time the vandalism started at Franklin West. Then a few weeks after Sydney's murder, he was arrested for the vandalism. He was expelled, obviously. The damage to school property was so extensive, he was charged with a felony count of third-degree criminal mischief. He pleaded down and spent eighteen months in prison. But listen, everything fits. Francine had plenty of access to him and plenty of time to cultivate a sick, inappropriate relationship with this kid. Then his mother dies, and he's even more vulnerable to her manipulations. His mom died of a drug overdose, so we can assume his home life wasn't perfect. He murders Sydney, and then he goes to prison for something else, effectively taking him out of the picture—and the suspect pool at that time—completely."

Trent frowned and crossed his arms over his chest. "Francine Rigo had this kid over for dinner one time after his mom died, and that makes you think he killed Sydney Adams? Rush, you get how much of a stretch this is, right?"

She groaned in frustration. It wasn't a stretch to her, not since Whitman helped her put the pieces together, but she really didn't want to have to discuss her relationship with Whitman at all. Ever. With anyone. So she just said, "I talked to a criminologist who used to be with the University of Pennsylvania. He's very — " the word *good* stuck in the back of her throat like a bitter pill that wouldn't go down. She settled on, "Knowledgeable. Just hear me out."

She recapped her conversation with Whitman. Trent's posture loosened as she spoke, but he kept one brow raised skeptically.

"Plus, Francine told Knox she was responsible for the bees in Becky Wu's gym bag, but she said a former student had done it for her. She said he was troubled and probably in prison. Cash told me that Davey Pantalone was working with a contracting company at Franklin West at the time Becky Wu was murdered. He'd already killed once for Francine. She had that over him already. I think he put the bees in Wu's gym bag."

"So now we're looking at this guy for two unsolved murders, based on nothing more than a dead woman's husband's claim that they had dinner once. Oh, and a criminologist's theory." He stepped toward her, index finger extended toward her heart. "You know that nothing you heard Knox and Francine say is even admissible in court. Rush, you're on thin ice. That shit that went down at the Rigos' house? If you weren't a cop, if you didn't have friends in the DA's office, if Knox wasn't my friend —" His breath caught. He looked down momentarily then back up at her, his voice quieter. "You've got credibility, but you're on very thin ice. Now you want me to talk to this guy, based on shit. That's what you got, Rush. Shit."

She put her other hand on her hip and narrowed her eyes at him. "Maybe it's shit, but it's more than anyone's had in fourteen years." She thought again of the night she'd spent doubling as a vomit spray hose and of Knox taking his last labored breaths in her lap. Anger ignited inside her. She could practically hear it, like the sound a flame makes when you set your lighter to a blown pilot light. *Whoosh.* She poked his chest, hard. "You know what, Trent? Fuck you. I'm closing this goddamn case with or without you. I'm tired of waiting around for you to take a fucking minute. I'm going to talk to this guy. If what I've got is really shit, then I've lost nothing but a little bit of my time. But if it's not shit, I'm fucking going for it. You can come and maybe solve two murders, or you can stay here and sulk like a fucking toddler. So what's it going to be?"

CHAPTER 50

November 20, 2014

In and around Jocelyn's Roxborough neighborhood, new homes were popping up like a fast-moving rash. It was a great neighborhood, she had to admit. She wasn't surprised that people wanted to live there. Now, it seemed wherever there was a square inch of unattended ground, some contractor tried to slap a trendy three or four-story home on top of it. The new homes towered over the neighboring twin and row houses. They were tall and exceedingly narrow with no yards to speak of. The lots they were built on were barely large enough to accommodate the houses themselves.

One day, after a week-long Dr. Seuss obsession, which culminated in three days of watching *Horton Hears a Who* on a DVR'd loop, Olivia had pointed to one of the houses while they drove past and said, "Look, Mommy! A Dr. Seuss house!" Jocelyn knew her daughter identified the houses that way because they were so tall, narrow, and unusual-looking compared to every other house in the area. That was how Jocelyn came to think of them, and it made her laugh every time she passed one after that.

Until today.

She and Trent stood before a half-finished row of four Dr. Seuss houses that had been thrown up in an empty lot in Roxborough. They were four stories each and sat crammed onto a one-way street between the neighborhood's two main thoroughfares, Ridge and Henry Avenues. Two of the houses already had windows and tan siding. The other two were just framed two-by-fours and plywood. Dirt spilled out over the sidewalks and into the street from where they'd dropped the concrete foundations. It was late in the day, and the job site was quiet. Three beat-up pickup trucks sat half on the pavement, half in the street, their dusty beds empty, save for one, which was filled with clean, new lumber. The truck in the middle had small, black capital letters stenciled on its side, spelling out NORMAN SCHMECK CONTRACTING with a 610 phone number beside it. The R in Norman was missing so that it read: NO MAN SCHMECK CONTRACTING.

As they got closer, they heard voices from the houses — a shout here or there. Impossible to make out from where they stood.

"You sure this is it?" Trent asked.

"Yeah. Anita found him. She called the contracting company earlier to see where Pantalone would be. This is the job site."

Trent looked again at the towering houses before them, trepidation tightening his features. Then he sighed and shook his head. "Well, let's give it a try then. If I think this guy has something to say that's worth hearing, I'm asking him to come downtown. If not, we roll."

They picked their way over mounds of dirt and rocks and up the set of concrete steps leading to the front door of the house where the voices seemed to come from. Trent opened it, and they stepped into a barren room with wooden floors and freshly sheet-rocked walls. To their right were a set of steps. "Yo," Trent called as they started up the stairs.

On the second floor, they found a man at work. He was in his fifties, wearing spackle-stained jeans and a long-sleeved Eagles T-shirt. His head was swathed in a dark green bandana. He stood beside a large bucket of joint compound and used a spackle knife to slop it onto the wall and smooth it over the seams in the drywall. Near his feet, a small black radio played country music.

The man sang along until he noticed them. He froze, the blade extended halfway between him and the wall.

At first, he looked as though he was going to tell them to get the fuck off the job site, but then he clamped his mouth shut and looked them over carefully from head to toe. Trent had changed into a suit with a long navy blue winter coat over top. The man was still taking them in when Trent flashed his badge and said, "How many guys you got in here?"

The man lifted his chin toward the ceiling. "Got two guys running wire on the top floor and one guy sheet-rocking the third floor."

"There are three trucks outside," Jocelyn said.

The man's eyes darted toward her. She knew she looked the part still—black dress pants, a white blouse with a black suit jacket, and a black leather coat over that. She'd pulled her hair back into a bun. "Plumbers went to get parts," he offered.

"We're here to talk to Davey Pantalone," Trent said.

With his free hand, the man pointed his finger at the ceiling. "Next floor. Drywall."

Trent gave him a mock salute as they turned to find the stairs.

"Davey getting locked up?" the man asked.

Trent stopped and looked back at the man. "Nah," he said. "We just came to talk."

They started up the steps again. The man slapped a glop of spackle onto the wall in front of him. "They don't send the suits unless it's a felony."

"Now that's just not true," Jocelyn said. "I once arrested a guy for making love to a block of cheese in a public place. Misdemeanor." She winked at him as they moved out of sight.

The third floor was open, the walls meant to separate the floor into individual rooms unfinished, just two-by-four frames waiting to be wired, insulated, and dry-walled. Bundles of pink insulation lay on the floor like great wrapped hay bales. Against one wall stood two black-and-red plastic saw horses. An assortment of tools lay scattered across the floor. Toward the back of the house, a man stood with his back to them, a large, squared-off tool that looked like a clunky gun in one hand. Nausea spiraled up from Jocelyn's stomach. She put a hand on Trent's forearm to stop him from going any further. "Oh my God," she said. "Is that a nail gun?"

He looked at her, his face twisted in confusion. Then he looked back at the man. "No," he said. "It's a screw gun."

It wasn't much better, but it was some relief. She watched as the man made quick work of the screw gun, securing a panel of drywall, positioning the tip of the screw gun where the drywall rested against the studs, and pushing the screw into the wall with a high-pitched squeal. It was still a little unsettling.

"*That's* a nail gun," Trent added, pointing to the corner of the room. She saw a red toolbox, a level, and the offending nail gun. It was large and yellow and unlike the screw gun, in front of its handgrip it had what looked almost like a gun's magazine, a long one like the kind an AK-47 might have. A twenty-round mag, she thought. Nails, nails, and more nails. The object of her nightmares. Trent was staring at her.

"I have some issues with nails," she said. She realized she was stroking her scar again and stopped, putting her hands at her sides.

Trent frowned. "Right," he said.

The screech of the screw gun sent a cluster of butterflies flurrying in Jocelyn's stomach as they crossed the open space toward the man. He was only slightly taller than Trent but flabbier in all the places that Trent was lean muscle. His torn jeans sagged in the back, and his large stomach hung over the front of them. He wore a red, zipped hoodie over a white T-shirt. His long brown scraggly hair hung down his back. On the top of his head was a backward baseball cap with a worn Flyers logo on it. He looked nothing like the skinny, pimple-faced kid whose mug shot Trent had pulled up on their way there.

He had no radio. He whistled a tune Jocelyn couldn't place, and when he turned and saw them, he had much the same reaction as the man downstairs—a look of intense annoyance at their intrusion that morphed into nervousness the closer he looked at them. It was then that Jocelyn realized that something was off. Pantalone and his coworker were nervous, which meant that one, or both of them, was probably armed, with no concealed carry permit. Either that or they had drugs on them. They already knew that Davey Pantalone, at least, had no outstanding warrants. They'd checked before coming to talk to him.

As if of its own volition, Jocelyn's hand reached for her shoulder holster, patting it furtively to reassure herself that it was still there. But it wasn't. She didn't have her gun. It had been taken into evidence after she shot Francine with it. She suppressed a whispered, "Fuck," and studied Pantalone. His face was ruddy and pitted from acne. The outline of a beard grew on the very bottom of his chin. He had big, wary brown eyes and thick, bushy eyebrows. He wasn't at all what Jocelyn had expected. She tried envisioning him as the teenager from the mug shot—a thinner, slightly better groomed version of this man. Still, she couldn't imagine Francine locked in anything resembling an embrace with this man. Maybe it had been quick and dirty. Come to think of it, she wasn't able to imagine Francine with Craig Hubbard either. But maybe that was the point. Francine's advances must have been so unexpected. That in itself was probably a turn-on.

Davey Pantalone stared at them without speaking.

"Mr. Pantalone?" Trent asked. "Davey Pantalone?"

The man nodded. He looked from Trent to Jocelyn and back to Trent again. He licked his lips. "You're here because of Francine Rigo, aren't you?"

Jocelyn gave Trent a sideways glance. A muscle ticked in his jaw. He stepped closer to Pantalone, smiling. "Mr. Pantalone, my name is Trent Razmus. I'm a detective with the Philadelphia Homicide Unit. This is Jocelyn Rush. I just have a few questions for you. How about if you come with us where we can talk in private?"

Pantalone didn't respond. Slowly, as if he were in a standoff and they'd told him to put his weapon down, he lowered the screw gun to the floor. The uneasy feeling in Jocelyn's stomach intensified. A voice in her head screamed, *This is going to go bad!*

Trent tried again, "Mr. Pantalone? Why don't you come with us." By Trent's tone, it wasn't a suggestion.

Then all hell broke loose.

CHAPTER 51

November 20, 2014

It happened in seconds. Maybe less than seconds. It was all lightning fast, like every action was being delivered in the flash of a strobe light. Pantalone reached behind him, beneath his shirt, and pulled a handgun out of his waistband. He fired as he swung it toward them. His bringing it up and around seemed to happen at the same time as the muzzle flash. The gunshot was so loud, it rattled Jocelyn's teeth. Trent shouted something. Both of them reached for their guns. Hers wasn't there, of course. Then a hot spray of blood arced through the air and landed across Jocelyn's face. Trent dropped on top of her feet. She half stumbled, half fell, pulling her feet out from under Trent's body and going to her knees. Her hands raked across his clothes, digging frantically for his gun.

He hadn't even gotten it out of the holster. She pushed him from his side onto his back, registering his groan with relief, and wrenched his Glock from the holster at his waist. She brought it up, prepared to empty the magazine into Davey Pantalone's fat ass. She'd had just about all she could take of assholes pointing guns at her.

But then the barrel of Pantalone's gun was pressed into her forehead. It seared a hot circle into her flesh, still hot from the shot he'd fired at Trent. She flinched. Then her body froze. At first, her heartbeat thundered so loudly in her head it sounded like a jet taking off right there in the room. Then the calm came over her. A detachment of sorts. Everything went quiet and slow, as though she had plunged into the depths of a deep pool. She was in the room with Trent bleeding at her feet and Pantalone pressing a gun to her forehead, and the woman who was so fraught with hysteria that she could not even form words was somewhere else, pushed down somewhere inside Jocelyn where her screams would not be heard and her panic would not be felt. That woman had been walled off, compartmentalized, and silenced by the part of Jocelyn that had saved herself from a sadistic home invader the year before. What existed now, in the room with Pantalone, was the part of Jocelyn that vowed she would return home to her daughter that night, no matter who she had to kill. She tasted Trent's blood on her lips.

"Gimme that," Pantalone said.

Jocelyn made some calculations. She had Trent's gun pointed at Pantalone's crotch. She could definitely get a shot off but so could he, and his gun dug into the skin of her head. She couldn't take the chance of him firing. The man had no hesitation, and that made him extremely dangerous. He could easily blow her head off in the same amount of time it would take her to shoot his dick off.

It physically hurt her—like a skewer through her chest—to relinquish the gun. But she had to. There was Olivia to think of, Caleb, Camille, Kevin, Inez, and Anita. Her people. There was Trent dying at her feet. She had to give up the gun and back down, regroup. She took her right hand away from the hand grip and put it in the air, a gesture of surrender. "Okay, okay. Take it."

His breathing was labored as he reached for the gun. He gripped the barrel and turned the gun so the top of her left hand was visible. "What happened to your hand?" he asked.

She didn't answer. As he stepped backward, away from her, she felt a measure of relief flood her body. With a gun no longer pressed to her forehead, she turned her attention to Trent. His eyes were open, his face lined with pain and graying with shock. The bullet had hit him in the chest, but high and to the right. Blood bloomed from the hole in his jacket, pooling below his shoulder already. Pantalone stood a few feet away, watching Jocelyn, his gun loose in his hand but still pointed in her general direction. He tucked Trent's gun into his waistband. Jocelyn pressed her palms over Trent's wound, but it didn't help. The blood found the seams between her fingers and spilled over.

"Jesus Christ, Trent. Hold on." She pulled off her coat, folded it, and haphazardly pressed it to his wound. His eyelids fluttered. "Trent," Jocelyn said. "Stay with me."

"That . . . that fucker shot me," he said, his voice low and weak.

"I know."

With all of her attention focused on Trent and Pantalone's attention on her, neither one of them heard the man from the floor below come up the steps. But then he was in the doorway at the top of the steps, his eyes bulging out of his head as he took in the scene. "What the fuck, Davey?"

Without warning, Pantalone swung his gun toward the man and fired once again. The boom was deafening. The bullet punctured the drywall next to the man's head. He jumped and yelped like an injured animal. Then he was gone.

Jocelyn took off her suit jacket and used it to cover Trent. Then she pressed her coat against his wound again, praying like hell he wouldn't bleed out before they got out of this. She looked up at Pantalone. "What's your plan, Davey?"

He paced back and forth before them, his free hand on the top of his head like he was trying to keep his hat from blowing off in the wind. Jocelyn heard shouts from elsewhere in the house, although she couldn't be sure if they were coming from above or below.

"I knew it. As soon as I saw on the news that bitch was dead, I knew you'd be coming for me. She used to threaten me. She said if anyone ever tried to kill her, a letter would be mailed to the police telling them. I always had the tape, but it don't mean shit if she's dead. That crazy fucking bitch."

A tape? A damning letter triggered by Francine's death? Jocelyn didn't know where to start. It sounded like the stuff of a B-grade crime-thriller movie. Did those things happen in real life? No wonder Francine had chosen Davey to do her bidding. If he still believed such outlandish things as a grown man, Jocelyn could only imagine how easy it had been for Francine to manipulate him as a teenager.

"Davey," Jocelyn said. "My friend needs help. He needs medical care. What is your plan?"

"Like I give a shit about your friend."

"You should. If he doesn't get to a hospital soon, he could die. Killing teenage girls is one thing, but killing a cop? In Philadelphia? You do not want to be a cop killer in this city."

"Shut up," he said. He made a noise deep in his throat and shook his head. "Teenage girls." He pointed a finger at her. "It wasn't my fault. She made me do those things. You don't understand what she was like."

If she wasn't dealing with someone so unstable, with such a hair trigger, she might have pointed out to him that ultimately, he was responsible for his own choices, but nothing she said would get through. Francine had indoctrinated him early, and she'd done a good enough job that now, as a thirty-two-year-old man, Pantalone was still living under the specter of the delusions she'd created in his mind.

That was where Jocelyn needed to go.

"I do know what she was like," she said calmly. "She poisoned us. We had another friend, his name was Knox. She killed him."

Again, Pantalone stopped pacing and stared right at her. In spite of the cold in the house, sweat ran down his face. At that moment, his cell phone rang. At first, Jocelyn didn't recognize the noise. It was faint, a digitized beat, like the kind old keyboards made. Then Pantalone pulled a cell phone from his hoodie pocket and looked at it. "It's Norm," he said. "My boss."

Jocelyn glanced down at Trent. His breathing was shallow, his eyes at half-mast. She used one hand to slap his cheek lightly. "Trent," she whispered. "Stay with me."

He opened his eyes and stared at her. She nodded her head

toward Pantalone. "Stay with me," she said again. "I'm going to get you out of here."

He said nothing but nodded. Again, his eyes fought to stay open.

Pantalone let the call go to voicemail, but it rang again only seconds later. "Norm again." He silenced the ring.

"Davey," Jocelyn said. "The police are outside. They got your number from your boss. Whoever is calling is the police negotiator. They're calling to talk to you. You need to answer."

She was only speculating, of course. She knew that Trent hadn't alerted any of his colleagues about the Pantalone situation. But she imagined that between Pantalone shooting Trent and almost shooting his coworker, the police had been called.

"No," he said, shaking his head vehemently.

"If you don't answer, they're going to come in, and believe me, they'll be coming in hard."

"I'm not talking to them. They'll just try to trick me."

"Davey, this isn't about tricking anyone. You shot a cop—he's going to die if we don't get him help. You can make this situation better for yourself if you let us go right now so my friend can go to the hospital."

He ignored her and walked over to the window. He looked down at the street. "Oh shit," he said.

She felt a measure of relief—they were out there. She pressed harder on Trent's wound and prayed this wouldn't take long. She was freezing, covered in Trent's blood, and even though she was outwardly calm, she was terrified. The chirp of another cell phone sounded from Trent's coat pocket. Pantalone strode over and pointed the gun at Trent's chest. "What the fuck is that?"

"It's his phone," Jocelyn said. "They'll call me next."

"Give it to me," Pantalone demanded.

She fished inside Trent's pocket until her hand closed around it. She held it out to Pantalone. He stared at the blood smeared across the cover, his upper lip curling in disgust. "Throw it over there," he said, pointing to the corner of the room where the sawhorses and other tools lay scattered about. Jocelyn leaned across Trent's body and slid the phone along the wood floor and into the corner of the room.

"Yours too," he said just as her cell phone began to vibrate. She had set it to vibrate before they went to interview Pantalone. Pulling it from her back pocket, she looked at the screen. Kevin was calling. Thinking of Knox, she pressed answer and slid her phone over to where Trent's phone lay. Trent's phone rang several more times before stopping.

Pantalone's pacing began again in earnest. Droplets of sweat fell from his face, making tiny wet circles on the floor. He took his hoodie off and tossed it onto the floor.

"You don't like the sight of blood," Jocelyn said.

"I can handle it."

"Was it hard when you shot Sydney? Seeing the blood?"

He went to the window again. Jocelyn hoped he would stay there long enough for a sniper to take him out, but then she remembered that the damn houses were so much taller than the surrounding houses. It would be hard for a sniper to find a good position.

Pantalone shrugged. "I don't know, not really. I never killed anyone before. It was . . . easier than I thought. Except she was late. She didn't come at six-thirty like Francine said she would. I almost left, but I knew if I didn't do it . . ." he trailed off.

"She would make you pay."

He turned back to look at her. "Yeah. Everything had to be done just the way she wanted."

"Is that why you covered Sydney's head? Did Francine tell you to do that?"

He moved away from the window, leaning his back against the wall beside it. "She wanted me to rape her and put her pants over her head. She wanted . . . wanted to embarrass Sydney."

He pressed down on his hat again. His other hand tapped the barrel of his gun against his outer thigh. "But I wasn't into that," he said. "I'm not like that. I don't rape girls."

Such a gentleman. It was just like a criminal. Murder was okay, but he turned his nose up to rape. "Where did you get the gun—the one you shot Sydney with?"

"It was my grandfather's. It was some old-ass revolver. When he died, my mom took it. Then she died . . ."

The more talking he did, the less he pointed his gun at her head. Jocelyn forged ahead, thinking of Knox, wishing he was still alive so she could finally deliver the answers that had eluded him for so long. "What did you do with it?" she asked. "Is that it?"

He glanced down at the gun in his hand and laughed. "This? Nah. Got this from some kid in the Northeast. I threw my grandfather's gun in the Schuylkill. Francine said if they ever found it, they'd know right away who killed Sydney. So I went right down to the riverbank, walked up Kelly Drive a ways, and tossed it in."

"But you kept the jewelry."

He shook his head and took a sideways glance out the window. Beneath Jocelyn's hands, Trent shivered. "No, not me," Pantalone said. "Francine kept it. She wanted it, she said. Whatever Sydney had on her, she said. So I took it back to her. Then there was nothing to tie me to it. Nothing but her."

"She held that over you." Jocelyn put a palm to Trent's cheek. His skin was cool and clammy.

"She tried. At first I didn't mind. I thought I . . . I thought I loved her. She was the first girl, I mean the first woman I ever fucked." He looked at his feet and scratched at his beard. "She was wild, man. Kinky as fuck. You know, when you're seventeen, a stiff breeze will get your cock up. Just thinking about what she let me do to her got me rock hard. Then I went away for the vandalism and shit. That was fucked up. When I got out, for a long time, I still wanted to be with her. She kept me around like, what's that called when someone won't shit or get off the pot?"

"She strung you along?"

He poked an index finger in the air. "Yeah! That's it. She was just stringing me along. She wasn't going to leave her husband. After that Asian girl died, the way Francine just wanted to be around him even though he cheated, I realized she was never going to just be with me."

"She was using you."

A look of pain crossed his face. "Yeah. You know, at first I wanted to do whatever she wanted. I didn't care what it was. I wanted her to love me back. She got me, you know? All that shit with my mom—the drugs and the men—Francine wasn't disgusted by it at all. She liked me anyway. She really got me. She tried to help. She did help. I wanted to do the same for her, but she took shit too far.

"The longer I stayed away from her, the clearer my head got, you know? I felt like maybe she wasn't the greatest thing ever. The next time I saw her, she just seemed old and kind of, I don't know, pathetic. All she cared about was hurting people. I mean it was fun at first, but you know, it was like *all* the time with her. She never shut up about it—complaining about everyone and saying what she wanted to do to them. I don't know. I just got tired of it. I had this job, finally had some money in my pocket, my own place. I didn't want to do her dirty work anymore. For once, I just wanted her to go away."

"But she didn't want to go away."

He laughed. "I was so dumb, you know? I never knew all I had to do to get her was push her away. As soon as I tried to get rid of her, she was all over me again. But by that time, she just gave me the creeps, especially after that shit with the bees. I saw her after that girl died. She looked so happy. Like for-real happy. Like she would get after . . ." his cheeks flamed red. He looked away from her.

"After an orgasm," Jocelyn supplied.

He looked back at her, his brow crinkled. "Yeah, how did you know?"

She sighed and wiped a wisp of blood-crusted hair from her eyes with the back of her hand. "I saw that look on her face while my friend was dying on her kitchen floor."

She wasn't sure just how deep and twisted his attachment to Francine was, even though he had spent years disentangling himself from her, so Jocelyn didn't mention the fact that she was the person who killed Francine.

Pantalone's face softened. "I thought you were bullshitting me about that."

Jocelyn shook her head. "I wish I was bullshitting you. Maybe my friend would still be alive."

"How—how'd you say she did it?"

"Some kind of poison in his coffee."

He nodded gravely. "Of course she did. That was her thing. She couldn't ever really hurt someone—I mean not, like, violently. She couldn't shoot someone, not like me. She didn't have it in her."

He said this with some pride, and it made Jocelyn want to wrap her fingers around his fat throat and squeeze the life out of him. At the same time, the image of Francine raising her gun at Jocelyn flashed in her mind. She changed the subject. "How did you get her to back off?"

"The tape," he said.

His phone rang again. He wiped at the sweat pouring from his face and looked at his phone again. "Fuck."

Trent's body spasmed. His eyes rolled into the back of his head. "Trent," Jocelyn said, trying to keep the hysteria out of her voice. She didn't know how much time he had left. She was going to have to do something, and soon. She shifted from her knees onto the balls of her feet and cupped his cheek with one hand. "Trent," she said again. "Stay. With. Me."

No response.

CHAPTER
52

November 20, 2014

She looked up to see Pantalone looking out the window again. Both of his hands hung at his sides, one holding his phone, the other holding his gun. There was no more time. No more time to think about it, to consider her options. The options were Trent died or she got them both the hell out of there. How dare this piece of shit stand between Trent and the help he so desperately needed?

Rage propelled her over top of Trent's body and across the room. Using her forearm as a bar, and throwing the weight of her entire body behind it, she rammed Pantalone below his shoulder blades. His face flew into the glass, his hat falling into her face. Before he could react, she batted the hat out of the way, grabbed a fistful of hair, and slammed his face as hard as she could into the glass.

He cried out. The glass broke, fine cracks webbing outward from where his nose had made impact. Blood sprayed from his face. She slammed it again a few more times for good measure. Then she pulled his head all the way back, as far as she could, until he fell to the ground. She didn't give him even a second to react. She couldn't. He was bigger than her. She knew from what had happened to her the year before that stopping was not an option. Not if she wanted to live. Or come out of this without scars.

He had dropped his phone but not the gun. She stomped on his wrist as hard as she could with her heel until he screamed and his fingers sprung open. She bent at the waist and reached for the gun, but his other arm swung upward wildly, catching her on the side of her head. Momentarily disoriented, she stumbled away from him. Her hands reached for the gun again, but her feet weren't moving in tandem with the rest of her body. They lurched forward as if they were their own separate entities, moving a split second faster than her hands. Her left foot came into contact with the gun first, a clumsy, unintentional kick. The gun skidded away from both of them. Then Pantalone's good hand wrapped around her calf, pulling her down. He had strong, meaty hands. His fingers were like steel pokers, squeezing her calf muscles until her eyes watered. He made a guttural sound deep in his throat. Blood continued to gush from his nose. As she tried to pull her leg away, he turned onto his stomach. He tried to get onto his knees but kept slipping in the blood.

Jocelyn used both hands to brace herself against the floor. With her free leg, she kicked and kicked until she felt flesh behind her. She made solid contact three times, and then her leg was free. She half limped, half ran toward the gun, vaguely aware of Pantalone's writhing in her periphery. She heard her own breath, her own heartbeat, and Pantalone's high-pitched moans. It was a cacophony, which is why it was a miracle when she heard Trent's voice, low and like the scrape of sandpaper.

"Jocelyn."

She froze and turned in time to see Pantalone on his back like a landed fish, struggling to get Trent's gun out of his own waistband. His right hand, the one she had stomped, didn't work. His fingers wouldn't close around the handgrip. Blood was in his eyes, on his clothes, everywhere. It slowed him down. She ran at him as he pulled it out with his left hand.

He dropped it.

With a shriek, she dove over him, going for the gun at the same time he turned onto his side, in the direction of the gun. Then they were a tangle of blood-soaked, slippery limbs, both grunting and swearing, both trying to gain control of the gun. His left hand closed around the barrel. She slid both of her own hands over his, feeling for his pinky finger. She found its fleshy tip, worked her own fingers beneath it, and pulled back as hard and fast as she could. Somewhere deep inside, the sound of his bone snapping filled her with glee. Pantalone howled in pain. Jocelyn scrambled to her feet, Trent's gun in her hand. Her chest felt full, and her head throbbed. Standing on wobbly legs, she turned, sighted in on Pantalone's center mass, and fired.

The gun jammed.

"No," she shrieked. "No, no, no, no."

She stared at it momentarily, like it was a part of her own body that had betrayed her. Then Pantalone was on her, raging like a wild animal, like a bear, his paws swatting the gun out of her hand. He whacked her on the side of the head with a half-closed fist. Her skin stung, and a pain streaked down the back of her neck. She moved backward, away from him, until her hips hit against one of the sawhorses in the corner. She fell backward, ass over head, landing hard on her right shoulder. The pain took her breath away. The sawhorse had fallen on top of her. She thrashed, trying to get free of it, to gain purchase, to put some distance between her and Pantalone. But it was too late.

He straddled her and wrapped his hands around her throat.

"You fucking bitch," he said as he squeezed.

Even with his grip weakened from her beating, the pressure on her windpipe was torture. With one hand, she yanked his hands down, and with the other, she reached blindly beside her, searching for anything she could use. As his weight settled more fully over her hips and stomach, she flashed back to the year before. Suddenly she was in her living room with a man on top of her. Her lungs screamed. Then, the nail—

Her hand closed around something hard and edged. It felt like aluminum. As she swung it wildly toward Pantalone's head, she saw that it was the level. It glanced off his shoulder, only making

285

him angrier. Making him squeeze harder. She wriggled beneath him, reaching, reaching, reaching.

Goddammit, a voice in her head said. *You are not going out like this.*

Her hand closed around something else. Something heavy and squared off and long. In an instant, she knew it was the nail gun. Her fingers scrabbled over it, like a blind person feeling someone's face, looking for something familiar. Then she felt a trigger. She knew what a trigger felt like. She slid her fingers beneath it, fitting her hand around it like it was her own gun. It was so heavy, so much heavier than her Glock. But it was all she had.

She brought it up, found soft flesh, and pulled the trigger. Pantalone's body jerked, his hands loosening around her neck. She sucked in a deep breath, her chest burning, and pulled the trigger again. And again.

Then Davey Pantalone's skull exploded, raining hot blood, bone and brain all over her. His body slumped to the side, and she kicked at it, up on her elbows, trying to get as far from it as she could. Through the red mist all around her, she saw Kevin.

He stood in a shooter's stance, both arms extended, his brow drawn down in concentration. A thin coil of smoke rose from the barrel of his Glock. He wore a black Kevlar vest over top of his dress shirt. She hadn't seen him in one of those in years. It was disconcerting. For a moment, he seemed frozen, suspended in time, like a still life. Or an apparition. Then he lowered his gun, holstered it, and walked toward her, stepping over the sawhorse, the level, and Pantalone's body. He reached out a hand.

"Rush," he said.

She took his hand and let him pull her to her feet. "Kevin?"

He smiled. "I told you. I got your back."

She looked behind him. SWAT team members and EMTs began pouring into the room. A few feet away, two paramedics knelt and started working on Trent. Jocelyn felt a flood of relief as they strapped an oxygen mask to his face. That meant he was still alive.

"You didn't—you didn't identify yourself," she said to Kevin in a quiet voice. "You didn't give him a chance to surrender."

Kevin leaned in. "Sure I did." He winked and handed her a handkerchief. "You just didn't hear me."

She looked around until her eyes found her phone, discarded on the floor. "But the call," she said. "You were listening."

"Yes," Kevin said. "Very smart. We were listening. Until I hung up." He took her elbow and guided her toward the door. "Let's go. Inez is downstairs, and I promised her I'd bring you out alive."

CHAPTER 53

December 3, 2014

"Maybe for our next big case we don't take a murder," Anita said. She stood in a slant of sunlight streaming into their conference room as she pulled thumbtacks out of the wall and tossed evidence and notes into a box on the table. "Maybe for our next big case, we could do something like a missing cat."

She looked over her shoulder and winked at Jocelyn. Jocelyn laughed and twisted the lid on her Dunkin Donuts coffee. She sat across from the seat Knox used to sit in, the untouched cup of coffee and the flirty photos of Sydney Adams fanned out before her.

"I think I could handle Fluffy the Cat," she mused.

Anita moved down the wall, removing more items. In the space she just vacated, dust motes floated lazily. "I thought you said this case wasn't going to beat you. Oh wait, you said you weren't going to let it fuck with your head."

Jocelyn picked up one of the photos of Sydney and put it back down. "I'm not," she replied.

She didn't need to look at Anita to know that her friend's brow was severely arched. "Best drink that coffee then," Anita told her.

"Before it gets cold."

Jocelyn felt a small tick of annoyance. Not at Anita. Her friend was right, she had said that she was going to start drinking coffee again. She had also said she wasn't leaving the table until she did.

Because fuck Francine Rigo.

That woman had taken daughters away from their parents. She'd taken bright, accomplished young women with unlimited potential from a world sorely in need of brilliance. She'd taken Davey Pantalone's free will and any chance he had at a normal life. She'd nearly killed Jocelyn—thrice if you counted the confrontation with Pantalone.

She wasn't taking Jocelyn's coffee.

"Go on," Anita prodded.

Jocelyn pulled the lid all the way off. She'd watched the clerk at Dunkin Donuts prepare it. She knew it was just a coffee. She dipped a finger into the caramel-colored liquid. Lukewarm. She lifted the cup to her lips and chugged it until the foam cup was three-quarters empty. It tasted exactly like she remembered. From across the room, Anita gave her a slow clap.

They had taken the week of Thanksgiving off, and even though they'd been back in the office for two days, they hadn't been able to face Sydney's file until today. Just seeing Sydney's photos brought back Knox's death and the ugly clash with Pantalone. Jocelyn was lucky that she hadn't broken any bones. She was scraped and bruised, and her shoulder still hurt like hell, but she would be fine. Except for the skull-exploding, red-mist nightmares. She could add those to her collection of Schoolteacher Attacker nightmares. It had taken hours of bathing at Caleb's house to clean all the blood from her body. She hadn't wanted to go home to Olivia looking like something out of a horror movie, and Caleb was all too happy to have her for the evening, so relieved that she was alive.

The ping of the door alarm snapped Jocelyn to attention. A moment later, Trent appeared in the doorway of the conference room. He still looked exhausted. His arm was in a sling and would be for some time, but he was finally out of the hospital. In his free hand, he held a padded manila envelope.

"Ladies," he said.

Jocelyn pointed to the envelope. "Is that what I think it is?"

From behind her, Anita said, "Is that the tape?"

Trent's expression was half scowl, half smile. "Yeah," he said. "This is Davey Pantalone's tape, all right. You guys got a VCR?"

They hadn't yet returned Kevin's VCR. "As a matter of fact, we do," Jocelyn said.

"I have to put this into evidence as part of the investigation, but I figured you'd want to see it."

Anita grimaced. "I don't think Rush needs to see it. She's already traumatized. How about you just tell us what's on it?"

Jocelyn laughed. "I'm fine. Besides, what's a little more trauma?"

"All right, let me start again," Trent said. "I need you to watch this tape so I don't have to be the only one carrying around this awful knowledge of it."

Jocelyn and Anita exchanged a look. "Well," Anita said sardonically. "Since you put it that way."

They locked the front door, pulled the mini blinds down, and situated themselves around the conference room table. "Coffee?" Jocelyn asked Trent.

He glared at her. She downed the rest of her cold Dunkin Donuts coffee, feeling accomplished.

The footage was grainy, or maybe they'd all become so accustomed to seeing everything in high-definition that it made old, standard-definition videos look blurry. It opened on a large bed in a dimly lit room. Part of the frame was obscured by what looked like a bottle of perfume, as if someone had set the camera on a dresser and tried to hide it. The bedsheets were rumpled. On the nightstands, candles burned, casting flickering shadows over the room. Two women entered the frame, giggling, their bodies fused together in a passionate embrace. Jocelyn recognized a much younger, thinner Francine Rigo. The other woman was waiflike, pasty and exceptionally slender, with waist-length black hair. When she turned in the direction of the camera, Jocelyn could see how sunken her cheeks were.

"The other lady is Davey Pantalone's mom, Delilah," Trent

supplied. "I'll fast-forward."

Anita slid him the VCR remote, and he forwarded through the two women tumbling onto the bed, kissing, touching, and removing each other's clothes. Various sex acts followed. Once they appeared to be finished, Delilah lay on her back, a sheet pulled to her waist. Her eyes were half-closed, a satisfied smile on her face. Naked, Francine sat beside the woman, her calves tucked beneath her. She looked toward the camera and smiled. Jocelyn had a horrible feeling in her stomach.

Francine beckoned someone from beyond the camera. A shadowy figure entered the frame. It took Jocelyn a moment to realize the tall, gangly boy was a seventeen-year-old Davey Pantalone. He was all bony angles and awkward, jerky movements. His hair was cut short but unevenly, and it stuck up in places. His chalky skin seemed to glow in the dark room. He wore a T-shirt and sweatpants. His erection strained against the soft material of the sweats. He gave Francine a handful of items, and she spread them on the bed.

"Heroin," Anita said.

"Jesus," Jocelyn murmured.

Francine reached out of the frame, to one of the nightstands. Davey's eyes were glued to her bare ass. Jocelyn was sure Francine intended it that way. She came back to her seated position with a belt in her hand, which she cinched around Delilah's skinny arm. The woman's eyes widened in confusion. "What's going on?"

Francine smiled and leaned down to kiss the woman. She held up a syringe. "Just having some more fun is all."

Delilah smiled and closed her eyes. "Okay. Just don't give any to Davey."

Francine made quick work of preparing and injecting the drugs into Delilah's veins.

"That's enough H to kill a large horse," Anita remarked.

Trent nodded. "Exactly."

Francine left the needle dangling from Delilah's arm. She turned away from the woman and faced Davey.

"You—you sure this will work?" he asked.

Francine smiled her wicked smile. She rose up so she was on her knees and inched to the edge of the bed where Davey stood, his eyes roving her nakedness. Francine pulled him closer and placed both of his hands on her ass. His breathing became rushed and shallow.

"It's already working," she assured him. She kissed him hard on the mouth like she was trying to steal the air from his lungs. Or his soul from his body, more likely. Afterward, she cupped his face with her hands. "Now that I've done what you asked, will you do something for me?"

"Anything," he breathed.

"Good boy," Francine said. "There's a girl I'd like you to get rid of."

"Get rid of?"

She thrust a hand into his sweatpants, and he nearly doubled over. "Yes, you know. Kill her." She drew out the word kill, sending a shiver up Jocelyn's spine.

"Who?" he gasped as she worked him over.

"She's in your class. Her name is Sydney Adams."

Davey's face scrunched up. "Sydney? But I—"

She silenced him with the deft movements of her hand. He was reduced to a series of grunts and moans. "Take off your clothes," she commanded, and he quickly obeyed.

While Delilah took her last breath beside them, Francine and Davey fucked like rabbits. Trent pressed STOP on the remote, and the screen went mercifully blank.

Jocelyn couldn't find any words. She felt cold all over. Of course, she had seen Francine's psychosis up close and personal and had heard her admit to all kinds of unimaginable things. Jocelyn had been there when both Craig Hubbard and Davey discussed the things she'd done, what she had really been like, but still. There had always been a part of Jocelyn that couldn't reconcile the sweet, pitiful Francine she'd initially met with the raging psychopath she now knew her to be.

But here was a tape.

Beside her, Anita shuddered and hugged herself. "That was so fucked up, I don't even know where to start. I mean I have seen some fucked up shit in my life. Shit that will make your hair turn gray overnight, but that—that's really fucked up."

Trent nodded. "I took five showers after I watched it, and I still feel dirty. Look, I'm glad we solved Sydney's case, but there are a shit-ton of things I found out working on this one that I wish I could un-know. You know what I mean?"

"Or un-see," Anita added.

A loud buzzer sounded outside the conference room door, like the kind a dryer makes when it's finished with a load of clothes. All three of them startled.

"What the hell is that?" Trent asked.

"Doorbell," Jocelyn and Anita said in unison.

Jocelyn stood. "I'll go."

CHAPTER
54

December 3, 2014

Knox's daughter stood on the other side of the door, clutching a white envelope and a set of car keys. Her purse hung from her shoulder. She was dressed all in black, like she had been at her father's funeral the day before Thanksgiving. The service had been short and to the point. It had taken place in the cemetery, just before Knox's casket was lowered into the ground. No church, no funeral home. Jocelyn, Anita, and Kevin had gone. Trent had still been hospitalized. Jynx and her husband had come bearing flowers. Knox's daughter, who had said nothing other than to introduce herself to them, had cried quietly during the pastor's short bible reading, but from where Jocelyn stood, she looked more angry than grief-stricken.

Now, as she stepped over the threshold, her face was haggard, her expression tight and strained. "Miss Rush?" she said. "Do you remember me from the funeral?"

"Of course," Jocelyn said. She motioned to the cushy chairs loosely assembled around a coffee table. "Have a seat, Bianca."

"I'd rather not. I just came to give you these." She thrust the envelope and keys at Jocelyn.

Jocelyn took them. "What is this?"

"My dad left you a letter, apparently. One for you, one for Trent, and one for me. I only read mine. Yours and Trent's are in the envelope."

"Did it help? The letter? I know things weren't good between the two of you."

Tears brimmed in the woman's eyes. "I don't know. It . . . it said a lot of things. Must have taken him a long time to compose it. The gist was that he was sorry—for everything."

"I'm sure he was."

Bianca laughed bitterly. "He was always a day late and a dollar short. He might as well have died the day Sydney Adams died."

Jocelyn grimaced. She had no doubt Knox had scarred his daughter, that his absence and unreliability had wounded Bianca deeply and irreparably, but Jocelyn had known a different man, a man consumed with getting justice for a young woman who had been permanently silenced. That quest had touched her in her core.

"Parents hold a lot of power, don't they? The power to destroy our lives with their bad decisions. I know you're angry with your dad. Maybe you always will be. But I've seen a lot, and as shitty dads go, Knox, well, I think if he could have gone back and changed things, he would have."

"He said that in his letter. But it doesn't matter. All of it is too late. Anyway, I know it's hard for people to understand."

Jocelyn said, "Not for some. My dad was a psychopath. My sister was gang-raped when she was fifteen. My dad brushed it under the carpet. He paid people off to keep quiet about it. He blackmailed the families of the boys who did it, and he had no remorse. I was seventeen, just like you were when Sydney Adams was murdered and your dad disappeared from your life."

Bianca's eyes were wide as saucers. "Holy shit," she blurted.

"Yeah. It destroyed my family. I didn't even go to my dad's funeral. Look, I'm not trying to play who has the shittier dad here. I know it's too late for you and your dad. I'm just saying you should remember that your dad—he was trying to do a good thing."

A tear slid down Bianca's cheek. "Thank you," she said.

Jocelyn held up the car keys. "What are these for?"

Bianca wiped her cheek with the back of her hand. "He left you his car."

"The one that he lost?"

Bianca laughed. "The very same."

Jocelyn saw the woman out and locked the office door. Anita and Trent came into the reception area and stood in silence while Jocelyn opened her letter from Knox and read it. It was short and sweet.

> *Jocelyn,*
>
> *If you're reading this, it means I died before you solved Sydney's case. That's okay because I know you'll close the case, so I want to say thank you for fulfilling a dying drunk's last wish. Maybe I didn't deserve it but Sydney Adams did. You did a good thing.*
>
> *-Augustus Knox*
>
> *P.S. If you can find my car, you can have it. Thanks for all the rides.*

CHAPTER
55

December 23, 2014

Jocelyn's tiny row house had never smelled so good, been so clean, or so packed with people. She rarely had parties. Her house was too small to entertain more than two or three people at a time, but this year Olivia had asked for a tree-decorating party, and after closing the Sydney Adams case in such dramatic fashion, Jocelyn could think of nothing more enticing than having all the people she loved under her roof to celebrate the coming holiday. Caleb had helped her pick out a real tree this year instead of the pre-lit, artificial one she usually put up. They had put the lights on a few days earlier, under Olivia's close supervision, of course. Jocelyn could do without vacuuming the needles every day, but the crisp pine smell was refreshing. Later, after everyone arrived, they'd decorate it together. Caleb had promised Olivia that she could put the star on the top.

Inez and Raquel had shown up bearing gifts and Santa hats for everyone. Anita had brought her children along with a bin of cookie-decorating items. The girls had a blast with the cookie dough—cutting shapes from it and dumping copious amounts of sprinkles atop them. Anita had a pretty efficient system in place, rotating trays from decorating table to the oven and back to the table with a short cooling period in between. Judging by the number of cookies they'd already baked, Jocelyn would be sending everyone home with a Tupperware container filled with them. She propped open her front door to get some cold air into the house. Baking cookies had seemed like a great idea until they had to turn on the oven.

On the porch, Anita's fifteen-year-old son, Terrence, stood chatting with Caleb's son Brian, who was nineteen and a sophomore at Temple University. They looked up when she opened the door and smiled at her. She had finally met Brian a few days earlier. He was tall and thin like his father, but he must have taken after his mother because, other than his dark, soulful brown eyes, he didn't much resemble Caleb. He did, however, have Caleb's easy charm and biting sense of humor. Olivia took to him instantly.

Jocelyn gave the boys a little wave and went back inside, taking a seat next to Olivia at the dining room table. Olivia turned to Jocelyn, cookie batter clumped in her brown locks, and red and green sprinkles cascading down the front of her shirt. She grinned, and Jocelyn leaned in to kiss her nose. "Where's Uncle Kevin?" Olivia asked.

"On his way."

"Is he bringing Kim?"

"Of course."

"Where's Aunt Camille?"

Jocelyn smiled. "She'll be here in about an hour. Her flight was delayed. Are you almost done with cookies? I need to get dinner started."

Caleb appeared behind her, sliding a warm palm across the nape of her neck. "You didn't hear?" he asked. "We're having cookies for dinner."

Across the table, Pia and Raquel giggled convulsively at a joke that Jocelyn wasn't privy to. "Yeah," Pia said. "We're having cookies with a side of cookies."

"And cookies on top," Raquel piped in.

Olivia tipped her head back and laughed loudly. Then she said,

"Then we'll have cookies for dessert."

"With cookie crumbs on top," Pia said.

Caleb sat down next to Jocelyn, a mischievous smile on his face. He leaned forward and lowered his voice to a near whisper, immediately gaining the girls' undivided attention. Their little sprinkle-covered hands hung suspended in mid-air, their faces bright and rapt, smiles frozen in place as they listened. "Are you girls sure you want cookies for dinner?"

"Yes," they cried in unison.

"With cookies on the side?"

"And on top!" Olivia shouted.

"Okay, okay," Caleb said. "But the real question is: do you want cookies with that?"

"Yes!" the girls hollered before dissolving into laughter, their little bodies going loose with hysteria.

Jocelyn saw Anita standing in the kitchen doorway. Anita rolled her eyes but smiled nevertheless. "Cookies it is," Anita said.

Caleb slid a hand across Jocelyn's shoulders and pulled her in closer. She caught a dizzying whiff of his cologne and was glad to be sitting down. He still made her knees weak. "So," he went on, addressing the girls. "What do you think of mashed cookies with cookie gravy?"

Before they could answer, Kevin's voice boomed from the front door. "Cookies? Who's making cookies?"

Olivia climbed down from her chair and ran over to him, leaping into his arms, recapping the entire cookie conversation, stuttering at times in her frantic effort to tell him as fast as she possibly could. Kim stood beside Kevin. Between them sat two huge garbage bags.

"You guys," Jocelyn joked. "I said bring a dish, not your trash."

Kim rolled her eyes, motioning toward the bags. "I told him what you said about not going crazy with gifts, but he cannot be stopped."

"You brought presents?" Olivia said, head tilted toward the bags like a pointing dog.

"Of course I did," Kevin said. "It's Christmas! Now go get Raquel and Pia. Uncle Kevin Claus brought something for all you kids, even the sulky teenage boys outside."

Cookies forgotten, the girls herded into the living room and gathered around Kim as she distributed the gifts. Brian and Terrence slipped quietly into the room and sat on the couch. The other adults made a loose semi-circle around the edge of the room, watching the girls open their gifts—every one of them extravagant. Kevin always spent ridiculous amounts of money on the kids for birthdays and holidays. He had no children of his own and loved being an honorary uncle.

Jocelyn sidled up to him. "No word on Knox's car?"

Kevin shook his head. "Nope, nothing. I'm sure it'll turn up. Why? You ready to get rid of that old, ugly Ford?"

"Not for anything Knox used to drive," she said, thinking of the faint smell of vomit that still clung to her backseat from the day Knox had thrown up in it.

Kevin laughed. "Well, it'll turn up eventually. Put it out of your mind for now, Rush. Enjoy the holidays." He motioned around the room. "Enjoy this."

Jocelyn linked her arm with his and rested her head on his shoulder, a feeling of contentment washing over her. "I will," she said. "I absolutely will."

ACKNOWLEDGEMENTS

First and foremost, I must thank my readers. You guys are awesome. Thank you for being so passionate, so supportive, and so encouraging. You make everything that's hard about writing worth it. I can never thank you enough for reading my books, recommending them to others, leaving reviews, sending me emails, Facebook messages, tweets or sometimes even pulling me aside when you see me in person! I am continuously amazed and humbled by your enthusiasm. Please know that I deeply appreciate every message, every email, every tweet, every Facebook post and every kind word. As long as you keep reading, I'll keep telling stories. While I was writing this book, there were so many times that I felt like throwing in the towel, but I knew that I couldn't because you readers were there cheering me on the whole way. From the bottom of my heart, thank you.

Thank you, as always, to my wonderful husband Fred and my lovely daughter, Morgan, who sacrificed many hours of time spent with me for this book. Thank you to my CPs and first readers, Michael Infinito, Jr., Nancy Thompson, Dana Mason, Carrie Butler and Jeff O'Handley. You are all extraordinary writers and human beings and I am privileged to know you. I am constantly astounded by your generosity and humbled by your brilliance. Thank you as well to Carrie at Forward Authority Design Services for being my go-to person for just about anything that crosses my mind. You have an astonishing ability to take my ideas and make them reality. I am in awe of your talent, kindness, patience and good humor.

Thank you to Jennifer Thomson, researcher extraordinaire, for finding out all kinds of strange and obscure things for me!

Thank you to my beta readers whose valuable input helped work out all the kinks: Torese Hummel, M.K. Harkins, Joyce Regan, Renee Crabill, Trisha Turner, Laura Aiello, Marcie Riebe. Thank you to Lilly Billarrial for helping me make up fake business names.

Thank you, as always, to my parents and siblings for your constant and unwavering support and encouragement as well as for spreading the word: William & Joyce Regan, Donna House, Rusty House & Julie House, Sean & Cassie House, Andy Brock, Kevin & Christine Brock, Grace & Kirk House.

Thank you also to Jana Dean, Steve Boyd, Nancy Frederick, Elaine Boris, Jewell Cartwright, and Sue Herwig, Judy LaMay, and Tanya Anderson. You keep me going!

Thank you to my constant cheerleaders and sharers of all things book-related: Melissia McKittrick, Ava & Tom McKittrick, Kerry Graham, Jeanie Loiacono, Katie Henson, Elizabeth Kaminski, Helen Conlen and the entire Conlen family, Jean and Dennis Regan and the entire Regan family, the Funk family, my in-laws, the Tralies, the McDowells, the Dauphins, the Kays, the Bottingers, the Spinellis and the Bowmans. So many of my friends and family help spread the word about my books, it would be tough to name you all individually but please know that I am so grateful to you, and every day I feel blessed to have you all in my life and in my corner.

Thank you to James D. McGinnis for taking so much time to help me with my various questions about private investigators, police procedure and the interplay between the two. Thank you to my sisters at DAMN and also the Delaware Valley chapter of Sisters in Crime for all your unwavering support! Thank you to Forward Authority Design for the amazing cover, to T.S. Tate for the content edit and Tajare Taylor for the final copy-edit. Thank you to Melissa Maygrove for the final proofread and for your eagle-eye precision. Finally, thank you to Integrity Formatting for the interior design.

ABOUT THE AUTHOR

Lisa Regan is an Amazon bestselling crime/suspense novelist. She has a Bachelor's Degree in English and Master of Education Degree from Bloomsburg University. She is a member of Sisters In Crime, Mystery Writers of America and International Thriller Writers. She lives in Philadelphia with her husband and daughter. Her debut novel, *Finding Claire Fletcher* won Best Heroine and was runner up in Best Novel in the eFestival of Words Best of the Independent eBook Awards for 2013. Her second novel, *Aberration* won Best Twist in the 2014 eFestival of Words Best of the Independent Book Awards. Her third novel, *Hold Still* was released by Thomas & Mercer in 2014 and has been translated into German. She is at work on her fifth novel.

Find her at www.lisaregan.com